Before the credits roll, and the story begins, a respectful dip of my board to the past, and to a place, I wish was part of my life...

To Charlise –
Stephen King might have sold more books, but he doesn't SURF!
Thanks
Love Ken

From the reviewers

On Surf Dot Com.

"With *Gidget Must Die!* and now *Surf.Com*, Fred Reiss has emerged as a sort of surfy Hunter S. Thompson, a vicious, merciless, ridiculous social documentarian with a distinct flair for drawing unforgettable characters. Fred Reiss is nuts. But mainly, he is very very funny."

- Allan Weisbecker, author of "Searching for Captain Zero

On Gidget Must Die

"*Gidget Must Die* is witty, surreal, and insulting text laced with keen perceptions and dead-on portraits of our sport's archetypes. Make no mistake about it, this guy Fred Reiss is sick. I recommended GMD for a hundred or so other reasons--compelling passages, acerbic truths, and the kind of outrageous and absurd exaggerations that help you remember it's just stand up comedy."

- Drew Kampion, author of "The Book of Waves" and "The History of Surfing."

"Fred made me laugh and squirm through the Malibu culturati. I choked on the asphalt fumes of PCH, and breathed the salt spray of the "Bu" again. I'm with him in the pre-dawn perfection, taking off until...but let Reiss tell it. He'll suck you over-the-falls with his wild surf yarn (or is it?)."

- John Severson, Founder of Surfer magazine, artist, author, and nice guy.

On Reiss' insult books

"If you need an insult, buy Reiss!"

- Playboy Magazine

Common people like you and me
We're the builders of eternity
Each is given a bag of tools
A shapeless mass and the book of rules

– *The Heptones*

SURF.COM

by

Fred Reiss

As always, this book is dedicated to the charm bracelet formed by the love of Laurie Roberts, Mom and Dad, my two sisters, and my brother.

Special thanks line-up (In no particular pecking order):childhood buddy Frank Doyle and Jef-with-one-f Gunion for the cover design (who polished and clarified the' big picture), Ken "Tomato Pie" Dixon for editing (Any mistakes are his not mine, ha!), Big Bad Johnny Severson for his generous art-work and correspondence (Fortunately, we have never met in the flesh, which is why we get along.), Ray Franklin for his computer worm-like insights into hacking, my departed point man Mikel Herrington (who taught me all about being me), Da Pitts Girls,Tsunami Tommy for fleshing out financial weasel deals), Joe Hernandez for his bartender's view of dot-comers, Hal "The Gardener" Stanger, Barbecue Bob, Ernie, Odwallah Ken, Bags, Coors Ricky, George Dumas, Michelle Scott, B.B Bond, Marshal, Lenny, Safeway Judy, Jack "Shut-in" Roddy, Maureen who locked herself in her own car changing into a wetsuit, Christina, Jenno Farley, Surf Dogs (AK, Huey, and Ambush), Hook Ruler and etiquette handler Shannon (alias Shandor), Antonio who knows and sees all, The Fish, The Twins, Einstein, Terry "Fabio" Arnaud, Respirator Mike, the "real" General and Michelle, Cowboy, Lurch, Patrick, Subpoena Greg (Who served a few for me!), Scary Larry, Allan "Trailer Trash" Borgo, the lions den of Farley Brothers, Gino, Reservists Lenny, By-Pass Bill, The Flea, Johnny and Rosemary Rice, Bobby "Aipa" Mills, reformed Dirt Farmer E.J, Chuck Bursey, Shop Rat Garrett, Doctor Digesto for the polyp pluck, Marsha and Gwen and all the cool people at the Capitola Book Café, Grateful Dead Steve, Mike Medina, Clamper Gary (for his killer java and generous everything), John "The Loud" Young, Larry "Unix Breath" Levers, Kevin Randick, The Floyd family (especially Deb with her Beenie Baby knowledge), Johnny with the Greek last name I can't spell, Ed Man "tree surgeon MacWorld geek" Cravalho, Joe an d his killer poodle, special guest stars Hap Jacobs and Mike Eaton, Bad Golfer Rapid Robert for construction tips. Plus, all the people who came in and hung out at Pat Farley's old Santa Cruz'n surf shop, and the crew of guys and women I shared waves with at 38th and everywhere else, along with all the snakes, burn artists, greedy surf class instructors, two-year Instant Locals who yell at real locals, name-brand wannabes, aggro girlfriends of surf-stars, rude beginners, and wave-hogging, souless pros who hurt my feelings enough to made this book necessary.

This is a work of fiction. With the *exception* of Ranger, all the characters, companies, and events portrayed in this novel are products of the author's imagination or are used fictitiously. For detail mongers, the author knows the Dream Inn didn't exist in 1999, but I love the name. And, that 'Saving Private Ryan' came out in 1998. Outside of those two basics, everything stands.

ISBN 0-9623869-3-6

FIRST EDITION

For
Pat Farley, Wayne Kenney,
and the
life–altering spirit
of the Santa Cruz'n Surf Shop

Santa Cruz, California
1999

Surf.com

1

THEY CAME FROM SILICON VALLEY. The dot-comers arrived at Bings the same way they downloaded the surf spots, the streets, and the shops of Santa Cruz. Suddenly, rudely, and in groups. The rapid pace of their invasive half conversations was blaring, cocky, intense, tightly clipped, and more focused than it needed to be. And God were these dot-comers loud! The static gibbering of their high-tech voices drowned out the yow-ing cries of seagulls, the damp barking of seals under the municipal wharf, and the waves slapping against the pier's pilings. At least thirty-five dot-comers sat on long wooden benches, which were positioned around several wooden tables, draped with red-and-white checkered cloths. Each table setting had plates filled with a three-egg omelet, toast, along with huge side orders of bacon, sausage, or tofu. But the food was getting cold. Instead of eating, the dot-comers sat with their backs to the tables, and hunched over laptops on metal folding chairs in front of them. My patented stinkeye hardened on these trannies. Most were embedded in their twenties, obviously single—and probably not by choice. The guys were dumpy dorks or wiry geeks, and the women were attractive, but only when they were compared to the guys. The dot-comers even looked uncomfortable *within* themselves—they rubbed their chins, pulled at the skin around their eyes, rapidly moved one leg up and down, or squirmed in chairs, as if they were trying to work their way out of their own flesh. Just about all of them had that soft-white bulb office tan. Laminated company badges were clipped like hunting permits on their belts or pockets. They yammered on cell phones, headsets, and only took a break from clicking their keyboards to check beepers and palm pilots for incoming calls or e-mails. Their hand-held devices might have been communicating online, but for people who took pride in their networking skills, none of the dot-comers looked like they were connecting with one another or the world around them. I couldn't tell if they were talking to themselves, speaking on a telephone headset, having a conversation with the person across from them, or babbling incoherently to an imaginary playmate...

"It's all about perceived value."

"IPO—"

"An eBay secretary got rich on her stock options. A secretary! She didn't know until she got back from vacation."

"HTML—"

"I bet this gets the business up to four million and a deal to sell to Microsoft for twelve."

"TCP/IP—"

"Pre-emptive multi-tasking is duplicating traffic..."

"JAVA—"

"A Boulder Creek guy sold his Loans.Com domain name for over a million dollars."

"Oh that's so Q-4! So Q-4."

"Hold down the option key and hit restart."

I wished *I* could hold down the option key on them and hit restart. Q-4. HTML. JAVA IPO. TCP/IP. All I thought was B-F-D: Big Fucking Deal. It was nauseating. I swear, if aliens came to this planet, I would volunteer to be a slave trader.

I ordered my breakfast from a new menu that displayed computer graphics of surfers riding waves around the point breaks of increased food prices. The $3.99 special was now $6.99 and no longer came with a choice of bacon or sausage. The print was difficult to read because the fonts were several different sizes and colors (Sometimes the same color type was positioned on a digital illustration of a similar color and completely disappeared.). I absently spun my Dad's gold ring on the finger above my right thumb and waited for Shiloh to bring me my Pepsi. It was a Tuesday. I planned to start it quietly on the outside deck of

Bings, a well-run dump at the end of the wharf on the Westside of town. I usually powered down a "Locals Only" breakfast special with a cold Pepsi, then did my surf check at Pleasure Point, and—if the waves were good—I'd get a session in, and possibly, open my surf shop before noon. Unfortunately, there was nothing quiet about the start of this day. Quiet just wasn't happening. The broadband of dot-comers overran my place and made it their own. They had some catered deal with a bar set-up. There were posts with silver metal poles topped with flying-saucer shaped hooded heaters positioned all around to remove the morning chill. They even had a massage table to give body-toneless geeks neck or shoulder rubs. I knew the masseuse, her name was Zoof, but she looked busy so I didn't bother her. The geek she rubbed was face down with his head within an oval, sponge cradle that extended beyond the edge of the table. He watched a DVD-movie on his laptop, which was placed on the floor. His cell phone beeped on a small table near him. Without moving his head, he asked, "Can you get that?" Positioned on the wharf railing, behind Zoof's set-up, was a one-foot high plastic windmill. The device blew a steady stream of tiny bubbles between revolving blades. I slightly suspected the machine produced bubbles by sucking out the air and replacing it with an atmosphere only the dot-comers could breathe.

"Does everyone have some bubbly?" the Über Geek asked, rising from his seat in the middle of the group and holding up his hand for silence. "It's the latest nineties vintage from my own label, Clos La Tech."

The dot-comers lifted their champagne glasses upwards through their bubble-laced air. The forty-minus something Über Geek climbed up on a table with the lumbering grace of an elephant seal. And what a geek he was. He looked like he got up too early and put his face on inside out and backwards. His forehead was indented in the middle and resembled a two-button computer mouse. His hairline receded well past the mid-point above his ears. His sidewalls were buzz cut. The remaining hairs on the back of his neck were stretched into a taut wire-thin strand that looked like a barbed, four-inch stinger. He wore round, steel-rimed glasses. His skin was pasty and toneless. He had a powder blue polo shirt with the words "Surf Dot Com" below a logo of a surfer on a wave. A beeper, palm pilot, and cell phone were clipped on the belt of his pleated khakis, which were pulled up higher than his waist. A headset looked like scaffolding around his skull. The devices seemed to restrain him into a semblance of human form—without the straps and wires he'd probably lose his shape and become one giant gelid blob.

The Über Geek glowed with benevolence as he proudly proclaimed, "In 1998 when I launched Surf Dot Com as a start-up, I told this team if SDC's stock price went over 50, I'd get a tattoo on my butt." He paused. "Well, it's 1999, and a value-added promise is a promise." He turned around and pulled the rear of his pants down. Across the middle section, displayed above his two mealy butt cheeks, were the two-inch high blue letters of 'Surf Dot Com.' Just what I wanted to see first thing in the morning: an asshole's asshole. The dot-comers rabidly applauded. The Über Geek pulled up his pants and turned around. "One more thing," said the Über Geek, which for some stupid reason drew a laugh from the crowd. "Before I get up to speed, you know how your team leader is with peripherals..." He waited for chuckles. They obediently came. "After posing in a picture with President Clinton, I picked this little gizmo up at the Comdex show in Las Vegas." He tapped a finger against a small square device attached to the base of his cell phone, which was lodged in its belt holster. "It's a voice-stress analyzer. It picks up inaudible vibrations that speed up uncontrollably, and these tremors trigger the device to emit a high-piercing eeee-ing sound when it detects a lie. And the really cool thing is this analyzer's preferences give me the option to make a noise that corresponds to the intensity of the lie. I can use it on tape recordings, phone conversations, television shows—and on Zander when he gives me his reasons why the server is down." This inter-office crack got a huge laugh. Evidently nobody liked this Zander guy. "Let's ramp up, and see if this lie-detector works." The dot-comers giggled in anticipation. "Oh, one more thing..." and again got a laugh. He cleared his throat and bellowed melodramatically, "Surf Dot Com's stock did *not* triple in value today."

The voice activator issued a harsh eeeeeeeeeee-ing alarm.

The dot-comers erupted in applause.

He paused and said, "One more thing..." Again the digital laughter. "Today we issued two million shares at $14, and on the strength of our contracts with Adapient and Sapient we have built out a multi-million dollar telecommunications strategic relationship with Expient to create a virtual private network service, which drove our stock to open at $28, and shoot up to $84 at the close. Surf Dot Com is valued at $936 million..."

"Surf Dot Com, Surf Dot Com, Surf Dot Com," chanted the dot-comers, who clapped soft hands, and stomped feet, as if they wanted to be fed. The seals on the cross beams beneath the pier barked too. Seagulls landed on the railings and cried.

I overheard one dot-comer say with admiration and awe to another co-worker, "He's having a good day." And the co-worker replied raptly, "Yeah, he's on."

Über paused again. "Oh, and—"

"One more thing" shouted the dot-comers, laughing.

"And this is absolutely true," continued the Über Geek. "When our employer-owner equity start-up does its second offering in six months..." He spread his arms out, beamed, and proclaimed, "We're all going to be rich!"

The Über Geek's lie detector issued a harsh eeeeeeeeee-ing sound. His brilliant team didn't hear it. The dot-comers continuous self-congratulatory applause drowned out the alarm. They were too busy cheering and looking at the sunlight slanting through the bubbles and imagining the clear globes were filled with money. The Über Geek seemed relieved his techie disciples failed to detect his lie. But he spotted me and knew I caught it.

"Surf Dot Com, Surf Dot Com, Surf Dot Com," chanted the dot-comers, but the team's clapping and stomping lost its group rhythm, everyone was off by one clap or stomp.

"You people rock!" shouted the Über Geek, shooting out his right fist, which caused him to lose his balance on the table. He awkwardly regained it. "And why does Surf Dot Com rock? Because we get it! Brick-and-mortar types don't get it. Why? Their gray-haired mindset needs..." He paused and disparagingly spat out, "...business models." The dot-comers laughed, but it was more of a braying taunt. "Surf Dot Com is like all on-line businesses, we have no history of past earnings because our drive geometry is a new market for the millennium with no precedent in Western Civilization. This is about vision, not profits. Price-to-earnings ratios and discounted cash flows don't apply to us. Surf Dot Com is beyond niche play. We're pure play. We're the bleeding edge. The prestigious investment firm of First Credit San Jose Suisse has rated SDC's stock as a 'buy.' The brick-and-mortar types claim we don't have a bottom line. We do. We have just redefined the bottom line. The e-bottom line is investors are still kicking themselves in the ass for not buying our stock when we IPO-ed. They're chomping at the bit to get at our second offering." The smart mob smugly laughed. "Our Surf Dot Com team sees the Internet for what it truly is, the coming of a second Industrial Revolution," the Über Geek continued, weaving his hands through the circulating bubbles as if he were casting a spell. "The Internet is the most important tool for information and altering the world since Gutenberg's printing press. No one can anticipate our future growth. Technology frames it all into a coherent picture. The tech industry is the third largest behind real estate and health care. Look at the comparables. There are 83 million Internet users. It took radio 39 years to get 50 million, and it took television 13 years. And the number of people on the Internet will double from 83 million to 157 million. In this deep future, there's no limit to the web's unparalleled growth. SDC's forward best-of-breed thinking encompasses every aspect of the global and domestic economy. Our new world has no borders! Nothing can stop us." The Über Geek imperiously threw out his arms to the glory sky. "Our upward trend is invincible!"

"Surf Dot Com, Surf Dot Com," the dot-comers chanted.

"Whoa!" said the Über Geek, wobbling, losing his balance, and flipping backwards. His head thudded twice on the planks, and sounded like a badly rolled bowling ball whacking the gutter. Packets of dot comers quickly rose, spread out from their seats, reassembled, and uprighted their fallen icon. The Über Geek realigned his head harness, which was tilted at an angle. His wire-rim glasses were bent. His shirt was pulled up. His belly looked mushy, like he had two guts. Then I realized what the second bulge was. The guy was packing a money belt—and it was thick too. I was the only one who spotted it. The Über Geek noticed the money belt was showing. He frantically pulled down his shirt to conceal it. The dot-comers perceived nothing.

A skeptical but soft voice came over my shoulder.

"I remember my grandmother told me something," Shiloh said. 'If you want to know what God thinks of money, look who He gives it to.'"

Shiloh and I went way back. She was in her late thirties. She was a home-grown local, an artist who supported herself as a waitress and a part-time caterer. She had a keen eye for beach colors and made some really cool paintings she sold at the Capitola Art and Wine festival. She was thin, had thick and long hair, and keen wrinkles in her face from living in Hawaii. Her smile just jumped out. She was a damn good surfer. She grew up on the Westside. Her Dad was a legendary big wave rider in Hawaii who died from cancer. Her Mom still lived in town. Shiloh's two brothers surfed. They worked as sales reps for surf companies. I purchased wetsuits from them for the shop.

"Check out these trannie women in their crisp blouses but they don't use the same colors we use on our clothes, they have hues," said Shiloh who nodded her head at the dot-com women. "Like charcoal gray, marled tan, raisin with burnt red, pale lilac, flecked rose, sage, slate, orchid frost, or cement, and, you can't leave out, *hunter* green. And look at their hair, it's always layered so every little piece fits right when they flip it." She jerked her head back and demonstrated the move. "These execudivas—"

"Executives?"

"No execu*divas*. Women who absolutely must have their diva mics. One of those headsets where they talk on the phone without making a mundane effort to actually hold a phone. They conduct business and think they're diva singers, like Madonna or Cher, who wear headsets instead of hold microphones when they perform. These trannie women are not divas. They're harness trained." She paused and rolled her eyes. "I'm so over it."

"What about the guys? Are they execudivas too?"

"No, they're execu-*deviants*."

I laughed.

"Here," she said, placing a napkin-wrapped object on the table.

"What am I suppose to do with this?" I said rudely, knowing full well what it was. But I didn't want to be nice.

"It's a bone for Ranger."

"Thanks," I said indifferently and turned my Dad's ring once again on my finger.

"You surfing today?" she asked.

I gave her my extremely sarcastic what-the-hell-else–do-I-do-after-eating-here-every-morning look. I said, "Surfed last night. It'll take a while to get used to the cold water again. Closed up the shop. I've been in Hawaii for the last three weeks."

"Poor baby, I feel your pain."

"I ran into Chuck there," I said. "He has his own boat now."

Shiloh said nothing. Years ago, she stood me up on a date, because this guy, Chuck Bystrom made a run at her. I was just an ex-nail banger who shaped boards and owned a surf shop. Chuck was a successful flooring contractor. She wound up living with him in Hawaii for a year. It didn't work out. She stopped in the shop, about a month ago, just to let me know she was around again. But I didn't act on it. And I wasn't about too now, either.

"Chuck said to say hi," I added, neglecting to mention Chuck was living with a new honey on his boat, a 19-year old redhead.

"I was listening to the buoy readings on my scanner," she said. "There's definitely swell."

"I'll hit 38th." I paused. "It'll probably be packed with idiots."

"Yeah, now, it's like Silicon Beach. I'm so over it."

"Server, these eggs aren't juicy enough," grunted a dot-comer.

Shiloh rolled her eyes and said to me, "That's the sixth person to send back their order. These people positively *live* to send back their orders, because that's what they think real important people and rock stars do. And then, when I bring it back, they barely touch the food." She walked away and said, "Vic, your food will be up soon, I'll—oh, I forgot your Pepsi."

"No big deal, I'll get one from Reddo at the bar."

Reddo was in his fifties. He tended bar and sculpted. He had traveled around the world. His left eye was shot out in Vietnam. The side of his face with the glass eye was flatter than the other side, and had a waxy complexion. His brittle gray hair was short, full, and parted on the left side. I had surfed with him for years. I shaped Reddo a ten-foot stepdeck with a kick tail, I gave him a break on it, and in return, Reddo always took care of me.

"Yo, Vic," Reddo said, who saw me coming. He pushed a tall glass of Pepsi with ice across the counter, and waved me off.

"Howz'it?"

"I have thirty days to get out of my place in Boulder Creek," said Reddo. "My wife and I have been renting from this guy for eighteen years. Nice house in the woods. We treated it like a home. And I came home and on the message machine the landlord says I have thirty days to get out. I mean I know I'm just a renter, but I get a letter from him telling us if we don't leave how we will get charged for trespassing or some shit. And then two days later, I come back to my house and the door is wide open. He left it open when he was showing the place to the buyer. I mean the door was wide open! And there are some real dirtballs who live near me. Trolls cut through my yard to sleep in Big Basin Park. A couple days later the landlord shows up with his son, and they give me a bottle of wine to apologize for leaving the door open. They didn't care about where we were going to go. And the landlord's son—who isn't good at doing anything except finding ways for his Dad to save money—drove up in some Beamer and acted like he knew how to make a living. But it was like neither one of them even saw me. You should have seen those eyes. All they saw was the money they were making from some dot-com piece of shit." He shook his head. "I mean you should have seen these people, you should have seen those eyes."

"Sorry to hear that, I'll put the word out."

"Get a load of Chad and Duane over there," said Reddo, who quickly pointed to the dot-comers at the corner of the bar.

The geeks were in their mid-twenties. They had short-spiked hair with orange-tinted tips. They wore khaki pants and denim shirts with a Surf Dot Com logo on them. The geeks had glasses with frames so small, they had to squint to see through the lenses. One dot-comer unbuckled a strap from his waist. He put it down on the bar. It was a high-tech tool belt with a pager, palm pilot, and two cell phones—the one on the left was marked "Home," and the one on the right was marked "Office."

Reddo went over to them.

One of the geeks said, "I'm the VP of graphic design for Surf Dot Com, my options are worth over 2.5 million dollars. I just closed on a cottage my wife wants at Pebble." He paused, like he was waiting for applause; it didn't come. "I want a sidewinder."

"You mean a side*car*?" Reddo asked.

"Uh," said the dot-comer.

"I've never made a sidewinder, what's in it?"

"A sidecar, I want a sidecar."

"Well, maybe you have it confused with another drink," said Reddo. "Perhaps you can tell me what's in a sidecar, and I'll let you know if that's the right drink or not."

"Yeah," said the dot-comer, who hesitated, "No, I—er, I want a sidewinder. I mean, a sidecar. Yeah."

"And I want a martini," piped in the other one, who loudly added, "With the *blue* vodka."

"That's 'Sky Blue' vodka—that's the color of the bottle. The bottle is blue. There is no blue vodka."

"Yeah," blankly said the other dot-comer. "That's what I meant. And I take my martini like Hemingway—"

"That's interesting," said Reddo, who cleared his throat. "I know about Hemingway. And I've been behind the duckboards for a while. And Hemingway had his martinis the same way Montgomery did his troop movements. Fifteen-to-one. Fifteen parts gin—not vodka—to one part vermouth."

"This is so uncool," sternly said the dot-comer, clearly irritated his attempt to be a sophisticated guy in front of his dot-com buddy was ruined by an hourly wage earner. "Bartender, I don't think that's the proper way for you to talk to a customer."

"Sir, my job as a bartender is to give you the drink you want, and the drink you asked for was not the drink you wanted, I was merely providing you with the proper information so you could make a decision based on my expertise." Reddo sharply smiled. "I'm here to give you the drink you deserve." He paused. "I'll mix your drink. Let me know if it isn't what you want."

"Oh, *I* will," threatened the guy. "Anyway, another round."

"Of what?" said Reddo.

"Funding," he chirped, holding up his empty glass as bubbles drifted around him.

Reddo came back to me, began mixing drinks, and said, "The geek was looking forward to being pretentious and I wasn't going to let him get away with it." He laughed. "Hey, it was *my* turn." He paused. "One thing about all these guys, being cool is the most important thing to them. They don't mind being called geeks; in fact, they *like* being called geeks. They've taken it to another level. Call them a geek, but don't say they're not cool."

"Is being cool having a martini in the morning?" I asked.

"They think they're rock stars, and rock stars are cool," said Reddo. "And they don't even know what they're drinking. They'll order an extra spicy Bloody Mary with Belvedere vodka—what a waste. You don't mix expensive vodka in tomato juice. That's for well-drink vodka." He lowered his voice. "I give them the well drink vodka anyway, they can't tell." He shrugged. "When I work downtown at 'The 99,' these guys are ordering expensive wine they don't have the experience to appreciate, but they have to have the best, and the best is the most expensive."

"I bet they don't even tip."

"You kidding? The dot-comers throw money at me! They think that's how successful people act," he smirked. "At 'The 99' on Friday and Saturday, it's packed with dot-comers. One guy threw down twenty bucks just for me to get him a glass of water. And ten minutes later he gave me another twenty bucks to turn up the music. I figure if someone doesn't understand the value of money, and they want to give me twenty dollars for water that's fine by me." He paused. "It's kinda funny. All the geeks have money. And their money has given them a set of brass balls for the first time in their lives."

A woman placed down a credit card with a hard snap and said, "All the drinks go on this, Reddo."

I scoped her. She had long auburn hair and used her sunglasses as a hair band. She wore make-up, a green blouse, a slit skirt, nylons, and red leather-strapped shoes with three-inch heels. Her perfume smelled like an approaching storm. She was taller than me. I liked that. She was either banking a tight turn and barely holding onto her late-twenties, or skidding into the wall of her early thirties. But she definitely had stopping power. And that ass, Jesus. That ass.

"Okay," Reddo said, taking the credit card without looking.

"Excuse me, that is *my* credit card," she said, raising her voice.

"Yeah, I know, you gave it to me," he grunted, shrugging. He slid the credit card through a slot in a machine to run it.

"Yes, but it's my credit card, I'm the one who gave it to you," she persisted, as if he was supposed to genuflect in awe.

Reddo turned around, gave her back the card and the receipt, and said, "Yeah, you gave me the card, people give me credit cards all the time."

"Just because I'm a woman doesn't mean I don't have stuff," she said, taking up her plastic and slowly walking away. She turned and flicked a look at me. It registered. Her phone bipped the opening chords of "My Heart Will Go On" from the movie "Titanic." She flipped it open and said, cheerfully, "Hey you!"

"Nasty," I said to Reddo, hawk-eying her exit.

"No matter how pretty they are, and some of these women are fucking beautiful man, kinda like new millennium hookers," said Reddo, laughing. "But no matter how good looking they are, they all have this techie thing about them like you just saw." He showed me his wedding ring. "I'm not even tempted. But they see the ring. And I make *sure* they see it. But they don't care. They view it as a challenge. It's like they're trying to make sure the ring means nothing." He shrugged. "It doesn't surprise me, you know. The shallowest pool has the most vicious fish."

"Later," I said, walking away. "Thanks for the Pepsi."

I passed two dot-comers who did a shot of Jagermeister and shouted, "All right now!" and followed it with a separate, quick rhythmic handclap, stopped, made one fist, lightly tapped each other's knuckles and said, "Go Cardinal!"

When I got back to my seat, the Über Geek remounted the unsteady table.

"There's a groundswell from Silicon Valley, a wave of change rolling underneath us," shouted the Über Geek. "And who is in perfect sync and sees this wave of the future?"

"We do!" shouted the dot-comers in unison.

"And who is paddling into this wave of change?"

"We are!"

"And what are we going to do?" he asked in a louder voice.

"Go for it!" shouted the dot-comers.

"Surf's Up!" said the Über Geek, crouching into his concept of a surfing stance. He extended his left arm straight out and held up his right arm. His potbelly protruded from beneath his Surf Dot Com powder blue polo shirt, and slightly overlapped the edge of his money belt.

"Surf Dot Com, Surf Dot Com, Surf Dot Com," chanted the dot-comers.

I twisted my Dad's ring around my finger. I couldn't stand their cheering any longer.

"This is not happenin'!" I wailed, bolting up to my feet. "Stop with the surfing. Surfing? You're not paddling for a fucking wave. Surfing? Surfing the Internet is not surfing." My outburst silenced the dot comers. They studied me. I was clearly not one of them. I was in my very late forties. I had thick red hair down to the middle of my back, a walnut-dark tan, and a tight swimmer's build. I wore a Vic's Surf Shop sweatshirt with the sleeves cut off, faded jeans, and sandals. A tattoo of the first 19th Infantry Rangers division was on my right upper arm. "Stop saying you're surfing. Surfing the web. That's not surfing. You're not surfing! You are sitting on your butts and clicking a mouse. You only move one finger. That's not a surfing move—that's how patients signal the nurse for more morphine in the hospital. Surfing? There's not a single thing any of you do that couldn't be done by a quad blowing through a tube! Surfing! Be serious. If there's one thing you people are definitely not. And one thing you'll never be. And that's a surfer."

I sat back down at the table, folded my arms across my chest, and poured my patented stinkeye deeply into the dot-comers eyes. My glare intimidated them. I had cultivated my welcome-to-Vietnam stinkeye over the years. A true stinkeye is a glare without the light. There's a deep flatness to it, an unresponsive darkness you can't see all the way into, and won't go near, because it conceals an ominous force that says to any possible intrusion: don't even think about it. I was pissed off.

The Über Geek held a steady bead on me. He wasn't offended. He was amused. He was sizing me up.

Shiloh put my plate on the table, and said, "Your shark."

The dot comers applauded and laughed. They thought I was part of the catered affair's entertainment. But one of them didn't laugh: the woman who had given Reddo a hard time. Our beams met. Her green eyes brightened and comfortably held their predatory focus. Her stare had a one-word vocabulary. It stirred me. And she held it. Her locked-in look said, "I'll go with you on a trip to Mexico—or anywhere for a week. And, I'll do whatever and anything you want me to do." I damn well couldn't keep up with *her* for sure. She arched her shoulders against the back of a chair, her hips tilted over the seat's very edge. Her expression was between a scowl and a pout. She was stunning. A Princess of The Walk. I mean I looked at her and thought what would I have to give up out of my life to get a piece of that? God, did I want to mad dog her.

"What do you think?"

"Huh?" I asked, recovering from my fantasy. "About what?"

"What do you think? About the shark?" repeated Shiloh, who smiled. "Is the shark moist enough for you? That's how you like it, right? I even threw in some extra bacon for Ranger."

"Looks great, um, fine, yeah," I said, but my glance went to the dot-com woman, who was walking towards me.

Shiloh studied the woman and said, "French nail manicure, solitaire gold earrings one karat each, Channel perfume, seven-hundred dollar Prada handbag." She cautiously whispered, "Warning: execudiva. Warning: execudiva." The woman turned her head. "Nice hair flip too." Shiloh territorially remained near my table. "Red heels, green shirt, Santa Hooker, ho, ho, ho."

The execudiva casually sat down across from me as if she were just returning to my table. She sipped a coffee drink topped with whipped cream, and asked, "So are you having a good time?"

"Yeah," I said, taken aback by the direct question.

"Then tell your face about it," she said, pointing at my stinkeye and scowl. She laughed, stopped, then directed a comment to herself, "That wasn't polite was it?"

I brushed a yellow jacket off my tartar sauce, dipped a piece of the shark into it, and I popped the chunk into my mouth.

"Isn't eating shark bad karma for a surfer?" asked the execudiva, whose voice had a light but brittle intelligent edge.

"No, eating shark is good karma," I said. "I eat shark because I figure if I'm out in the water the shark will sense there's something that will also eat them and the shark will leave."

"You know sharks are endangered."

"So am I."

The woman caught Shiloh's disapproving look.

"Excuse me, server, but can I have what you would call a spoon?" she haughtily asked and lifted her cup at a slight angle.

"Yes, I have what you would call a *spoon*," tartly said Shiloh, withdrawing a metal utensil from her apron, loudly snapping it on the table. "That dress—that's a nice color. What's that color?"

"Hunter green," she replied and flipped her hair. "I'd like a Pellegrino."

"We only have Crystal Geyser or Evian?"

"I don't think so?" the execudiva said, turning away. "I'll have a Bloody Mary with Belvedere vodka—or Ketle One. Reddo knows how I take it." She said to me. "Reddo's my bartender person at 'The 99'. I use Reddo at all my off-site events." She started singing, "Party like it's 1999." Then she suddenly stopped. "Reddo makes great Cosmos—Cosmopolitans. I was at a launch where he poured them through the grooves of a block of ice. But that would be a little too decadent at this hour."

"So, a Bloody Mary then," said Shiloh, who did a mock servant girl curtsy behind the woman's back, smirked, and muttered a warning to me, "High maintenance."

The execudiva studied the lettering on the front of my sweatshirt. "So you are the Vic of Vic's Surf Shop? I always thought it would be *kewl* to surf. It's on my checklist of things to do. I just achieved horseback riding."

"Checklist of things to do?"

"Fire walking was another. I mean, we are the directors of our own movie," she smiled, leaned forward, and flipped her hair.

"I run my own shop. Shape my own boards. I live in Santa Cruz. I'm not like these trannie maggots."

"What's a trannie?" she asked, amused.

"Transplant," I said. "Someone from Over The Hill."

"Over The Hill?"

"Over The Hill—that's what locals call people from San Jose.

It's 'Over The Hill' because when you go north from Santa Cruz up Highway 17 you have to climb the summit of about eighteen-hundred feet, then you go down into Silicon Valley."

"So you're a real local. Were you born in Santa Cruz?"

"San Jose," I grimly replied. I paused, and firmly added. "I don't like to talk about that."

She laughed.

"You look like a local. Not many men look like you, you're kinda sexy," she said. She quickly noticed I was taken aback by the forwardness of her remark, and rapidly added. "I'm not coming onto you, I just broke up with somebody. But we stayed friends. I insist on always staying friends." She tapped her finger on the tattoo on my upper right arm. "What's with your tat?"

"It was a division I was in—in Vietnam."

"I can't read it. It's kinda blurred."

"Actually, it's clear. My skin just hardened over it."

She laughed, glanced at my hand and said. "That's a nice gold ring on your finger. It looks like an old ring."

"It used to be my Dad's," I said sharply. "He's dead."

"Ooooh, don't want to go there. I can relate. Been there done that. I just spent a week in the war zone."

"War zone?"

"Home with my parents," she said sadly.

"What's your connection with these clowns?"

"IJS," she said, angled her head, and then flipped her hair off her shoulder. Her answer irritated me. She was one of them. She sensed it. "I'm sorry, I'm just used to geek speak," she assured me. "We acronym everything. IJS stands for 'I just started.' I left my job in Palo Alto to come down here. I went to BrassRing Dot Com's job Fair in San Jose. Surf Dot Com was one of 520 companies there. They offered me more money than I was making at my old job. And the recruiter gave me a trip to Key West just to take the position. And I got a five-figure signing bonus. OK? I mean O-K-A-Y. This is my seventh job in three years. I'm bright. When someone offers you a better opportunity you have to take it. You want to laugh? When I went to the credit union, they almost wouldn't give me a loan because they thought I was *losing* my job every six months. They said my employment record 'looked shady.'" She leaned forward to give me an angle on her cleavage. Jesus, she had no bra. She crossed and recrossed her legs. The webbed-fabric of her nylons sounded like the soft crackling of kindling. "Me, shady. Do I look shady?"

"God, yes."

When she laughed, I noticed all the dot-com guys in the place were checking her out. I knew they were jealous. Surfer guys like me weren't supposed to get their women.

"I was afraid to talk to you," she casually said and sipped her weird coffee drink. "With all that red hair you look like a lion."

"What is that thing you're drinking?"

"A low-fat double espresso caramel macchiato I got from StokaMocha. I'm useless without it." She paused than sang to the tune of the Macarena song "Hey macchiato!" She laughed. "My barista person Juan makes them perfecto." She looked off at the ocean and said, "God, the eye candy in Santa Cruz is great."

"Eye candy?"

"And you know what's ironic?" she said in a soft confiding voice. "I hate the Internet and these PDA—er, pardon, Personal-Digital-Assistant-carrying e-holes. They all dress in this real expensive casual. You know, the guys with the khaki pants and the same three-hundred-dollar sneakers that looked like boat sneakers but aren't or those ridiculous black military shoes. They're all Banana-Republicaned-maxed-out people, like they are oh so hip and mod but not caught up in being professional. And they're way anal." She looked away. "No business smarts at all. If it wasn't for dot-coms, these geeks would be hanging out in comic book shops, collecting stamps, flying with radio-controlled planes or in ham-radio clubs." She examined my food. "Wow. Six strips of bacon. Your arteries must be solid as licorice."

"The bacon is for Ranger," I said, wrapping up the crisp strips.

"Ranger? I hope that's not the name of your girlfriend?" She smiled. "I mean if that's her name she can't be too attractive."

"She's my dog. A German shepherd."

"Bacon for your dog?"

"Ranger eats what I eat," I said, smiling, but not all the way because I didn't want her to see my missing back teeth. "Range doesn't know she's a dog. She thinks she's human."

The woman unrolled the paper towel and examined the bone Shiloh left for Ranger.

"So, I guess, the bone is for you?" she archly said. She laughed and because she was attractive I laughed too. "So Vic of Vic's Surf Shop, when were you born?"

"November—"

"Ooooh," she cooed with pleasure. "A Scorpio."

"I'm Westsider. But, maybe my shop makes me an Eastsider."

"What's an Eastsider?" she asked, acting enchanted. "Is that the name of the dish you're eating?"

"Eastsider means I surf Pleasure Point. Right now, we're on the Westside. The San Lorenzo River is considered the dividing line in Santa Cruz between the Westside and Eastside. Years ago, Westsiders and Eastsiders used to get into fighting over surf spots. Westsiders are still pretty hard-core locals. Out there by the Lighthouse is Steamer Lane. The Lane, if you surf, you've got to know what you're doing out there. In those days, you didn't mess with Westsiders who grew up here or you'd get beefed on. They have time and grade. Out by that stupid surfer statue on the cliff is Indicators, and inside is Cowells, where I learned to surf. It took me ten years to work my way into the Killer Cowells surf group. It's a nice longboarding spot, sandy bottom, not much kelp. It doesn't break year-round anymore. The Yacht Harbor they built in the mid-sixties screwed-up the sand flow. I hate surfing this side of town. It's UCSC-ed out.."

"Now who's speaking in acronyms?"

"UCSC is an abbreviation," interrupted Shiloh, standing near us.

"And?" sarcastically asked the execudiva.

"It's not an acronym."

"Your point?" she said in a condescending way.

"You *pronounce* acronyms," replied Shiloh.

"Whatever," she said in a bored drawling. "Duh. Hello? Did someone call the grammar sheriff? Abbreviation—that's what *I* said, anyway." She studied Shiloh's glare. "Don't look at me like that, what are you going to do home girl, hit me?"

Shiloh stood still for a moment, as if she was mulling over doing just that. Then, she sharply turned, and walked away.

I said, "Shiloh is a scrapper, and you don't go rail-to-rail on a Westsider who had history. She just might take you out."

The execudiva grimaced and muttered to herself. "I guess I should stick to smaller words." Her beeper went off. She took out a Palm Pilot, hit a few buttons, smiled, and closed it. She said, "Our stock price is still climbing." She nickered and purred to herself, "Ehhhh-xcellent."

I said nothing.

She filled up the silence by spinning her key ring on the table. It had a blanched out, twisted curled rock attached to it.

"What's that white thing on your key chain?"

"Oh this," she said proudly. "Ever been down to Key West? This is part of a coral reef. I was snorkeling on this tour. The guide said not to touch the reef, but that's his job. I wanted to have something to prove I was there. Like taking one little piece is going to hurt anything."

"Huh."

"BTW," she stopped, sensing my irritation at the abbreviation, and quickly corrected herself. "By the way...our campus is right near the ocean—"

"Campus? You're go to UCSC? I thought you worked—"

"Campus is what we call our office."

"Huh."

"Ours is in an old surf shop."

"Where?" I asked, irritated.

"Across the street at the entrance of the wharf."

"The old building, looks like an old forties gas station?"

"Yeah, you know it? It used to be a place called, um—"

"Slap's," I said, looking off at Cowells beach.

"Yeah, I guess that's it. You know it, huh? Surf Dot Com in an old surf shop. That's rad!"

I grabbed the bacon and bone. I wanted out of there big time. I counted off a few bucks to pay the bill.

"Hey you fucked up!" yelled someone. "This is definitely not cool. Not cool at all. Not even close to cool."

It was the Über Geek. He was dressing down Shiloh, who was standing next to him, her head bowed.

"I did not ask for fucking onions with my fish," the Über

Geek loudly lashed out, spitting the food in his mouth to his plate. "I never have onions on my fish. Everybody knows that."

"I thought you did say onions. I'm sorry," said Shiloh, who scratched her head. "Can't you just scrape them off?"

"Didn't you hear me? I placed a simple order: broiled ahi with a twist of lemon, a Thomas' English muffin, and a Bloody Mary with Belevedere vodka from the bar," snapped the Über Geek, who pointed his finger in her face. "Why should my money award fuck-ups? You fucking didn't do your job. You fucked up. Why an untrained chimpanzee could handle my order."

I muttered to the execudiva, "Who is that idiot?"

"Drake Sather," she said. "Drake already has a couple companies under his belt. He can be a pain in the ass, and he knows it. And he wouldn't mind me saying it either. He's the germ of the company. He's brilliant, brilliant, brilliant. He never wears suits. He doesn't even have an office. He has a cubicle like everyone else. We're all on the same level."

"This is fucked, this is bullshit," continued Drake.

"He's a genius," she said.

"If that's how a genius talks, I've been surfing with them my whole life."

"You have to extend yourself to understand him."

"I'd extend something, all right," I said, putting in an extra dollar tip with the rest of my bill for Shiloh, which I placed under my dish to prevent the sea breeze from blowing it away.

"Drake really is a genius," she insisted. "He pitched a deal to an incubator in the Valley. He got the seed money for SDC after a twenty-minute Power Point presentation. They knew if they didn't give him funds for Surf Dot Com someone else would."

I stared at her, paused, and said, "I didn't understand a single thing you were saying to me."

This amused her.

"An incubator—"

"I didn't say I wanted to understand what you were saying," I said, getting up and turning to leave.

"Ba-bye," she said, surprised at my abrupt exit. "Hello? Something I said?"

"Yes."

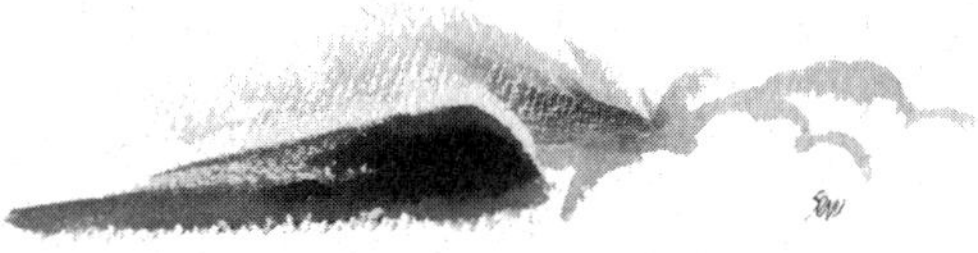

I withdrew from Bings and walked on the wharf. The light breeze had a slight bite. I kept my hands in the pouch pocket of my surf shop sweatshirt. It was a little cool, but the sun was warm. A cloudburst of fog puffed out along the distant Monterey coastline. The salt-water air contained the mingling aromas of kelp, fish, and a touch of freshly opened watermelon. The surf made a muffled crumple like the distant march of an unseen enemy. I passed closed souvenir, T-shirt and swimwear shops, seafood restaurants, and ice cream stores. Parked on the wharf were the dot-comers' vehicles—SUVs, Lexuses, Mercedes, and BMWs—all with activated car alarms that blinked with little red lights on the dashboards. The owners were only ten feet away!

A horn tapped. A hand waved at me from within a beat-up green van that had 'Mark The Mobile Vet' written on its side. I shaped him a 9'6" pintail with soft rails. Mobile Mark was in his late fifties. He had long hair but was completely bald on top. He never trimmed his ear or nose hairs. He was thin. He always wore jeans, a flannel shirt, and work boots. He'd park in one of three gas station locations around the county and treat people's pets. He was qualified and all. Mark just didn't like the overhead of an office, and wanted to run on his own schedule around the tides to surf. He had taken care of Ranger since she was a puppy.

"Burr, whattup?" he said, stopping his van in one of the two lanes on the wood-planked road that went through the center of the wharf. He looked at me with concern. "How'z Ranger?"

"Good days, bad days," I said, looking down.

Mobile Mark realized he upset me by bringing up Ranger's condition. She had been around sixteen years. I had other dogs, but Ranger was different. Her right leg was starting to go. And she was favoring her other leg too much. I didn't even want to think about what it meant. I couldn't bear it. I just couldn't.

A SUV driver behind Mark leaned on his horn. Instead of just simply passing us on the left, the driver leaned on his horn again, threw his hands up in the air and started yelling. We couldn't hear him. His windows were rolled up. But the guy was going ballistic over nothing. Mark waved him by, which seemed to infuriate the guy more. The SUV driver flipped us off, quickly passed on the left, but slowed down the all-terrain vehicle to go over a miniscule speed bump. He drove ten feet, and angled his car across two parking spaces, so no one would scratch his off-road vehicle. He stayed in the SUV and talked on a cell phone.

"Look at that guy, he could have just passed us, but no, he went out of his way to be miserable," Mark said, laughing. "Yeah, top-of-the-line SUV. That world just keeps coming here."

"Surf yesterday?"

"Went out with Barbecue Bob, got yelled at by people in the water I never saw before," he glumly said. "I had a terrible time and Bob had a whatever. It was so crowded. What I'm looking for isn't there anymore. I got in three arguments that I didn't start. It's not like back in the day of '83 at Rivermouth, we had to fight to get our waves, and when we did they were good ones."

Mark was right. I remembered how the storms of 83' pushed sand out from the San Lorenzo rivermouth, and created a perfect bar that extended hundreds of yards out, where perfect right-and-left handers peeled off it. If you watched it from the cliffs, the waves broke off the distant bar's tip, and rolled into shore: it resembled a giant Christmas tree. It was the best I have ever seen it break—and it broke that way for several months that year.

"It was at Rivermouth when those two guys who kept burning you said, 'Let's take it to the beach.' You paddled in. Then you and Ranger kicked their butts for stuffing you on a set wave."

"Yeah, Ranger was just a puppy then. But she still went after them. They were assholes." I paused. "But they never burned me anywhere, and they never came back to Rivermouth."

"And guess what? They're still assholes. I ran into them when I had to put down one of their guard dogs. Those two guys do corporate security stuff." He paused. "The assholes especially remembered Ranger. One of them still had a chin scar."

"Back then, a scar was a receipt," I said. "Send them our love."

"Plant you now, dig you later," said Mobile Mark, who pulled away. "Surf should be good today. See ya." When he said 'see ya,' it sounded like 'seizure.'

His truck made the wooden-planked roadway thump out a drum roll, which vibrated underneath the parked dot-comers cars, and set off a rolling wave of car alarms.

I passed two Mexican fishermen who stood on the seagull-dung splattered concrete walk. They flatly stared at their poles. In their buckets, were a few decent sized halibut. I watched the waves break on the beach along the half-mile stretch of the Santa Cruz Beach boardwalk. The amusement park rides on it were stilled and resembled giant pieces of discarded weaponry. I looked out across the bay. Farther out in the ocean, thousands of sooty shearwaters formed an endless swarming trail through the sky. The birds came from New Zealand and Australia to feast on the anchovies. A swirling spray of sprinkling blackness dipped into the water and than rose above it. The flapping flock almost looked like a funnel cloud vacuuming up fluttering chunks of black flecks off the ocean's surface. The ravenous birds were systematically following and slaughtering schools of anchovies. The anchovies had no choice. Run or be eaten. When you're overrun, you're overrun. Not much choice there.

I walked to the Burr Mobile. It was a mustard-colored VW truck with white bumpers, and a camper shell over its bed. The VW was so riddled with brown-ringed holes of rust, I think the only things keeping the vehicle in one piece was its primer coat, decals, dents and possibly the fumes from its bad muffler. The passenger and driver windows were down and the doors were unlocked. A longboard's tail with its fin up, stuck out of the open rear window of the camper shell. In the passenger seat, I could just make out the rising, vigilant tips of Ranger's black ears.

A dreamless bum approached me from the public bathrooms. A soiled sleeping bag formed a shroud over his head. He wore a grungy multi-stained poncho, dirty jeans with heavily frayed bottoms, and flattened-out faded brown shoes, which gave the impression he was wading in two ankle-deep puddles of dried gravy. His unwashed and uncombed beard looked like someone had glued fifty-separate strands of beef jerky on his face. His flesh resembled badly poured brown dough that had baked unevenly. And sticking out of his hair, just over his forehead, was a white feather. I briefly wondered if he had recently been shot with a crossbow. He clenched some flowers he wanted to sell me, which he probably stole from a park or someone's lawn. I was in no mood to deal with this troll. I turned on my stinkeye and quickly tried to walk past him.

"Hey man, don't ignore me, man," the troll accusingly said and walked alongside me. "I said, 'Don't ignore me,' man."

I stopped, fired my stinkeye into him at point-blank range, and firmly said, "Don't bother me and I won't ignore you."

The troll advanced toward me. I made a low and soft whistle. In the truck, Ranger's pointed ears rose higher over the low edge of the passenger-side window.

"You see that German shepherd?"

Ranger stuck her head out the passenger window and tilted her head to the right. She barked once. The bum studied Ranger.

"What you are about to do is just not happenin'," I cautioned. "You make one more move toward me, and I will kick you in the chest, knock you to the ground, and then my dog will jump out of the window and go for your balls. And if you try to hit her, she'll grab your hand and work her way up to your throat." I paused. "And once she does that, she goes crazy and I'm not responsible for her actions." The bum retreated. "Hey, dog breath." The bum stopped. "When you walk away, don't call me an asshole either. And when you go away, you go away quiet." The bum spotted the 'Vic's Surf Shop' lettering on the side of the bus. I knew what he was contemplating. "And don't go thinking you can go to my shop and throw a brick through a window or scratch them up, or piss on my doorway, or harass my customers. Ask around, I'll find you—and so will my dog."

He said nothing and left.

I went to the VW. Ranger proudly barked twice, tilted her head to the left, looked at me, and opened her mouth like she was trying to smile. Her tongue slightly hung off the right side.

"Rangey! You're looking out for Daddy weren't you?" I said, and smiled and sang in baby talk, "Rangey."

I enjoyed how every inflection of my voice made Ranger tilt her head a different direction. When I got her as a puppy, she was all black. Over the years, her coat turned to brown with saddle-shaped pattern of black on her back, along with just a few brush dark strokes on her back ears and the top of her head. But now, her black fur had fringes of gray where it met the fading brown.

"Whup, whups," I said in my baby-talk voice, opening the passenger door. "Whuppers, Daddy's got breakfast." She jumped out. "Stay, Range!" I tried to block her. Ranger slipped through my arms and landed on the pavement. Her right back leg gave out. She yelped. I felt the pain. "Okay, Rangey, here you go," I said, unwrapping the napkin, and placing the bacon in front of her. She hobbled up and happily gobbled down the crunchy strips. "Yes, Rangey." I stroked her back a few times. "Yes, Range. Who's a good whup whups?"

We crossed the street. I heard Ranger's nails from her paw drag and slightly scrape on the asphalt. The depressing sound nicked a sharp pain inside me. Mark told me Ranger should rest. But when I went some place she *had* to be with me. It was what made her live, and was probably going to cut her life short. But not being with me would make her fade faster. Ranger still had her moments left. I was going to make damn sure she got them.

I stood in front of Surf Dot Com's new headquarters. The blue pastel painted building was trimmed around the edges with a rose tint. Along the roof, was a glowing neon sign slowly illuminating letter after letter until it spelled out "Surf Dot Com." The name changed from blue to green to red then disappeared and respelled again. To the right of the name, was a digital animation of a breaking wave and a surfer just barely in front of it. "Ahead of the curve" in blue neon tube letters flashed beneath the waverider. The sand-rutted and pot-holed lot was recently paved and painted with white lines for parking spaces, which were occupied by BMWs, Mercedes, Ferraris, Lexuses, Vespa scooters, VW bugs, Porsches, Jaguars, one yellow and one red Japanese motorcycle, a blue Hummer with a "Surf

Dot Com" vanity plate on it, as well as three mini-vans with "Surf Dot Com" logos wrapped around their sides. I went up to the front door that had a small, black-square pad thing for people to pass a magnetic card over to gain entrance to the building. Inside, I heard the fast tha-thumping of electronic music. The workplace resembled a combination arcade and day-care center for dorks. The walls were coated with glistening pink salmon-colored paint, hip-hop graffiti, and some drawings of the cartoon characters Rocky and Bullwinkle. The floor had a smooth, light brown-clay carpet. A mirrored disco ball hung from the middle of the ceiling. All the light within the building came from tiny black wrist-bone looking desk lamps in the cubicles, which were surrounded by those paper-thin walls you usually see in Japanese restaurants. Lodged inside each cubicle were hunched-over geeks sitting in large black chairs at oddly curved futuristic desks. They rapidly jabbed keyboards and intently peered into the lead-shielded glass of their cathode-ray computer terminals. The cubicles seemed more like playpens. They contained mountain bikes, skateboards, rollerblades, squirt guns, tennis racquets, golf clubs, scooters, or surfboards (which really pissed me off). Mounted on a center support beam was a miniature replica of a backboard and basketball hoop with a net. A small foam ball flew from one of the cubicles; the ball rolled off the rim. In a far corner, four dot-comers intensely played foosball. Amid all this, a miniature radio-controlled race car made a tight turn by a black bean-bag couch, and collided with an inflated globe, which rolled against a chair where a geek sat in front of a wide-screen TV and played a video game. The racer sped away down hallways into a back left hand corner room, where several geeks stood in a kitchen near an espresso machine.

A horn tapped.

"Watcha think of my new ride?" Bobby Weever said, sitting behind the wheel. He stuck out his right hand in a fist with his pinkie and thumb extended out, and slightly rocked it up and down in a gesture to his brand-new van, which was angled into a parking space near me. The van's windows were plastered with surf stickers. Stickers were okay if you just had one for the surf shop or board shaper you supported, but this guy had no loyalty to anyone. There were several surf shops, board shapers, surf club stickers on his van, all because Weever thought it was cool to put as many surf stickers as he could on his windows. He got out of his van, admired it, and said, "It's da kine."

"Hello Robert," I paused a beat and contemptuously stretched out the pronunciation of his last name. "Weeeeeee-*ver*."

I said Weever's name that way to mock him. Basically, he was a perfectly decent guy who I couldn't stand; in fact, a lot of locals couldn't stand him either, and showed their contempt by stretching out the pronunciation of his last name the same way I did. He was in his late forties, and had dyed blonde hair. Weever claimed he surfed Santa Cruz as a kid but I never remembered seeing him out in the water. He viewed himself as a surf legend because he had surfed every day for the last twenty-five years. He lived in San Jose, and would drive to Santa Cruz, dip in the water, then jump back into his car and go to work. And some newspaper actually did a story on him. First off, there was no reason at all for surfing every day because there aren't waves every day. And, Weever couldn't even surf for shit. Even the character lines on his face looked like a swell that wasn't working. The guy was really overly theme-ed out. He wore a "Surf Dot Com" logo-ed baseball cap, a stonewashed denim herringbone shirt, pleated khaki pants, brown loafers, and strapped over his right shoulder was a black computer bag with the words "Surf Dot Com" stitched on its flap, an 'Industry Standard' magazine stuck out of a half-zipped pouch. He held a 'Surf Dot Com' travel coffee cup coffee. The guy was Valley before there was a Valley.

"I'm selling my place in San Jose, and getting a beach house in Pleasure Point. I'm a local," he said, smirking. "My dad had to wait forty years to get what I'm going to have in less than three." Weever paused. I knew he was trying to soften me up. But for what I didn't know. "I'm living large. I've been sitting on the sidelines for a long time, watching these dot-comers getting rich on stock options. I mean gosh, I figured, they're young and getting rich, and I'm not. Years ago, I started out of college at $18,000. But kids out of high school are starting out anywhere from at $80,000 to $120,000 without any job experience, some only know how to link a web page. I'm bright. It's my chance.

I'm not missing out on this! I went to a BrassRing Dot Com job fair. I got hired on...I forgot the date. Oh, wait, it's on the back of my Rolex." Weever pulled the watch off this wrist and read the inscription on the back. "Drake gave me this for signing on with the team." He smiled and put his watch back on. "I started on March 19, 1998." I half expected the watch to start boasting about Weever too. "This isn't data processing, this is different." He flicked his right hand, which had a multi-colored beaded wrist bracelet his kid made for him. "I mean I put in my time at Intel and HP. I topped out. Time to ratchet up the game plan. I'm Da Man! No more electronic time sheets, billable hours, or dry cleaning bills for me." He paused and loudly vowed. "I'll *never* wear a tie again."

"There you go," I said, flatly. "That's you."

A few bubbles drifted between us. I was hoping Weever would sit on one and float away, but he wasn't finished with me.

"Yeah it is! I'm going to put in a special surf room in my new place," he rapidly continued. "How about selling me one of those old classic sixties longboards you have hanging in your shop? What do you think, bro?"

Bro.

Bro was short for brother. And from running a surf shop, I knew anyone who called me bro wanted something I had. Can I have some of your fries, bro? Give me a lift, bro? Hey, can I bum a cigarette, bro? Do you have any spare change, bro? Whattup, you still seeing that girl, bro? Hey, you and me on this wave, whaddayasay bro?

"They're shop boards. You know I don't sell shop boards," I replied firmly, giving him the same pat answer I'd been giving to him—and jerks like him—for years. "I put them there for display. They're part of the shop. A shop board is never for sale."

"Come on, a bro deal."

Bro deal.

The Bro deal was a pure Santa Cruz transaction. It meant a guy wanted something I had, and expected me to charge them less than what it was worth. Why? Because they were my bro, right? Bro dealers typically hang out in the shop and haggle for hours. They'd missed the best part of a swell, just to grind me down twenty-five bucks on a board. And, if I did cut them a break, they'd keep pushing the deal further to get a leash cord thrown in. If I did that, then the bro dealer would try to get fifteen percent off some shirt because he found some flaw in it. And what's even worse is, bro dealers *have* the money. After spending hours trying to save just a few dollars, they'd pull out a wad of hundreds just to get to the fifties to pay for it—or, they just throw down their Gold Card. I learned early on that when you give these bro dealers price breaks they don't appreciate it.. They attributed the discount to their ability to talk you down. God, there were a lot of them. They never put it together a regular customer always get a better deal in the long run.

"Well, no harm in asking," Weever said. "Hey, I'm no different than a million other guys, it never hurts to ask."

But there was harm in asking. It was rude. And who the hell would want to be like a million other guys? That's the last thing I would want to be. But, it didn't bother him, or guys like him.

Weever hit his key chain button. The van locked itself and electronically chirped. He hurried to the wharf, following the trail of bubbles leading to the promised land of a tie-less job.

I turned and caught sight of a familiar, rounded-edged, red sign, which stuck out of the dumpster. It was faded, and covered with dust and dried mouse droppings. The white letters of 'Slap's' were barely visible on it. Slap's Surf Center was long gone. Slap never really called it a surf shop. I guess it was a "center" because the place sold everything—umbrellas, beach chairs, maps, towels, lotions, inflatable mats, and candy bars. I don't think he even carried T-shirts with the shop logo (which was a monkey knee-paddling on a longboard for a wave within a circular border, and wrapped around it were the words 'Slap's Surf Center.'). Back in the day, Slaps was a seedy soulful sixties place crammed within an old forties-style filling station, which had white stucco, red trim, and a slanted black metal roof. It even had the remnants of a small oblong concrete island and red gas pumps. Its damp, salt-water concrete floor was coated with wax, resin splatters, sand fleas, and ancient oil stains. Behind the counter, past the front door, the garage bays had two hundred longboards stacked against the walls. The decor was done in the style of those old Tiki lounges, with bamboo poles and palm fronds. There was a lime-green couch where anyone could hang (the couch wasn't lime; it was faded.). The windows of the place were always plastered with flyers. Slaps occupied a small triangular corner lot at a four-way intersection opposite the municipal wharf entrance, up the street from the boardwalk, and catty corner to a stretch of Cowells beach where the 10-story, 125-room Dream Inn hotel is now, and nearby was a drive-in hamburger joint. Painted in red on a side of the building were the words "Surf and Sand." There was a "Rentals" sign placed near the window. And on the roof, was a broken "Sea and Ski" clock next to a sign that said, "Follow the Washington Senators." Outside the front door was a wooden flagpole with a screeching monkey in a triangular steel cage who threw his shit at the customers. The monkey weighed about twenty pounds. He was one of those circus-type monkeys that do tricks. The one thing you didn't do was try to stare this monkey down. If he even sensed you were challenging him, he'd start throwing shit. I admired his stinkeye. Slap had to hang the cage—with a straw food basket next to it—high atop a flagpole outside the shop, because the kids would try to get back at the monkey for hitting them with shit. When Slap kept the monkey inside at night, there were quarter-size welts on the windows from guys firing pellet guns at the chimp. During the day someone actually tried using a bow and arrow at him. The arrow was stuck in the post just below the cage. I don't remember the monkey's name. I never ran into anyone who did. All I remember was he stunk, jerked off a lot, and he was mean to everybody. Even Slap had long white scars on his lower arms from where the animal scratched him. But, actually, I never really understood the monkey thing.

I loved Slap's. Slap made it possible for me to grow up in the sand under the sun in Santa Cruz. I worked part-time there, rinsing out wetsuits and renting surfboards. I had it aced, hitting on girls, drinking a Pepsi on the beach, eating a sandwich, catching waves, and just getting baked in the heat. I could surf all day and sleep on the beach at night. Cops didn't bother you then. Santa Cruz was a wide-open coastal town of only 20,583—funny, I still remember that number. It was mainly a retirement community. And Slap was all right, but was kinda on the ornery side, but never chased us out of his shop. He liked kids. He let us hang. We were always cutting up, burning tires on the beach, shooting rats in the rocks with guns, whatever, anything to get a rise out of anyone. Slap would yell but he'd never get really mad at us because he knew we didn't want to be anywhere else. He had reddish-white skin, wore thick black-framed glasses. He was in his fifties, bald and overweight, and constantly smoked cigars. He wore Hawaiian shirts, baggy white painter pants, and black sneakers spattered with blue paint. If he surfed, it was years ago. I think he was Scandinavia and German or Greek something. He landed at the beach on D Day. And he came down from Seattle or Portland or somewhere like that and had run a center for delinquents. He even played major league ball on the Washington Senators for a few months; in fact, he never talked about surfing, he was always talking about home run hitters like Harmon Killebrew and Frank Howard. I think the only reason Slap started a surf shop was simply because the building was near the ocean. The place's rental boards were used piles, if you got there late in the day, the leftovers were so cracked, when you sat on the board, it'd cut up the sides of your legs. Slap was cheap, when he rented you a board, he'd give you a piece of wax for it that wasn't enough to wipe your ass with. When Slap got his lunch at the hamburger place across the street, he never tipped. And if he bought hamburgers to pay some of the kids for helping around the shop, he'd drive to McDonald's and give us cheaper burgers; or, after we worked three hours he'd let us use a board. A lot of older teenagers would act like the place wasn't cool. Anytime the subject of Slap's place came up, they shook their heads, flicked their hands at the topic like they were swatting a fly away, and grunted, "Ah, arh." But every one of them was tied into that shop—a lot of people were. Slap's wife was a weird lady always reading the Watchtower and talking about Jesus. She took board deposits and zealously guarded the register as only a true Christian can. Slap wasn't religious. Slap said he stopped believing in God at the beach on D Day. He said there was a conscientious objector who was a medic, and who preached about the immorality of the war to the soldiers. Then on D Day, when they were taking so much fire, he saw the medic drop to his knees and start praying. A bomb came down and scored a direct it on the guy, blasting him to nothing. That was enough God for Slap. He didn't care. But there was one thing in the shop he did care about. It was a surfboard Slap never rented out, or sold, or allowed anyone to use. The board was white and in the middle of its deck someone had drawn and air-brushed a figure of Superman in the center. And it looked so classic: the red, white, and blue uniform, and his arms on his hips, with the cape flying behind him. It was Slap's shop board and hung from straps in the ceiling at the shop entrance. I never knew what happened to it. Every afternoon, between the shop and the garage bay building, Slap set up two resin buckets, placed a piece of plywood across it, and lied in the sun. He'd lounge out there and talk to his buddies about baseball, or nap with his sunglasses pushed back on his forehead. I didn't know it, but at the time Slap was sick. I thought it was because of his back and he was tired. I was just a kid, you know. I didn't know, I was caught up in other things.

I went to Vietnam in 1968, and a year and a day later, I came back to Santa Cruz, and stood in front of Slap's abandoned shop. The white paint flaked off the stucco. Jagged glass edged the few windows, which weren't boarded up. Inside I could see a few wrecked pieces of furniture, a bare mattress, and beer cans. There were pigeon and gull droppings on the sidewalk by the door. A chain clip attached to a rope tolled a chinging sound against the flagpole. The monkey cage was gone. The cracked-asphalt and sand-filled lot was used for $10-a-day beach parking. Slap died from cancer. The monkey was dead too. But, I really didn't know Slap at all. It was the feeling of the shop I missed. And on that bright summer day, I took my nine-ten O'Neill Intruder and paddled out to Cowells. I sat on my board and thought I am home and this was bliss. But everything had changed within a year. The surfers in the line-up were my age but had long hair and rode short boards and I had short hair and a longboard. I missed the transition from longboard to shortboard. Longboards were no longer cool. They were logs. I was no longer cool. The surfers called me a trannie. I wanted to mangle them. And on land, my friends approached me at parties and called me a warmonger, a murderer, and a baby killer. They isolated me. And, I decided to stay that way. I closed-up shop too. Before the war I was the center of every activity, but now I wanted to be left alone. I lived in a Plymouth Valiant off Steamer Lane on West Cliff Drive, did construction work and surfed at night. Throughout the years different people owned Slap's building and expanded it, burned it for insurance, rebuilt it, put another addition on it again, but nothing really took off. The place drifted from owner to owner, and would stay vacant for a year or two in between. I always thought one day I would get my crack at opening the old shop up again. Maybe I could come full circle. But there was no chance for that now. It was bad enough the dot-comers were ruining my town. They were ruining my dreams too. I clasped my hands together, spun Dad's ring on my finger and studied the dot-comers through the huge front window. The full reflections of Ranger and I on the glass were like translucent ghosts of an icon on a computer desktop screen, just waiting for a dot-comer to place a cursor on our image, click their mouse, and drag us like a file to the trash.

I DROVE MY VOLKSWAGEN past Seabright Avenue on West Cliff Drive, a two-lane stretch lined by huge cypress trees on one side, and railroad tracks on the other. A procession of six bums marched down the tracks, they were in their forties, had scraggly stained clothing, and long hair. The trolls' bandleader carried a case of beer. He had a big smile on his face and so did all his followers. In front of me, was a Mexican guy in a yellow baseball cap on a beat-up bike. He glanced back, saw me, smiled, and rapidly pedaled onto to the shoulder. I stuck my arm out the window and gave him a thank-you wave. The oldies radio station played 'Sixteen Tons' by Tennessee Ernie Ford. I looked in the rear-view mirror. An SUV was tailgating me. There was no point in accelerating. Ahead was a traffic jam of new SUVs, mini-vans, luxury cars or sporty foreign jobs, which were interspersed between concrete mixers, utility and gravel trucks, painter and contractor vans, as well as pick-ups with black metal rack frames above their beds going to job sites with either landscaping equipment, window panes, lumber, ladders, carpets, or long white PVC pipes. Only a few years ago, it used to just take ten minutes to drive a couple miles from the Westside to the Eastside of Santa Cruz, but now, almost every morning, it took me twenty-five minutes because everyone used the side streets to get around the slow-moving rush hour traffic on Highway

One. I turned right onto 7th Street toward the coast, and eventually made a left at Twin Lakes onto East Cliff Drive, I glanced at the ocean and the short stretch of beach just to the left of the Santa Cruz Yacht Harbor mouth. The jetty rocks resembled a giant stack of children's jacks. I stopped to let a group of ducks and geese cross the street to the small tidal marsh on the other side of the road. I liked the ducks. Especially how the mother duck led the way. Soon, I was driving through a neighborhood of mobile-home parks, and a healthy, offbeat combination of well-kept or rundown one-story cottages, some with several cars parked on small front yards with overgrown lawns and beautiful hydrangea bushes. But as I kept going, dirt paths became sidewalks, curb cuts, and catch basins. The roads were torn up, partially repaved, or streaked with tractor mud tracks. Hydrangea bushes turned into tall redwood fencing. There were "For Sale" and "Sold" signs everywhere. I heard hammering, electric saws, pneumatic drills, and the beeping of heavy hydraulic construction equipment driving backwards, and dumping dirt into large trucks. Bulldozers demolished Victorian homes, bungalows, and seaside cottages. Orange netting wrapped around the trees. Freshly scraped vacant lots were roped off with two-inch wide, yellow plastic strips marked "caution"—the ones police used to mark crime scenes. Each block had a starter castle, a three-story McMansion built out to four-feet from the edge of their property lines and bordered by stupid banana plants. Every other side street had rows of completed tract homes or condo units, paved driveways with shiny new SUVs, and trimmed lawns. More homes were going up, their wood-sheeted roofs topped with stacks of half-cylindrical, Spanish mission-style, terra-cotta shingles. The Instant Locals didn't want to blend into the neighborhood. If the could take down the ocean views and the sunsets and put them inside their homes, they would have.

The traffic was still stop-and-go, but the SUV kept tailgating me. The throttled-out vehicle was ridiculously huge. For a second, I thought it was actually growing. I could only see its flared chrome front bumpers in my rear-view mirror. Years ago, when Santa Cruz was more of a retirement community, I'd get stuck in traffic behind blue-haired old ladies who sat low behind the wheel and drove too slow in old cars. Now, I was stuck in front of blue-haired young ladies who sat high in the front seat of SUVs, drove too fast, and tailgated me. The SUV passed me on the shoulder, then cut in front of me. I braked. The driver did all this just to advance one space between my VW and a SUV in front of me. I slowed down to negotiate orange cones merging two lanes into one. And a sign near it said "Flagman Ahead." The SUV that passed me was also stopped in front of me.

"Hurry up and wait," I said. "Nice move, maggot."

The SUV people who cut me off were dead-on Instant Local trannies. Their SUV had two surfboards in gold reflective board bags lashed the wrong way onto the roof racks (These trannies didn't even know the proper way to put the boards on their cars. Instead of having the tail of the board toward the front of the car, they always had the nose of the board over their windshield, which increased wind resistance.). The couple in front of me sat on flowered seat covers. A Hawaiian lei hung from the rear-view mirror. The guy driving was on a cell phone. And the woman on the passenger side was *also* on a cell phone. They wore huge sports watches on their wrists—these clowns were always into these waterproof watches. The back window of their SUV had three basic stickers that identified an Instant Local: one had to say Santa Cruz, the other was KPIG radio, and the third sticker was either The Surfrider Foundation (to show they *more* than just surfers, they were environmentally responsible surfers), or a local surf club they joined, or created (because they couldn't get into a local club yet). The SUV also had bumper stickers that said, "Women Rip," "Got aloha?," and a white Roxie clothing logo in the shape of a heart bordered by white hibiscus decals.

"Look at us because we're cool because I have a surfboard on the roof of my car and look at us because we're cool because we surf together," I said contemptuously. "What idiots."

"Eleanor Rigby" by The Beatles lunged out of the radio. First off, I hate The Beatles; second, I hate the cello. I popped 'The Doors' cassette into the player.

A horn honked behind me. In my rear-view mirror was a barge-like, brand-new, white pick-up truck. For a second, the front grill looked like it could open and devour my VW whole.

I lifted up my hands in a what-do-you-want-me-to-do? gesture. A twenty-two year old girl was driving it. She wore a hooded sweatshirt, a knit cap, and sunglasses. She chiseled her face into a nobody's-going-to-give-me-shit expression. I mean I've seen shell-shocked guys come out the jungle who looked more cheerful than her. But someone told her that was the way she had to look if you were going surfing, and didn't want anyone to mess with you. It seemed like everyone was coming down to the ocean preparing for a fight, and getting angrier and angrier.

"Oh you're bad, the Roxie You-Go Girl is going to kick my ass, yeah," I said. "You're bad—"

A hand rapped on the glass of my driver's side. I looked over. It was the flagman. I rolled down the window. Ranger barked.

"Easy Range," I said, blocking her with my right arm.

"Vic!"

"Duffy!"

When we were teenagers Duffy was a madman. Once, when we were in high school and went trick-or-treating, he dressed up as a bug with goggles and when people opened the door, he would run around in their house and jump on all the furniture, and go "Gee ga ga geem ga ga gee." And people would scream and yell, and chase him then he'd run out the back door. He used to work part-time detailing cars so he would have time to surf. On every car he pinstriped he would put a "Fuck you" somewhere on it—it would be real small and in ultra-fine detail. Before he got married, he spent winters down in Baja. And now, Duffy landed a job in the Department of Public Works for Santa Cruz County. He divided his time between his family, and going up to Lake Shasta to fish, water ski, or wake board.

"How you doing, Vic?"

"I'm still me."

"Me too."

"Who were you talking to in there?"

"Ranger," I lied, paused, and said, "I heard about your Mom."

"Yeah Mom passed on a couple weeks ago."

"Sorry," I said. "She was a nice lady. When we were growing up, after my Mom died, I always knew I could walk into your kitchen and get a sandwich. She loved having kids around."

"Yeah, she was. My Mom loved kids. But hey, ninety-six, what can you do? My wife and I were taking care of her at her house. What was really odd, is that she was fine until her sister died, and then when she was the last one left, she just faded real fast. After her obit appeared in the Sentinel, some dot-com guy knocks on the door of her house, you know, the one she bought for $15,000 in the seventies? He says he wants to buy the place. I tell him, we're not interested. Then he hands me a blank check and tells me to write whatever amount I wanted. I figured what the fuck? I wrote $2.5 million. And he went for it! Now, all my neighbors are going nuts. They're cleaning up their properties and yelling at the people who aren't. Then they put up their places for $750,000 and they ask the buyer how much they're willing to pay over list price for the house. They're all trying to get the money I got." He laughed. "I got $2.5 million, man! Fuck, remember in the sixties when we had $65 a month rent on that house at 37th? And we heard an earthquake was supposed to be coming, so we had a party and waited for it? That party lasted six days. Shit, we had over 200 people in that house. Naked people laying on the roof." He laughed and shrugged. "There were waves everywhere. Before they built the harbor in the mid-sixties, there was enough sand and beach to walk from the Westside of town to the Eastside. All so a bunch of boat drunks could have a floating trailer park. Anything that generates revenues." He shrugged, assumed a resigned look, laughed, and added, "Hey, I don't care, right now I'm King Shit. I just have a few more years with the county, they'll offer me a buy out, and with the pension—you know, move out to Gold country."

"Gold Country?"

"You know where the 49ers Gold Rush used to be? All those abandoned mining camps. It's nice up there. Only problem is some of the rivers are still polluted from the mercury they used back then to separate the gold from the sediments or whatever. The miners are gone, but the mercury they used is still there."

"Does Gold Country have a beach?"

"No," he said, laughing.

"Then I don't think I'll go there," I said. "I haven't seen you in the water much."

"Every time I paddled out I got into fights. I was tired of getting unwound. Totally losing it. Talking to myself in the car going down to the beach! I was going to give myself a heart attack. When your source of recreation becomes your source of frustration it's time to find another game. We've been jabbing that surf's-up needle in our arms for forty years. Vic, we're on the retirement plan. We're being driven out by the next group."

Two guys in red and yellow leather jumpsuits on red and yellow Japanese motorcycles recklessly sped in the narrow openings between stopped cars and the cars driving in the other direction. The bikes were ridiculously loud.

"Dot-goons on rice rockets that sound like hair dryers," scoffed Duffy. "I guess they can afford them so they don't have to ask Mommy for money so they can buy one."

The woman in the huge truck behind us, leaned on her horn for a few seconds.

"God, what's that about?" said Duffy. "Pushy, pushy."

"They're worse in the water," I said. "You know Tanner's daughter, Crystal—"

"Too bad about her Mom dying of cancer like that. She was a great surfer and a nice lady. Crystal's a nice girl. A good surfer."

"Yeah she is. She went down South to surf in a contest. The women in her heat, kept paddling to prevent her from getting into waves and giving her shit, saying, 'What are you doing here? You're not a home girl. You can't surf for shit, and why are you out here? You have no one to impress, you're mother's dead.'"

"That's more than giving someone shit. That's black soul stuff," said Duffy.. "It's why I don't miss surfing, what I want is not there. I don't know why you put yourself through it."

"What's going on here?" I asked, not wanting to go there.

"We're digging up the street to put in sidewalks," Duffy said with a smile. "Then next year, when we bury the power lines, we'll dig up the whole thing and start all over again—a real bro deal." He rapped his knuckles on the side door, waved me through, and walked away. "Close enough for government work. That's why I love being employed by the County: job security"

It was cool running into Duffy. We were 100 percent us, and hadn't deducted any points since. A lot of people forget who they start out to be. And I have to take off points. Hell, I've taken off points on people in my own family. It's nice when you see someone and you don't take anything away from them because nothing has really changed.

I caught up to the Instant Local's SUV at the three-way stop where East Cliff narrowed from two lanes to a single one-way street along Pleasure Point (It was once two lanes in each direction, but the cliffs had eroded, and took out part of the road.). That wasn't the only change. The County undertook a "beautification project" that built a bike lane on the ocean side, sidewalks, and wooden railings, as well as stairways that went to the ocean. A sign near a bent and rusted guardrail along part of the cliff's edge read "Adopt a Beach. This area cleaned by Surf Dot Com." I looked to my right at StokaMocha, an upscale coffee cafe/grocery store, which replaced a rundown market named Kongs owned by some Chinese or Japanese guys. The parking lot used to be filled with hand-painted vans, beat-up pick-up trucks with ripped tarp over their beds, loaded with pool-cleaning or landscaping equipment or firewood. The cars were beater Chevys and Dodges from the sixties or seventies, covered with splotches a dark gray primer coat, equipped with salt-water rotted un-upholstered seats, balding tires, clothes hangers for an antennae, heavily scraped hoods, and at least one missing window covered with either plastic, cardboard, duct tape, or a piece of wood. The low-life surf cars were replaced with high-end BMWs, Passats, Mercedes, Porsches, Jaguars, and Land Rovers with African lights. Every other car had Stanford and East Coast college alumni decal on rear windows, along with silver plastic license-plate frames of Southern California car dealerships, which bordered vanity plates that said: "MyJag," "Prez," "Myothcar," "Jaded," "Maryz," "Cr8Tiv," "Thksdad," "InrBlis," "4adrmr," "2Satori," "Xceed," "Tru2Nun," "OurBMW," and worse. And what a scene! A well-groomed couple in blue jumpsuits walked out of the cafe acting like country gentry out for a stroll, along with their latest accessory, a Chocolate Labrador on a leash. Three thirtyish women jogged with a determined stride and frozen faces past the self-anointed Instant Locals. The women had on clean, bright running outfits and wore baseball hats with pony tails sticking out of the cap's rear opening. The arms of their sweatshirts were tied around their hips (the shirt's 'Santa Cruz' logo was perfectly centered over their black Lycra-sealed butts). Their running jackets were zippered halfway down, revealing their pastel colored sports bras. As the women ran in black leggings, they glared at me for checking out their cleavage. It was really hard to tell what they were angry about. I mean, I didn't force them to dress like that. Another group of women, dressed exactly like the joggers but moving at a slower pace, quickly sipped lattes from paper cups with brown cardboard heat-protective jackets around them, and pushed their babies on large metal tricycle-type strollers with huge rubber wheels. Lycra-clad geeks dismounted unscratched thousand-plus dollar mountain bikes and swaggered in for their mochas. Spa-muscle toned Instant locals lounged at tables. The trannies wore T-shirts or sweatshirts with the name of a surf shop or local fitness gym, jeans, drawstring sweatpants, with sneakers, sandals or sheepskin Ugg boots. Others had pressed pleated khakis with polo shirts and dot-com logos. They drank coffee, wheat grass, Chia tea, nibbled on muffins, intensely typed on laptops, read their newspapers, and thought they mattered.

Ranger barked. She was primed for the beach. She panted faster. She uttered a muffled high-pitched mmmmmm-cry. She stuck her head out the window and groaned.

I laughed and said, "Okay we're going. We're going. Calm down, whups." Then I looked over at what was coming down the road, and said with disgust, "Oh please, go away."

Two dot-com guys and a girl crossed the street. They were in their tan-less twenties. I could tell they had rarely been in the water. Their styled hair didn't have a broken strand, or a highlight from the sun. Instead of straining against their shoulders, their wetsuits sagged toward their hips. Sports watches on their wrists bulged beneath the neon-orange-paneled neoprene. If you told me a bank had a dress code where people had to work wearing wetsuits and carrying surfboards, I'd believe that's where these people were heading, because they had that on-the-way-through-the-office-to-my-desk walk. They thought they were cool because they were surfers. Their faces positively radiated cluelessness with a smile. They didn't connect. They viewed surfing as a wholesome activity, a way to stay in shape, as if the ocean was no different than a ball field, a jogging trail, a basketball court, or a park. They carried their surfboards sideways against their hips, like serving platters. They gazed at the surf and pointed at the waves, then glanced at me to see if I was watching them. I thought, if no one was looking at these people, they wouldn't even be doing this. No matter what the dot-com Instant Locals did, whether it was surfing, jogging, or walking their dogs, they always looked around to make sure people saw them. But there's one thing all of dot-comers and Instant Locals had in common: not one of them ever had a surfboard worth looking at. Usually, a surfer had a board shaped to their specifications out of a foam blank, which was coated with a shell of fiberglas. A board reflected a surfer's ability, their style of surfing, and the waves they enjoyed riding—some boards were customized for speed, others for noseriding, even the board's fins gave you an idea about the person. That's why the surfboards used by dot-comers and Instant Locals revealed all I ever needed to know about them. The dot-comers exclusively rode three types of surfboards: a blue polyethylene foam board, which was sponge board with a plastic fin; a soft top, an epoxy blank topped with foam and a hard plastic base, which was a stage between a real surfboard and a sponge board (it was a basically a sponge board with a callous); or the dreaded, all-epoxy board, which was designed from a template of a computer program and mass produced from molds in Southeast Asian plants by sweatshop laborers. Not one of these boards was shaped by a human touch. They were boards without souls carried by soulless people. So, I guess it was a perfect match.

"Why are you staring at the ocean?" I muttered and watched the dot-comers. "You don't know what you're looking at."

I *knew* what I was looking at. Pleasure Point was a quarter-mile stretch of a jagged cliff-edged coastline with a narrow beach along East Cliff Drive. Pleasure faces south. The reef breaks were an average of a hundred to two hundred yards apart, and just slightly over that distance from the shore. Each surf spot possessed a distinctive identity and personality based on the regulars who surfed it. Sewer Peak was straight out from StokaMocha. Superb shortboarders or longboarders looking for the fastest and hollowest waves rode Sewers. The break was called Sewer Peak because years ago there was an open sewer pipe out there; the water always had a clear, blue-bubbling chemical look. A lot of guys who surfed the place back then have since died from all different types of cancers. The next break I passed was First Peak, where highly competitive hard-core longboarders and hot shortboarders yelled, splashed, shoved, and burned each other for beautiful and juicy waves, which sometimes connected for longer rides through the next break, Second Peak. Second Peak was slightly closer toward shore. Shortboarders and longboarders who weren't as skilled or competitive or cruel enough to catch waves at First Peak or Sewers, settled for intimidating and fighting each other over the scraps that rolled through or around First Peak. The next inside reef was called 38th because it was located where 38th Avenue t-eed into East Cliff Drive. The wave that broke here wasn't consistent or as good as First or Second Peak. The rides weren't longer. The spot was occupied mainly by longboarders willing to take less quality but at least get a few waves without the hassles out at First or Second Peak. Past 38th Street, where East Cliff Drive bent away inland and became 41st Avenue, was The Hook. The Hook was a pure break of fast, snappy, tight, hollow waves that allowed few mistakes. The wave peaked in a very small take-off zone filled with a tightly condensed pack of aggressive and intensely possessive, seasoned shortboarders who acquired a reputation for instinctively shooting their boards or lunging at anyone who tried to drop in or burn them on a wave. The different peaks still broke the same and some of the remaining hard-core locals surfed those breaks, but when the dot-com thing hit, the Point's surface was tiled with a trannie-urban sprawl of neon wetsuits, shiny epoxy, soft-tops, and blue foam boards. They filled in every open space from Sewer Peak to The Hook the same way they were occupying every available vacant lot and ocean view from Santa Cruz to Watsonville. There were over two hundred new people on boards out. Ten barely knew how to surf. The locals were outnumbered. They couldn't police their breaks. Pleasure was no longer pleasurable. It lost its logic. It was a Point without reason. Before, beginners who didn't have the ability to surf well wouldn't even think of paddling out to Pleasure Point. They stayed on the Westside at Cowells and rode small waves, or stayed on the inside at better surf spots to stay out of the way. Everyone in the water started out the same, and took their lumps. Eventually, you improved, and worked up to better surf spots, When you paddled out to those spots, you humbly respected and followed the rules and waited your turn in the rotation of waves. The proper way to surf is to take off at the peak where the wave starts to break, split open and peel to shore. But for a surfer to ride it right, the others in the lineup had to practice wave etiquette. The first surfer up at the peak is who gets the wave. And once the surfer is on the wave, no one is supposed to drop in front of them on the way to shore. If someone else mistakenly gets in front of the surfer, they're supposed to kick out of the wave. With no one else on the wave, the surfer can trim the board parallel across the wave until its face starts to lose its steepness. Then the surfer cuts back to the curl, which is a curved pocket just ahead of the breaking water. This move allows the wave to rise and reform into a steeper and more deeply banked curved wall ahead, and the surfer shoots across it again, and cuts back again, until the wave ends. Getting along in the water was all about respect and developing friendships because you wanted to surf for the rest of your life. By following the rules, you learned to compromise and know people, you made connections with them, their jobs, where they lived. But, this new squad didn't want to learn the proper way to surf and a develop respect for locals and the ocean. They didn't want to build relationships with people for the long run. They didn't believe in history. They didn't believe in a learning curve. They didn't give a rat's ass about locals. They cared even less about the ocean. They just wanted to surf *now*. Like surfing was suddenly part of their own inner-personal growth program or something like that. Everything in the water was just a backdrop for them to get their rides and attain their personal "wave quota" (which usually meant getting more than everyone else). As far as they were concerned, when they paddled out, there was no pecking order—unless of course, *they* were the ones doing the pecking. They never waited their turn. They went for everything. After all, in their professional lives, the dot-comers believed in—and seemed to be achieving—-a shortcut to success. They never had to work their way up at anything. So, in the water, they applied those same ambitious principles to surfing, and took the quickest shortcut to get waves: they became burn artists and snakes. A burn artist is someone who drops in front of a surfer who is already up and riding the wave. A burn job is like cutting someone off in traffic—they assume you will slow down to avoid collision. But eventually, burn artists get hurt because people *do* collide with them. So, most burn artists evolve into snakes. A snake is subtler, more conniving. When a wave is approaching, the snake goes to your left a little further out, spins around, angles their board, and tries to prevent you from dropping into the wave by cutting you off; or, after you're up on a wave, the snake takes off behind you, angles and trims through the foam, catches up, and tailgates you out of the curl by squeezing you up higher on the face so you can't get enough speed to cutback. You have been driven off it. The wave rolls underneath you. The snake cuts back to the curl and surfs your wave to shore, leaving you, sitting on your board in the flatness.

I made a left onto 37th Avenue to park in my usual spot. The dirt shoulder was gone. In its place, a homeowner planted flowers and stuck in a small square black sign with orange lettering that stated: 'No parking. Private Property.'

"That's just not happenin'," I said, and parked my VW on the spot, cracking the sign, and crushing the plants.

The construction crew framing a McMansion on the corner lot stopped pounding nails, applauded and hooted me. I got out of my VW and acknowledged their approval with a nod, hand flourish, and a smile. They went back to working.

"You're cold, Burr," said Driveway Dave in a tone roughed out by years of cigars and booze.

He was called Driveway Dave because for the past two years he lived in a trailer, which was mounted on a rusty, pick-up truck, and parked in the driveway of The General's one-story rundown cottage. The vehicle had been there so long, someone had written in the grime of its back windows: "Dirt restoration project in progress." Dave wore a frayed T-shirt with 'Farley Surfboards' logo on it and cut-off shorts. He held a beer and smoked a large cigar. His thick brown hair was fringed with gray. He had a bushy mustache that required a trim, and the rest of his tanned hide of a face needed a shave. He always looked like he was mulling over his displacement from the world in a quiet amused way. Dave was a lawyer for some corporation, got divorced, gave his job up, surfed, and picked up a few bucks doing grunt work. He was just burning time because he had no money.

"Vic, you need anger management," Dave said dryly, walking away from his trailer.

"Fuck that shit," I said, gently lowering Ranger down onto the uprooted plants. She sniffed and urinated on them. "When it comes to anger, I don't need management. I'm my own boss." I paused. "Who would do a move like this?"

"The same dot-com guy who's circulating a petition to get this street turned into a private road. He doesn't want anyone parking in front of his house. He's trying to set a precedent."

"For years, I've parked here, slept in my van between sessions and waited for the surf to come up. I was sitting on this place long before some trannie Instant Local piece of shit didn't want me to park here anymore. The guy doesn't even live here yet!"

"Go figure," said Dave.

I looked at the skeletal two-story frame, and its four-hundred-and-thirty square-foot tower, which was 28-feet high and framed.

"Who owns this beast of nothing?"

"Drake Sather, the Surf Dot Com guy—"

"You mean the asshole who bought Slap's?"

"When it comes to hating that guy there's no short list, you'd be at the end of a very long line," said Dave, leaning against his truck. "That tower obstructs the entire block's view of the ocean. It looks into everyone's back yards. It's going to be his study. He wants to put a beacon on it. Last night at midnight he was drunk and driving golf balls into the ocean from the second floor."

"How big does he want to make this place?"

"Three stories," shouted a worker's voice from the second floor of the McMansion.

It was Contractor Rick. I once shaped him a 7'10"' thruster with hard rails, a pintail, pointed nose. He rode Moss Landing a lot. He was in his mid-forties, about five six, long hair, and wore a bandanna to conceal his receding hairline. He was all muscle. He wore a sleeveless shirt, steel-toe boots, and had a tool bag strapped around his cut-off, white-paint spattered shorts.

"Three stories?" asked Dave.

"It'll never get that far," said Contractor Rick, laughing. "By the time this guy gets to that, the county will make him tear this whole thing down. Check it out, I'll give you the Cook's tour."

We walked through a framed wall's opening and stood on the first floor. Contractor Rick came down a wide flight of temporary stairs to welcome us.

"Can you believe this shit?" said Contractor Rick, spreading his arms around. "This the foyer, which is going to have some church-type window and a chandelier for that big first impression. See that turret tower deal? That's the first thing he wants completed. It has a vault and a safe room—you know, one of those rooms with reinforced steel walls. Gives you an idea of what he thinks people will want to do to him after he builds this scenic eyesore. The rest of this McMansion is stupid. The guy thinks he's Frank Lloyd Crap. Never built anything. You can tell by the way he designed this place. I went through all the engineering drawings. He has different measurements on each page. I don't even know how this got through the Planning Department. Probably, a little ca-ching." He rubbed his index finger on his thumb to indicate a political exchange of cash. "And, you wanna laugh?" He pointed to the studs that framed one of the first story's four corners. "Check this nail schedule out."

"No way," I said, seeing the spider-line cracks forming from the nails into the frame. "I can't believe he used nails like this. What is he, an idiot? These are what? Twenties?"

"What are you guys talking about?" asked Dave, sipping his beer. "I'm a lawyer. I only know how to sue people. My job is to keep the wound open. I never build anything, except distrust."

"Framing is usually put up with sixteen-penny nails" explained Contractor Rick to Dave, pulling a nail from his tool bag. "Sixteen-penny nails are three and a half inches long, and pretty much look like regular nails. But the studs on this frame were put together with twenty-penny nails." He pointed at the nails in the frame. "Twenty-penny nails are six inches long and look like railroad spikes. See! The nails are already splitting the wood studs. Cracks are spreading from every nail in all this framing."

"You can't build three floors with this," I said, shaking my head in disbelief. "The whole building will come down. I'm surprised it's even holding a second floor."

"Before we started building this thing, I even told the dot-com engineer guy who designed it, that this building won't hold," said Contractor Rick, flicking his arms up in the air. "I said, 'You only got ninety percent of an idea.' He didn't want to know nothing. He tells me, 'You don't get what I'm doing. It'll all come together later.' So, now we've elevated the discussion to the blow-me mode. I mean if this brilliant idiot figures that before he came along no one was ever smart enough to figure out that 20-penny nails would hold more weight than the sixteen penny nails, fine by me. None of the guys on the job are saying word one." He took a hammer from his belt hook. "I'm milking this job for all it's worth. Man, it's a TM—time and materials. What a dream job. I draw on the job, we start sheetrock. He has to pay me for sheetrocking. We start painting the outside of the building, and he has to pay me. We start electrical, insulation, plumbing, and he has to pay me. I tell him we have to do one floor or one different section first and he believes me. I'm following his plans so there's nothing I'm doing wrong. I'll build the first two stories, and his tower first, and frame the third. I mean at two floors, I can always jump sixteen feet if it goes, but no way am I jumping twenty-four. When we complete everything and have to finish off the third floor, we'll all walk off the job. I'll drop the dime on him, the county will red tag it, and the dot-com asshole will have to tear it down." He smiled, laughed, and added, "The whole thing is unstable, but on paper it looks good."

We looked through the framing down to East Cliff Drive and the side streets. Every parking spot was taken by an SUV, a Minivan, or huge jacked-up, off-road, four-wheel drive vehicle that had never been off a paved street. We watched a SUV cruise by; its roof racks had four surfboards in reflective bags.

The vehicle contained a family. A mid-thirties couple had a nine-year old boy and a twelve-year old girl in the back. The Dad driving was eating a Power Bar. The Mom was on a cell phone. They both had huge sports watches.

"There goes the neighborhood," said Dave, who sipped his beer, lifted up his shirt and scratched his tan, hairy gut.

"Now we're getting entire families," I snarled. "I mean look at them, with their tennis shoes and surfboards. Moms. Dads. Kids. God, they even have matching boards. They think surfing is mainstream. It's just not. These people make me ill. Maybe it's just a fad and they'll get tired of it."

"That's what I said about rap fifteen years ago," said Dave. "And rap's still here."

Contractor Rick watched SUV after SUV after SUV go by with six-to-eight surfboards in silver reflective board bags piled on their roof racks, and he sagely said, "I remember gyms used to be cool places for tough guys to work out, then they became the place for everyone to go. Harleys used to be the tough guy thing to do. Now yuppies are all on motorcycles. And surfing used to be the cool thing to do, and I can guarantee you that there are a lot of dot-comers with surfboards out there who have a real nice house, a motorcycle in the garage, and belong to a gym."

"Huh."

"I'll tell you one thing, though, there's one big difference between them and us, they'd never sacrifice anything to surf or whatever they do," said Driveway Dave. "They're only riding a motorcycle or surfing because they can *afford* to do it. They'd never give up money to do those things. So when they do get in financial trouble, the first things to go are the surfboard, the bike, and then the gym membership."

"You can only hope," said Contractor Rick.

We parted. As Driveway Dave and I stepped back onto the sidewalk, we heard derisive howls. We looked across the street. A block over, The Crew leaned on the railing along the cliff.

"I'd suit up before I went over there," said Dave. "If you don't, those guys will talk you out of a go out."

"Yeah, I know," I replied. "They didn't used to be that way."

"Surf was good yesterday at his time," Driveway Dave said,

exhaling smoke through his yellow teeth. He reached through the broken butterfly window on the truck's door, grabbed the inside handle, and opened it. "In an hour it'll be yesterday."

"You're not going out?"

"Early daylight, I'm a sunrise guy," he said. "I don't want to fight the crowds, can't deal with it. Burr, you can't fight against the world. I already tried."

"What happened?"

"You're looking at it," he said gesturing to his van. He laughed, coughed, and went inside his trailer.

I wanted to get wet, so, instead of going over to The Crew to say hello first, I took off my clothes, and put on my wetsuit.

Ranger and I went across the street toward The Crew at Heckler's Point. The Crew sullenly stood side by side along a four-foot high wooden-slat railing on the jutting cliff's edge, which overlooked Pleasure Point from 38th Avenue. The Crew had their backs to us. Larry The Legend, The General, Chops, and Skin Dog, were home-grown guys in their mid-thirties to the fifty-plus range, who had all been bounced off the bottom a few times. They wore sweat pants and stained shirts with my surf shop logo, and either had on sandals or sneakers. Just a few years ago, the area was called The Cliff, and I'd see boards angled against it, and guys laughing in wetsuits excitedly pointing at waves and jabbering about their rides. But as more and more people took up surfing, everything changed about The Cliff scene. No one was in wetsuits. There were no surfboards. The Crew sorrowfully leaned against the railing. Their shoulders slumped. They looked down at the ocean like they were viewing a old friend in an open-casket. The Cliff was called Heckler's

Point because The Crew surfed less and less, and seemed more and more content to limit their activities to planting their elbows on the railing and do a crash-by-crash commentary that ridiculed the surf-related collisions in the water:

"T-boned him!"

"Holy shit balls, it's way out of control."

"Yeah, it is. There must be three hundred people out there—"

"Two hundred and thirty six— and their mothers. I know. I counted them."

"Nobody knows what they're doing out there."

"Ya think?"

They nudged each other, shook their heads, and laughed.

"Howz'it?" I asked, stepping from the street over the metal guardrail and around a wooden bench.

The Crew turned around and their words backwashed over each other like waves: "Hey, yo, Vic...Wattup?...Shape any new boards, yet?...You off, today?...Squirrel watching the shop?"

"You know, same old same old," I replied and smiled. "I just thought I'd get in a session before I open the shop. Throw the ball around for Range."

I wore a cracked, black, two-mil wetsuit with short sleeves; its knee patches were peeled halfway off. I held a longboard tucked under my right arm. My left hand gripped Ranger's dry-wet bag, which contained a plastic half-gallon jug of water, some dog food, two plastic bowls, a tennis racquet and ball, a leash, and a plastic bag to clean up her poop. I leaned the board on the railing and put down the bag near it. Ranger brushed against The Crew's legs, looked for pets, and received them.

Ridiculously loud whoops, hoots, and cheers, came from the water. The Crew turned to its depressingly enthusiastic source: the You-Go Girls. They were a group of girls, middle-aged women, and Moms with their daughters. They sat on the inside, paddled as a group for every wave, and took off in front of everybody. They slid straight down, crawled up into kneeling positions, and stiffly stood in the middle of their blue foam boards. Then they assumed some stupid surfer pose they picked up from a bad beach movie: sticking up their right arm like they were taking an oath, and angling their left arm straight off their hip. These women didn't care who they burned. They only acknowledged each other's efforts with supportive cheers: "You go, girl...Chick wave...Paddle, paddle girlfriend... Gnarly...You're a shredder... Awesome...*Mack*eral it...Go-fer it, girl...Girl power."

"The You-Go Girls are out in force," said The Legend, nodding at the spongy mass of women "Yeah, instead of being outside at the peak like everyone else, the You-Go Girls just create their own peak." He shook his head "They don't surf the wave, the gang up on it. Somebody's going to get hurt soon."

"It's crunch time," said Skin Dog, pointing at a pot-bellied dork in a neon-lime-green paneled full-length wetsuit and a white protective helmet, who was trimming across the face of a four-foot wave on a longboard. "This guy has been running everyone over. He's like a punchline to bad joke you can see coming."

The dork stiffly stood in the middle of his board. Skin Dog was right. This guy obviously didn't know how to turn, but figured everyone else would simply just get out of his way. "Hey, hey, hey," the dork yelled. The You-Go Girls saw him, but kept paddling for his wave anyway, believing he would avoid them. The women slid straight down in the path of the oncoming dork. Without a qualm, the dork dove off his board, which plowed directly into the You-Go Girls, who also dove off their boards, which were attached by ten-foot leash cords to their ankles, and swept wide semi-circular swaths on the water, and took out surfers who were paddling out, who also dove for safety and let their boards go too, which took out even more people on the surface. The white water of the breaking wave turned the churning mass of them into a clueless chowder.

"Nice kick out," said The Legend. "God it's like watching people trying to drive without steering wheels."

"What gets me is they never even make the effort to even hang onto their boards," said Skin Dog. "I don't get it, don't they think they can get cut by their fins, don't care if their boards hit or hurt anyone, and don't think they can drown or drown someone else."

"Well, they obviously don't want to get hit by their own board," observed The General. "And if they can't get a wave, they know just enough to ruin a it for somebody else. They're making mistakes in their favor, so they must know something."

"Oh, look at this coming," said The Legend, staring at ten pale and puffy people descending the steps. Their wetsuits fit them like sausage casings. They awkwardly carried blue foam, soft-top, or epoxy surfboards. "They arrive at the same time like the tides table is a train schedule. They checked the Internet surf report and read that there were waves. Before, you'd have to get to know people, so you'd have someone to call and ask what the ocean was doing. These people don't have to get to know anyone, it's a free ride just there for them. We're in the way."

"They're walking down the steps with their leash cords attached to their ankles," I said, bewildered. "Don't they realize they can trip over those things? Common sense would tell you that it's better to put a ten-foot long cord that you attach to your ankle after you reach the bottom of a set of stairs instead of at the top of a set of stairs." I paused. "A conveyor belt of idiots."

"I used to like everyone I met at the beach," said The Legend. "And now, I'm beginning to dislike people I don't know for no reason at all." He paused, then added, "And without much effort." He laughed. "Surfing's making me hate people!"

"If you need a reason, here comes one now," said The General, looking at a group of bicyclists on East Cliff Drive.

There was a bike lane, but the pack of forty Lycra-coated geeks on bicycles used the one-way road. They created a traffic jam behind them. They didn't even glance at the ocean.

"Use the bike lane!" shouted Skin Dog.

"Tell me about it!" a biker sarcastically jeered as he went by and flipped us off.

"Come on back here and do that," said Chops.

"I'll kick your ass," said the biker, pedaling away.

"You can't do it from there," shouted Chops, drawing a laugh from us. He shook his head and muttered, "I swear the more Lycra the bigger the asshole."

Behind the bikers was an attractive woman in a sports car. She looked over at us.

"She's checking you out Larry," said Surf Dog.

"Yes, but is she in love with me or—The Legend?" he replied.

The Crew laughed, leaned back against the railing, and faced the ocean. The water still had a high-tide bounce, and had a slight warble. But when the tide dropped, the shape of the waves would get better defined and start cracking.

I picked up my board and bag, motioned toward the surf, and said, "You on it? Right now is the best shot at it, I checked the tides, it's low at nine, and at three it will be a five."

The Crew grumbled: "Eh, too crowded for me. I'd need my reading glasses out there to find an opening...By the time we get our boards and come back there will be another fifty people out there...Too dangerous. Yeah, it is. Some guy got his jaw broke....I think I'll just pull some weeds around the trailer...We'll come back in a six hours, and watch the idiots with their boards get washed up on the rocks on the high tide."

The dour Crew turned their backs on the ocean and walked down the middle of 38th Avenue. They were side by side, and either hung their heads, glared at surfers they had never seen, or scowled at the endless procession of people in SUVs topped with stacks of foam, soft-tops, and epoxy boards. The Crew pointed in the street gutter at litter—surf-wax wrappers, bottles, and cigarette butts dumped from car ashtrays. They barked at people who drove too fast, rolled through Stop signs, or weren't cleaning up after their dogs. The Crew just wasn't getting their water time in. It was like they were in mourning. They were all starting to get fatter too. Pretty soon they'd take themselves out of the line-up. We had given up better jobs and even relationships to surf and stay close to the ocean. Surfing, no matter what humiliation life dealt us, was always part of the circle we could go to and make it all right. We had all come down alone to the beach and met each other surfing. None of us could really locate on the map where our friendship began. The water brought us together. We were drifting away on land. The lack of ocean was slowly breaking us apart.

I never took the flight of wooden stairs leading from the one-hundred-foot cliff down to the ocean—that was for Instant Locals, dot-comers, You-Go Girls, and trannies. I carefully threaded down the two-foot wide, knee-deep narrow trench through the ice plants and rebar-laden concrete chunks dumped on the eroding slope. The path ended at a shelf of wet boulders that looked like huge slabs of gray meat. I had taken this route for so long I remembered when it was a level path. I even knew which one of the many smooth rounded grooves in the boulders to use as toe holds to get down to the beach. I took a short two-foot jump and landed on the damp cove of sand, near a chunk of washed-up kelp. Sand fleas rose up from it. Ranger came over, gently placed the ball at my feet, and looked up at me.

"You want me to throw the ball?" I said, goading Ranger into barking. "Is that what you want, Range?" She barked three times and expectantly stared at me. I laughed. "Okay, whups."

I reached into the bag and took out my bent metal tennis racquet with its chewed-up handle. I used two fingers to pick up the saliva-soaked ball, released it, and swung the racquet. It made a flat wet sound at impact. The ball spun, sprayed its contents outward. Ranger went after it. The sand gave a little so she ran at almost ninety percent. I deeply hoped it would make her bad leg stronger. The ball landed into the shore break. Ranger stopped at the edge of the wet sand. She barked at the ball. She didn't pursue it. She never went into the ocean—even when I finished my surf session and paddled in, she'd see me coming, run up to the edge of the water, bark and cry, but she would never swim out to me. Ranger was a beach dog. While she patiently waited for the ocean to wash the ball into shore, I waxed up my board. The air was cool but the sun was already heating up the back of my black wetsuit. My knees settled deeper into the sand. I sunk into the rhythm of moving my arms and rubbing the wax onto the board's deck. I deeply inhaled the cool breeze and smelled the kelp's vegetal rot mixing with a tinge of salt in the lingering mist from the spray of snapping and sizzling waves; it cracked out a fishy tang.

"Oh, man," cried out a middle-aged pudgy guy, who was so exhausted, he panted in gasps between vowels. He staggered out of the ocean. His longboard slipped from his grasp and thumped on the beach—the board was one of mine, a 10'6". The leash cord was still wrapped around his ankle. He dropped to his knees beside his board. His lungs wheezed. His face was white and his wet hair wound around his bald spot. The guy was worked. I thought I was going to lose him right there.

I stared at him and asked, "You all right?"

"Still pulling air," he said, heaving again. "Guess, I'm out of shape." He coughed and eventually got his breath back. "I been busy. Too busy." He reflectively stared at the ocean. "It's a long story. I won't bore you with it."

"Thank you."

He laughed and said, "I'm scraping off the rust, I used to surf years ago, but I'm weak now."

"Divorced and have kids?"

"Been there," he looked at me. "Ever been married?"

"No."

"Don't start," he said firmly, peeling the wetsuit down to his waist. His skin was pale, his chest hairs were gray, and his wetsuit bunched up his belly into three defined rolls of fat. He took out a clear plastic baggie containing a cigarette and matches.

"A little hectic out there, huh?"

"Eh, everybody is everywhere. I lived down South. What are you going to do? The one thing I've learned is no matter what activity you choose it starts to resemble life no matter what. Once the money comes in—it's over.. Malibu, Pacific Palisades, can't create more dirt in those places can you? Same thing here," he said, lighting his cigarette. He was exhausted, but then I noticed his eyes were gleaming with stoke. This guy's pupils looked like they were going to quiver right off the whites of his eyes. He was more than stoked. He was off the chart. It was like he not only found Jesus, but was also given a hundred bucks by Him. "It was great out there. I owe you for it. Thanks."

"Thank me?"

"I was just floating out at The Hook, and I was sitting there on my board, just floating," he said, shivering but clearly not feeling the cold. "And as I sat out there, these Air Force jets flew over, and I remembered something I forgot. Just before I went into the Army, was my last time surfing. I was sitting out there in the water at that exact spot and the jets flew over the same way, and I was seventeen." He stopped and thought about the two moments converging into one. "It all came back to me. It all came back to me. Yeah, thanks, man." He grabbed his board, looked back at me. "You know, out of all the surf shops I went to, you were the only one who told me the truth. Some scowling, young girl at some trendy shop, who clearly didn't give a rip, tried to sell me an eight-foot board. You were the only one who was straight-up enough to tell me a two-hundred-and-twenty pound guy who was wearing a wetsuit would probably weigh another fifteen pounds more in the water. So, you said, 'You need a 10'6" longboard. It might look big on land, but it's never big enough in the water.' And you were dead-on right. I needed it." He paused. "I'm Ralph." He smiled. He waved off my gesture of apology for not knowing him. "It's okay, I don't expect you to remember me just because I bought a board. I know you meet a lot of people. I don't take anything personal, anymore. I'm past that. Who has the time? Life's too short." The guy sensed I wanted to surf. He took off his leash, picked up his board, and walked away. "I might go out again this afternoon, later."

"You can always leave your stick at the shop, then come back, pick it up, and go for a second session. Or, you can just hang out on the couch and have lunch and watch a surf video."

"Really?" he said, surprised and touched by my offer. He coughed. "I just might take you up on that." He paused. "I liked your shop. It has a link to the past, it has... a *soul*."

"Thank you."

He limped away.

A damp tennis ball soggily thumped on my longboard's deck. I looked straight into Ranger's brown eyes. She tilted her head to the right and barked.

"All right, one more, whups," I said, grabbing the bent metal tennis racquet and hitting another shot.

A couple in their late twenties came down the beach. They were in new wetsuits and carrying epoxy boards. One was a short woman who was easily sixty pounds overweight. The guy had one of those mellow, yoga-like faces, black hair, and had a gaunt but flexible build.

"I went on a one-month surf safari," loudly said the woman. "I surfed Australia in Victoria at Bells Beach. And Sunset—that's Hawaii, and Tavarua in Fiji." When she said the famous and challenging surf breaks, it was like she was name-dropping, as if the surf spots were status symbols that ranked her higher than people who merely surfed 38th. There was no way she surfed those spots—especially, Tavarua, which was a break for the quick and the dead; if you didn't get up quick on the thick, pitching, fifteen-foot wave that threw out stand-up barrels, you'd wipe out, and either get impaled or have your flesh scraped off on the coral bottom. No way she surfed it with *that* butt. The only way she could make a name for herself at those spots was lying in the shallow water and hope someone would call her a reef break.

I kept waxing my board. I looked out in the ocean. Finally, a young guy somehow got up on one knee and stood up. Instead of getting more relaxed on the wave, he tensed up. He became stiffer and stiffer, bent his knees lower and lower, widened his stance, and extended one arm forward in front of him like a low punch, and the other behind him like a backward jab.

I shook my head and softly grunted in disgust, "Fall already."

The guy fell off the tail of his board, as if he had been shot. His board flew out in the air. He surfaced and whew-hooed himself. In the rocks above me, a young girl whew-hooed back to him. It was his twenty-nothing girlfriend. She waved a camera and gave the guy a thumbs up. Man, I thought, why would anyone want a picture of that ride?

A judgmental shadow hovered over my board. I looked up.

"When was the last time you changed the wax on that log? It's black," said Sonny.

"Like my heart," I said, laughing. "Trunking it again?"

Sonny was only wearing swim trunks. He proudly held a new red nine-foot longboard under his right armpit. He always trunked it, which was pretty hard when the water got in the fifties, but he only came out for short sessions. I guess it was his statement. Who knew? Sonny's board had fresh puffs of wax coating the deck. He never waxed the nose of his board because he didn't believe noseriding was functional, which meant he couldn't do it. He was in his late fifties and had an enviable thick pelt of gray hair. He did a lot of martial arts. He was superbly proportioned. We surfed tons of spots for over thirty years, but outside of the water and the shop, we never hung out much. His divorce changed him. I assumed it was bitter because shortly after the ruling, Sonny was arrested for getting drunk and repeatedly ramming his car into the front door of their house. On top of that, his wife left him for another woman, a fact we never let him forget. And all of us in The Crew, even though we surfed with him on trips to Baja and Hawaii, noticed Sonny started going his own way. After he stopped dealing marijuana, he made as much money as he could under the table from part-time construction jobs, and spent his spare time out of the water, attending theology and sociology and other ology-sounding classes at UCSC and Cabrillo College. I sometimes thought he took all these courses so no one could come close to ever understanding him again. He was always going to art films, jazz clubs, and talking politics. But as he got more interesting, and the more he had to say, the more he alienated those who knew him best. He became jarringly blunt. Sonny would get in moods where he'd disappear for days, leave the water without saying goodbye, refuse to return phone calls, or even acknowledge a passing greeting. A lot of people stopped speaking to Sonny. And it didn't bother him. His shorthand response was to casually say, "I don't have friends." It was too bad, because he was a charming guy, who was very intelligent. The Crew and I just took Sonny as he came, which was the only way to get along with him, because you didn't have a choice. He was like a dog that acts real friendly, then all of a sudden you pet him in the wrong spot and he goes for you. I just enjoyed hearing him talk—even when he was rude to me, which was frequent because underneath all his philosophy, Sonny was a real competitive Italian guy. I liked him, admired him actually. Sonny even raised two sons, who were both great surfers. They were attending college: one was going to be a cardiologist; the other, an engineer. I mean he was always on his sons in a good way, you know, making sure who their friends were and all that stuff. But, he just didn't seem to have any use for people, which oddly attracted more people to him.

Ranger protectively came over. She never warmed to Sonny.

"That board is pretty dinged up. It's taking in water," disapprovingly said Sonny, pointing to the open fiberglas gashes on the rails of my board. "Your equipment is a reflection of yourself as a surfer. It's like a samurai with his sword. It's not right."

"I learned that some of the idiots out there won't get in my way because they see the board's dings and know I don't care what happens to my stick—or, them."

"So you're driving without insurance," he snorted, smiling. "How long is this airplane wing? It looks bigger than ten-feet."

"I've shifted over to an eleven-footer. Lately, I've been needing an extra foot of indifference."

He proudly flipped around his new stick, placed its tail in the sand, and stood it up. The board wasn't shaped by me. Sonny never purchased a board from me, which was fine.

"Check it out.," he said, extending the upright surfboard.

I stood up and took the board from him. I ran my hands along the rails. I stopped halfway down. They were off. I said nothing.

"Nice," I lied. "I'm surprised you're taking a new stick out in this crowd." I paused. "It'll get dinged up today. Those people don't know what they're doing out there, and they don't care."

We turned and looked over at the surfers on the waves. The dot-comers were so busy jockeying for a better position to snake or burn a wave off someone else, when the snakes and burn artists finally got what they wanted, they didn't know what to *do* with it. Instead of going with the shape of each particular wave, the dot-comers brought what they wanted to do to the wave. They went for noserides where there was no wall to support it, and lost their balance and fell. They torqued their upper body instead of their lower body to turn, then lost their balance and fell. They really thought this was surfing. And that they were cool even though they weren't even close to getting it right. Their style was hideous. The ocean looked like it was trying to snap them off its surface.

"Even when I was gremmie in the sixties," I said. "I don't even remember anybody being as bad as these people. They are absolutely the worst surfers I have ever seen in my life."

"Those people are in denial out in the water, but you have to realize they are in denial *before* they paddle out," said Sonny. "Don't get pulled down into their world, let them get pulled down by their world. They're circles without a center, traveling in circles, and the circle gets smaller and smaller, they're like a boa constrictor choking itself. Self love hugs itself to death."

"Do you have one ya?" I asked.

Ranger took a poop. I got a clear plastic bag and scooped it up.

"You have to understand the Tao, the energy they're giving off, and you just don't become part of it. Otherwise you're on a narrowing highway of ambition lined with violins playing the tunes of self-pity. Everything becomes butter to the toast of your misery. They're not people they're reruns. You have to paddle out, if you don't paddle out, you become like them, half-dead, floating face down on the sea of compromise. Let their ambition consume them. Alcohol and drugs, that's nothing. You want to see what causes short-term memory loss? It's not smoking dope, it's wearing a suit. These people are on the ultimate form of substance abuse—a better car, a bigger house, a higher salary. You don't believe me? Get in between them when they're tying off for a hit of income. Now *there's* a narrowing highway if there ever was one. You have to see where they're coming from on that level and just go with it. It's all a circle, Burr. The Indians were here first, then came the missionaries, then the traders—shit every other road in this town is named for someone who ran a lumber mill, a farm, railroad, a quarry. There was even a Chinatown here. Santa Cruz was an Italian fishing village, then it became a tourist town, a retirement town, and when UCSC—"

"Want a beach muffin? Fresh out of Ranger's oven," I said, extending the clear plastic bag with brown dog poop mashed inside it. Sonny wasn't pleased, but I wanted to change the subject. He was being way too open minded to be interesting. But, Sonny kept on, he was still riding high on some recent brain buzz from a lecture he received at one of his ology courses.

"Tao doesn't see cliffs, hills. It flows. The Tao is like water."

"That's great if you're water, I guess."

"You can't abdicate to the crowd. Look at The Crew. They're water-logged. They're sinking. They're giving up. You have to hit it. When you go out in the ocean to surf, the sharks lurk, but the angels sing."

"I can guarantee you one thing, if they're singing out there, you're not going to like the tune."

"It doesn't matter what anyone says out there to me," said Sonny, laughing. He walked towards The Hook. "I have no friends."

I picked up my board and looked out in the water. Ms. Bell's Beach-Sunset-and-Tavarua and her pal were struggling on their surfboards to get through 38th's three-foot shorebreak.

I grimly paddled out. The ocean was colder than it usually was. Each time I dipped my bare arms into it, I felt like I was reaching down into ice-cube filled water for the last soda at the bottom of the cooler. I figured I'd get used to it. I glided like a crocodile and stared with distrustful reptilian eyes at the drifting crowd of obstacle delusions. I didn't know one of them. It seemed like every day there were new faces. They replaced each other like shark's teeth. I resented them. These people would not be here in two, five, or ten years from now, but I would be. All they were doing out in the water was taking my time from me. I paddled through a chorus line of You-Go Girls. I smelled perfume. The You-Go Girls twittered over other people's heads to talk to each other: "The school is starting up a soccer uniform fundraiser...I just got my realtor's license, I'll give you my card...You're practicing for the contest too? I entered for a novice heat....I wore the same dress I wore at Bill's service...When can I make a hair appointment with you?... The last thing I want to hear is the whining of a teenager, so I let her get the piercing." The last thing *you* want to hear, I thought. God, I felt like I was in a shopping mall. They weren't the only ones who wanted validation for whatever they thought they had to be. Everyone held forth loud hey-let-me-tell-you-what-I-do-for-a-living-so-I-must-make-a-lot-of-money-because-I-live-in-a-house-I-paid-this-much-for-after-all-there's-no-reason-not-to-be-friendly-and-let-me-tell-you-about-this-great-restaurant-and-isn't-it-great-to-live-in-a-place-where-I'm-just-a-few-hours-from-the-snow-or-the-ocean-because-I'm-originally-from-etc conversations. I just kept thinking, 'Will you people just shut the fuck up!' I sat up, and looked beyond the kelp line. The sooty shearwaters were in the distance, chasing down anchovies.

"Hi, bro," intrusively said a friendly but hollow voice to me. "Great day to be out surfing, huh, bro?"

Bro.

I never responded to anyone who called me bro. My friends flat-out know my name and call me by it. Hey, Vic. Not hey, bro. I looked over. It was the Bro Dork who had plowed into the You-Go Girls. In his protective helmet, neon-orange wetsuit, white webbed-gloves, and green-tinted goggles, Bro Dork resembled a bloated wingless beetle.

"Bro, isn't being out here just great!" Bro Dork said. "The energy you get from the ocean..."

The *energy* of the ocean. He should stick his head under the water. There wasn't one thing below the surface that wasn't staying alive by eating something else.

I ignored him. He even wore cologne. What an idiot.

"Guess I said the wrong thing," he said to someone else like him. He was miffed at my slight. "Pardon me for being friendly."

I never acknowledged the existence of these idiots. If I did, Bro Dork or one of his buddies would think we bonded and it was okay to go in front of me on a wave, because, after all, I was a bro and wouldn't mind. That was their concept of friendship. I figured, if you want to show me you're a nice person, surf like one. Until then, I viewed it simply: If I don't know you, I don't owe you. But I still had to listen to their land conversations on water.

"Yes, it's at 3.3 and went from a 4.3," said one out-of-shape surfer in his thirties to another one. I figured they were talking about the tides. "I was offered 3.8," replied the other guy.

God, they were comparing interest rates! I didn't want to hear this. I paddled past some young surfers who had shaved heads and beards. They sat on shortboards, which immediately gave them away as clueless idiots. Most of the time—and today was one of those days—the break at 38th was a longboard wave. It wasn't steep and hollow or fast enough to surf a board under nine feet. These Instant Locals were on seven-foot boards, which meant they obviously couldn't surf, because anyone with the skill to ride boards that short would be at The Hook, First Peak, or Sewers. But these two Instant Local trannies thought they were cooler than everyone else because they had the same brightly colored shortboards the pros used. They defiantly looked down at me, as if I was the one who didn't belong. They thought acting tough would intimidate others. There was no way these wannabes were going to come close to catching a wave on those boards, and if they did, I was still going to fry them.

One of the shortboarders said, "Dude, the swell is coming from the west. See how the waves coming straight into the beach? It has to be a total west, dude."

"Yeah, dude, a west," replied his buddy, who had trouble straddling his narrow, partially submerged board.

In their effort to look cool, these guys revealed they weren't even close to room temperature. They thought looking straight out at the ocean meant you were facing west. They didn't know Santa Cruz's coastline faced south. More morons in denial.

I studied the outside waves. In the distance from First and Second Peak, I hawk-eyed a slight purplish bruise of a rolling hump straining the tight strands of kelp that laced the ocean. The bulge flexed against the kelp. The sun glinted briefly on it. My local knowledge knew the roll wasn't going to break out there. It would come right into 38th. Normally, I would let the first wave go out of respect for the lineup, but these trannies had no time and grade on me. I spun around and started paddling. Bro Dork sat upright on his board and stared through me at the approaching wave. After I paddled past him, he spun around and paddled behind me for the same wave. My snake detector went off. Bro Dork was going to pull the go-behind move. He looked straight ahead like he didn't see me, which cracked me up, I mean we were both floating on the surface, how could I not see what he was doing? He was going rail-to-rail on me. And I had history. The Bro Dork didn't have the raw ability to keep up with my pace. His hands seemed to slap and slide off the surface, as if he was wiping it off. I penetrated the water up to my elbow. He dragged. I glided. The water rose beneath us, creating a sharp ledge. It lifted up into a four-foot banking slope to my right. I gave my paddle an extra hut hut. This trannie piece of burn-artist-snake shit get my wave? That was just not happenin'.

"Mine," Bro Dork shouted, as if claiming the wave was going to make me give up. "I got it, I got it!"

I made a quick, high turn at the peak. Bro Dork was up on one knee, lost his balance, fell, and let his board go. I slid across the rising and curving chute of water and looked down the line. The You-Go Girls saw me coming on the wave, and furiously paddled to drop in and burn me.

They whooped and cheered each other's bad behavior on: "You go girl... Put your blinders on and paddle, that's what Mom says ...Whew-who!...Go-fer it, go-fer it...Yeah, girlfriend... Take it all the way in... paddle, paddle. You can get it, girl."

One of the You-Go Girls was a little faster than the pack. She wore a neon orange wetsuit, helmet, goggles, and webbed gloves. She was lying on a thick and wide ten-foot white epoxy board with a hibiscus-pattern across its deck. She looked right at me, smiled, and paddled even harder for my wave. She dropped straight down, trying to cut across my angled path. She hadn't even stood yet. She was still crawling. I kept going. I had enough speed to avoid her and continue down the line. But she thought we were going to collide. She panicked. She bailed from her board. It shot out and banged off my arm.

"Hang onto your stick!" I yelled, recovering my balance and did a smooth cutback around her surfacing head. I swung the board around, walked to the nose, and planted ten all the way to the beach. When I kicked out close to shore, Ranger spotted me. She expectantly stood on the edge of the water. Her tail was wagging. A ball was in her mouth. "No Rangey, not yet," I said, smiling. I paddled back out. My wrist was starting to throb.

"That was a great wave you got," cheerfully said a clueless guy on a blue foam board, looking at me with a glowing admiration. "You were on the nose and everything."

I didn't respond. I didn't want to share the joy of my ride with him. Why share it with someone who was probably going to use his compliment as a way to take advantage of me later? But then I looked at him, I could see he was one of the many people who adopted the Instant Local characteristics, only because they were genuinely excited about surfing and purchased the Roxie clothing and the decals because they sincerely wanted to be a part of the surfing scene. I was unjustly turning decent people away by not sharing my stoke. And what happened? My effort to contain my stoke without sharing it, was like putting a glass over a candle and snuffling a flame. It left me feeling empty. I was being reduced. I realized instead of projecting being mean and nasty, I was *becoming* mean and nasty. I didn't know what to do about it.

Then one of the You-Go Girls launched a comment at me.

"Well, that was rude," snapped a woman, paddling rail-to-rail with me. "I'm talking to you, Mister Rude. You're rude."

I looked to my right. It was the helmet-headed woman who hit me with her board. She was in her early forties. I ignored her kept paddling. She struggled to keep up with me.

"You hit me with your board," I grunted.

"I'm a beginner," she snapped. "Sorry Mr. Perfect, don't you ever make mistakes?"

"Yeah, and when I hit someone with my board, I apologize."

"Well, I don't appreciate you yelling at me."

"I don't care what you appreciate," I said, paddling. "You hit me with your board. You don't know what you're doing."

"Big strong man, trying to run down a *girl*," she jeered. "You saw me, you should have backed off. You get enough waves."

I stopped paddling. No one talks down to me at sea level. I sat up on my board, and said, "Fine, now you're a girl, before all you were was a snake trying to burn me on my wave."

"I thought we were out here to have fun," she huffed.

"Oh yeah, it's fun when you're in my way, but it's not fun when I'm in yours."

"This is 38th. It's not like it's a real surf spot. It's just 38th."

"38th *is* a real surf spot," I said, flaring on my stinkeye, which lanced through her. "You're dangerous. You shouldn't be wearing a helmet, you should be handing them out."

"Are you questioning my surfing ability?" she huffed.

"You're the one who just said were a beginner."

"I've been surfing for six months," she said, boasting. "I placed second in the Las Amigas Surferama last week in Capitola."

"Second? You mean there is somebody who placed third who is even worse than you?"

"I know what I'm doing."

"You do, huh? Well, when I'm screaming down the line in the slot on the nose, why do you look right into my face, smile, and try to drop in front of me on my wave? When you're driving and come to an intersection, do you just pull out in front of a speeding truck and expect it to stop for you?"

"Then don't take off *behind* me."

"Behind you?" I laughed. "You cut in front of me, then tell me I shouldn't go behind you. You're an idiot."

"You're supposed to share. We're all out here cheering each other on and sharing waves. That's what I do."

"Taking what other people have isn't sharing," I said, the paused. "So, are you going to apologize for hitting me with your board? Are you going to say you're sorry?"

"You don't know how to talk to people." She paused. "Fuck you."

"What did you say to me?"

"Fuck you."

"You're saying I don't know how to talk to people? And you tell me to go fuck myself?"

"Tell it to my husband," she snipped.

"Why should I tell it to your husband? You tried to burn me, let your board go, and hit me. You're an asshole."

"There's no need to talk to my wife Cathy like that," barked Bro Dork.

God, she was Bro Dork's wife. And what a couple! They wore identical white protective helmets, sports watches, goggles, orange-neon paneled wetsuits, and webbed gloves. If someone put holes in the top of their white helmets they would look like a matching set of floating salt-and-pepper shakers.

"I believe an apology is in order," Bro Dork said. "You called my wife, Cathy, an asshole. There's no call for that type of language. There are children out here."

"I'd call you an asshole too, but an asshole has a function."

They were stunned. Clearly no one had ever directly talked to them this way before. They had routinely turned and burned people their whole lives, moving on, and leaving the road-kill clean up to others. But surfing wasn't like turning and burning motorists in traffic, or turning and burning fellow co-workers to advance a career. When you turned and burned someone on a wave, they didn't go away. You had to paddle back out and deal with the consequences. This new crowd of people hated that.

"What are you doing out here?" said Bro Dork. "I'm the vice president of the Longboard Union and I have never seen you at our meetings." Bro Dork paused. He pompously added, "We believe in spreading the vibe of the surfing stoke."

"Then why did you try to snake me on that last wave?"

"I saw the wave first."

"No, you didn't."

"I spun around for the wave first."

"No, you didn't"

"I called the wave first."

"Called the wave? Called the wave? What does that mean?"

"You know, I think you should surf somewhere else."

"*I* should surf somewhere else?"

“What I’m trying to say is the people who surf this place all the time have rules here,” he said.

“Rules!” I snarled, throwing my arms up into the air. “Listen Dot-Com KahanaFucku, I'll tell you what the rules are. There are two rules. The first rule is: ‘Do unto others as you would have them do unto you.’ And the second rule is: ‘Do unto others as they did unto you.’ I snorted. “How long have you been surfing? A fucking week? And you’re making up new rules and telling me to go somewhere else? I’ve been here since 1959. I’m not going anywhere. And you come out here thinking you own the place? You’re not changing the rules. The rules aren’t going to change. Why don't you go back to where you came from?”

“I'm a local. I live here.”

“Yeah, right. You don't live here you *bought* here.”

Bro Dork pointed to shore, and said with great pride, “I paid three million dollars for that house over there.”

“You might have bought a house, but you didn't buy a surf spot,” I replied, leaning toward him. “And if you forked out three million dollars for a house with no backyard, or privacy, and bums who leave syringes in your ice plants, you’re a fool.”

“Hey guys, chill” interjected another surfer. I looked to my right. He was yet another out-of-shape guy in his mid-forties who I’d never seen before. “There are plenty of waves. Surfing is supposed to be a beautiful thing. There’s plenty for all of us.”

“Excuse me, was I talking to you?” I asked him.

“I’ve been surfing this spot for twenty years,” out-of-shape man said.

“Twenty years, huh? Okay, then what’s my name?”

The out-of-shape guy stared at me There was a long pause. He averted his eyes as he replied, “I don’t know.”

“Then you haven’t been surfing here for twenty years. If you were surfing here for twenty years, you would know who I was.” I paused. “Maybe you surfed here *once* twenty years ago, but that doesn’t add up in water time.”

He drifted away, and cowered off to the side.

“So what is your name?” demanded Bro Dork.

“I don’t want to tell you my name,” I said. I paused and flashed my stinkeye. “And, I don’t want to know yours either.”

"Well, whatever your name is, the ocean is for everyone, you don't have a proprietary interest in it," said Bro Dork, as if all his decisions were final.

"Oh, is that one of your rules too, *hombre*?" I barked, cupped my right palm and skimmed it across the water, splashing him directly in the face. "There's your share."

"It's cool, it's cool bro," Bro Dork nervously spluttered. I think my stinkeye gave him the impression I was going to hit him. He extended his hand and blurted out, "Friends?"

"You are so out of here," I said with disgust and pointed to shore. "There's the stairway."

"You're not going to take this type of behavior from this loser are you?" said Bro Dork's wife, Cathy, miffed.

"Yes," said Bro Dork rapidly paddling to shore.

Cathy straddled her board. She was a few feet away. She looked around, as if she were hoping a cop would float by and arrest me. We stared at each other.

"I'm sorry," she said.

"Sorry?" I said, stunned. An apology from her. Now, that was something I didn't expect.

"I'm sorry you have nothing else in your life," she snarled. "No wonder you're not going anywhere."

"That's the best you can come up with?" I asked, watching her paddle away. I had to say something, because I hated to admit by my silence that her remark stung. She was impervious. Her arrogance depressed me. I floated in neutral. It was the first time in my life, I didn't look forward to paddling back out for another wave. Sure, there were nice waves, but if I was going to have people yell at me, or hurt me with their boards, and then say *I* was the problem—well, then what was the point? The waves didn't matter. Surfing wasn't a whole meal. Surfing was dessert. And you looked forward to dessert. But when you looked forward to a dessert and found it covered with ants, would you eat it? I mean the dessert was still there, but you had to deal with the ants. You could brush them off, but then would you still eat the dessert? No, because it was no longer dessert. I just didn't want to get into it with these people anymore. To them, what they did in the water to others wasn't right or wrong, it was debatable to them. I didn't come out here to debate people I didn't like. That's not why I surfed. But, what option did I have? Did I want to end up like The Crew and give up? I looked at a lone pelican flying low along the ocean. The bird banked and went out to sea. I slowly turned my Dad's gold ring on my finger. My wrist ached from where the board hit it. I heard a splash. A sea otter rolled and twisted and then lolled on his back. He was casually eating a crab alive, breaking off one quivering leg at a time and crunching it down. Agony on a half shell. I don't think that's how the crab originally planned to start his day. I thought, me neither. I felt the throbbing pain grow in my wrist. Before, when I surfed, I'd come out of the water feeling better, now, I was feeling worse. The dot-comers had done something I never thought possible: they made surfing boring. Their California dream had become my nightmare.

THE SWELL STAYED AROUND most of the week, but today, its pulse was slowly dropping. I threw the ball for Ranger on the beach. and checked out the ocean. The grayish clouds looked like snakeskin. The sun streaked a silvery shadowed light through the high approaching fog, which gave the sky a smoking, haunting haze. A stale static drifted in the warm air. Cruising low above the ocean was a one thousand-foot long flock of sooty shearwaters moving across the kelp and heading to shore. The surf didn't look appealing. It was sectiony, backing off, and warbly. The few waves that broke, tented, quickly peaked, and closed out. Yet there were still seventy people out on epoxy, soft-top, or sponge boards, greedily scrambling for very meager ankle-biters. They whew-hooed and you-go-girled over nothing. They didn't even know what bad surf was. Suddenly, the water churned with splashing baitfish, and the sooty shearwaters rained down upon the clueless. The birds accurately dive-bombed for darting anchovies between the floundering surfers. I was surprised the birds could tell the two groups apart. The dot-comers were enthralled by the carnage, as if they were witnessing a natural miracle. The frantic anchovies schooled themselves into a ball to look like a big creature, but the larger fish in the water weren't fooled and drove them towards shore. The anchovies had only one escape route: land. The sooty shearwaters and seagulls lined the shore and gorged themselves on the seething, silvery swirls of flapping anchovies washing up on the beach. You know things have gotten bad when fish try to leave the water to survive.

"Have you given any further thought to the shop-board, bro?"

Bro

"No." I reflexively responded.

It was Weever. He held a plastic garbage bag filled with trash. He wore jeans, sneaks, a Surf Dot Com powder blue polo shirt, and a "Longboard Association" baseball cap. He said, "Surf Dot Com adopted Pleasure Point. We're cleaning up the beach."

"That's nice, I do it every day."

"We're even painting lettering over catch basins to say, 'Flows to the Ocean' so people become aware of the connection between the ocean and the land."

"I never knew that," I said. "You know one thing about 'aware' people in Santa Cruz? That's all I ever meet here. They're all aware. I think I'm even aware of something right now."

"Bro, you ought to get involved with the Longboard Association. It's a tipping point that generates business for your shop. I'm trying to get interscholastic surfing going too."

"You mean where high school teams come out here to practice, like the ocean is a football field? You shittin' me?"

"This Sunday, we're sponsoring 'Share A Wave.' The media will be there for the paddle out. Pro surfers do it to get press."

"'Share A Wave'. What is that?"

"We take physically disadvantaged people out on surfboards."

"Big deal, I'm in the water with people like that every day."

"No, these people are deaf and blind."

"Like I said, I surf with them every day."

"No, these are people who are physically unable to stand-up on a surfboard."

"Yeah, those people are out there all the time too."

Weever could tell he wasn't scoring any points, but he persisted in trying to impress me with what he and his idiot buddies perceived as their elevated status within the upper echelons of Santa Cruz's surfing community.

"You know I just got elected association president, bro."

Weever, President of the Santa Cruz Longboard Association. Man, in the old days it would have been impossible for him to even park near a meeting. Originally, the Association used to be the group for the hottest local surfers. Slowly, the membership was infiltrated by the Instant-Local trannies, who sponsored more trannies (They even inducted people who didn't surf, but were friends of members who did, if you could believe that.). Eventually, the Instant Locals began to dominate meetings and ran the surfers who originally formed the club out of it. The trannies elected themselves officers, and formed committees so they could represent the club at surf contests. After the contest, they'd go to some bar, and have raffle drawing for wetsuits and boards donated by surf shops, with the ticket sale proceeds going to some politically-correct scholarship (I heard Weever frequently won by purchasing tickets at the last minute, and crumpling them up, so they would sit up high in the drawing bowl's pile.). After the prizes were handed out, the club members got drunk, made speeches about each other, handed out trophies, and applauded themselves as cool Santa Cruz surfers.

"Vic, if you want to join, I'll sponsor you as a member, bro."

"Are you telling me that the trannies who can't even surf are going to vote on whether or not I can join their club?" I said, unable to conceal my contempt. "That's not happenin'." I was surprised I snapped at him. Normally, I'd just blow Weever off with a neutral comment. But today, just seeing him at the beach pissed me off. "You know, every time a club guy comes to my shop, and wants me to donate something for one of your stupid raffles that's the only time I ever see them in my place. Oh wait, I take it back, one guy came in, bought a fifty-cent bar of wax and asked for a ten-percent club discount."

"Bro, if you changed your way of thinking, club members might start going to your shop," said Weever. "BTW, did you check out our surfing etiquette sign?'

"The what?"

"It's up on the railing at the entrance of the stairway."

"I never come down those steps to the beach."

"That sign is another opportunity you missed, bro. Your shop could have been listed as a sponsor.," said Weever, who paused and picked up a cigarette butt. "Based on the way you're thinking, if everyone is an idiot in the water, and there are more of them than you, how are you going to be able to keep your shop if they hate you and won't come in? I mean wake up, bro. Look at the way start-ups are taking over office spaces and the way rents are going up in Santa Cruz. What will happen to you if you lose your shop? I'll tell you what will happen..." His eyes narrowed, and he added with an out-of-proportion malicious glee, "You'll have to get a *real* job like everybody else."

Weever was pleased he dropped a fart in my head. I watched him walk down the beach with his garbage bag. Were the bro-dealing Weevers of the world going to defeat me? I started third-personing and played a mental game of solitaire I called: woulda-coulda-shoulda. Maybe, if I woulda gone to UCSC instead of trying to hustle a dollar to buy an egg roll from Kongs between surf sessions, I'd have an edge on the bro dealers of the world. Maybe, I coulda put my efforts into shaping more boards and doing more carpentry jobs and not surfed my life away. Maybe I shoulda never turned my surf shop into a hangout. What did I have after seven years? I didn't have a savings or a personal checking account. My credit card debt was about two thousand dollars from trying to keep the shop going through last winter. I had no medical or dental coverage. My lease was up in three months. My landlord would probably raise my rent. I was losing. I imagined the shop going out of business. The stripped metal T-shirt racks looked like upright, twisted robot spines. There were no wetsuits left. The display counter's shelves were barren. The voices sounded hollow. I'd be at the register, standing near huge piles of plastic hangers on the floor, and watching the shop slowly become a bargain basement for scavenging bro dealers. And Weever would finally get the shop board he wanted. I just couldn't let that happen. I mean, what else did I know? This was my life. But Weever was right, my way of life was dying. I couldn't schedule shop hours around surf sessions, shape a few boards, and just get by. I was losing. My surf shop was the one thing I brought with me from the past that I knew was right. I thought there might come a day when I would have to leave the shop, but I didn't think the shop would leave without me.

Ranger and I walked up the dirt path to the cliff. No one was hanging out at Heckler's Point. A few cars honked their horns and the drivers waved hello to me—I had surfed or shaped boards for them. It made me feel good to be recognized. I had to throw away a small plastic baggie of Ranger poop. I walked to the garbage barrels, which were on either side of the entrance at the wooden steps that descended to the beach.

Weever's new wooden sign was posted on the railing:

Surf Etiquette

1. First surfer up, closest to the curl has right of way.

2. Paddle around the break to get out.

3. Hang onto your board, look out for other surfers.

4. Respect the beach and the ocean.

38th Avenue: Beginner and intermediate spot, if under head high.

Sponsored by The Longboard Association.

'Beginner and intermediate'? What were they trying to do? Turn the ocean into a golf course with a slope rating? And what was the point displaying rules? It would only enable the idiots to rationalize their bad behavior. They lived to set up rules just to bend them. What was interesting is I remembered the original rules from the sixties. They left out Rule Five: "If you want respect, give respect." In other words, respect the pecking order, which I guess wasn't considered a positive enough message. The stupid sign was posted so Weever and his surf club trannie pals could get an newspaper article or TV coverage so they could be known for their "contribution to surfing." They had to be known for their contributions. None of trannies were good enough to let their surfing do the talking. I tried to find a spot to deposit Ranger's beach muffin, but the huge plastic garbage tubs were filled to the brim with crushed beer cans, plastic six-pack rings, wine bottles, and 12-pack cardboard boxes. Piled around the bins were more cans, bottles, boxes, 64-ounce Big Gulp wax cups, and a torn-apart Styrofoam cooler. I put the clear plastic baggie of Ranger's freshly baked item atop a Styrofoam fragment.

I leaned against the railing. Ranger sat at my feet. I hung there hoping to run into one of The Crew, or just get a few more car honks and waves. Rangey growled. A thin and spry guy in his seventies walked past me and stopped. He wore sweats, a Giants baseball cap, and sneakers. He had a beagle on a leash.

"No Range," I said, knowing how jealous she was of any other dog getting near me. She barked. "Hey, quiet!"

"That's the way they get," said the man. "They're loyal."

I said apologetically, "I'd like to pet your dog, sir, but Range would go crazy." I paused. "Howz'it?"

"Like pulverized pepper," he replied. "Mighty fine."

"I—"

"Why does he ask for it, if all he does is complain? Fuck him!" harshly shouted a jogger into a diva mic as he ran by us. He checked his pace against his sports watch. "I'm out of the box."

"If he keeps living like that, he'll *be* in a box," commented the old guy, smiling. "You know young man, I see these computer people. They're on their cell phones. Their kids are playing video games. They've lost already and they don't know it."

"Before you'd only see jerks like that downtown—"

"I haven't been downtown in thirty-two years."

"Thirty-two years? Are you back in town visiting?"

"No, I live a couple houses down the street, been here for forty years, worked as a claim adjuster," he cheerfully said, but then added sourly. "I stopped going downtown after the college came in. All those snotty young people. And they're all communists! They voted out the local politicians and put in commies. That's why we have all the problems with the illegal Mexicans living in the Beach Flats neighborhood by the boardwalk and the drugs and the crime and the trolls panhandling. And the homeless! They come into Santa Cruz from Arkansas with a map that tells them where the shelters are. My daughter is a single Mom raising a kid and going to school at night and there's nothing for her. You're not supposed to kick a guy when he's down, but when he's down and kicking you, what are you supposed to do about that? The people running this town are socialists. I had to spend $13,000 just to get a permit from the Planning Commission for a retaining wall on my property. Then when I went down there, they nailed me for another $174 to process the permit! Did you know the Planning Commission here is larger than the one in Los Angeles? Santa Cruz is one of the smallest counties in the entire state. The only thing the Planning Commission is planning in the future is to charge us more so they can keep their jobs. I'm ashamed to tell people I live here. One time I was in a diner in Klamath Falls, Oregon. The owner found out I was from Santa Cruz, and as a joke he offered me a bowl of fruit and nuts. Now, I always say I'm from somewhere else." The dog pulled at its leash. "Okay, Caesar." He walked away. "Nice talking to you."

God, the guy was really bitter. I wondered if that's how grumpy I sounded to younger people when I talked about surfing. What was I turning into, a grouch?

"It sucked, but I had to get wet," said Shiloh, who came up the path with her surfboard. Her hair was plastered to her head. "I'm so over it."

Then Shiloh started to cry.

"You all right?" I asked, stepping back.

"I got fired. The dot-com guy got me fired," she said. "I went out to First Peak to work the edge off. Didn't help though, I was surfing slop and these tannie Roxie Instant Local You-Go Girls all cheering on each other and lipping off at me like I'm violating their air space. Clueless. And they're really mean. They make me mortified I'm a female. They can't even surf. I'd be embarrassed to be like them, really. They are so unocean. I'm over it."

"I might be able to throw you some hours in the shop," I said, knowing that's not what she hoped I'd offer.

"Thanks," Shiloh said dejectedly. She wiped her tears, and walked toward The Hook.

She didn't want a job offer from me. She wanted a hug. A voice told me to console her, and I usually followed my first nature, but this time I didn't. I withdrew. I thought about the Bystrom guy she dated. He was a complete jerk in the water, but he was strong and could get all the waves he wanted. Anyway, now I was planning on mad-dogging the dot-com execudiva.

"Come on, Rangey," I said. Ranger tried to get up too quickly and her back right leg gave out again. She yipped. It was a sharp yip. My heart jumped. Today was going to be one of her bad days. She laid her lower jaw flat on her front paws and looked directly at me with her tired brown eyes. She softly panted and cried at the same time. "I know Rangey," I sympathetically said, taking her in my arms. "I know." I gingerly carried Ranger to the VW and gently placed her in the passenger seat.

We drove a quarter mile down 38th Avenue. I made a right, and pulled in front of the shop. It was at the corner of 38th and Portola Avenue, just two minutes away from Pleasure Point. The neighborhood was still funky—a lumberyard, a couple breakfast places, bike shops, the closed-down Opal Cliffs market, and across the street was a small strip mall of Adobe-style buildings, which contained a liquor store, a tae kwon do place, The La Boca Mexican restaurant, a pizzeria, a lesbian-run coffee house, and a chiropractor's office. There were dirt paths instead of sidewalks, stop signs instead of traffic lights, and no bike lanes, or tree-lined safety islands in the middle of the street. I liked it.

My favorite part of the day was opening up the shop. And I never got tired of doing it. It was like waxing up my board and looking at the surf. It mentally prepared me for the way the day was going to break. The routine started with pulling up in my VW, and looking at "Vic's Surf Shop" on the front window against a backdrop of the shop boards hanging in straps from the ceiling beams. I helped Ranger out of the van, took out my keys and opened the front door. A strong wall of stale rubbery air from the wetsuits hit me. I even smelled wax. The security system panel buzzed. I had forty-five seconds before the alarm went off. I briskly stepped over the nine-foot pink surfboard laying on the wooden floor, made a tight turn around the fifteen-foot long bamboo-edge trimmed counter, and ducked under the palm frond roof suspended above it. I went to the wall, a few feet behind the register, moved aside the surf leashes that hung in front of an alarm panel, and entered the code on its ten-digit touch pad: my birthday 11650. Each digit beeped as I pressed it. The buzzing stopped. I switched on the ceiling lights. I went behind the display wall to a tiny little alcove that could barely hold a filing cabinet. I opened the top drawer, reached under a pile of several unopened Roxie Girl surf clothing catalogues (every cover had a picture of a young honey in a tropical-floral pattern bikini noseriding a longboard on a wave), and pulled out the small zippered leather pouch, which contained eighty-nine dollars, yesterday's register tape, and some checks. I looked at the grand total: $650.53. The money came from one consignment board sale, a wetsuit, some wax and a few T-shirts. Minus the cash I gave back to the guy for the consignment board, I cleared $240. After deducting my $8 an hour salary, yesterday penciled out to $176. I put the money in the register. I carried the nine-foot long pink surfboard outside. The log weighed forty pounds and had the word "Open" painted on it in black letters. I stood the board up on the right corner of the building, positioned it between two looped metal eyelets, and stretched the dangling bungee cord from one eyelet across the deck of the board to the other eyelet, which bound the stick flush against the wall. When I walked back into the shop, Ranger was settled in the far left corner by the front window. The sun hit that part of the place first. She curled up on a small rug, where I had a bowl of water and a dish of brown dry food.

"Getting your sun, whups?" I asked, wedging the front door open with half a brick that had been thrown a year ago through the window by a vengeful bum, who did it because I beat him up for trying to steal a customer's bike left in front of the shop.

I patrolled the six display racks of T-shirts, drawstring pants, hooded sweatshirts, and men's swimming trunks. I found a couple empty hangers on the rack, which meant a shoplifter had snagged some shirts. A chewed-up, faded green couch was in the middle of the shop. In front of the couch was a small low scuffed-up wooden table covered with surf magazines. Just beyond the table, was a TV set on a pile of wooden crates. Atop the TV was a VCR, an amplifier, a cable radio box a friend of mine illegally connected to a neighbor's house, and a police scanner, which flashed red as it searched for its channels. I turned on the TV. A news show came on. I was going to turn it off and put on a surf video, but then I saw shots of Santa Cruz. I turned up the volume. A balding, skinny business reporter in a suit spoke in front of a backdrop of changing images: bumper-to-bumper traffic on Highway 17 and Route One; industrial parks with high-tech logos on their buildings along 880 in Sunnyvale; line charts of rising housing prices and rents; a shot of the Coyote Valley open space and the word Cisco Systems imposed over it; and young dot-comers driving expensive cars, drinking champagne at launch parties, and constructing McMansions.

"There is no logical reason for the tech stocks to be booming," said the reporter. "But this second California gold rush began in 1995, when Netscape went from $28 a share to $58.25 a share, and overnight became a company worth $2.6 billion. And a year later in April, another mother lode was struck, it was a company called Yahoo, which went from $13 to $24, and that start-up was worth a billion. Today every day trader, money manager, and broker, and mutual and hedge fund, is placing chips on the NASDAQ roulette table to strike gold without using a shovel. Everyone is panning for the next big IPO for an eBay, Netscape, Yahoo, Sun Microsystems, Amazon.com, or Cisco. Everyone wants to be rich, so they're all coming out to Northern California. Instead of bringing picks and digging mine shafts, and staking claims, these dot-com prospectors are bringing routers and building web sites, and acquiring domain names. The average income of a Silicon Valley techie with stock options is between $89,000 to $145,000 a year. The latest flashpoint is Cisco's Coyote Valley Research project, which would take the last expanse of open space in San Jose. A 688-acre area in the city's southernmost limits. Cisco calls it an 'industry-government collaborative' that will respect the area's 'agrarian past.' Cisco predicted its creation of 20,000 jobs would solve the county housing shortage. The company planners claim the project will bring $242 million to the area. But critics ask is an information super highway worth the trade off in the loss of quality in lives and farmland? Critics question how low-and-middle income families in Santa Cruz and Monterey County can compete for housing against the needs of Cisco employees making six-figures. Currently, Silicon Valley and Santa Cruz are rated the most expensive places to live in the nation. Santa Cruz, California, is situated on the northern part of Monterey Bay about 74 miles south of San Francisco and 30 miles from Silicon Valley. Santa Cruz has an area of 12 square miles with a population of 53,200. The median price for a house in Santa Cruz County is $540,000. A few years ago, the median price tag was $240,000. In 1993, only 12 Santa Cruz homes sold for one million dollars, but in 1999 with the infusion of dot-com money, and the ratcheting up of home prices, 96 homes sold for over one million dollars. Santa Cruz perfectly illustrates the digital divide. This town that was once known for its laid-back quality, its surfers, UCSC-Birkenstock-wearing-tree-huggers, and clove-cigarette-smoking vegans, is experiencing a sea change. For years, the progressive-majority serving on the Santa Cruz County Board of Supervisors virulently opposed commercial growth and mass-transportation to protect this beach town's quality of life from urban sprawl. Ironically, the board's progressive policies backfired and increased property values due to the shortage of housing and businesses for the middle-class to work, and created an urban sprawl of bedroom communities and industries in surrounding areas, which has lowered the quality of life for the people who have always lived here. Thanks to the supervisors, these workers only have one-way to commute to Silicon Valley, by car, in bumper-to-bumper traffic on Highway 1 all the way from Watsonville to where it fishooks and goes north to Highway 17. Ironically, Santa Cruz had is becoming a second-home community for the rich, a party-college town for children of Los Angeles' upper-middle class, and a playground for Silicon Valley. Unless you work for or attend the university, owned a house before the boom, or happen to be one of those Santa Cruz County Supervisors who pull down $87,000 a year plus perks (the median California income by the way is $35,000), the average Santa Cruzan can no longer afford to live here, unless they supplement their income with a second or a third job, rent out part of their home, or live in a trailer park. Some residents I spoke to are actually moving to Hawaii because the cost-of-living and housing is cheaper. Many are selling their homes for huge profits, but once they do, they can't buy a better house in Santa Cruz, they have to either purchase a condo or leave and never be able to move back to Santa Cruz. It's the American Dream stuck in reverse. Not much joy in seeing a beautiful California sunset when you're stuck in a traffic jam on the Coast Highway. Back to you, Wolf, on the rise of the Taliban regime in Afghanistan—"

I quickly slid an old surf video from the sixties into the VCR. The news was replaced by Phil Edwards surfing uncrowded waves at Hawaii in the early sixties. I turned down the volume of the movie, flicked on the amplifier, and punched in the oldies channel on the cable radio box. 'I Feel Free' by Cream came over the huge speakers in each corner of the shop. The tune took me back to 1969. It was my last day in the army. I was in the barracks at Fort Ord. I had that Cream song cranked up on my stereo. I was dancing and jumping around. I was still in uniform, but I had those discharge papers in my hand and I wasn't going to let them go. Nobody in a military uniform would ever have any say in my life again. And 'I Feel Free' was cranked at full volume to let everyone on the base know just that. Some rear-echelon sergeant busted in. He was an asshole who resented I had a Combat Infantry Badge. He gurred, "You're going to be a hippie aren't you?" And I smiled and replied, "I'm going to grow my hair long and surf in Santa Cruz for the rest of my life." And I shook and waved those discharge papers in the air.

"Yo Vic, you need me today?" asked Squirrel, who walked into the shop, carrying his laptop computer. "I came by at ten and the shop was closed." He paused. "Open at noon? I guess you're working hard, huh?"

"I had to get some blanks to shape for boards," I said. "And what were you doing here around at ten in the morning on a week day, Squirrel? Get thrown out of school again?"

"They got me in home study three days a week."

"That's the same thing isn't it?"

"I don't know," Squirrel said, shrugging.

His real name wasn't Squirrel. I called him Squirrel because it seemed like a good name for a short fuck-up. He was dressed in hip-hop clothing—baseball cap turned backwards, baggy shorts hung low, underwear band showing, and sneakers with untied laces. Squirrel was a thin kid who was self-conscious about being short, and bad at sports. He was fourteen years old and he lived nearby. He hung out at the shop more than his home. He was on probation for using credit card receipts on the Internet to order computer games, porno, CDs, and some MP3 players. When he was arrested, his mother came into the shop crying, telling me her daughter had decided to become a homeless person and she didn't want to lose her son the same way, and would I watch Squirrel because he respected me. Obviously, the mom wasn't all there either and viewed herself as some saint. She was divorced and according to her, all of Squirrel's problems started when she recently remarried. She said he resented the attention his stepfather's two kids were getting, and the time she spent with her new husband. All I knew was she never held a job, and she was this frumpy, unattractive mess, and the guy she married had a type of disability from emphysema or something and only worked part-time, and they used credit cards to go on trips, and owned four TVs, got a new car every year, and complained about being broke. And everything was always a drama. Since Squirrel was going to hang out at the shop anyway, and play on his computer. I paid him to vacuum, clean the glass counters, sweep the sidewalk, and take out the garbage. I trusted him. The last kid I hired floated wetsuit deals to his bros in exchange for dope. Squirrel was content to sit in front of his laptop, watch the store, and let the guys hang out. It was odd. I had a beach dog that didn't like the ocean and a surf shop rat who didn't surf.

I walked around the shop straightening the black-and-white eight-by-ten inch surfing photos of Santa Cruz in the sixties, displayed on the walls and support beams. I stopped at a shot of me lying in the sand at Cowells in 1966. I was smiling.

"Black is Black" by Los Bravos came on.

Squirrel said, "Don't you listen to anything that's not old?"

"I'm not going to play that rap-ghetto shit you listen to, G," I said, grabbing the cap off his head, twisting it on backwards, and pulling my pants low. "I'm bad, homey, yeah, essay"

"You musta heard these retarded songs a thousand times," said Squirrel, jumping up and grabbing his hat back. "Don't you get tired of hearing them?" As he spoke to me, he moved both his hands in the air like he was petting an invisible animal. "Get DSL in here. I won't have to use my wireless connection. It'd be hella cool, with broadband you'd have a large enough pipe to download all the music you want. I can get it on the Internet for nothing, and burn a CD, or play it on a computer like this."

"Out of that little thing?" I asked, pointing at his laptop.

"Damn Skippy," said Squirrel. "Sixty gigs. It's da bomb."

"What's that mean?"

"Gigs, they're—"

"No, I don't care about that shit, what's 'damn Skippy' mean?"

"Damn Skippy means something like damn straight."

"Oh."

"Hook up with this," said Squirrel, connecting his computer to the stereo's amplifier.

A rap song with heavy bass thumped, a guy yo-yo-ed, and the tune's hook was a sample from a sixties top-forty hit, but I just couldn't place its title. And then the rapper vocalist shouted, "If you don't like my shit, you can suck my dick."

"Turn that off," I said. "You can hear that out in the street."

"If you don't like my shit you can suck my dick," cheerfully sang out Squirrel, who stuck his hands in front of his chest, with his thumb up and two forefingers extended, and moved them opposite each other like he was caught in an invisible pair of Chinese handcuffs. He declared, "In the house."

"Off!" I yelled, but Squirrel put his fist near his mouth like he was jamming a microphone against his lips, and kept rapping. "Hey, turn this stuff off. People outside this shop can hear this! I don't want to scare people away. People can hear this!"

"Downtown!" Squirrel shouted, completely and thoroughly enjoying my rage. He jabbed his hands out and in, then put both his hands together and acted like he was stirring a huge pot. "It's on, it's on." Ranger heard my shouting, came over, and barked. "Let's get it started, let's get it started." I flicked my finger, knowing exactly where to thump his forehead with Dad's ring to inflict maximum pain. Ranger's jaws lightly clamped on the inside fabric of Squirrel's shorts. I think it was a competitive thing because Ranger viewed Squirrel as the other shop pet.

"Hey!" he said, rubbing his head where I thumped him. He tried to shake himself free of Ranger, who was tugging his pants down. I laughed. Ranger let go. "That's so weak," he grunted, hurt and upset. Ranger barked. Squirrel disconnected his laptop, but did one last face-saving bob and shoulder weave, and said in a rap voice to Ranger "You playa hata, nobody disses me, ho. You want the upside-hand bitch slap? For real, girlfriend."

I laughed. The kid was just a cornhead.

'Cara Mia' by Jay and The Americans played. I was back in the sixties again.

A voice came from the front of the shop.

"Hi. Um, you told me I could come by and have my lunch?" tentatively said a guy, who was in his mid-fifties, balding, and had glasses. He wore jeans, one of my surf shirts, and sneakers. The shirt was tucked in and his gut hung out. He carried a bag from Der Wienerschnitzel. I couldn't place him.

"Ralph," he said. "From the beach, I met you—"

"I didn't recognize ya, I'm used to seeing everyone damp and in wetsuits. When people are dried out they look different. Make yourself at home on the couch, have your lunch, watch a surf video, look at a magazine, stay as long as you want."

"I got hot dogs," Ralph said, sitting on the couch and opening the bag on the low table in front of it. "My treat."

"I'll pass, I'm burned out on Der Wienerschnitzel."

"I'll eat it," volunteered Squirrel, walking over to Ralph.

"Wait until you're asked." I said.

A voice slurred at the front door, "Need your windows done?"

It was Broadway. Broadway was an excellent surfer who went to Vietnam after me. His real name was Danny Billings. He was in Special Forces. On Christmas Eve he returned to the states. His wife and child were killed in a car accident coming to pick him up. State troopers met him at the airport. Broadway flipped out the following Christmas Eve. That night he did seventeen shots of ouzo at some bar, and went to the store on his motorcycle for cigarettes. He was heading down Broadway Street. Someone called out to him. He looked back and waved.

He drifted in the opposite lane, he turned, a car was right there, and plowed into him. His head hit the bumper. Blood exploded. He stood up, looked around, and held up his fists. Then he went down. When asked why he held up his fists after the crash, he said, "I thought someone hit me." There was nothing left in him except to keep drinking or get high so he wouldn't feel the physical pain. His teeth were rotten. His face was puffy and orange, like the inside of a clam. He had long hair and beard. He wore faded jeans, a tie-dyed shirt with tiny holes around its collar stitching, and wafer-thin sandals on his dirty feet. He carried a bucket filled with dirty water. Broadway never accepted handouts. He worked odd jobs. He lived in a storage shed. If you could get past his looks, he was relatively harmless.

"I want a couple stickers for my bike," said Broadway, who pointed to his shiny, red bicycle, which had a large black-bulb silver horn on its handlebars, a paint-splattered, brown, ghetto blaster in a front metal basket, which was held in place with gray duct tape. The bike had new tires, and a banana-shaped seat. He looked like a nine-year old as he moved his finger over the display case and pointed at the stack of "Vic's Surf Shop' stickers. "I want a shop sticker, the big one, for my banana seat."

I took out an oval sticker, along with three other surf decals some sales reps gave me and said, "These others are free. You can have them. The shop one is seventy cents."

"Oh," Broadway said, holding a few dollars in his hand. He looked at the case, perplexed. He spoke like he was carefully stacking his words one on top of the other, and feared they would teeter, fall, and he'd lose one. "I want to spend three dollars here." He pointed at a can of wetsuit-repair glue in the display case. His eyes lit up within the deep redness and wrinkles. I caught a brief glimpse of the man he once was. "How much is the glue?"

It was four dollars, but I took it out of the case, slid it towards him and said, "$2.25 and with the sticker it comes out to a flat three dollars. I got the tax."

On the speakers, Keith sang the song "98.6."

"Man, this is boss, these sticks are so cherry," Broadway said, drifting about the shop, and gazing at the shop boards hanging from the rafters. He spoke as if the boards were stars and he was reverently naming different constellations that somehow held his universe together. “Man, a Velzy, a Jacobs 422, a Dewey Weber Performer. A Phil Edwards signature model—a Phil! Now there’s a guy who is a true surfer. Phil was my hero. I mean Phil said, ‘Surfing is not about the waves, if it was, we’d all be living in Hawaii. It’s the act of just doing it.’ I remember that. Man, classic sixties longboards.” He scrunched his face. “I was in a bar.” He paused again. “A lot of my stories start that way. Anyway, I was on R&R and in Australia. And I'm in this bar. There was a monk in it. He was in his early thirties, longish hair. Looked like he didn't take himself too serious, and for a being a monk in a bar that's pretty good. He looked over at me. I was just wearing my trunks and all tan. ‘You surf?’ he asked, looking at the board on my car. I said, ‘Whenever it’s necessary, right?’ And the monk guy says he's in a monastery in Raglan and said all they did is pray. I said, ‘Yeah.’ Then he says, ‘I'm a monk. I had to give up all my earthly possessions. I did. But I left my Con Ugly, a Curran gun, and a Tom Blake paddleboard with my Mom in Dana Point.’” Broadway jerked his head. “I guess it showed the monk really believed in something.” He looked around. “This shop is a cool place. I like the music. It’s all tricked out the way surf shops used to be, like Slap’s was, kinda. It’s there for me, a place I feel I can always come to. It’s like a...”

“Sanctuary,” said Ralph. “A special place.”

“Yeah, something the world doesn’t have, yeah, something that should be preserved,” said Broadway, who snorted back some mucous in his nose. “Vic, you want me to do your windows?”

“Maybe, when you get some cleaner water.”

“Oh,” he said absently, looking vacantly down at the gray water sloshing around in the plastic bucket. “Yeah.”

“What are you up to?” I asked.

“Nothing,” Broadway replied, as he went outside to his bike. “But I’m going to fix it right now.”

“Fucking troll derelict,” snorted Squirrel, his mouth half filled with a hot dog as he tapped on his computer.

“You keep going the way you’re going, Squirrel, cutting up in class so you can get home study and not do anything, and one day you’ll be fighting Broadway for his bucket.”

"Yeah, right," said Squirrel, staring at the screen.

Broadway honked his bike horn, waved, and pedaled away.

A mom and her teenage-age daughter entered the shop. She wore a running outfit. She was in pretty good shape. Her daughter had on a shell choker, and a brightly colored island style Roxie board shorts, sandals, and knit cap. The cheerful colors contrasted sharply with the scornful look crouched on her face. She also wore a gray, hooded sweatshirt with a drawing of a huge wave. The word "Team" was above the wave, and the word "Tola" was across the wave's face, which was a real joke, because most of the year, the break at Capitola was considered a lame wave for kids, old farts, girls, and clueless surfers. Very few excellent surfers rode the place, so by default, women surf clubs took it over, and used it as a contest site, which was fine, but it definitely wasn't cool.

"Feel free to look around," I said, hospitably "If you have any questions, I'll be glad to answer them."

'You're The One' by The Vogues played on the speakers. The mother-daughter combo didn't respond to the upbeat song. They tentatively sniffed around the shop. They looked uncomfortable. The daughter didn't conceal that fact she was bored. Anytime the mother stopped, she alternately lifted one of the heels but kept the balls of her feet on the floor, like she was running in place, as if she always had to be going somewhere.

"Do you carry anything besides these clothes?" patronizingly asked the woman, who touched one of the shirts on a hanger, then let go like it irritated her flesh. She grimaced. "This is your total selection? Just T-shirts, drawstring sweatpants, wetsuits?"

"Yeah, shop clothes—"

"Do you know where they carry the Roxie line of apparel?" she asked, slowly running in place again.

"Probably at Macy's in the Capitola Mall, I—"

"Got it," she said, quickly pivoted around, and left with her foot-dragging daughter trailing behind her.

Just as the mother-daughter Team Tola combo drove off in an SUV, two cars pulled up in front, a pick-up truck, and a van. It was the 38th Crew. Larry The Legend, The General, Driveway Dave, and Chops. They paraded in with small grease-stained brown bags filled with burritos and tacos from La Boca. The Crew spread about thc place like it was their home. They nodded at Ralph to acknowledge him, but said nothing.

"I got the sodas," said The Legend, rolling quarter after quarter into the machine. The Legend was a slightly pudgy guy in his mid-fifties. He had a goatee, and a shaved head. He wore sweat pants, a sleeveless shirt, and sandals. He was called The Legend because he only rode classic longboards from the sixties. He made a living as a surf photographer and worked part-time at his father's liquor store. "It's coming up a little, the Westside is starting to show."

"Why aren't you over at The Lane shooting?" I asked.

"Fuck, I was there and these dot-com idiots I've never seen before, are setting up with the same digital camera and tripod I have," said The Legend, who sat on the couch, and placed a tin-foil wrapped chicken taco and a bean-and-cheese burrito on the table. "My camera is a forty-five-hundred dollar camera, man. My lens is fifteen hundred. These dot-com trannies with their beaucoup bucks are coming out of the sand with these big-buck digital cameras or video cameras. I mean, I remember the first day it started. It was early in the morning last Spring when and a North swell was still coming in. I can stand on the end of the wharf, and get great shots. They were there, all of them. Then later in the afternoon, when I'm on the cliff at the Lane, with the light behind me, they're there too. Last Winter, I go up to Mavericks to get big-wave shots at Half Moon Bay, and the trannie photogs are in my spots too. They'd follow me, and wherever I went that's where they'd go. God forbid they should think for themselves, you know? And they're selling their photos for nearly nothing so they to get exposure in the magazine so they can get in with the local surfers and say they're cool to their friends because they got their shots published in a surf magazine. Fuck me with a sharp stick. With everyone sending wave pictures to surf magazines, there's just a glut. And what's worse, before when I gave the surf mags a picture they ran it, now they hold on to it just to make sure the other magazines can't use it, and then they give it back to me, and say they don't want it. And it's all because of those guys! And they're all making surf videos, the community cable channels are always showing them. They're filming their friends and none of them can surf worth a shit." He paused. "But they're cool! They're surf photographers. Oooooh."

"Did someone call the Waaaaaaaaahm-bulance?" said Chops, smiling. He listened the music. "Hey, who does this song?"

"'Pata Pata' by Miriam Makeba," said Skin Dog, who knew his oldies better than The Gospel. "A cool tune. She was married to Hugh Masekela, and Stokely Carmichael. She never got a cent from this song, she was ripped off."

"Picked you up a shredded beef burrito, Vic," said The General, who flipped a rolled-up tin-foil burrito on the counter.

"Cool, thanks."

"Say brutha, did you tell Burr, he's famous?" asked Skin Dog, heavily flopping his 250-pound plus body on the couch.

"I figured I'd let him digest his food first," said Chops, clearing away the magazines, and using a bag as a placemat. "If I read it to him when he was eating, his meal might come up."

"What's this about?" I asked, looking at the smirking Crew. They shared a joke I wasn't in on yet. "What?" I said. "What?"

"You're in the paper, brutha," said Skin Dog, laughing as he opened and held up a page of Good Times, a local weekly.

It was a picture of Bro Dork's wife above an op-ed column she wrote. Her full name was Cathy Deborah Hopwell.

Skin Dog extended the paper at full arm-length from his eyes it and read aloud: "Women today are breaking the mold by challenging stereotypes in the male dominated world of surfing. I was out on a beautiful day, surfing, and sharing waves to experience walking on the energy of Mother Ocean, promoting surfing no matter what level our abilities or age. It was a great atmosphere that said 'Yeah, for women.'"

I groaned and softly said, "Why are you hurting me?"

"Wait, it gets better," said Skin Dog, who continued reading. "'And I was with a group of women feeling the feminine stoke of being supportive and cheering each other on waves in our graceful spindrift of estrogen with da-kine camaraderie—"

"'Da kine'? If she pulled what she did to me in Hawaii, those da-kine Hawaiians would beef her ass and burn her SUV. Where are these people coming from? Even in ancient Hawaiian times, the Kings and Queens kept the best breaks for themselves. I bet there were a lot of heads on stakes lining those perimeters. God, and look at her picture, with her dried out face, her head would look more natural on a stake that on her neck."

"Please brutha, this is classic journalism, here," said Skin Dog, who continued, "...'this old long-haired hippie local...'" He stopped and looked up from the newspaper. "I think that just might be you." He read on, "'...whose testosterone-laden vibe was based on the assumption of false ownership that all waves were his, bullied us and ordered us to leave—'"

"Does she say how she burned me and hit me and how she and her estrogen gracefully told me to fuck off?"

"You know she left that part out," Skin Dog said, "She's a last-word person, typical reporter. But she does conclude it's a positive thing for women to be aggressive and notes 'men can't handle it' because women are 'breaking new ground.'"

"How can you break ground in the water?"

"That's why she's 'breaking the mold'."

"How can you break the mold when you're riding a board made from a mold?" I asked, realizing how The Crew enjoyed setting me off for their amusement. I didn't disappoint them. "I'd like to write an article. You know why there were so few women surfing back in the sixties? Because most of the women back then didn't want to surf. Nothing was stopping them. They thought guys who surfed were flakes, losers and derelicts. Women didn't want to bother with us bums. I know, I was one of them. The only good-looking women who hung down at the beach were jogging and living with the guys who were drug dealers. We didn't have the money to take them to clubs or to dinner or to concerts, and we wouldn't take the jobs to make that kind of money because we didn't want to miss waves. But all these clueless dot-comers, lawyers, and doctors have made all this money and bought houses here and they paddle out with their two-year trannie badges and have made surfing *acceptable*. Who stopped women from surfing before? We had women out there! Those women didn't need to come out in packs or with a boyfriend to block out people so they could get waves. They were independent. Look at Shiloh. But it's all these trannie

Instant local Roxied-out women who paddle out, because they're either married to these trannies or want to date them. They feel it's safer out there because they know those types of people. They're with their friends, husbands, boyfriends, and kids. The same women who called us deadbeats and derelicts for surfing, and said any grown man who surfed was stupid and never wanted to grow up, these are the same women who see surfing as cool now because *they* want to do it. They're trying to make the water like their neighborhoods. What's next? Street signs, traffic lights? Anything, that makes it easier for them to take over. Shit, it's not my fault, she took up surfing when she was forty."

"Yeah," added Chops. "I mean it's so *unusual* to find a hostile woman in Santa Cruz."

The Crew laughed.

Dusty Springfield's "Wishin' and Hopin" came on.

"Hostile, my Ex is a prime example of that, in fact my Ex is in perpetual relapse," said Skin Dog. "Back in the day, she was this cool hippie girl who drove around with me in a beat-up truck. We sold muffins she made. Then she got this job at a hospital and she started getting promoted and making money and she began wanting all these things. I kept saying, 'Hey, where's the girl I knew in the truck?' We divorced. She has the house and drives a Mercedes and I'm driving a truck and paying child support and she's complaining she needs more money to raise the child and she's making more money than me. And she starts referring to herself as a 'single mother.' I said, 'No, widows are single mothers. Our daughter has a father.' But you know what still gets her mad? And what always got her mad? Was that I could swim better than her and when I came back from surfing she just hated it. We're divorced, but she still talks to me like we're still married. My daughter is eighteen now. As far as support goes, I shook that hook. I'm still living in a mobile home. But my Ex wants me to pay for college. Says I'm not being a good father. When the kid came to live with me for two years, do you think my Ex coughed up any child support? No way. So now she doesn't have money for the kid's college. Yeah, because of what? The repairs on the Mercedes or all the vacations she took? And, you know, my daughter is turning out to be just like my wife. They both expect more from me, and for what? I mean I'll probably kick in something for school." He paused. "But, I learned my lesson." He paused, then said with great conviction. "I learned I'll never, ever, get married again!"

We laughed.

"Girls don't seem to be interested in you when you're older and haven't had your success," said The General, who was in his early sixties. "What people see in you when you're young is more of your earning potential. It's a socio-economic thing. All I can tell you is there's one thing the women out there don't want, and that's me."

"I don't want to know them," I said, but suddenly flashed on the executiva crossing her legs at Bings. "I don't know."

"I got into surfing because of this one girl," said Chops. "We'd run together and I ran better, we stopped that. We took up racquetball and I got better at that. We stopped doing that too. We went surfing and I got better at that." He paused. "Then, I broke up with her."

Everyone laughed.

"You know, around that time of month when women can become irritable?" said The Legend. "That's the one time I feel I can talk to them. I mean being irritable I can understand."

We laughed, stopped. Laughed again, and stopped.

Squirrel's laptop speakers blasted out screams, followed by the clanging of swords.

"Zander is going down," shouted Squirrel.

"Who?" I asked. "What's a Zander?"

"Zander. He's one of the geeks I'm playing war games against on the web," said Squirrel, intently focusing on the screen as he rapidly hit keys. "I can write code to slip into God mode and the idiot doesn't know it." There were more screams, explosions, and the crackling sound of fires. "I'm going to rock his world."

"Help Yourself" by Tom Jones came on.

We gathered behind Squirrel. He was moving knights on horses around castles that resembled chess rooks. We didn't know what he was doing, but he was clearly kicking somebody's ass. Thatched huts were engulfed in flames. He shifted between numerous menu bars, clicked different icons to use various weapons, and based his offensive movements on an aerial topographical map that depicted the enemy's advance in the form of approaching dots. It was pretty realistic.

"This guy who calls himself Zander is stupid," said Squirrel. "He's not using his hero points. He's coming right into my base. He doesn't know I offloaded all my weapons. I have my scouts out. I know he's used up all his gold and lumber. Zander thinks I have weapons in my camp. After his troops find nothing, I'll ambush him at his base with his munitions and annihilate him."

"What's the game's point?" I asked. "You just kill everything?"

"No, I don't just kill everything. It's Warblood. I fight the Undead. It's hella cool. It puts the DeathRattle game to shame."

"Must be set in downtown Santa Cruz," said Chop, drawing a laugh. "Which means the universe lost, huh?"

"So it's just a game where you kill people," I said.

"I stop the Forces of Chaos from taking over the universe."

"So," I said. "You stop those forces by killing them, right?"

"There are death coils, night elves, wizards, druids, and they have different abilities and can cast spells—"

"How do you win?" asked The Legend.

"When everyone else is dead but you," Squirrel said.

I smiled and said, "So, it is a game where you just kill people."

"It's more than a game the *way* I play it," cunningly said Squirrel, who suddenly scowled. "Damn, he went off-line, Zander must have had to go back to work." The Crew drifted to the couch. "Hey, I can get into a gay chat room!"

The Crew remained on the couch..

A rusted late seventies Dodge van with second-floor camper shell atop it parked out front.

"Sonny," said Driveway Dave, nodding at the van.

"Yeah," I said, unwrapping a barbecue pork burrito. "Before I paddled out, Sonny was going off about the power of the Tao."

"The Dow?" asked The Legend, putting a key in his right ear.

"The Tao, one of those go-with-the-flow religions," I said. "Where you become water that flows over rocks—"

"Oh Tao, go with the flow?" said The Legend, turning the key to scrape wax out his ear's opening. "Sounds like a laxative

"You look like you're trying to start your head," said Squirrel.

"I wish my head worked that way," replied The Legend, who stuck the key deeper. "It would make my life a lot easier."

"You have hair in your ears, too."

"Thanks for being so kind to point that out, I appreciate that... needledick."

We laughed.

Ralph sat on the couch with an amused expression on his face. I could tell he wanted to belong.

"Fucking stupid cocksucking motherfuckers," spewed Sonny, stomping into the shop with his red surfboard, which had a three-inch wide strip of fiberglas dangling eight inches from underneath the board's nose. Sonny's face was a deep purple. His pupils slid back and forth. The veins in his neck bulged and looked like they were the only things that supported his head, which was going up and down. He was seething. The guy was seriously spun.

"So life is just one big smile of God for you today isn't it?" observed Chops, who always enjoyed digging into Sonny.

Sonny flashed a look at Chops and continued, "I'm waiting outside for a wave for twenty minutes, and one is coming, I go for it. And this snake who has just paddled out, spins around, and goes for it to my right. He stands and falls, let's his board go. The guy wasn't even wearing a leash and he could barely surf."

"Yeah, I've seen that," said The Legend. "They see the guys who can surf don't have leashes so they don't wear them because it makes them look cool."

"Hey, I have the floor, here" said Sonny, who paused and resumed his story. "So, he doesn't apologize and gets back on his board and tries to paddle away like nothing happened. I said, 'Look what you did to my board. You just paddle out, and take a wave that I waited twenty minutes for?' And he goes, "I was the first one up. First one up gets the wave. That's what the rules say on the sign by the stairs.' So, now, it's supposed to be my fault!"

Ranger heard Sonny's raised voice. Any time voices were raised near me, Ranger came between me and the voice's source. She sensed everything was fine, but laid near my feet just in case.

"Yeah, but the Tao, the river, the rocks?" I asked, smiling. "You know, the water, the flow—"

"Fuck the stream, fuck the rocks, and fuck him," rapidly said Sonny, his body fully involved with rage. "These people are the Valleys we threw rocks at on the beach in the sixties." He paused. "We're the locals. We're the ones who chose to live here. We're the surfers with soul. We possess a fire deep inside us."

"Yeah, they're called hemorrhoids," said Chops.

"That's not funny," said Sonny, who was still worked up. "There's nothing to these people. They're bad novels. And they have only been surfing for what? Tops two years? And they're walking around acting like they know what it's about. You have to surf thirty years before you know what it's about." He paused and significantly added, "I knew a guy who went to college and said it took him seven years to understand what clay is."

"Clay? Couldn't have been much of a college," said Chops, who we called Chops because he was from New Jersey and busted everyone's chops, even his own.

The Crew laughed. Sonny didn't. He stared off.

"I don't find you funny," said Sonny. "And I never will."

"Looks like he got your fin box too," The Legend said.

Sonny turned the wet board over, and gently laid it on the rug by the table. He pushed the fin with his fingertips. Instead of being firm, the fin rocked back and forth.

"Brutha, that board is duh-stroyed," said Skin Dog.

"Yeah it is," said The General.

"I am chafed," Sonny said, shaking his head and looking at the damaged fin. "The dot-comers are the ones who should be on the beach watching us. Instead these trannie Instant Locals are in the water and we're on land. They're surfing the prime times and the best point breaks, and we've been driven out and have to settle with trying to snag a few rides on the inside, or find a window when we can paddle out when the tide is too high or too low just so we can snag a couple rides without a crowd. But it's all backasswards. They're beginners. They should be the ones doing that. Not us." He paused. Sonny flopped down on the couch, folded his arms across his chest, and said in a ripe sulk, "They remind me of when I fell out of love with life."

"Oh, did someone call for a waaaaaaaaah-ambulance?" asked Chops in mock pity.

"You're not funny," snapped Sonny. "And I didn't like your smile-of-God crack, either." He paused. "Do you think those jerks in the water would let us hang out in their neighborhoods and play touch football in the street? They'd call a cop. Are those dot-com people sharing their stock tips? No, because they put their cubicle time in. So, I put in water time, I'm not sharing my point breaks. I worked hard to get my hook into Santa Cruz."

"Oh, yeah, how many crops did you have to plant in the mountains that year?" asked Chops, drawing a laugh.

"Again, not funny," said Sonny. "But effective."

Ralph smiled and said to Sonny, "You want a hot dog and fries? I got some extras."

"Only if you're not going to eat them," Sonny said firmly. "It doesn't mean I owe you anything. You offered them to me. I didn't ask for them." He reached into the bag. "Because I—"

The Crew finished Sonny's sentence,"...don't have friends!"

"And you don't have a surfboard either," added Chops.

"You're full of not funny, today," said Sonny.

"Consider it a gift," said Ralph, giving the hot dog to him.

"It's only a gift if I accept it," Sonny said brusquely.

"Right."

"Fuck it then," said Sonny, pushing the food away. "I refuse."

Ranger stood up, her leg gave out. She yelped. I went over to her, bent down, and pet her. The Crew looked on, concerned.

"Bad hips, that's how shepherd's go," someone behind me said callously. "One leg fades, they favor the other leg too much, then it goes out. They start losing their bowel functions and the best thing is to put them down earlier—if you really love them."

It was Drake Sather. The Surf Dot Com Über Geek. He was dressed in khaki pants, a woven belt, tasseled loafers, and a v-neck sweater with a Pasatiempo Golf Club logo on it, and under the shirt, I spotted the bulge of his money belt.

There are two things no one criticizes me about, my surfing and my dog. So far, Drake was one out of two. Ranger stayed between us. She sensed I didn't like this guy.

'Liar, Liar' by The Castaways played.

Drake walked around the shop and said with complete disgust, "How can you stand this?"

"The shop?" I asked, puzzled.

"No," said Drake glaring at the merchandise. "Inventory."

"Oh well, what can I tell you?"

"I came here to establish some face time," said Drake, who handed out his business cards to The Crew. "When you tilt the card it's got a holograph wave on it that moves. And I have T-shirts, polo shirts, and caps too. SDC is a real company. And I'm the CEO, a player, a mover, a shaker, a—" A belt-holstered cell phone beeped the tune 'Play That Funky Music White Boy.' He flipped open the phone. "I'm interrupt driven."

"No cell phones in the shop," I said. "Take it outside."

Drake ignored me, and answered, "Drake here—" Feedback came out of the scanner. "What the fuck is that?"

"Feedback," I replied. "The scanner picks up cellular calls."

"Yeah, yeah, yeah," Drake said, who reached over, turned down the scanner's volume knob, and continued talking on the cell phone. "I landed that Sand Hill Road cache. I waited outside in a hallway for an hour in this four-star Froggie-Pepe-Le-Phew-Francois-chic restaurant, I throw down my red herring and make my pitch in front of a bunch of VC who are eating salmon with a dill sauce and asking me about 'e-mail reads'. But, I make things happen. I'm the rainmaker. I'm the rainmaker. The rainmaker! I reel in the whales. I kill everything I eat. I'm the wood behind the arrow. I've been crawling through broken glass prospecting needs and accelerating and pioneering this deal. So don't fuck this deal up. If Surf Dot Com goes down, I go down too."

The lie-detector activator attached to Drake's phone eeeeee-d.

"Hey, Funky White Boy," Chops said sarcastically, "do you have a call-waiting buzzer on your phone?"

"It's just a short," Drake said.

The lie detector eeee-ed again.

"Still buzzing," Chops said.

"That's not the phone," said Drake, who composed himself and continued his business call. "It's on my radar. I'll go through the 'Bros of Drake' at Adapient, and Sapient, and Expient."

"Excrement?" asked The Legend.

"No Expient, you moron," snapped Drake, clicking off the call. He briefly closed his eyes and said to himself. "Why?"

"Expient? That's a word?" said The Legend, looking to The Crew for support.

"No, it's a company, brutha. If it was a word, it would mean something," said Skin Dog, who snapped a nacho chip but spit it out into the palm of his hand. "Hey, these are stale."

"I have a question," said Ralph who wiped mustard off his lips. He looked at Drake and asked, "Kodak sold cameras. Ford sold cars. And you're Surf Dot Com. What do you make?"

"Reboot," said Drake, who paused, as if he were downloading the answer. He drew a deep breath and rapidly rattled off, "Surf Dot Com provides the platform to connect the data processing operations of companies within an interactive application which works with an existing web site to match skill sets of consumers to their content needs and interfaces a better profile recruiting tool to generate e-market profitability in real time."

There was a silence.

"Well, thanks for clearing that up," said Chops.

The Crew laughed, except Sonny, of course.

"You don't *get* it," Drake said with a slight trace of impatience. He scanned everyone's shirt, as if he was searching for a name badge on an employee. "Our— "

"Hey, if you're going to lie, be brief," Sonny cautioned, drawing a laugh. He looked at Chops and authoratively said, "See, now that's funny."

Drake merely continued, "Our paradigm shift is redefining the medium with a new global-enabling tool. The Web is evolving and elevating man's whole way of thinking on a higher plane..."

"Yo, yo, yo! I got two women doing each other on line," shouted Squirrel. "The vibrator is huge! I think they're dykes."

The General and Chops quickly got up and scurried over to look. It wasn't as easy for Skin Dog. He had to rock his two-hundred-and-fifty pound bulk back and forth to gain enough momentum to rise from the sunken couch. When he stood, a few stray beans that fell from his burrito into the folds of his shirt dropped on the rug. Skin Dog wobbled, regained his balance, and joined the group around Squirrel.

"What do you want?" I asked Drake.

"Your look and feel," said Drake, holding a document.

"Brutha, we got heavy 'look and feel' going on over here," said Skin Dog, engrossed in the porno. "How do they do that?"

"You have sour cream in your beard," said Squirrel, laughing as he pointed at Skin Dog, who wiped it off.

"Look and *feel*?" I asked Drake, confused. "What's that mean?"

"The long-hair-sixties thing you have going. The muscled body. The Vietnam division tattoo. Look at you. The beat-up truck, a dog, and a can of Pepsi. You're image ready. Jesus, slap a bar code on your ass and you're a living product placement. Now, *that's* look and feel. Your look and feel is Surf Dot Com—"

"It's just not happenin'."

"Reboot," Drake said, reassembling his composure, and placed a document atop the magazines on the table. "Take a look at that contract and sign it. Broaden your bandwidth. Leverage the moment. Who else would pay you just to be you?" He paused and significantly added, "It's all about thinking out of the box. I'm a success because I don't live in the past or the future. There is only the now."

"Yeah, it's called Alzheimer's," said Chops.

The Crew laughed.

"This look and feel is a once-in-a-lifetime deal," continued Drake in an urgent tone. "You gotta be there. It's all about speed and insight partnering to co-venture."

"Is that a fist?" asked Skin Dog, staring at the screen.

"She's elbow deep!" gasped Squirrel.

Whatever happened next on-line clearly made The Crew queasy. They drifted from the computer back to the couch.

"You're Surf Dot Com's branding. When we portal out with Yahoo, we will need a surf identity create a heavy mind share and monetize eyeballs to our site. Branding is first-mover advantage. It's all about brand-name recognition."

Chops looked over and said, "Brand names? You mean brand names like the Edsel, Titanic, swastika, Michael Dukakis?"

"Reboot," said Drake. He paused. "Liaison your needs. If you don't you're cutting your nose off to spite your face."

"In your case that would be an improvement," said Chops.

The Crew laughed.

"Why are you so sarcastic?" snapped Drake, glaring at Chops.

"I didn't mean anything by it," replied Chops, who smiled, then added, "Except just then."

"I'm trying to be a nice guy," said Drake like a threat.

"Really, what are you using for a point of reference?" said Chops, who drew high fives from The Crew. He laughed and commented on himself, "Hey, I'm on a roll."

"Maybe you ought to butter it," said Sonny.

"Good one," said Chops, smiling appreciatively.

"Reboot!" Drake barked. He pointed at The Crew and scolded me. "Come on, Vinnie, it's a digital world. Going digital is— "

"It's Vic. Not Vincent."

"So?" Drake said dismissively, "Take a look and feel around. Is this a shop or a rehab center? Do you think these low-life, developmentally-disabled couch guys will to keep you in business?"

There was a silence.

"Hey, we got him this far," said The Legend.

"You're right, it's a digital world. In fact, I'm going to go digital right now," Chops said, extending his middle finger. "This is my digit going digital." The Crew laughed. "Hold on," continued Chops, sticking up his other middle finger. "Looks like I'm getting my 2.0 upgrade."

Drake dealt with criticism the same way all dot-comers reacted to any comment that required a clarification: he ignored it and kept talking, "Vinnie, how much would you charge me to teach my team how to surf?"

"Teach what to surf?"

"I'll pay you," quickly said Drake, smiling. "You'll need boards I'll buy boards. You'll need wetsuits, I'll buy wetsuits. You give me your look and feel, and I'll set you up. Think of all the other people you could give surf classes to? People want you to respect them. I have a sense about people, and you're the kind of guy people *want* to have like them, because knowing you makes them feel they're cool. I could care less—and do. Still, that's what you have. Why waste it on your own life and just be a failure?" He paused. "Don't be a small player on a minority platform."

We stared at him, expecting a translation. But then the focus in the room shifted to another intrusion.

"Excuse me! Waiting," said a perturbed male at the counter.

The name-brand wannabe wore a designer Hawaiian shirt tucked into sharply creased khaki slacks. He had polished leather sandals, and round gold-rimmed glasses with thick lenses that barely covered his pupils. His gray ponytail was curled up in a conch-shell shape, and resembled a parasite feeding on his neck. A wetsuit was draped over the thin guy's cocked right arm.

"I was here yesterday but you weren't open," he said in an aggressive tone, as if he were my boss. He snapped the wetsuit in my direction. "I was here waiting for you at ten in the morning."

"I was surfing."

"Your hours say ten to five."

"Can I help you?"

"I purchased this wetsuit from your shop and it's defective."

I walked over to him, examined the inside of wetsuit and said, "Did the tape or stitches come apart?"

"Nothing ripped out, I was out in the ocean, and I got cold."

The Crew leaned forward. They couldn't believe what they were hearing. I couldn't either, actually. This was a first.

"You got cold?"

"Yes, you said the wetsuit would keep me warm. I was out in the ocean for three hours and I got cold."

"You were out in an ocean that has a temperature in the 50's for three hours in a wetsuit on a foggy day with maybe some wind coming off the water and then got cold. You're supposed to get cold. A wetsuit doesn't prevent that. When you go skiing and get cold do you take your jacket back? What are you telling me?"

"I'm saying you lied to me."

I slowly spun my Dad's ring around my finger and said in a low voice, "Are you calling me a liar in my shop, *hombre*?"

The guy stiffened, but said nothing.

"Fire" by The Crazy World of Arthur Brown came on.

Ranger stirred, sensing my anger.

I flashed on my stinkeye. I was used to losing. I had been losing my whole life. But I always had my waves and my life in Santa Cruz. And now, I didn't even have that because of idiots like this. Even if I minded my own business, they launched at me. I mean this guy went out of his way to come into my shop to give me shit. I had my fill of these dot-comers debating me about their bad manners in the water, ruining my peaceful meals by holding loud cell phone conversations in restaurants, and stressing me out on a casual drive by tailgating me in their SUVs. This guy wasn't the first rude person launching at me. He wasn't the fiftieth. He was the fifty-first one in the last few days. And he was in my face, going rail-to-rail, and calling me a liar in the shop I created—and, that was just one rude too many for me to take. It just wasn't happenin'. I lunged toward him. Ranger barked and followed me. The guy dropped his wetsuit. I grabbed the back of his shirt, and pushed him toward the open front door.

"Do you know who I am?" he indignantly blurted, looking over his shoulder at me as I shoved him from behind.

"Yeah, you're the guy who is on his way out of here," I said and heaved him out on his ass. Ranger stood protectively by me at the shop entrance. She barked several times. He started to get up. I pointed at him and issued a warning, "If you get up and make one a move back into this shop. I will kick you in the chest, knock you to the ground, and then my dog will go for your balls. If you hit her, she will grab your hand and work her way up to your throat." I paused. "And once she does that, she goes crazy and I'm not responsible for her actions."

The guy slowly stood, brushed himself off, and said in a slighted tone, "Do you know what you're missing?"

"No, dog breath, what am I missing?"

"This is what you're missing," he said, holding up a one-hundred-dollar bill between his two hands and snapping it. "If you treated me properly, I would have purchased a board. Now, I'll go somewhere else. I'll tell other people about you. You'll lose their business too. I will cost you more than you cost me. I'll—"

His next words were muffled by his wetsuit., which I threw at him. It draped over his head like a dead four-legged octopus.

"Keep your money, you need it more than I do," I said.

I pivoted and went back into the shop.

"Oh, good God, just give me your ask!" implored Drake, blocking me. "Just give me your ask! Talk about conflict resolution. Nobody heaves rude customers out of their shops. They're afraid of getting sued. You've got pop! Just give me your ask. I must have your look and feel. You *are* Surf Dot Com."

"No one calls me a liar in this shop," I said.

"Give me your ask. I'll, I'll..." excitedly babbled Drake, struggling to recall a phrase. "Damn, I lost my buffer."

"You suffer?" asked The Legend, puzzled.

"No, buffer," said Skin Dog.

"Buffer. What's that mean?" asked The Legend.

"It means he's an idiot," grunted Chops.

"Word," said Squirrel, who kept staring at his monitor.

"I'm losing money standing here wasting time over this nickel and dime bullshit," said Drake, shaking his head like he pitied us. "Would a hundred and twenty five thousand cover you, bro?"

Bro.

"It's just not happenin'," I said decisively, but I noticed Drake's offer wiped the smirks off The Crew. They were thrown by it.

Ranger growled at the Über Geek .

"I can see we will have to revisit this," Drake said, nervously glancing at Ranger. He retreated and protectively moved his hand over the money belt beneath his shirt. He left punching numbers into his cell phone. "Your surf shop phone number is on my speed dial."

Nobody said anything. The Crew pretended to watch the surf video. Squirrel rapidly clicked the keyboard of his laptop.

"He offered $125,000," said The Legend. "Even *I* heard that."

"We can make a lot of money," Sonny said.

Drake drove away in his Surf Dot Com Hummer. The police scanner's flashing light stopped on a number and Drake's voice squawked out of it: "This is all about our second offering. The 'Bros of Drake' file is locked and loaded. You get 20 to 30 percent of the carry and 2 to 2.5 from guys investing with you. What do you have to lose by handling SDC's second offering compared to that? I'm working on a twisted Vietnam vet for branding..."

"Twisted? Did he call me twisted?" I said. "Turn it off. It's even worse hearing him when he's not here."

"No, no, leave it on, leave it on," loudly insisted Driveway Dave, who jumped up from the couch.

"You understand that shit?" I asked.

"Quiet! Let me hear what they're saying," Dave uncharacteristically snapped, leaning over the scanner and listening intensely.

"... the Bros of Drake on the board are giving me a loan so I don't have to sell my stock yet. This is truly a stand-alone deal and not a firm-wide focus. You get compensation of stock for your investment, the money from the IPO, and a retainer fee plus equity for pushing the stock in our second offering. First Credit San Jose Suisse is the linchpin to our exit strategy—"

Then Drake's cut out into static.

'Time' by the Chambers Brothers played.

"Exit strategy?" I said. "What's an exit strategy?"

"It's a business term," Ralph said, who was eager to contribute to the conversation. "But basically it's when you're thinking of an excuse for not spending the night at someone's house while you're fucking them."

Dave put on his half-framed reading glasses, grabbed Drake's contract from the table, thumbed through it, and said, "Let me peruse this agreement."

"Drake made a interesting offer," said Sonny.

"The guy's a puke," I grunted.

"There's definitely something rather disingenuous about him," Sonny added, stroking his square chin.

"Disingenuous?" Skin Dog asked. "Can you translate that from UCSC to English, brutha?"

"Yeah, it means—"

"He's a bag of snakes," said Ralph, dabbing several French fries in the ketchup puddle on a hot dog wrapper. "And I can tell you, from first-hand dealings with that guy. I work as a loan officer at First Savings, man. I handle mortgages and stuff. He's such a self-centered idiot he doesn't remember me. Years ago, I worked as a stockbroker on Wall Street, I played in their arena and I was good at it. And they can have it. Hey, no matter what these wannabe CEO Type-A's say, if some tech geek who lives at home with his parents, can design a computer program in the garage that can put your high-tech company out of business, then you don't have a company. My back-of-the envelope analysis says this surf shop is a more secure investment than Surf Dot Com."

"But all I have is a surf shop, a dog, and a VW truck."

"Yes, but they're vested," said Ralph..

"Vested?" I asked.

"You're still a real business. You make products. Your shop is dependent on making quarters, meeting revenue targets, and hitting profitability. Dot coms aren't close. This Drake guy is leveraged up the ass. He came into the bank looking for a house loan. I went through Surf Dot Com's S-1 initial registration document—it's a stock financial report thing. I couldn't believe it. Surf Dot Com had $21.7 million of sales but a revenue of $9.4 million, and came out with cumulative loss of $147 million since the second quarter of 1998. It's all there for anybody to see. They're weren't hiding it. And First Credit San Jose Suisse backs their stock. And because Surf Dot Com is projecting a profit with all its mergers and acquisitions. Their stock is up to over $145 a share. So what? SDC's P-to-E ratio is still abysmal."

"P-to-E? That's real?" I asked. "What is P-to-E?"

"We used to cut PE in high school to smoke dope," said The Legend. "I hated gym class. The guy made us square dance."

"No, not PE." said Ralph, chuckling. "PE isn't Physical Education. This P-to-E stands for Price-to-Earnings ratio."

I rubbed my forehead, winced in frustration and said, "Now *you* sound like you're making stuff up."

"No, no, no, you guys have to know this stuff" said Ralph who seemed eager to use his knowledge to be a part of The Crew. "I've been tracking this clown, he's projecting all these high numbers and profits down the line. But I went through Surf Dot Com's original numbers. Even if I assumed a net profit margin of twenty percent—and again that's more than Surf Dot Com has ever made because every number they show is negative—it would still take the company over ten years for them to hit those numbers and end up in the black. Even if I assumed Surf Dot Com would grow into the market valuations through other companies, their profitability is still contingent on the ability to sell off their stakes in the markets. I don't get it. But Surf Dot Com is one of many start-ups that sell for 200 times their earnings. To give you a comparison: GM sells at seven times earnings. And GM has a product, plants. But these start-ups are losing money and their stock is worth more than GM? It doesn't make sense. But every time I deal with these dot-com guys they just call me a dinosaur. They say it's a new thing. Hey, trees don't grow in the sky and you can't divide by zero. But somehow their world has escaped math and gravity."

"Ralph is simply saying Surf Dot Com's stock is overvalued," said Driveway Dave.

"Then how do these start-ups get their money?" asked Sonny, clearly trying to grasp the topic.

"Okay, I'll give you an example," said Ralph. "Let's say Vic didn't have a shop, but Vic wanted to start-up a surf shop and you went to a VC—"

"VC? There's only one kind of VC I know," I said. "I mean I don't ever see me crawling down a tunnel to ask for a business loan from some slope-headed gook who just tried to kill me."

"Okay," said Dave. "Think of VC as VIC without the I..."

"Shit, I can't even smell cooked rice in a Chinese joint, I get flashbacks. I even start hearing Vietnamese voices. I—"

"Are you sure those voices didn't belong to the kitchen help?" said Chops.

"No, when I smell cooked white rice I go back. Back. I—"

"Burr, enough with the war, already," interrupted Sonny. "Save the post traumatic stress for your counselor. Let the guy talk. I want to hear this."

"A VC is a venture capitalist," continued Ralph.

"So he's a suit?" The General distrustfully said.

"Yes, but an expensive suit," answered Ralph. "Vic, let's use your shop as an example. You want to start up a surf shop with an old-sixties atmosphere that only sells surfboards shaped by you. And the VC gives you the money for your start-up because the VC believes he can get a higher return on his investment."

"But how can I give him a return on money I don't have?"

"The VC takes it in equity. You're putting up all your money, everything you own, and giving him shares of stock in your surf shop in exchange for cash," said Ralph.

"I give the VC stock in a company I don't own for his money," I slowly said, baffled.

"It's *not* his money—it's other people's money," said Dave, still perusing the contract. "Investors."

"Then you go IPO."

"Again with initials," I said, exasperated. "What is an IPO?"

"Initial Public Offering," said Ralph.

"Huh," I said, then thought for five seconds. "So what is an IPO?"

"Okay, let's stick with my example of Vic's Surf Shop being a start-up. Right now the only business partners who own stock are Vic and the VC," Ralph calmly explained, resting his arms in his lap. "You want to go public, which means you offer shares of your surf shop for sale. That's where the IPO comes in. But to do that, you need a bank that will guarantee a minimum value of what the stock is worth and give you an approval rating."

"So the banking guys put up the money?"

"Yes, but again, it's still other people's money. The investors."

"Okay, then where does the IPO come in?" asked Sonny.

"Let's say for simplicity's sake, Vic's shop has a total of ten thousand shares. But Vic and the VC put only two thousand shares out for sale. That's a thousand shares each. They only release a small portion of stock at a low price—"

"So then the public buys it," concluded Sonny.

Ralph and Dave laughed.

"Hey, what's the joke?" asked Sonny, irritated he delivered a punchline because he missed a subtle point.

"I guess Sonny doesn't think you two guys are funny either," said Chops, laughing at his own observation. "That's funny."

"The public *never* gets first shot to buy the stock!" Ralph said. "So you offer the stock at ten dollars a share, the brokers spin it."

*Bro*kers

"Spin?" I asked.

"Brokers have already given out the stock to their special clients at ten dollars in exchange for other deals. But because you only sold a small portion of stock, the demand is higher than the supply, and the stock shoots up to two hundred dollars a share. The clients who get in early flip their stock—"

"Flip?" asked The General.

"Flip means they sell it," said Dave.

"Yeah, after only hanging onto it for maybe a total of forty seconds," Ralph said. "Based on those figures, investors make $190 in profit on a $10 investment on each share." He paused. "The end result: Vic and the VC become millionaires."

"How can I be a millionaire if I sold my stock for ten dollars? Those other guys made all the money, not me."

"But you didn't sell all your shares. You and the VC still have eighty thousand shares valued at two hundred dollars apiece. You're worth one million six hundred thousand—on paper."

"I don't have the money, but I'm rich?"

"Yes, on paper. But there are regulations in place that say you can't dump your stock," said Ralph. "It's business ethics."

"Business ethics?" said Sonny. "Now there's an oxymoron."

"Axe the moron?" said The Legend.

"It doesn't matter if you can't sell right away, usually it's six months," continued Ralph. "You can power real money based on the value of your stock on margin as collateral."

"Boring," said Squirrel, imitating Homer Simpson.

"So what's this second offering deal?" asked Sonny.

"A second offering is the same thing as an IPO in a way, except now with the stock price higher for Vic's Surf Shop, the stock is worth more," said Ralph. "Vic and the VC can't sell their stock, but as long as they can keep the venture capital coming in to support the business and hire people, they hire more staff but pay them less by offering them stock-options instead of cash. And because investors have read about how other investors got rich on your IPO, they're really hungry for the second stock offering. Your stockholders won't unload their stock because they assume you'll put the money into the business and diversify—"

"Wait," Sonny said skeptically, "you're telling me, investors actually believe a guy who doesn't put a dime of his own money into a company is going look out for someone *else's* money?"

"Yeah," said Driveway Dave, who added. "These dot-com burn artists and snakes created the ultimate bro deal,"

The Crew was quiet, trying to take it all in.

"That Drake guy wore a money belt," Sonny, said. "Old habit from my drug days, I can spot a money belt or a gun on anyone."

"Drake has a salary," said Ralph. "He expenses flights, meals, he gets company loans. And he just bonuses himself out with investors' cash for whatever he wants to buy for himself."

"He's getting paid to steal on the company's time," said Skin Dog, who slapped his hands on his knees and laughed.

"I have a motto," said The General. "Never steal anything from the company if you bring it home and it reminds you of work." He paused. "I mean, what would I steal? A shovel?"

"Shovels? What are you?" said Sonny. "Jesus, we're not talking about shovels. We're talking about Drake's money."

"It's not Drake's money," said Ralph. "Investors are giving him cash, little old ladies, day traders, money-market managers, city fiscal officers, whatever. These people know better. But it's like watching a roulette wheel and the number ten keeps on coming up over and over again. The people betting on ten win, and leave their bet on it, and win even more! So you put you money down on ten too. And when you win, you leave it there."

Sonny turned his attention back to Ralph and asked, "So there's no way to lose at this game?"

"Well, there is *one* way to lose," said Ralph. "You have to keep your stock market price high. If you don't, then that's where you get hit by AMT."

"ATM, the cash machine?" asked The Legend.

"Not ATM. A*M*T. Alternative Minimum Tax," said Ralph. "Let's say, you take a salary at a dot-com and as an added incentive to remain at the company for a few years, you're given a stock option of 5,000 shares. A stock option is the chance to purchase the stock at let's say...a strike price of 50 cents a share."

"Strike price?"

"That's the price you have the option to purchase the stock at," said Ralph, who clearly enjoyed educating us. "You see, even if the stock is going for a hundred dollars a share. Your agreement says in six months or whatever set time, you can buy those 5,000 shares at 50 cents from the company. You decide to exercise your stock option when the offering price for the stock hits $300 a share, and you make a profit of $299.50 a share."

"But, where does the stock come from?" asked Sonny.

"What's funny is there is no stock," said Ralph. "All these dot-com companies do is just print up more paper. Those new shares dilute the holdings of the other stockholders. The stockholders go for it based on the theory that an employee with company equity will produce more, which will increase the company's value."

"Smart people actually believe this?" Sonny asked.

"No smart people who with money riding on number ten do."

"Brutha, let me follow what you are saying," said Skin Dog. "If I had 5,000 shares of stock which I optioned at a strike price of 50 cents, and sold each share for $300, I'd make a profit of, um, a thousand times three hundred is three hundred thousand. Five times three hundred thousand is—"

"One point five million dollars," rapidly said Driveway Dave. "Minus what the IRS takes out as capital gains."

"But you have to minus a lot of those fifty cents," pointlessly cited The Legend.

"Why wouldn't the employees just sell?' said Sonny. "Shit, I'd cash out right away. End of game Elvis has left the building."

"Sure, you would, and so would I. We know these things don't last," rapidly said Ralph. "But not the dot-comers. They don't have that floor in their building. We've been around the block a few times. But the dot-comers have never had to. They've only been around the block in a chauffeur-driven limousine. Nothing bad has happen to them—ever. All they know is boom. When we hear a boom, it means someone is firing at us with a weapon. We duck. They're not afraid of explosions. When the dot-comers hear a boom, they think they're the boom everyone fears. After all, they're rich and they have complete faith the stock can only go up higher. Sure, they can sell, but if they sell, they only think of all the money they will be losing. These techies have no frame of reference because they never needed one. Imagine if you were a teenager and could have whatever you wanted, would you ever mature and listen to anybody if everything is coming your way?"

"I hope not," said Skin Dog.

"So what's the incentive for these people to think any other way?" said Ralph, concluding. "It's not in them. It's not there."

"I don't see what the big deal is," said Sonny, shrugging. "The stock tanks. So it goes from three hundred dollars a share down to fifty cents a share. So they break even. No blood."

"But, that's where the AMT rears its ugly head," said Ralph. "When you exercised your stock option, the dot-com stock was valued at $300 a share, that's considered income by the IRS. It doesn't matter if your stock is underwater. You still owe taxes on $1.5 million."

"Minus all the fifty-cent guys," added The Legend.

"Huh," I said.

"I have our exit strategy," proclaimed Sonny, standing up.

"*Our* exit strategy?" I asked.

'Mr. Businessman' by Ray Stevens played.

"Why should dot-comers make all the money?" said Sonny. "We have a real first-mover advantage. We're locals. We have the experience. We have the surfboards."

"Therefore, we have the technology," said Chops.

"Right," said Sonny. "The dot-comers have nothing on us but the software. We can take these guys."

"I'd have to get paid to hang be with those people," I said.

"That's precisely the point, Burr. They *are* willing to pay you," said Sonny, raising his arms up. "These are people who don't want to make a life, they want it given to them. I read about them in magazines all the time. They pay people to take them to Mount Everest, or to fly a MiG-25, or drive stock cars, or go to some Rocky Mountain trout school. Now, they want to be surfers. I can organize the curriculum and teach the class. You know, surfing as a 'fear resolution clinic,' a 'team-building' exercise. We can package it as part of some motivational development to be a better person. Assholes love to think they're becoming a better person when they're paying to get what they want."

"Sonny is dead-on right, Burr," said Chops, stoked.

"You left out the other half of the formula," said a voice at the front door. We turned. It was Shiloh. Ranger went to her.

"What's the other half of the formula?" asked Sonny.

"Women. You have to have women's classes to draw in all those Roxie Trannie You-Go Girls," said Shiloh, who gave Ranger a new bone. She walked over to the couch, and sat down. "These women all paddle out with this hot-shit cool attitude. They just want to take over. Hey, when I started surfing I knew I wasn't cool. I was embarrassed. I knew I had to start on a longboard, and they weren't making longboards then, just shortboards. The General had one in his back yard. Its nose was sawed off and it was a real beater board. I mean there were snails on it. It was gross. But I knew I wasn't cool. I mean I went to Cowells and surfed the inside. It was like people were saying,

'What are you doing?' You know, cause only old people and kids surfed there. I mean, it was embarrassing surfing with old people. And there were only a few girls who surfed then, guy-girls who were super strong athletes. I didn't think I was hot-shit cool. I knew I was starting off from scratch because we watched from the beach as the guys got better and saw how they progressed. We had something to compare it to. But, when these You-Go Girls paddle out there, they're thinking they're in the groove and they're not. Do you think that kind of women is ever going to listen to men? They think a support group for a man is a jail. These women hate guys more than lesbians do."

"I like lesbians," said Chops. "First off, they have such a great sense of humor." The Crew laughed. "Really. I'm not threatened by them—except physically," continued Chops. We laughed. "Actually, I'd like to be a lesbian. There's nothing they do to a woman that I can't do. And, there's no performance pressure at all. It would be like collecting unemployment."

"Who cares if they're UCSC snail lesbians or You-Go Girls?" said Shiloh. "These trannie women shop! The Roxie stuff is huge. It's all right to wear one kind of Roxie thing, but they're Roxied-out in those Hawaiian prints and bright-island colored bikinis, sandals, blouses, and cargo pants. The women are like uncool guys, but don't want to admit it. They need to elevate themselves above others. Soccer Moms hate being Soccer Moms. They'll take a surf class so they can say, 'I'm not a Soccer Mom—I *surf*.' They want to convince everyone they're cool. Just put a price tag on surfing. And they'll pay to be cool as long as they can buy their way in. I'll be able to sell them anything."

"Shiloh's right," said Sonny. "Women-discovering-themselves-as-women in classes taught by women is key. It's a cult at UCSC. They're not breaking ground in surfing. They're breaking ground for a mall. We can sell that. Santa Cruz women live for stuff like discovering another aspect of themselves."

"Or be like you, be married and coming home early and discovering your wife discovering herself as a woman with another woman," said Chops, drawing a laugh.

"We surf with the dot-comers, anyway," said The Legend, "We might as well get paid."

Sonny picked up the tempo of his appeal, "The You-Go Girls and the dot-comers all share the same thing, they're taking a piece of our Santa Cruz, so let's get a piece of them."

"Build a surf mall and they will come," said Chops.

"He's right," chimed in The Legend. "We might as well."

"In the water, I have to deal with them because they launch at me," I said firmly. "In my shop I have a choice. I make my own boards. This shop is all me. This shop taught me if I'm straight up with people, I'll always have a place to spend the night."

"Yeah, they're called tents," Sonny somberly observed. "Vic, your shop should be doing killer. I mean people are buying boards, and you're only shaping three or four a month. There are hardly any boards here. This shop is dying."

"In three weeks I can redesign this shop, order some Roxie apparel and girl surfboards and we'll all cash in," said Shiloh.

"I'll design a web page," said Squirrel. "If I get a new laptop."

"I could help you deal with the vendors and the orders," said Chops. "I know you don't like doing that stuff on the phone."

"Yeah, brutha, Chops is right" said Skin Dog. "I saw you break your reading glasses once doing inventory on T-shirts."

"I can draw up the business plan," said Driveway Dave.

"And I'll help you on the financial end," said Ralph.

"I'm not in on this deal," said The General, shaking his head. "You guys are going the wrong way. I eat off the low end of the food chain—fruits, vegetables. Even when I catch a halibut—and I pull in some beauties—I'm thinking, 'Do I need to eat him tonight?' I just take what I can eat. But some people always have to take their limit—or go over it. Have you ever noticed that it's something like a small percentage of people who are rich in this world? And it's the exact same percent of the people in the world who screw it up for the rest of us?" He paused. "I hear these dot-comers talk about the latest technology, well the latest technology gets replaced every six months, then it's junk. I have Singer sewing machine that's forty years old, and I can still use it. These people think everything disposable. They accept it"

"Well, right now, we're disposable," Sonny said then added harshly. "General, you're sixty, never married, live in a your mom's old house. My rent is going up five-hundred bucks."

"I can't afford a place in Santa Cruz—ever," said The Legend. "And I grew up here, well as close as I could get, anyway."

"The company that bought our trailer park is suing the county so they don't have to obey the rent-control laws , brutha," said Skin Dog. "They knew rent control was there when they bought us. They're just going to use their big bucks to change it. They'll win, money always wins. And I'll lose all equity in my place."

"I'm living in a driveway," said Dave. "It's not even paved."

"All I'm saying is when you make a lot of money, you also have real expensive problems," said The General.

"Thorsten Verblan has spoken on the leisure class," Sonny said sarcastically. "All decisions are final, huh?"

"Thurston?" asked The Legend. "Thurston Howell. Wasn't he that rich guy in the 'Gilligan's Island' show?" .

"Yeah, you know he did Mister MaGoo," said Skin Dog. "I hated Mister MaGoo. A blind cartoon character. Stupid."

"Jim Backus, yeah," said Chops. "He also played the wimp dad in 'Rebel Without a Cause.'"

"Would you guys, shuttup!" snapped Sonny. "We're talking big money and you're babbling about blind cartoon characters."

"All I'm saying," said The General, "is money takes care of money, and people take care of each other.. But these people don't care what they're doing to Santa Cruz. They came here for the money. They expect services. They're bringing the world they left. Their condos, houses, restaurants, factory outlets, malls, Home Depots, Cinema-plexes, and the traffic that along with it. They don't care what makes Santa Cruz special. Over The Hill wants Silicon Valley with an ocean view. They don't want Santa Cruz, they don't want us, they want what they want."

"I'm with The General," I said. "It's just not happen—"

"Vic, I hear we're going to be together on the same SDC team," piped out a woman from the front of the shop.

It was the Surf Dot Com execudiva from Bings.

Ranger immediately got up and ate all the food in her dish, which was odd, because she only ate all her food if there was another dog in the shop who Ranger didn't want to get her food. Shiloh folded her arms across her chest and glared. The Crew looked her over. Ranger guarded her bone.

"Drake was here, I can tell, everyone is agitated," she said, assertively strutting over to me. "You know, you never asked me for my name?" She paused. "Andrea Kanable."

"Lucretia McEvil?" said The Legend.

"Where did you hear Lucretia McEvil in Andrea Kanable?" she asked, puzzled.

"Larry The Legend has real bad surfer's ear."

"Surfer's ear?"

The General explained, "The wind and the cold narrow the ear's opening and thicken the bone so it's harder to hear."

"Actually the world is narrowing," said The Legend.

"And who's Lucretia McEvil?"

"It's an old Blood Sweat and Tears song."

"I think my Dad listens to them," she said, as if anything old was useless. Then added, "Of course, your mileage may vary."

"Lucretia McEvil," said The Legend, who suddenly didn't like her. "Andrea Cannibal sounds like it that's all." He shrugged and said with a mouthful of carnitas. "It's a lousy song."

Andrea had an empty paper cup in her hand, she gave it to me and said, "Can you dispose of this for me? I've flapped all the wings out of this low-fat double espresso caramel macchiato."

"Sure," I quickly said, chucking the yellow cup into the rusted wastebasket behind the counter.

"What's that song playing? It's an oldie isn't it?" she asked.

"The name of this song?" said Chops, who quipped, "It's 'Low-Fat Double-Espresso-Caramel-Macchiato-Shot of My Baby's Love' by The Swinging Medallions."

The Crew laughed. Andrea didn't, which surprised me. I expected her to like Chops. They both had sharp tongues. But she was clearly offended by any clever crack made about her. And, I could tell he didn't like her very much either. Weird.

"*You're* on line?" she incredulously said. She walked over to Squirrel, who didn't notice her. He was absorbed in his laptop.

"They threw me out of the gay chat room just because I misspelled douche bag," said Squirrel. "That blows."

"TMI," she said, walking away. Then she added to me. "Translation: Too much information." Andrea kept talking, "I was hoping to catch Drake here and say hi to you—you know, multi-task." She looked around the shop. "This, this is so *kewl*. The sixties music. It's so retro."

Ranger protectively and loudly gnawed on her bone.

Andrea watched Ranger, frowned, and said, "I don't like eating around bones. Bones bore me,"

"How can bones be boring?" asked Shiloh, rolling her eyes. "Everyone has bones."

"Nice wheels out there," said Skin Dog, nodding outside to Andrea's convertible.

"It's my fly-by ride," she chirped, pointing the key chain with the coral reef fragment at her car. "I got it at the Grand Concourse in Monterey. It's a gull Mercedes. A classic car. The one Tippi Hedren had in 'The Birds.' I saw it and it really jazzed me. They said I couldn't find one. I did. I have my lesbian mechanic person tune it up. The car cost sixty-thousand dollars." I was surprised she quoted the price. She haughtily added. "You certainly don't think I'd put surf racks on a car like that?"

"I think it would be *kewl*," said Shiloh, imitating Andrea. "I mean, I think it would be cool."

"What's your license plate say?" asked Chops. "'Ms. Angry?'"

"No," snapped Andrea. "Ms. Energy—E-N-R-G-Y not A-N-G-E-R! Duh, hello?" Her beeper went off. She checked its number and said, "Gotta bail. The Singapore system is down." The said to herself. "All those H-1Bs will be knee deep in code."

"HIVs?" asked The Legend, pulling on his ear.

"No, H-1B," said Andrea. "It's a type of visa. All these geeks from India come here. They're cheap, only hang out with each other, and they live like eight in an apartment because they spend all their time at work, never shower. They smell like curry, and talk about soccer." She said to herself. "I'm so Un-PC." She paused. "I have to hook up with my 1:30-pm chocolate cookie with macadamia nuts and get a new set of wings with a low-fat double espresso caramel macchiato at StokaMocha.."

I followed her outside. She walked to the silver convertible. Its top was down. Mardi Gras beads dangled from the rear-view mirror. A pink traffic ticket was on the leather passenger seat.

"Did you get nailed by a meter maid for a ticket?"

"No, no, no, when I was coming back from the Dylan show at

the Civic, where I paid a scalper $200 to see the show because I have never seen Dylan. His voice was shot. I didn't understand a fucking word, never did anyway. Anyway, after Mr. Mumbles' concert, I went downtown to The 99' and some control-freak-macho-small-town cop on some type of power trip nailed me for rolling through a stop sign." Andrea clicked her tongue against the roof of her mouth. "I slowed down. I looked. No one was coming. I went. I told the cop I would have stopped if someone was there. One hundred and one dollars. The cop should have given me a warning. I cried but that didn't work either."

"Crying, I never tried that."

She got into her car, shrugged and said, "And giving me a ticket the way people drive here. Yeah, space-out people in Santa Cruz drive in traffic following the signs—Aquarius, Scorpio, and Virgo." On the horn of her steering wheel, was a yellow Post-It note with the phrase 'Run with the thinkers.' She revved up the car. The stereo blared out an alternative-rock song, a chorus sang, "I get knocked down, but I get up again."

"Who's that?"

"It's 'Tubthumping' by Chumbawamba," she shouted. Then she danced a little in the front seat and sang, "He takes a whiskey drink. He takes a vodka drink." She turned down the music, angled her body for the tightest curves, and smiled at me.

I blurted out, "You wanna see a movie sometime?"

"Sure, where?"

"Cinema 9. Downtown. 'Saving Private Ryan'."

"Isn't that pretty violent?"

"Yeah, I've seen it twice."

"I'll 411 you," she said, opening a Dave Mathews CD case.

"Wait, you'll 411 me?"

"411—give you the information. You know, you dial 411 so you can get information for a phone number? Maybe we can hit the matinee some time," she said, did another hair flip, and added in her affected California-girl voice. "Then like we can totally go out to some super trendy sushi place and cap on people."

Her phone beeped and she unfolded it.

"Hey you," Andrea said into her phone. "Isn't that what I said? I told you the two systems would work. It's all about backward compatibility." She waved goodbye and drove off. When she reached the four-way Stop intersection, she jumped her turn ahead of the other cars. Man, did I want a piece of her.

When I walked back into the shop, The Crew was talking about Andrea.

"She's bad news. I don't even get it," said The General. "High maintenance. What does Vic see in her?"

"You're kidding me, your flesh has really cooled, brutha."

"Hey," said Chops, raising his hands as if he was afraid of being robbed. "You won't see me going near that."

"Oh like none of us have chased down women we had nothing in common with," said Sonny. "How about that ass for starters?"

"Hey, Shiloh is here. A little courtesy," said The General.

"Over it," said Shiloh. "I'm so used to Sonny."

"But it's the truth," Sonny said. "Oh, like she would be one to talk. She took off with Bystrom and lived on his boat in Hawaii. And what did she have in common with Bystrom?"

"That's wrong," said Shiloh, looking down. "That's so wrong."

"Well, since Sonny's not going to say he's sorry," said The General to Shiloh. "I'll say he's sorry for him."

"Thank you."

I went back into the shop. I was pleased with what Sonny said to Shiloh, it was what I always wanted to throw in her face.

'Well Respected Man' by The Kinks played.

"Wait! There *is* a catch in what Drake wants you to sign here," said Driveway Dave said, pointing at the contract "It's this 'senior liquidation preference' clause. It says if a company is sold or goes bankrupt, the investors get their money back first, the rank and file, i.e., you, get diddily squat."

"But he's giving us $125,000," Sonny said. "That's not stock. We could bankroll surf classes and teach other dot-com idiots how to surf and make three or four times that amount of money."

"But you heard what that Drake guy said on the scanner," said Dave. "He's playing this game at another level. If the stock drops and he cashes out, his creditors will come after Vic and us."

"What do we have that anyone would want, brutha?" asked Skin Dog.

"Well, Vic could lose his name, his image, and his shop."

"I'm losing that now."

"So what if this Drake guy and his bros are playing this game at another level?" said Sonny, gesturing wildly with his hands. "But we have something the dot-comers don't have. We have something the dot-comers want. We have something to sell them they can't purchase any other way but through us..."

"And what might that be?" I asked, wondering where Sonny was going with his logic. I continued, "These dot-comers have everything. They can own everything. What could we possibly have that the dot-comers don't have?"

"A life," Sonny clipped out. "There's nothing inside them. The dot-comers have driven us off the land to the water. And now they're paddling out into the ocean to finish us off. We have nowhere to go. They have the land and the sea. We're not even surrounded. You know what we are? Anchovies." He paused. "Well, so what do you say, Vic?" He paused. "Do you want to be an anchovy?"

"I hate anchovies, not the fish, just the way they taste."

"Well, it's all your call Vic, is it happenin'?" asked Sonny, looking straight at me. "Or is it just not happenin'?"

I lifted up my arms and limply dropped them. They slapped against the sides of my legs. I thought of my lease, the shop, my debts—and, Andrea's ass.

"It's happenin'," I said, nodding. "It's happenin'."

The Crew cheered and high fived. The General stood outside the group and stared at us. Ranger went to the front door and barked. I walked outside. Whatever she was yapping at was nowhere to be seen.

A FEW WEEKS LATER, PLEASURE POINT was glassy. The sky was clear blue and the sun showed all the colors that were in the ocean. The water had a major glitter factor. The sunlight bounced off the surface with sharp and piercing crystal sparkles, as if God were heavily salting it. The glistening waves were three feet and peeling nicely to shore. It was a Thursday morning, and already, there were sixty people out at 38th Avenue, and twice that number at the other spots. The scattered specks of wetsuits floating on the surface looked like aquarium food left for sharks. The You-Go Girls and Whew-hoos dug for every wave, cut each other off, and fell off their boards. But this time the crowd was not an issue. We were armed with a beginning crowd—a paying crowd. The Crew and I stood ten feet behind our first surf class and listened to Sonny's lecture.

"In this expression session we have re-invented the board meeting with a separate modality of team building configured with self confidence and camaraderie so co-workers can learn about each other as an individual group," said Sonny, pacing in the sand before twenty people in wetsuits, who were lined up in two-rows, holding blue foam boards. "Surfing is about making a commitment, testing limits and life." A few students peeled back the wetsuits from their wrists to check the time on their sports watches. "When I'm in the water, the ocean is the bottom line."

"I had no idea Sonny could be so insincere," I said.

Driveway Dave whispered. "Yeah, it's really impressive."

"Surfing is good for you. There's nothing virtual about this reality. It gives you an appreciation for your body and the ocean environment," said Sonny, who downshifted into a supportive-Dad mode. "Surfing is a copasetic way to develop an upper body, strong shoulders and abs. One hour of surfing is like doing two hundred push-ups. This is not a school of hard knocks. We are using blue foam boards. They are soft-skull friendly." The dot-comers laughed. "Surfing is about fun, being together, meeting people, and getting in tune the ocean's rhythm." He smiled. "And it all comes with my money-back guarantee that you will stand up on your first wave. Now, let's apply these concepts in real time. That's high-tech talk for: 'Surf's up!'"

Sonny ran out to the ocean. The class cheered and followed him. When the dot-comers paddled on their boards, they squirmed like bugs blown into pudding.

"What idiots," I said in disgust.

"You want idiots?" said Chops, nodding at the stairway leading to the beach. "I think The Idiot King has just arrived."

A fat-as-a-tick geek thumped down the stairs. He had long and thinning black hair, which he pulled back into a pony tail that was as thick as fives strands of piano wire. His wetsuit was on backwards: the zipper in the front instead of the back. The leash cord of his foam board was attached to his wrist instead of his ankle. He was on a cell phone, "Why are you taking up Zander's valuable time with lame-ass questions? RTFM is your answer. Zander is busy. Zander's implementing a packet-sniffer security program to find the moronic ass-wiping borg responsible for the hole in our network's firewall. This is not like you finding spam in your e-mails! Do you understand what this means? There is proprietary data being accessed by an outside database. Your printer not working is a low-priority in the big picture. Right now, Zander's plate is full. Oh, what's RTFM mean? Zander will mentor you on this. R-T-F-M? RTFM means: Read The Fucking Manual." He clicked off. "God, users are such dark meat."

Chops met Zander by the stairs and quietly said, "I'll take your cell phone for you. I don't want to embarrass you, but...ah, the wetsuit goes the other way. The leash—"

"How the fuck is Zander to know this?" the geek snarled,

wiping his mouth with fingers covered with orange powder from cheese doodles. “Zander is not native to this version. Zander is the guardian of Surf Dot Com’s database.”

After we suited up Zander, it didn’t take us long to catch up to the class, who were in such bad shape they probably got out of breath eating chocolate. The class was only twenty yards out and we were already losing some of them. Most were tired from paddling. Others wobbled on their boards or kept sliding off them. A few kept their face planted down into the board and glided off in the wrong direction. Somehow, Zander managed to swallow some salt water, clung to his board and threw up.

“Probably the most intelligent thing he’s said all day,” said Chops, drawing a laugh from us.

We herded the surf class to the outside peak in the middle of the pack. The Crew and I wore large, floppy, yellow canvas hats. We figured it would help the students identify us in the water.

“Bringing an instant crowd right into the line-up, you know better,” reproachfully said The General, sitting on his board, and staring down our group. “It’s all about getting your waves, isn’t it? You look at waves the same way these people look at money. You’re pissing in your own drinking water. This is cold, Burr.”

“Cry me a river,” grunted Sonny. “Surf somewhere else.”

The General left.

A set of three-foot waves came through. It was crunch time.

Sonny paddled alongside a dot-comer, and urged him, “Okay, here’s one, let’s go for it.”

At this juncture, The Crew and I mobilized into a solid war machine running on stinkeye, push, and shove. I felt like I was a sergeant with a squad again. My assignment was to walked point on the first teacher-pupil wave. I paddled to the right of Sonny, who was guiding our first geek. My mission was to clear a path ahead and prevent burn artists from dropping in on us. On Sonny’s left, Skin Dog rode on an eleven-foot green board, positioned to prevent anyone from snaking the wave. Our rear was covered by Driveway Dave and Chops, who formed a defensive line with remainder of the class to interdict surfers from threading between us. There were no openings in our line-up for anyone else except us and the students.

"Timing," said Sonny to the pupil as the wave rose and broke behind them. They slid down the face. The dot-comer was on his belly. "Position," added Sonny, standing and hoisting the geek to his feet. "Trim," he continued, angling the student's foam board into the wave. They rode side by side, trimming parallel across the face. Sonny used one arm to help the dot-comer balance on the board. "Go for it!" commanded Sonny, releasing the pupil into the curved chute of the wall. For five unappealing seconds, the dot-comer shot down the line. He was a goofy foot, so he stood sideways on the board with his right leg forward. The wave broke from left to the right, his back was to the wave. He didn't even see it. His arms were bent at the elbow and stuck out from his hips—it looked like he had forgotten to remove the hanger from inside the wetsuit—actually, he looked more like a human-shaped hanger supporting a wetsuit.

"I'm surfing! I'm surfing!" the geek joyously shouted.

The Legend was stationed with a camera and tripod on the beach. He quickly snapped a shot of the horrid sight.

The dot-comer fell off his board, and yelled, "Whew-hoo!"

Skin Dog and Sonny kicked out of the wave and rejoined the class. I was left all alone with a choice three-foot peeler. I cutback to the curl, let the wall reform, and rode it to shore. I paddled back out. The students cheered my noseride.

We deployed variations on the same maneuver to student after student. The Crew rotated posts of either surfing point, rear guard, being human shields, or doing the timing-position-trim drill with a student. And it always ended with the same result. After we successfully drove everyone else off the wave, the student fell, and we'd take turns surfing the wave to shore. The Crew and I couldn't believe it. We were using the dot-comers to get our waves back—and make money, *their* money.

Then the ocean fucked us big time...

"Hot wheels from hell here comes a set," shouted Skin Dog, pointing outside.

At least ten, six-to-eight foot waves were rolling. We paddled with our students to scratch over the first wave.

"Dig, dig, dig," urged Sonny to the students. The Crew and I just made it over the wave. It closed behind us. We turned. Our entire class was swept to shore. Sonny looked around at the ocean surface minus students and concluded, "Well, I guess that didn't work."

Within minutes, the class members were either getting carried off by currents to The Hook, washing up to shore and staggering on the beach, or getting bashed against the rocks. But most desperately hugged their boards and coughed up water. The ocean looked like a ship sunk and everyone was clutching wreckage. A few students were probably still below the surface. The waves weren't really that huge, but the majority of the surfers in the water were so bad, the waves were beyond their meager abilities. Most of them were actually afraid of waves over three feet. So, The Crew and I were the only ones left outside.

"They're all gone! What are we going to do now?" I asked.

"Timing, position, trim," cheerfully answered Chops, who spun around and snagged a wave. I saw his head just above the wave as he shot across it. He triumphantly howled.

"Fuck it, brutha," said Skin Dog, pointing outside. "It's great out here. Nobody wants it. Let's take it."

We surfed for the next hour. When we paddled in, there was no sign of our surf class. Ranger came over with a ball.

"Not now Range," I said, walking past her.

"I guess they left," said Driveway Dave, looking around.

"Or they're all dead," said Chops.

"I bet one of them probably was stupid enough to die and take us to court," I said. "I wonder where The Legend is."

"They probably stole his camera," added Chops. "And beat him to a pulp with his tripod and ate him."

"This was my way out, man," Sonny said bitterly.

"Did somebody call the Waaaaaaaahm-bulance?" said Chops, who smirked.

"Will you knock off that Waaaaaaaahm-bulance, shit?" said Sonny. "It's old and you're not funny."

"Kinda like you," snapped Chops.

"Fuck you," said Sonny.

"What's it to you, Dr Tao?" said Chop, who got angry. "You don't have to worry: You have no friends."

We hung our heads and walked with our longboards back to

Heckler's Point. We spotted our class milling around my new white van, which was parked halfway down 38th Avenue. The class had their wetsuits peeled down to their hips, ate from box lunches, and drank bottles of Odwallah fruit juices.

"There they are!" said a dot-comer, pointing in our direction.

The class charged at us.

"They signed waivers, right?" I nervously asked.

"Yeah," wearily said Dave. "But, anybody can sue you, man."

"Oh we are so fucked," I quietly sighed. "A mega cluster fuck."

We angled our boards across our chests, ready to shield ourselves from blows, food, or plastic fruit juice bottles. But instead, the dot-comers eagerly handed over checks and jabbered: "Wassup? That's was so bitching...Awesome...Wassup? It was sick out there...That was just like—eh, whoa!...Hella fat...Wassup? I need a wetsuit...Do you sell board bags?...Do you give individual instruction? I'll pay extra...Wassup?"

The Crew and I lowered our boards and looked at each other, completely aghast. We stared at the dry checks and cash in our wet, cold hands.

"Hey look, I hurt myself surfing," boasted a damp, stringy haired dot-comer girl, pointing to a small cut above her nose, which was bleeding pretty good.

"That's so cool," someone said.

The group cheered her.

"One-hundred and twenty five, right?" said the exhilarated dot-comer, who wasn't bothered by her bleeding. "Can I pay you later with a credit card so I can get my airplane miles?"

"Sure."

The class went back to the van.

The Crew and I exchanged looks. We couldn't believe what was happening. In a few minutes, we had over a thousand dollars of dot-comer money in our hands for one hour of doing what we usually did: surf and ignore them.

My cell phone beeped out the opening chords of 'Purple Haze' by Mister Jimi Hendrix.

"Yeah," I answered.

"Hey you," said a voice. "Andrea."

My heartbeat spiked. A quick rush of energy hit my brain.

"Hi!" I said with an excitement I couldn't control.

"Can you come over to Surf Dot Com?"

"Let me check my schedule," I said. I looked up at the sky for a few seconds. "Yeah, when?"

"The Webmasters need to repurpose you for our web site," said Andrea. "We're getting a great response to your image—focus groups love the German shepherd. Who knew?"

"You're talking about Ranger."

"I guess," she said. "We're making Surf Dot Com shirts with a picture of you and the dog on them." There was a call-waiting click on her line. "I have to take that call, it's Drake probably bitching about his hotel room. Gotta fly, bye."

"Fine," I said, struggling to find the button to end my call. Then it occurred to me. I didn't know what a Webmaster was, or the meaning of the word 'repurpose.'

"Okay guys, group photo," said The Legend, who walked down toward the railing at Heckler's Point.

The Legend lined them up. They stood in front of their boards along the Heckler's Point railing. The class treated it like a graduation ceremony. Some pulled down the middle three fingers of their hands and shot their thumb and pinkie out in a Hawaiian hang-loose gesture of coolness. Others extended their arms like they were riding a wave. They were smiling, laughing.

"See, I told you this would be easy," said Sonny.

"I don't get it, why did they pay us? " I asked.

"They surfed so think they're cool now," said Sonny. "That's what they paid for. They think they're surfers."

"But don't they know they had a miserable time?" I said and uncomprehendingly looked at the gleeful dot-comers. "All they did was get beat on."

"Their lives are so miserable, they don't *know* the difference," Sonny said. "They don't get it."

"But they seem different now than when they came," I said, amazed at how wired these people were.

"Yeah, they are."

We turned to see The General studying us. His gray hair and mustache were wet. He held his longboard under his arm and said, "You planted a seed. They got on the wave. They defied time and they defied gravity. They don't get it—yet. But it's a feeling that's in them unconsciously. They feel good and they don't know why. They'll get addicted just like you and me. You planted a seed, you planted a seed." He paused. "But this happiness will hunt them down. And if these people ever wake up, and the blind pupils see, actually see their lives, their foundations will be gone. Buildings will fall. Buildings will fall."

I was within Andrea's cubicle at Surf Dot Com. I indifferently listened to the steady, sucking, vascular tha-thump of electronic music by Banco De Gia from the office speakers. In a corner, foosball-playing dot-comers shouted, slammed rods and banged a wooden white ball back and forth. Two young guys with short, dyed-red hair played against two older guys who had shaved heads and trimmed Billy-goat beards. They all wore polo shirts, khakis, and shiny black square-toed shoes. I heard someone taking a shower in a side room near a kitchen. A microwave dinged. I smelled popcorn. The achingly beautiful day outside didn't distract the dot-comers. Everyone contentedly stared at monitors and typed on keyboards and talked on cell phones. It almost looked like a form of animal experimentation. They seemed so happy in this habitat. There was a certainty to them. Within the nesting areas of their workstations, the dot-comers squawked and cheeped out an arrogant intellectual crispness...

"Unify the brand..."

"Push it as an internal P2P document-sharing solution..."

"Really simple tags..."

"The discoverability is a proven. Too many upsells."

"I left my ICQ and my IRC handle at the bottom."

"If it groups that way, subsets are cool."

"I feel functionally responsible on this path to develop a delivery model."

"Interpolate? There are way few shadow structures."

"The ISP tightly scoped..."

"Blessing the system folder..."

"Where's my Think Pad"?"

English was a second language at Surf Dot Com, actually, it was probably a third language. It was like these dot-comers were from another solar system. And this office was their mother ship on a mission in cyberspace. Everything outside was just passing scenery. The geeky guys walked around with the cockiness of action heroes. The misshapen, thin or just plain peculiar women strutted with a professionalism they mistakenly thought made them sexy and beautiful. Besides each other, the only thing the dot-comers seemed to fear was daylight.

In the office, Andrea looked uptight from the outside in. She wore red, small framed, cat's-eye angular glasses. Her hair was tightly wound against the back of her head; it resembled an angry ball of yarn. She had on Capri pants and a tied-off blouse that ended just below her ribs, and revealed a pearl-naval piercing on her flat stomach. But she still had those spiked red heels. It was pretty weird. Talk about mixed signals. She looked like a collision between a hooker and a career woman. Oddly, she seemed relaxed, but uncomfortable in her clothes.

"How do you like my cube?" Andrea proudly said, spinning around in the chair.

"Huh," I said. "Nice."

Her cubicle's light-gray fabric walls were plastered with pinned-up Post-It notes. The yellow one-inch square pieces of paper had motivational phrases like "Stay Hungry," "Take No For An Answer," and "Be The Newest Thing Under The Sun." There were a few pictures. One of her with four girlfriends hoisting beers in a Mexican bar; another of her with seven bridesmaids all in their twenties, who had low-cut gowns that revealed cleavage as well as portions of purple and red tattoos across their upper arms or shoulders; and, one of her in Paris hugging a beret–wearing, geeky guy; a Post-it said 'Tucker' below it. On her desk were a few self-help books, which looked like they had never been opened. Atop her tangerine computer sat small, bendable, green figures of Gumby and a Pokey, and between them was yet another yellow note that said: "Do it." Her screensaver was a shot of Kevin Costner in 'Dancing With Wolves.' A stock ticker ran along the bottom of the monitor.

"We have the best of everything. Ultra fast computers. Cool 21-inch monitors. I put in all the furniture here. I went with a lot of green, browns, grays, and oak finishes to give the place earth tone decors. A little Feng Shui. Balances out the energy of the right and left brained." She spun around in her chair again. "Aeron chairs—four hundred dollars a piece." Her eyes suddenly widened in remembrance of something. "I keep the refrigerator stocked in the break room. Just got some yogurt-covered pretzels and Odwallah fruit juices from Costco. And some boss Krispy Kremes!" Andrea jumped up and circled me. She looked impressed. "And check out the Vic-Burr makeover! A whole new look. I like the pleated khakis, the denim shirt and the sandals. Your hair tied up in a nice ponytail. You could pass for a vice-president at most of the dot-coms I've worked at." I didn't know how to take that. I said nothing. Andrea rapidly filled our silence like it was an enemy. "How'd your class go?"

"Great," I said. "Did you do Shiloh's all-girl surf class this morning down at Cowells?"

"Yeah, but I didn't like it. That girl is all mega 'tude."

"We'll go out together, I'll make sure you get your waves."

"Check this poster out," she said, pointing to her cube's wall. "It's a satellite shot of Santa Cruz taken from space, which I think is redundant."

The poster was an aerial view of the turquoise blue Monterey Bay penetrating into the brown and green coastline—the bay's shape actually resembled the tip of a penis trying to enter the land. Outside of the penis penetration, it was really a great photograph. I could see the San Lorenzo River, downtown Santa Cruz, and all the neighborhoods along the cliff-edged shore stretching to the south. I could even make out the two stacks of the Moss Landing power plant, Point Pines, Asilomar, Monterey, and the beginning of the Salinas Valley.

Andrea pointed at map where downtown Santa Cruz was and said, "There's The 99', StokaMocha, and Mobu Godzilla, where I go for sushi, an Asian named Yoshi is my sushi person."

"There's the Holy Cross Church," I said.

"Are you religious or something?"

"No, I've always figured anything God got me into, God will get me out of." I paused. "That's about the extent of it, I guess."

"Did you know that Santa Cruz means like 'Holy Cross'?"

"I didn't think it mattered," I said, shrugging. "Holy Cross. Some Spanish missionary guy came up with it after he probably killed a bunch of Indians. It never has much to do with anything in the long run." I paused. "Pretty cool picture, though."

"It's virtual. Computer enhanced and you can see everything."

"So it's not real?"

"As long as reality is virtual, it's undoable."

"What does that mean?"

She repositioned her finger on the poster and said, "This is where we are." She slightly turned and brushed my chest with one of her firm breasts. "Feel my finger?" She smiled and tapped her perfect butt. "New Capri pants. Like the color? Marled tan."

"Since when do you wear glasses?" I asked.

"I took my contacts out," she said. "Glasses make me look more professional. My Mom told me getting into the door as a woman is easy, but then look twice as tough as the guys."

"That can't be too hard *here*."

Andrea laughed, smiled, and studied the stock ticker on the monitor. She nickered and purred to herself, "Ehhhh-xcellent." She looked at me and casually announced, "I'm a millionaire." I stared at her. I didn't know how to respond, probably because I didn't ask her if she was a millionaire. It's just not something I bring up right away. Then she corrected herself, "Well, I will be one. It's inevitable. After our second offering, everyone here is going to be a millionaire." She added with great significance. "What we're doing is changing the world into a place no one has ever seen before. We're starting a revolution."

"Huh," I said, and glanced at someone was left out of the

revolution: a Mexican man struggling with two large, unwieldy garbage bags at the front door. None of the dot-comers helped him. I knew him. I excused myself, went over, and held the door for him. He didn't notice me yet.

"Hombre," I said menacingly over his shoulder.

"A-meeee-go?," Fernando said, quickly turning to face me.

"Fernando! Como esta?"

"A-meeeee-go!" cheerfully said the man, dropping the bag and hugging me.

I hadn't seen Fernando in a year. But he always looked the same. He had gray peppered hair, a thin mustache, and was missing three top front teeth. He was short and thin. He looked like he was in his mid-fifties, but was probably in his mid-sixties. Fernando did all his shopping at the Salvation Army so his clothes always had a logo from a charity run, a radio station, a movie promotion, a product, or golf tournament. He lived in California for twenty years. He graduated from the University of Mexico City, and worked for the Sears there. He got promoted and did retail for Sears in Chicago. When he visited his sister in California he told me, "A-meeego, I went to Chicago, it was the first time I was in this country. I thought all the United States was the same as Chicago. I came out here and it was paradise." He moved here and worked as a janitor at a Catholic School in Scotts Valley for twenty years. He retired and picked up under-the-table money landscaping. I met him on a construction job years ago. Fernando was putting in gutters. I didn't like the way the foreman talked down to him, so I offered him a Pepsi out of my cooler. He taught me dirty phrases in Spanish and I taught him more English, which definitely meant I was getting the better part of the deal. He had a lot of wisdom. And he always came up with these Spanish proverbs. The guy was amazing—he could butcher any animal, break-in horses, put in drainage systems, grow any crop, do electrical and plumbing, and fix almost any kind of car. He even played guitar in a mariachi band. And he was a hell of a cook—I still remember the pig he cooked all night in a pit, and his chili verde, which he made with roasted vegetables. Fernando's solution to any meal that didn't taste good was to just throw a "leeetle salsa" on it. His earnings went toward building a place in Purisima, a village in Baja. I made sure I found him work on every job I did. When I was renovating a building for my shop, Fernando came out of nowhere, and helped put in sheetrock and did dump runs. The day the shop opened he bought his band down and played. He was divorced because he had a problem with the bottle. He had three sons, but got along with his ex-wife. A year ago, he claimed his body wanted alcohol and he started drinking again. He'd get into arguments, and threatened to get one of his guns. I found him sitting at a park bench near some tennis courts off Ocean Street. He was drinking tequila from a bottle in a paper bag. He slurred his words and told me he and his buddies got drunk, stole a cow from a County Fair petting zoo and ate it. He pointed at a pigeon and said," See that bird, you want me to catch it and break its neck? I can. I can kill that bird for you, a-meee-go." I called Manuel, his son. We got Fernando into a rehab center.

"No barracho?"

"No, no, barracho, a-meee-go, I drink I die," he said, and smiled, showing his missing front teeth. "No barracho, I don't have that problem."

"Finally using your head?"

"I don't have that problem anymore either," he smiled. "Pinche, a-meee-go."

It was good to see him.

"So you're working here, Fernando?"

"I was working at a horse farm, but the man I worked for, he was not a good man, a-mee-go," Fernando said. "He wanted me to work for so little. I left. I told him I didn't want his money. I work with my sister's husband. It's his company. Mucho tabajo. They clean up these people's messes. They're a lot of them."

"You have to come over to the shop."

"You need help? I help you."

"I'm fine."

"Nobody is bothering you?"

"No."

"You still say 'hombre' when you're angry, a-meee-go?"

"Como, hombre?" I said, smiling.

"Pinche a-meee-go," Fernando said and laughed.

A young, Asian dot-comer geeky guy, rudely cut between us. His cell phone beeped out the opening notes of "The Raiders March" from the Indiana Jones "Raiders of The Lost Ark" movie. He went outside to his red Lamborghini.

Fernando studied the dot-comer, shook his head and said, "Se hizo miel y se lo comieron las moscas."

He turned himself into honey and he was eaten up by flies.

I laughed.

"Vic," said Andrea from her cubicle.

"A-meeee-go, senorita," he approvingly said.

"Hasta," I said, smiling.

"Vic," Fernando said, mimicking Andrea's voice. "Vic."

Fernando laughed. He joined four other Mexicans out front, who had vacuum cleaners and mops, pails, and plastic garbage bags. They were waiting for a friend to pick them up.

I walked back to Andrea's cube. She was on a call, "Yeah, I feel relaxed, I had a massage earlier from Zoof, my massage person. Ring me." She clicked off, smiled, and tilted her head. "Who was that cleaning person you were talking to?"

"His name is Fernando, he is a friend of mine.

"You're so PC," she said, taking out a metal box from her small shoulder bag. "Altoid?" I stared at it. "It's a mint."

"Do I look like a mint guy?"

"No."

"Is Drake here?"

"Drake? Drake's almost never here. He's out at one of those dog-and-pony shows to get more investors," she said, her eyes widened. "Oh, oh oh! Sometimes Drake puts down his cell or sits on it and sets off the speed dial, and I get these messages." She hit a button on her answering machine. "Check this out: Drake's being read the riot act by his wife, she spells her name E-l-a-i-n-e, but pronounces it 'Élan. Puh-leeeze. Make me hurl." The recorded message came on. It was a woman who brayed, "How come we didn't get the house I wanted? I thought you had equity! And why couldn't I get the first class tickets to London?" Andrea stopped the machine, and said, "Pretty trippy? Those are very real problems to her. I have a whole collection of them."

"Do you guys have showers here?"

"We even have a fitness gym," she replied, pointing to an open door at the rear of the building. An unattractive skinny woman was doggedly running on one of three treadmills. In front of each treadmill, angled from the ceiling, was a TV tuned to the CNBC business channel. The woman had a purple Prince Valiant haircut and small glasses. She listened to music on headphones, skimmed a newspaper draped over the handlebars, checked her pace with her sports watch, and also watched TV. "Everything is in-house. This is like a dormitory in a way. This place is cool."

I pointed at the screensaver and said, "Kevin Costner. I hated that Indian movie. He killed a dog in it. Killed a dog in another movie too. You gotta be sick to do that. You don't kill a dog."

"He's definitely on my to-do list," Andrea said, narrowing her eyes at me. "But you Mr. Burr person, you're on my short list."

I assumed that was a good thing. Just then, a woman hopped on a pogo stick past Andrea's cubicle. She had an orange buzz cut with black spots scattered on her head, which made her hair look like a food mold. She wore an antique baby blue cardigan sweater over a REM concert T-shirt, a fifties-type skirt, white socks and clunky saddle shoes. With each bounce, a gold necklace with a diamond pendant flew out from her flat chest and hit her chin. An MP3 player was attached to her hip. She somehow listened to the music through a small pair of headphones and simultaneously held a phone conversation on her diva mic. She had those round steel-rimmed glasses Nazi adjutants wore in forties movies. She was about as attractive as a doorknob—that probably opened the door of a haunted house. But you could tell she thought she was beautiful, she had to.

"Wassup, Vic," said Pogo Woman, who had a small bandage on her forehead from her surf class injury. She continued her phone conversation. "Hey, the discoverability is enabled. It's end-to-end. All the dogs are hung, just get run of the press. We have so many internals in place. But once you get under the hood..."

Under the hood? I bet Pogo Woman didn't even know where the coolant was under the hood of her car. Under what hood?

"What was that?" I asked, watching her hop away.

"That's Aedhmer. She's that way all the time."

"Eczema?"

"No, Aedhmer. She's worse than 'the heartbreak of psoriasis. She spells it: A-E-D-H-M-E-R"

"Aedhmer. That's a name?" I asked, shaking my head.

"Yeah, I know, what were her parents thinking?" said Andrea, laughing. "Eczema. I'll have to use that one. You wouldn't believe how people here go ballistic over how you spell or pronounce their names. I deal with it all the time. We have a Maya but it's spelled M-a-i-j-a, and a Michael spelled M-y-k-e-l. Whattup? I don't get it. Big deal. Still sounds the same. But Aedhmer, she's one of the most case sensitive. She's Miss Electrical Science and Engineering of 1996. Sure, she's brilliant. Who isn't here? But, boy does she live in a bubble. Never helps anyone. She's a walking CYA alert—cover-your-ass alert. And she always sticks her nose into other departments and starts doing someone else's job and screws it up, but blames them. I mean, she'd throw you under the bus as soon as look at you. Graduated summa cum laude bitch-on-wheels with a double major in being a cunt. The woman's a mollusk. And you wouldn't know just to look at her, but, she acts like she's Ms. Feminist and talks about glass ceilings and how women don't get paid their true value in the industry, but she was down in Cabo at the Giggling Marlin being winched upside down while guys poured tequila on her tits."

I tried to imagine that. It wasn't easy. Then I wondered what Andrea in her red-spiked heels did at Cabo. I also couldn't believe how easily the c-word came to her.

"And, Aedhmer fucks everything that moves."

"Then, I'll try to stand real still," I said, making Andrea laugh. I paused. "So what is it you do here?"

"I'm a Vice President of Communications Administration, which means all I've been doing is just making it up as I go along. Everyone here is either a VP or a director (When we only had ten people we were all directors and VPs.). Trippy, huh? Basically, I'm a combination cruise director and happiness coordinator. But most of the time I have to put out fires among the web monkeys and the alpha brats and e-holes." She paused and said with great conviction. "I make things happen."

"I see," I said, not seeing.

Bobby Weever popped his head into the cubicle. He had on

khaki pants, a tight v-neck sweater and a Surf Dot Com T-shirt underneath it. He wore sunglasses. He ignored me, which was fine. He said, "Andrea, how are we coming along on content? I just wanted to touch base and get your thoughts—"

She said, "Hello Robert." She paused. "Weeeeeee—*ver*."

God, I thought, his own *kind* even hates him.

"I processed the first three action items. The other two are on task, okay?" she said, and looked away.

"I'm not taking issue with you here, this is our confront and debate space," Weever said, chopping his right hand into his open palm. "It'll impact our schedule. I'll get a memo into the mix so the rubber hits the road. We need to get some traction on this."

Weever turned and left.

"What does he do?" I asked.

"Nothing and very slowly," she said, rolling her eyes. "He's the VP of Human Resources. The guy's a click-through. He's always trawling through the office and escalating issues. But from what I can tell he just finds out what everyone is doing and then writes up memos. He's so snarky. He creates problems so he can solve them. I think he wears sunglasses so no one can see through him." I laughed. She took a pull on her mineral water and whispered to me, "How does he surf?"

"About as good as he works, I guess."

"Delivery," loudly shouted a Federal Express woman, who came through the front door carrying several envelopes. She extended a computer clipboard to a geek, who was positioned near the door. "Delivery."

"Zander doesn't sign for deliveries," the geek snapped without turning his head to look at her, and slurped a Mountain Dew soda. After he swallowed, he clamped his teeth on a leathery strip of beef jerky, but instead of biting it, turned his head to viciously tear a piece off with his grayish teeth. He was in his early thirties, I think. He had square, black-framed glasses with tinted lenses. He wore a 'Pinkie and the Brain' T-shirt that was splattered with red and orange food stains. His gray drawstring sweat pants were also heavily stained. Rainbow straps on his sandals set off his white socks. His arms limply hung at his sides.

"That Zander guy was just in my surf class, I was wondering

where he went. He wore his wetsuit on backwards in one of my classes. He was a real jerk about it too. He cut out early. He even calls himself Zander? Zander? That's his real name?"

"Yeah, Zander. Great name if you're made out of plutonium and from the future. A total e-hole. Zander talks about Zander in third person all the time," replied Andrea. "I think it's because Zander doesn't want to speak directly to Zander. He's our IT: Information Technology Officer. An IT is—"

"You don't have to tell me, I can see what an IT is."

"He's an engineering type. I deal with them all the time. They live in a bubble. They're closed-in people. They solve problems by thinking not feeling. There have been studies on it," said Andrea, as if that somehow justified his rude behavior. "Zander's another in a series of multi-taskers with no life. He birthed our site. The guy's a user manual wired for sound. He maintains the security of our network. He goes through attachments to make sure no one is putting a virus in our system—I think he really gets off on going through everybody's e-mails. He works 24-7. He even has a sleeping bag and spends nights here." She paused. "And he acts so smart—well, he didn't graduate high school." She shrugged. "I have to work next to him. He won't let anyone clean his cubicle. They both smell. Check out his cube."

I peered from Andrea's cubicle into Zander's workspace. The place was a mess. Zander's shelves were lined with empty Mountain Dew soda cans. His wastepaper basket overflowed with frozen-burrito microwave foils, candy bar wrappers, and several empty take-out cartons of Chinese food coated with a red sauce. Under his desk were discs, batteries, a spare hard drive, and modem cables. Several three-foot high piles of technical manuals were positioned maze-like about the floor. Comic books were scattered everywhere. His keyboard was covered with powdered doughnut sugar, dried smears of brown enchilada sauce, and orange cheese doodle dust. Alongside it was a wireless mouse, a joystick, and a miniature steering wheel with a wire connected to a brake and clutch pedal platform on the floor. The only clean item in his cubicle was the screen of his enormous monitor, which was twice as large as anyone else's in the building. It displayed a legion of horseback-riding knights awaiting orders. I recognized the game. So, *this* was the Zander Squirrel battled against on the Internet. Atop his computer were various alien stick figures and a picture of him camping with other fat dork system administrators—one held a mandolin (An instrument I despised almost as much as the cello.). On his desk, was a set of headphones emitting a bass pulse of rap music, which sounded like muffled Morse code. He had a shelf lined with numerous science fiction books by William Gibson, H.P. Lovecraft, J.R.R.Tolkien. Another wall had a "Tomb Raider" poster of a woman dressed in a tight fitting black leather bikini. Near it, and mounted on the wall was a four-foot long sword or stick resting on two ornate pewter hooks designed with a fleur-de-lis. The sword had a round bejeweled pommel engraved with a crescent moon looking at a star. The hilt was covered with leather, and the steel crossbar just above it was inscribed with medieval script: "God Wills It." Beyond that point, the weapon bore no resemblance to a knight's long sword. Instead of a gleaming sharp-edged and wide hand-hammered steel blade with full groove in the middle coming to a sharp tip, this weapon had a one-inch round wooden pole with silver-duct tape wound around it. Above the sword was a football helmet with white horns on its sides, and a wire cage face protector.

"What's the deal with the weird stick?" I asked, pointing over at Zander's weapon of choice.

"Oh, puh-leeeze," she said, looking away. "The guy's heavily into Dungeons-and-Dragons stuff. Zander actually got Drake to sponsor a Renaissance fair coming up at UCSC a few months from now. He's going to take on people in sword fights. Oooooh, hold me back! He's streaming it on our web page. I have to put an appearance. If we're still speaking, will you be my escort?"

"Medieval geeks with swords? You'd *never* get me near that."

"Can blame you, guys like him have to make up a world because they can't download the real one," she said. "Zander went ballistic when the Webmasters had a bigger monitor than him. Mr. IT has to have the best of everything. He doesn't even need a big screen to do his job. Believe me, I know. I work right next to him and hear him playing his stupid games. He actually has a finger callous from using his joystick. A real worldly guy."

Meanwhile, the duel between the Zander The IT and The FedEx Delivery Woman was still playing out.

"So you're refusing the package?" said the female carrier.

Zander ignored the carrier's question and spoke on his diva mic, "The lame-ass, powers-that-be told me I couldn't compete in this year's gamer contest because it's limited to fourteen years and under. Can you believe that shit? Just because I took first place last year by 490,000 points." He paused. "Man, did you check out the latest Drew Barrymore flick?" He opened his mouth, and belched loudly. "Yeah, she's a pig."

"Listen to him, *he* of all people has standards for a perfect woman," Andrea whispered. "Zander wouldn't know what to do with a woman unless she came with a pop-up menu and a scroll bar. He'd probably have to write code to get an erection."

"Fine, you refused the package?" the FedEx woman said, who pivoted to leave. "Thank you."

"Hold up!" shouted Andrea to the carrier, who left the cubicle and muttered to me, "This is why I get the big bucks."

She signed for the packages.

Zander stood between them and talked on his mic, "The cool thing about Renaissance fairs is you can become whoever you want to be. You get pumped up being someone else, totally into the fantasy. When Zander leaves, Zander realizes everyone in the real world lives in a fantasy. Zander can be and do anything!"

"Delivery," said a guy at the front door. He was carrying a thin, large, square white carton. "Who ordered the pizza?"

"Zander has that!" possessively declared The IT, who quickly thrust out his arms and grabbed the box.

Andrea returned with the packages and said, "Wouldn't you know it? All five packages are for him. Figures" She flipped the envelopes from her cubicle onto Zander's chair. She motioned me to follow her. "If you think our IT is lax on people skills, wait until you meet the Webmasters, those two guys are the real developmentally disabled kings of this dysfunctionasium."

As we wound through the maze of cubicles, dot-comers chattered and threw out high-tech phrases of toxic fairy dust: "The front end leverages functionality... Open the GL pipeline ...It's Protocol centric—it has to be a part of the same core code."

The steady combination of deadening computer language and thumping electronic music pummeled me and sapped my energy. "The interface is surprisingly unfriendly...Our inflection point...It's a Unix program bundled with...The cross platform is untethered" I felt leaden, drowsy, as if their phrases were tranquilizing me. "This model API could be a little difficult to use...There's a work-around because there's isolation between the operating systems...OCR applications." The disco ball flashed silver splinters of light that hurt my eyes and affected my vision. I was getting a headache. My arm bumped into the edge of a cubicle. "Everything but the interface in a promiscuous model... You can't find the config...Under the GUI." Did I just hear under the gooey? I didn't want to be on this killing floor. I started third-personing. The dot-com was a stomach and the phrases were its digestive juices breaking me down. The thumping music was its pulse. My first nature told me to bolt and paddle out into the ocean and keep going. But, I had to endure this to save the shop. I numbly drifted, struggling to keep my bearings. I got through it by keeping my eyes on Andrea's ass the whole time.

The Webmasters ignored Andrea and me. They sat with their backs towards us and designed Surf Dot Com's website page. One stared into a flat-screen monitor, deftly hit his keyboard, and rapidly clicked his mouse over a Captain Kirk mouse pad. Andrea and I stood at the opening of the cubicle, next to a life-size cardboard figure of a Klingon alien from Star Trek. The Webmasters were two chin-bearded guys in their mid-twenties. They had huge foreheads. Their jell-spiked, thinning, short hair resembled splintered debris swirling around drain-like bald spots on the back of their lopsided skulls. The Webmasters angular black glasses were so minutely designed, the frames partially obstructed the geeks' sight. Their puffy faces looked like they were pushed in, and slowly trying to reassume their original shape. The two ate out of the same box of 'Frosted Mini Wheats and slurped Red Bulls. One Webmaster wore an untucked rumpled dress shirt, black jeans, and sneakers with untied laces. The other wore a wrinkled Metallica T-shirt, black jeans, and scuffed cowboy boots. There were two motorcycle helmets on the floor; one was yellow, and the other red, which probably matched the red and yellow Yamaha bikes parked outside. Everything about these guys matched. Andrea and I watched the digital image on the Webmasters' huge screen. It was me! I surfed across a glassy wave. I wasn't wearing a wetsuit. I was trunking it. A pelican briefly flew near me. When I kicked out, water sprayed off the board, and splashed out "Surf Dot Com."

The Webmasters briefly looked back at us, but returned to the screen, and talked to each other.

"I dithered the GIF dude," said the young Webmaster, who spit some tobacco juice into the Red Bull can he held his left hand, then placed it back on the desk. "And dude, scope the edges of the pelican wings, no artifacts. This program totally rocks."

"Schweet, dude," said the other Webmaster, who stared with awe at the screen. "Perspective drop. Optimized color range."

"Am I cool or what, dude?" he said, raising his arms like a bodybuilder and kissing his thin left and right biceps.

"Dude, the bit-depth is so off-the-hook cool," said, the other one, who looked intently at the screen, and squeezed a sponge ball of Earth in his right palm. "Architected the rendering, dude."

"And dude, Blaine told me a shortcut, to change the opacity on the image say six percent hit the number 6, hit 6-6 and I get 66 percent, but if you hit 6-6-6 you reform the hard drive."

"It's phat. Yo, I hella dig it, dude. Blaine, yeah," he said, laughing at the digital joke. "That's cool. Who's Blaine, dude?"

"Dude, Blaine's the Tiburon guy who yakked out his cookies big time from too much Jager at the Cal game."

The two shouted, "All right now!" They followed it with a rhythmic handclap, stopped, made one fist, briefly tapped knuckles and said, "Go Cardinal!"

"Hello?" said Andrea, expressing her irritation.

“Andrea, like don’t you have to restock the Chill Out room with M&M's,” snidely said the Webmaster at the computer without glancing back. “I think the fruit bowl is getting low too.”

The Webmasters smiled, lightly pressed knuckles again, and spun around. They crossed skinny arms over sunken chests and studied us. A scaled-down model of Star Trek’s Enterprise hung on a thin wire from the ceiling and guarded the skies above them. What geeks! I couldn’t imagine these guys being paid to do anything else but this.

“Wassup?” they both said, doing the hang-loose Hawaiian hand move, but in a detached too-cool-gotta-go attitude.

“This is Jef with one f,” said Andrea, pointing to the one working the mouse. “And Gregg with two gs is the one who either has a gross chewing tobacco habit, or is leaking oil.”

“Greg with two gs?” I asked. “And Jeff with one f? What’s the point? Jef sounds the same as Jeff. I don’t get it. Hey, I thought Greg always had two gs.”

“It’s Gregg. And you spell it: G-r-e-g-g.”

“But that makes it three Gs.”

“My name *ends* in two gs—that’s the point.”

Gregg-with-two-gs spit an extra gob of tobacco juice in the Red Bull can and placed it on the wrap-around desk, which was covered with candy and junk food wrappers, zip discs, FedEx envelopes, small video game CD-Rom boxes, an Etch a Sketch, piles of graphic artists trade magazines, and a couple plastic Streetlight Record bags filled with unopened CDs and DVDs. Near the Webmaster’s feet were computer sacks stitched with the name of the company, and filled with disc-golf Frisbees marked ‘Beast,’ ‘Cheetah,’ and ‘Hawk.’ The cubicle walls were plastered with posters of rock groups, computer-graphic images of ridiculously proportioned females in thong bathing suits, a Nagel drawing, some Japanese animation stills, and a Bugs Bunny cartoon cell signed by Chuck Jones, as well as an assortment of business projects the webmasters designed (among the them was the revised Bings menu I could no longer read).

“You're the Vic guy we have to repurpose to add content,” said Jef-with-one-f, still staring at the screen.

“Repurpose?” I asked. “You lost me.”

"Yeah, repurpose, you're still at the beta stage to us," said Jef-with-one-f in the snot-nosed way all these dot-comer guys had. "We'll need more of your content to throw on the web." He paused. "I mean we're all just CPU units with a hard drive."

"Well, maybe you are," said Andrea, which drew glare from Jef-with-one-f. Obviously, Jef-with-one-f didn't think there was anything funny about Jef-with-one-f.

Andrea stood next to me and thrust her hips slightly forward. She languorously ran the finger of her right hand back and forth below her pierced navel, along the edge of her low-cut pants. She was trying to turn them both on. It was a weird office dynamic. They were like caged-cubicle animals taunting each other. But it was like she didn't know she was doing it.

"We haven't gotten any collateral material on you. So tell us about your life." drolly said the Gregg-with-two-gs, who tried but failed to conceal a lustful gawk at Andrea.

"Yeah," added the Jef-with-one-f, who was also trying to resist watching Andrea's finger slide. "Give us the Cliff Notes version."

"I have a surf shop, a VW, and a dog." I said. "I fought in Vietnam and when I—"

"Got it," interrupted Jef-with-one-f with a dismissive tone. He typed and said in an insensitive, intellectual shorthand, "Flashbacks, Post-traumatic stress. No parades when you came home. Isolated. Anger at authority and rules. Lived off the grid. Decided not to come home again because there was no home. So, you rebelled by surfing away your life."

"You know me better than I know myself," I said evenly. It was amazing he had gotten this far in life without someone punching the shit out of him. "I guess you have me figured out."

"What's the dog's name?" said Gregg-with-two-gs, who still deigned to face us.

"Ranger?"

"Why Ranger?"

"I was a Ranger in Vietnam."

"So you named your dog, Ranger? Isn't that's a little overkill?"

I spun my Dad's ring around my finger and looked at the two-gs guy. I wanted to thump him with in the unrendered, unoptimized, color-ranged plains of his dithered forehead.

"I don't think it's overkill," said Andrea. "Maybe it would be overkill if Ranger was spelled with two gs."

I liked her more for saying that.

"You attended school?" said Jef-with-one-f, typing.

"Yeah," I paused. "In Cupertino."

"We went to school in Palo Alto," Jef-with-one-f said loftily as he spun back around in his chair. The Webmasters smirked at each other in a cocky, collegial way.

"Which high school?" I innocently inquired.

Jef-with-one-f said, "So what's the deal with surfing?"

"The deal?"

"Surfing is supposed to be such a cool thing, but what's their ultimate high? Getting caught in a tube of water that swirls around you like a toilet bowl. I mean a turd experiences that on a flush." Then Jef-with-one-f looked at me like I was the turd. "Some of these guys, surfing is their whole identity. I mean, no offense, but if it wasn't for surfing, you wouldn't have a life."

I was jolted by his rudeness. But, my intense dislike for him helped me regain my composure. I flashed on a response.

"No offense, but what's the deal with the Star Trek thing?"

"Meaning?" impatiently said Gregg-with-two-gs as he tried to peep around the obstructed view of his small-framed glasses to follow Andrea's polished red-nail, fingertip-crotch dance recital.

"You know Star Trek," I said, pointing at the stupid spaceship model. "The mission of the Starship Enterprise is supposed to seek out bold new worlds and explore them. But almost all the time they wind up killing the people in those worlds, ruining their planet, and leaving." I paused. "What's the *deal* with that?"

The Webmasters said nothing. I thought they'd be offended. But then, when I thought about it, they probably assumed what I said was obviously the most effective way to make a new world; after all, look what they were doing to Santa Cruz.

"You fucknozzles did it again," shouted Zander as he barged between Andrea and me, using our elbows like they were a the rotating posts of a turnstile entrance to the Webmaster's cubicle.

"Oh, did someone place an order for fecal matter?" asked Jef-with-one-f, looking over his glasses.

The Webmasters laughed and tapped fists.

"It took me eighteen hours to get our server back up after you opened an e-mail attachment with a virus in it," vented Zander, who had tomato sauce on his scraggly beard. And Andrea was right. He did stink. His body odor smelled like stale food flossed from between teeth. "But you don't even give a flying fuck do you? We have to protect the robustness of my network. It took me hours to repair holes in the firewall that were so big, a fourteen year-old could have hacked into this system."

"If a fourteen-year old could do it, then you're just one way stupid fucking glorified security guard," retorted Jef-with-one-f.

His two-g's buddy added, "Last time we had to upgrade our system with one of your dick-ass lame programs you shit hosed everything in our hard drives. Your network security sucks ass, it lacks configuration. And you call yourself an IT? Your pussy-assed system runs at a crawl. One time it froze all my aps."

I whispered to Andrea, "Does anyone here like each other?"

"E-holes," she muttered.

The all-powerful IT wasn't offended by the Webmaster's comments. He just viewed this moment as an opportunity to retaliate in a more venomous way.

"You buzzword-spewing leeches don't understand the process," said Zander, bristling. "Zander can make a telephone switch handle more calls per minute than the number of lines of code you flaming turds have ever written. Zander can reduce everything you ankle-grabbing dead-weight motherfuckers have created your whole lives to under a 1k assembly. Zander is putting in a packet sniffer security system to find the borg who is creating a hole in my firewall. And you better hope it's not you." He stormed out from the Webmaster's lair like an angered God. Andrea and I parted for him. "Zander rocks!"

The IT's anger had no effect on the Webmasters.

"Dude, the only way that dickweed IT could rock is passing a gallstone," said one.

"Zander couldn't log off on a toilet bowl," replied the other.

They shouted "All right now!" and followed it with a separate, quick rhythmic handclap, stopped, made a fist, and lightly tapped each other's knuckles and said, "Go Cardinal!"

After the Webmasters concluded their cheer, they spun back

in their chairs to their monitors, and spoke to each other like we were no longer there.

"Dude, I got the Matrix on DVD," said Jef-with-one-f.

"Try a levels adjustment, dude," said Greg-with-two-gs, who watched his fellow Webmaster change to my image. "Cool, dude. Maybe you should blur it to make it more realistic."

We stood there. They ignored us.

"This is where we came in," Andrea, clearly rankled by these guys. She turned and left. I followed her.

When we got back to her cubicle, she spat out, "You catch that Palo Alto bullshit? Those e-holes always have to work in where they went to school. And the MBA guys are even worse. Their schools are soooooo important to them." Her body shivered. "It's bad enough I have to deal with programmers who are dysfunctional dropouts. But, Stanford University! That's the kiss of death. My God, Stanford! Those people are the worst. They'll never say Stanford but oh, do they have to let you know. They always find a way to work it in. You say, 'Hey, it's a nice day.' They go, 'Yeah, there were days like this at Palo Alto.' And the Harvard guys with their prep schools and Boston crap. You think they're bad about their names, get on them about their colleges."

"If they are so smart how come their education is the only thing they have going for them?" I said. She laughed. "So who are the Cardinals they're talking about?"

"Not Cardinals—Cardi*nal*, there is no s. Think they're trying to compensate for not being Harvard Crimson? Cardinal, it's not the bird. It's the color of the Stanford team. They were called the Indians but that was politically incorrect in the seventies so they asked the students to vote on the name and some wanted 'Robber Barons,' but the administration went back to Cardinal. Believe me I know the whole story. I've heard it ad infinitum from my father. My Dad is old, he's in his fifties and he religiously goes to the last football game of the season to *support* the seniors. He's never left that place. He even goes to Stanford basketball games in Arizona! He still has college textbooks on the shelves of his study. Get real! I mean he paid to go there, they didn't give him the education. Move on." She paused. "I can't believe you don't know about Cardinal. Didn't you play sports in high school?"

"I was on a basketball team once with the guys I surfed with, and we all made the team and were real good. The day of the first game, the surf came up, and we all cut out for Santa Cruz. The coach was pissed. He lost all his starters. He couldn't believe it. I wasn't going to miss a good surf for a basketball game."

Andrea laughed.

There was a loud crack followed by a "Woooah!" and a round ball from the foosball game rolled past us followed by an MBA.

"Fuck these bed-wetting JPEGGers," she said, getting angry again on a whole new level. "My exit strategy is to get my fuck-you money and fly." She rapidly added in an off-hand way. "The way our stock value keeps on doubling, I'll just cash in my chips, buy a house on the beach, and marry some guy who wants to raise my children while I become a Tennis Mom. You know, continue my arc—or, lob." She laughed at her own aside.

"A Tennis Mom? What's that?"

"I was just, um," she blurted, embarrassed because a suppressed truth slipped out from behind her dot-com mask. She punched my upper right arm, but it was more of a jab. Her knuckles were in it. The contact had a little bite. She giggled and added in an unconvincing playful tone, "I'm kidding."

"Hey, that hurt a little," I said, rubbing my arm.

"No, it didn't," she said authoritatively.

"Shouldn't *I* be the one to say that?"

"Don't worry, you don't fit a breeder profile. Besides, I have a lot to do before I turn thirty." Her pager beeped. I think she was relieved when it did. I followed her out from the cubicle as she said, "That's Drake, calling from Aspen. He's at some confab. My turn to be the weather vane for yet another shit storm."

We went into an empty conference room. There was a long, dark-brown shiny table in the center of the room. Arranged around it were metal-legged futuristic-type chairs of soft black leather. In the center of the table was a lava lamp, and around it were open styrofoam trays with half-eaten California rolls and dried-out green wasabi gobs beside puddles of soy sauce. In a corner, by a beanbag chair, was a six-foot, naked inflatable female doll, which actually had better muscle tone than most of the people who worked there. On the wall was a huge laminated white board. Scribbled on it were several multi-colored arrows linking two multi-colored circle: one was marked "Need;" and the other one was marked "Connection." There were numerous framed high-tech and business magazine covers on Drake. The largest photograph, was of Drake in a Hawaiian shirt, wearing a shark hat, singing with Jimmy Buffett on a stage.

"Checking out the Jimmy Buffett picture?"

"Not really."

"It was so *kewl*. Drake rented out the Paul Masson Winery in Saratoga and had Jimmy Buffett's whole band perform a special show for just us. The place is so trippy. Drake sang with them on stage throughout the whole show. He said it was his own Day On The Green—you know, where a band plays an outdoor concert, except he was the stage star. It was something he wanted to do his whole life. He bought Hawaiian shirts for everybody. There was Cuervo tequila, Corona Beer, and Margaritas. Inflatable sharks and beach balls." Andrea lifted her arms over her head and placed their palms together like she was going to do a dive. She moved side to side and sang, "Fins to the left, fins to the right, fins—" She stopped abruptly. "You're not really interested in any of this, are you?"

"No. I don't understand it."

"That's right, surfers don't like sharks."

"Especially on land," I said, looking at all the uneaten food on the table and asked, "What goes on here? Lunch?"

"This is the War Room," Andrea said, who had no problems shifting topics. She picked up the trays of sushi, along with four half-drunk bottles of Odwallah fruit juice near the speakerphone. "Nobody finishes what's in front of them in this place." She threw the food in the trash. "Like the desk?" She ran the flat palm of her hand on its surface. "It's an exotic wood milled in Maui—fifty thousand dollars." She pointed to some misshapen statue in the corner. "That piece is made from sandstone that came from Burma." She closed the door and dialed the phone.

"Drake," came from the speakerphone, which somehow made his voice seem more human.

"Hey you! So did you just get into the airport?" she said with a spunkiness that didn't equal the question.

"What are you, a pig fucker?" said Drake. The remark jarred me. But Andrea was unperturbed. She expected it. "I'm not in the fucking airport. I'm in my limo—and it's not the limo I asked for. What the fuck do I have to do, spell it out for the office?"

"I'm on it," said Andrea, who pantomimed sticking a finger down her throat to show me that Drake's statement made he want to hurl.

"Reboot," he said, and paused. "I'm under a lot of pressure on this road show to ramp up more funding for the team. I don't want to think about this crap." There was a call-waiting click on the speakerphone. "I have my therapist on the other line, hold." Drake came back on the line but he mistakenly thought he was confiding to his therapist. "Reboot," he said, and paused. "My wife? She understands nothing. It's not like she can't do anything she wanted. Our youngest is in day care. She doesn't cook. Hell, one time, I came home and the nanny was cooking frozen dinners for the kids on our Wolf stove. I mean I gave my wife everything. A six-car garage. A terraced swimming pool. We had four bedrooms with private baths. We can travel anywhere in the world. And she *left* me. My oldest kid got busted for doing drugs. I sent him to the best school, sent him to camp. God, I give my kid everything, how can he be so vacant? What's wrong with these people? Don't they see what I'm doing for them? I can pay for a Hummer in cash but I can't get my child to listen to me. And my wife left me. I hate my life! Doc, hold." There was a click. "Reboot," he said. "Andrea, c-c an e-mail to everyone, I can't find my Mount Blanc pen. That pen has sentimental value. Andrea? Andrea?" She looked at me and smiled. "Reboot, reboot, reboot, reboo—!" There was a click and he was gone.

"He'll be back," said Andrea, imitating Arnold in 'Terminator., then spoke in her own voice,' "Once in awhile us peons have to fuck with the king. God, Drake wondering how his wife could ever leave him? He's done everything for his family." She laughed. "I could hurl! Two weeks ago I saw Drake at MacArthur Park, a bar in Palo Alto. He was with an investor and they were both showing their kids' baby pictures to this woman at the bar and at the same time trying to hook her up into a three-way with them." The War Room phone bipped. "That's

Doctor Destructo now" She paused. "I've got to put this fire out." The phone bipped. "I can bail after this. Let's bounce and check out The Big Dipper. We have passes. Even better, I'll meet you in front of the roller coaster at the boardwalk?" She opened the door. "Okay?"

"Yeah."

"Is that all right?" she asked. She gave me a quick peck on the cheek. I walked away. The phone bipped.

"Hey you!" she said, softly kicking the door closed.

I walked passed the cubicle farm toward the Chill Out room.

"Wassup, Vic? You got to see this," excitedly said Aedhmer, alias the Pogo Stick Woman, who waved me into her cube. She was opening a small cardboard box on her lap. A silver Razor scooter was tilted against her cube's wall. A 'Scooby Do' lunchbox stood on a rhinestone-sprinkle covered white desktop. She resumed her diva-mic conversation. "My reservation is under Aedhmer. It's spelled like it sounds. A-E-D-H-M-E-R. My credit card number is..." she took out a gold card that had a picture of Snoopy on it, then rattled off, "7777 6869 5679 2341. No, it's 69 5679. Not 7769. Do I have to go through this again? It's a no-brainer." She repeated the numbers at a condescendingly slow pace. She clicked off. "Stupid." Aedhmer pulled out a tiny stuffed dinosaur out from the Styrofoam kernels. "My Beanie Babies!" she said, maternally. "My Mom also sent me my Tarantula polar fleece pullover!" She began talking like a nine-year old girl to the doll. "Hi-ya Rexy, pexy!" Then she spoke to me in her semi-adult voice. "This is Rex. He's not my favorite. Bronty, Bronty! Here she is." Aedhmer assumed the child-like voice again and clasped the stuffed brontosaurus to her chest. "Lonely for your buddy Steg?" She plucked a small stegosaurus out of the box and pressed Bronty and Steg's noses together and sang, "Bronty and Steg sitting in a tree, k-i-s-s-i-n-g." She smiled. I think this was her way of flirting with me. She put the dolls carefully back in the box. "Time for a nap. Now, you two behave." She made growling sounds. She giggled. "Rex, Bronty, and Steg, go for a thousand dollars as a trio. I even possess some of the *old* face Beanie Babies, which are also worth quite a lot." She spoke with increasing excitement. "I mean really, some of those ones are even worth more because they came out with red noses instead of black noses and Splash and Flash came out with the wrong tags attached to them. Some of my Beanie Babies have sold on eBay for three-hundred dollars a piece."

"You paid three hundred dollars for those dolls?"

"No. I got my Beanie Babies for $2.89. They're worth $300. I'm not selling. I'm holding out.."

"Why?"

"They'll go higher. I don't enter any situation with a losing mentality," she said. "Everyone here is bright and so aren't I."

"How's the head?" I asked, pointing at her forehead bandage.

"My what?" Her phone bipped. She turned from me. I exited as she spoke into her diva mic, "It's about wiggle room. It's all mods, hacks, and tweaks. A lot of that is ADP. I've got reports of Java errors. Cogeneration? There are layers of hierarchy." She paused, the literally shrieked, "What the fuck do you mean the scalability of the banner ad supported content page won't scale?"

One thing about all these bright or brilliant or genius people: they lived to talk crude and say "fuck" a lot. Weird.

No one was in the Chill Out room. I opened a huge stainless steel refrigerators. Its shelves were packed with fruit juices, sodas, and two cartons of Krispy Kreme doughnuts. The freezer was filled with ice cream, microwave dinners, and frozen yogurt cups. On the counter to the right of the cappuccino maker, were separate bowls of strawberries, apples, oranges, and candy bars. The cabinets were stocked with junk food. I grabbed a Pepsi, sipped it, and watched the dot-comers stir in the stable maze of cubicles. I studied a dot-com geek who wore a turned-around baseball cap and a puca shell necklace. The guy had the charisma of a plant. He stood in a cubicle, rested his flabby right elbow on the ledge, and absently sucked the palm of his hand. His eyes furtively searched the room. It was the same look that betrayed potential shoplifters who checked to make sure no one was watching them. Customers focused what they want to buy, they never looked around. What were these dot-comers were stealing, and what was Drake stealing from them?

"Vic, what are you doing here?" asked a familiar female voice, coming through the back door near the refrigerator.

"Howz'it Zoof?" I said, watching her tighten the straps of her portable massage table.

Zoof had frizzy black hair. Pale skin. I knew her in the seventies when she partied with my buddies at Pleasure Point. She pretty much had the same figure and face and dressed the same: a loose cotton blouse and black corduroy pants and black shoes. But over time, never wearing a bra definitely made her less appealing to look at. Zoof was always into holistic things. And she always made a big deal about being a vegetarian—and now it showed. She was losing her hair, her skin was pasty, and she had gotten heavier in the hips. Santa Cruz was the capital of the overweight vegetarian. Zoof spoke in this steel-plated, New-Age monotone mixed with a condescending tolerance and pity for anyone misguided enough to think differently than her on issues, such as women's rights, pesticides, animal experimentation, organic food vs. fast food, Republicans, off-shore drilling, and how the American public's views were being distorted because the mainstream media didn't give them all the facts (which was information she was somehow able to find, but never thought anyone else was clever enough to locate for themselves). For all of Zoof's fenced-in, open mindedness, the only taboo subject that made her get irrationally defensive, was suggesting her twelve-year old son was barely four feet tall because she never fed him meat and stunted his first three years of growth. I went there once for just the sheer enjoyment of pissing her off, but believe me, that was enough. Outside of tripping that particular claymore of a nerve, Zoof was easy to get along with. Zoof was a thoughtful, perceptive, and considerate person, as long as you agreed she was. She socialized with the yoga-and-body-movement-summer-Shakespeare-arts-and-craft-and-wine-festival-jazz-and-blues-concert-art-galley-author-poetry-book-reading-university-seminar-lecture-series-performance-artist-National-Public-radio listening-candle-vigil-tribal-elder-MSG-free crowd, which is why I rarely ran into her. We could handle doses of each other, we just didn't like being in close quarters for long periods of time, say an hour or so.

I smiled and said the same joke she hated, but always greeted her with, "Still rubbing people the wrong way?"

"About as much as you are," she said.

"Huh," I said. "I just surf in the water with these dot-comers, but you have to touch them."

"That's why I use oil," she said, thrusting out her hands. "It *separates* me from them." I laughed. "And it's easy to keep my distance. They come in talking on their phone. I don't speak to them until they are off the phone. The women either have to get a massage with a friend and talk to each other or they have to be on the phone and tell someone they're getting a massage. One woman calls me her massage person and schedules her next appointment as I'm massaging her and then checks her calendar and emails throughout the whole session. The geek guys and the women are pretty obnoxious when I first start working on them. But sometimes, when I have them on the table, as I put on the lavender oils and my music plays and I work into their necks and lower backs, they get quiet—real quiet. They're just so tapped out. I mean there's one thing they always say about themselves, 'I don't have a life.' Like it's part of their job. They accept it. God, can you imagine accepting you have no life? When I get deeper in the massage, it's like I've put them in touch with their bodies and who they are. I really say the term 'massage' loosely, because these dot-comers really like me to beat on them—they don't think they're getting a massage unless they feel pain. That's funny. And what's weird is, in the middle of the massage, the women have these mini-breakdowns, and cry and blubber about the hours they work and that the guys are dorks. The guys are a little different. They get jumpy. They don't cry. They just say all the women are after their money. When these people freak out, or do the no-life rap, I almost believe they look forward to it, like the breakdown is just all part of the massage. But, these people never completely let go. If I ever really get close to that last pressure point, their muscles actually shift into a reverse chain reaction and start tensing and knotting up faster than I can and loosen them. Strange. Then they suddenly get on their cell phones and say they have to get back to work. And they really have to get back to work because they're, they're..."

"They're what?"

"Scared."

I waited for Andrea on the boardwalk at the entrance of a Moorish-styled beige building, which had turrets, columns, and archway openings. It was the front facade for the Big Dipper, a wooden roller coaster with a white frame and red-trimmed track bed built in 1924. Riders screamed as they shot down the seventy-foot peak and wrapped around a tightly banked turn at around fifty-five miles an hour. The ride clattered and thundered with a contained rumble that vibrated the planks beneath me. I smelled fries from a nearby stand. It was daylight but a series of pulsating white bulbs outlined the buildings and the rides. Rock music and happy screams filled the air. I looked over toward the beach-blanket packed beach. The surf looked like it might be coming up. Armed security guards in blue shirts, gray pants, and black military shoes, stood along the railings with their backs to the ocean. They smiled, their flat and penetrating eyes profiled the crowd, everyone was a suspect—the excited kids, the bickering families struggling with melting ice cream cones, and the standard boardwalk human debris in the form of teenage punks, and shirtless dirtbags drinking 32-ounce beers and prowling (One guy actually had a tattoo of the crying face of Jesus Christ covering most of his chest, who might have actually really been crying because of who he was tattooed to.). Fifty feet above the crowd, lovers glided in bright candy-colored sky-tram cars suspended on the taut-wires stretched from one end of the boardwalk to the other. And above the tram wires, atop the highest car on the Ferris Wheel, undercover cops videotaped drug deals going on in the Beach Flats neighborhood a few blocks away. I was surprised by how warm the day was.

Andrea came over with the tokens for the roller coaster. We stood in line and watched the teenagers and little kids riding the hand-carved wooden horses and chariots on the gold-and-ivory merry-go-round. It was built in the early 1900's and still had its original pipe organ, which mechanically churned out tunes.

"I don't get it," she said sullenly. "They go around in circles and reach for a brass ring. It's not a brass ring—it's stainless steel. Don't they know what they're really reaching for?"

"If they get the ring, don't they get a free ride or something?"

"That's like getting paid in drugs—or, stock options," Andrea said, laughing, but followed it with a hard glare. The people enjoying the merry-go-round really irked her.

We entered through an arch, put our tokens in the turnstile and stood at the end of a long line, which wound up the circular cavernous cement walkway inside the building. After twenty minutes, we were finally in the next group to board the ride. A loud bell briefly sounded, signaling the arrival of the roller coaster pulling up on the track alongside of us. Andrea snaked through the crowd, cut in front of two adolescent kids, and burned them so she could get the second set of seats in the last car. She smiled, waved me over and lightly patted down the empty seat beside her. The kids stared at me like I was a jerk.

"The last car is the super fun way to ride a roller coaster. It's intense. A gasser. You get the most whip," said Andrea, ignoring the kids' angry stares. Her beeper hummed and vibrated. She glanced at it. "I have to get back to the campus after the ride."

A teenage attendant clamped the car's cushioned steel bar over our laps, and said, "There is no standing..." then he recognized me. His eyes lit up. It was The Fish. "Vic, whattup man? Wadell was going off this morning."

"Pleasure was good but crowded," I said.

"I usually surf out of town, too many Internet rippers at The Point, just too sketch" said The Fish, checking out Andrea. "I get all the waves I want. I was pulling into some barrels. The wind switched offshore out of the canyon something fierce. Had a little South. Sun was setting. The waves were backlit. It was Ep."

"Ep?" asked Andrea. "Hello? Duh. Translation, puh-leeeze."

"Ep is short for epic," I answered.

The Fish didn't notice my translation. He was caught up in his story. He acted out paddling and turning into a barrel with the wave throwing over him. He added hissing and sucking sounds. His eyes glowed and his jaw opened and closed. The Fish started growling. "I'm pulling into hell pits! And I'm going across it. 'Yaaaaaaaaaaaaaaaaaaaaah.' I said, 'Bring it on, bring it on.' I wanted it all, man, I wanted it all." He made a barking sound, "Rooow. Roooow. Roooow." He paused. "I'd paddle out, and re-up again. It was like, like..." He was unable to find a word, so, The Fish growled, "Yaaaar-raaaaaaaaah."

Andrea warily stared at the kid like he was an animal who might start humping her leg.

"Sounds bitchen'," I said, smiling. "I lost two back teeth in the Wadell shore pound. I was knocked out by my board. I came to on the beach. I was riding a 5'6" twinzer back then shaped by Joey Thomas. In the seventies all I wanted was juice."

"I work part-time at the cement plant up in Davenport, so I'm on Wadell before the word gets out," Fish said. "You still hang out at the Barnacle Point railing at 38th with all those old carp?"

"You mean Heckler's Point with The Crew?" I said.

"Yeah, the guys with the bald spots."

"Not me," I replied, fluffing my thick scalp of hair.

"They're just these old barnacles on the railing, all those guys just hang there and bitch," said Fish, smiling. "You know, I might longboard some day when I'm too old to really surf." He walked away but added. "Anything over seven foot is a gay board."

"Well there goes an argument against public schools," Andrea said, watching The Fish, and adding, "Some of us get older and grow and develop complexity, while others just become food groups." She looked curiously at me. "God, you know everyone in this town don't you? How do you know that guy?"

"That's The Fish. He's the son of Marty Mechanic. His Dad put a clutch in my Volkswagen because I shaped him an eleven-footer and a 7'0" for The Fish. I shaped boards for a lot of guys. I need help with the toilet, I shape a board for Plumber Pete. My shop roof leaks in the Winter. I call Roofer Bobby. I shape him a board. People have been pretty good to me actually. Phil the Doctor came by and gave me prescription medication for my ear infection. Don The Dentist worked on a cavity I had. When I was broke, which was often, Safeway Sam wouldn't ring up half my food purchases at Safeway by throwing them past the scanner. I'd pay $5.00 for $60 worth of groceries. It helped."

"No, that's not the whole reason, most people expect to break even, but if they go out of their way like that," she said, sliding closer to me so our hips touched. "They respect you. They must respect you. That Fish person respects you. I can see that. People like that don't have to fake liking people, it's the only luxury they can afford. But it's real."

"Basically, anyone who looks like me, probably knows me, and the only people who avoid me are the ones I don't want to talk to anyway." I paused. "I go way back in this town, way back."

"For a guy who knows everyone in town, you don't have many people in your life, do you?"

"Yeah, I'm just—"

But Andrea didn't want an answer.

"You do something for someone on a barter system," she quickly said, talking over me. "I guess that's how it all really ends up. Once people get what they want, even if they respect and like you, the phone always stops ringing because they got what they wanted. And because you traded it all off, it's a wash, and you never advance. The best thing about just paying people cash is you don't owe them. The transaction ends right there. They have nothing to hang over you. It's done. They have no emotional claim on you. You move on, but at your own pace, not theirs."

"Huh."

Andrea's phone beeped. The people in the same car with us, looked back, irritated. Andrea seemed to enjoy irritating them, like the negative reaction validated her success.

"Hey you," said Andrea, answering the phone. Then she did something I hadn't seen a dot-comer do in a while—she seemed to be actually listening to someone. "Yes, I went through all the IPO questions. BTW, I did ask if it was a non-incentive stock. And the unstatutory option? Yes, yada yada yada. And what were the vesting terms? Yes. What do you want from me? Yes, Father, we've already dotted all the i's and crossed the t's on all this. All FAQs. I'm definitely exercising my options ASAP." She paused. "Thank you. Goodbye." She snapped her cell phone shut. "He thinks I'm going to get ripped off. I have options—no wonder my mother left him with that passive aggressive behavior of his. He never forgave me for not finishing law school. How many times is he going to throw my life story into my face? It's history. I'm tired of it. I can do anything I set myself up to do." The roller coaster jerked us apart and started moving upwards. "My Dad still doesn't get it. He's old school. A total main frame. He's completely hardwired. He wants me to diversify, maybe get into pharmaceuticals. That's not part of my plan. I've already told him I have an option of ten thousand shares of Surf Dot Com, and another option for twenty thousand more on our second offering. If I don't know what I'm doing, how come I'm doing so well now?" The roller coaster teetered at the top of its highest point. A one-foot-figure of a plastic clown's head was positioned on the railing at the peak of the ride. The clown had a white face, was bald, and had two sharp triangles of red hair pulled out from the sides of its head. There was a meanness in its unblinking, black-circled, red eyes. Its wide open-mouthed smile was nasty. Every five seconds, a steady stream of small, rainbow oily bubbles propulsively heaved out of the opening between the clown's thick lips for ten seconds. The sound of an organ from the merry-go-round below played the spooky sound of Bach's 'Toccata and Fugue in D Minor,' which I remembered from Mr. Webb's fourth-grade music class. In the roller coaster, we overlooked the entire stretch of beach to the boardwalk and from the boardwalk to the city. But Andrea wasn't looking at the view. She was too busy seeing her expanding future. "My strike price—that's my option to buy the stock at—is only $6.50 a share," she said as a stream of bubbles fired over her head. "And Surf Dot Com's stock is up to a valuation of $120 a share. A share! I'm throwing all my salary into it and living off my credit cards, I'm no fool. But, I'm locked out until we do our second option, months from now. I'm just waiting my time out. It's like my mother said, 'Get the money first, the independence follows.' And that's so true. The only reason you finally do things for yourself is you realize no one is going to do it for you. Believe me, I've learned. Nobody lives rent free in this head. No one.

My life is set to default. Hey, as long as reality is virtual it's always undoable." She laughed. "I'm future proof." Just as the mechanical calliope played sustained and rising dark chords, the bottom seemed to fall out underneath us and the roller coaster dropped into its free fall as Santa Cruz and the beach and the surf blurred around us. Andrea lifted up her arms through the drifting swirl of bubbles and screamed recklessly.

"LET'S SEE WHO YOU GUYS are kissing," I gleefully said, fanning my face with a brick-thick pile of twenties in my hands. The Crew looked over at me and laughed. Over the last couple weeks, Andrea gave the place a high-tech makeover to get the surf class business "up to speed." Some of The Crew sat on spider-like Aeron chairs, positioned in front of computer terminals at each of the three new workstations located in the upgraded area of the former lounging section of the surf shop. Andrea removed the beat-up couch, and the old table, and put in a six-foot long maple table, with laser jet printers, scanners, an answering machine, and a CD burner. The old TV was replaced by a wide-screen TV in an entertainment-center cabinet that contained a combination DVD-CD, radio, VCR player, and the shop's old police scanner. The TV had the CNBC business channel on. But the volume was on mute. A stock ticker ran beneath it. The shop was on-line because Squirrel drilled through the floor, put in wires to set up routers, and created a network for our computers, and connected it all to a static IP address on a DSL line. He also designed a web page, registered our domain name, and set up a server. The surround-sound speakers played 'Lightning Strikes' by Lou Christie (one of thousands of oldies Squirrel downloaded from the Napster music site). The walls and the front window were racked out with over one hundred and fifty epoxy, soft-tops, and blue foam boards that blocked most of the natural light, so, I pulled down the shop boards from the rafters and installed the track lighting. Andrea handled the tech side and Shiloh managed the decoration part of the shop's makeover. Out went the wax-stained rug, and in came hardwood flooring. We threw up sheetrock and constructed two changing rooms. She painted the place in various beach-like shades of aqua, pale pink, tan, and sand. Shiloh went with an Islands decor—palms, petrogylphs, nicely framed photographs of native women surfing, as well as Hawaiian prints. She even threw in several translucent-paneled shoji screens, and artificial exotic flower arrangements. She even revamped the bathrooms with pictures, seashells, and potpourri. Shiloh set up elegant bamboo displays and racks, and she stocked them with Roxie women's apparel—bathing suits, low-waisted cargo pants, wrist scrunchies, body-length burnoose-like changing garments, bikinis, tropical-print pants in soft fabrics, board shorts, stretchy lavender skirts, even drapey, wrap-around Polynesian pareaus. On the display cases, she put small glass boxes filled with incense candles, jewelry, lotions, hair ties, anklets, and chokers. The place smelled exotic with the aromas of plumeria and pikaki. I expected guys to stop hanging out at the shop. But because more women were shopping here, more guys came to the shop hoping to lurk and hit on the women, and because guys came in, more women came in, and because it was Santa Cruz, even more *women* came in. The only thing remaining from my old shop was Ranger's spot. I refused to put boards in front of Ranger's corner because I wanted my whuppers to get her sun.

The shop was doing so well I actually looked forward to flat days, because it gave me the chance to do inventory, order epoxy surfboards, pick up blanks, and place orders. We were making more money than we had ever made our entire lives. The Crew and I had a full-on schedule of five separate sessions of twenty people a day. We charged them $1,750 tuition for five two-hour surfing lessons for the week that included a box lunch, a picture of their ride (A group photo cost ten dollars extra.), a silk-screened T-shirt with the words "Vic's Surf Shop," and a certificate stating they completed the course and had become a surfer. When the dot-comers discovered every hard-core Santa

Cruz local had a custom board shaped by me, they concluded the next logical step was a personalized surfboard. My boards became status symbols. The dot-comer's boards had to have every possible bell and whistle on it: special colors, air-brushed images on the bottom, fabric on the deck, wood tail and nose blocks, and even a glassed-in wooden fin. Sometimes a family would order three boards like that! But the joke was, a computerized machine shaped the foam blanks from a software template, then, the blank was roughed out by kids, and glassed. I just signed the wood stringer in the board (Sometimes I didn't even do that.). The dot-comers didn't know the difference. These trannies just wanted everyone to know they lived and surfed in Santa Cruz and personally knew a local shaper. They also had to have look-at-me-I'm-cool stuff. They snapped up any item with my surf shop logo on it. And man, did these trannies live to accessorize! They purchased wetsuits, surf racks, booties, sunglasses, gloves, protective helmets, wax combs, board bags, surf racks, instruction videos, magazines, leash cords, sunscreen, towels, sweat shirts, jogging pants, bathing suits, rash guards, and—a new item I just started carrying—a $125.95 "Vic's Surf Shop" sports watch.

'A Young Girl' by Noel Harrison played.

My cell phone beeped out Mister Hendrix.

"Yeah," I said, flipping it open.

"Hey you," said Andrea. "We still on for the film tonight?"

"Yeah."

"I'm running a little behind, so let's hook up in front of the StokaMocha downtown. I'm all low-fat double-espressoed-caramel-macchiato-ed out. But I still need some wings of caffeine. Could you grab me a French Roast? By the fly, I checked times for movies, the next showing for 'Saving Private Ryan' won't be for another two hours. There's another flick at Le Nick I'm really up for seeing. You'll like it."

"Shouldn't *I* be the one who says that?"

"Yeah, right. After the flick we can come back to the shop and I'll show you the surf video someone took of me."

"Le Nick?" I asked, debating about whether I should tell her why I hated Le Nick. But then again, she suggested coming back to the shop tonight in those red-spiked heels and with that ass. "Yeah, sure, sounds like a plan."

"See you there in an hour, gotta fly, bye," she said, clicking off.

"Hey, the wetsuits I ordered came in," Shiloh said, walking into the shop. "I already priced and put them out." She stood by a rack. "You have to check these out."

Ranger came over to Shiloh and barked, her friendly bark.

"Oh she knows, she knows," cooed Shiloh, bending down to Ranger. "Look what I have, Range. A bone." Shiloh took a bone from her sweatshirt pouch, and held it out. Ranger gently took the one-foot bone into her jaws and went back to her corner. "Good girl. You know when I take her to some of the classes she really likes the women, I almost think Ranger could be a lesbian." She laughed. "What are you doing tonight?"

"Shaping," I lied.

"So what do you think of the girl wetsuits?" she asked Skin Dog, who had just constructed a shop rack for the suits.

"Look like wetsuits to me, sistah," Skin Dog said, examining them. "They're brighter. I don't see any real difference."

"They are the same wetsuits—the *labels* are different," Shiloh said, smiling. "Women—especially older women—have wider hips. Women don't like to say the word 'Large,' so, the 'Medium' is a man's 'Large'." She paused. "Wetsuits aren't very flattering."

"You're shitting me," said Skin Dog, slapping his huge gut.

"That goes for large shirt sizes too," added Shiloh, reading a drop tag attached to a shirt button. "'Broad shouldered for athletic women with muscular backs.' Buzzwords for: fat. Women are vain. Guys will say what they weigh to get the right board to float them. Not women, no way. And, trannie women have to have color! They love their baby blue and pink" Her eyes widened. "Vic, did you see the latest write-up I got?"

"Another one?"

"I got the cover this time," Shiloh said, holding up an issue of Metro, a local weekly that had her picture on it. "They called me a 'pioneer in the business field of women's surfing.'"

My classes never got any coverage, but Shiloh's classes received an amazing amount of press because of her all-woman theme. For some reason, it was big news simply because women were taking up surfing, as if this never occurred before. Female reporters who worked for the two local weeklies, the Santa Cruz Sentinel, the San Jose Mercury News, the San Francisco Chronicle, as well as stringers for national magazines and newspapers (even The New York Times!) wrote these painful first-person articles—usually, with an unsubtle anti-male slants—that described their Santa Cruz'n Surf Diva lesson and how they learned to surf. And Shiloh covered every ovarian angle. She promoted her women's surf classes as "fun without the testosterone" and a "refuge from a male dominated sport." She organized "Women And Waves" surf contests at Capitola with the proceeds going to breast cancer research or a battered woman's resource center—a PR move that got her even more students by distributing surf class flyers to pumped-up female spectators at the event. She held special classes for bachelorette parties, weddings, and mother-daughter outings (Four of her classes got TV coverage: "Mothers who surf," "Pregnant Women who surf," "Lupus and Surfing," and "Menopause and Tidal Changes."). Shiloh ran her classes differently than us. She added massages, made reservations for groups at local bed and breakfast places, and even threw in yoga lessons. The Crew gave students sandwiches, power bars, soda, lasagna, barbecued burgers and hot dogs. But Shiloh went with chicken, pasta and Caesar salads, stir-fry dishes, low-fat snacks, and turkey or veggie patties. At the end of the day, she had all her classes get together and have cocoa and herbal tea by an evening campfire with sing-along. She designed a logo with a graphic of an Aphrodite-like woman surfer with flowing long hair, a hibiscus flower behind her left ear, and a wave breaking over her. Below the logo were the words 'Santa Cruz'n Diva.' Shiloh printed up the logo on sweatshirts, rash guards, polar-fleece zippered-jackets, baby clothes, tank tops, caps, T-shirts, bumper stickers, decals, and 3-D metallic-finished plastic auto plaques. The female-logo stuff sold four times more than guy merchandise. The You-Go Girls viewed the Santa Cruz'n Diva logo as an emblem, which they proudly displayed on their cars and clothing to proclaim their special place among a select breed of women who possessed a spiritual harmonic connection with the rhythms of the ocean, the moon, and the one-ness that is their embodiment of a true California Surfer Girl. These women were different. They were a special tribe. They were unique. But above all, they felt cool for displaying a 'Santa Cruz'n Surf Diva' logo. It set them apart. Shiloh had them nailed.

"I told the reporter how beautiful it is for women to learn about the ocean," said Shiloh. "But I did say, how I've noticed that as soon as these women learn to make a turn and get better, they become super bitches to everyone. And their aggro behavior is worse than the guys, because women don't think anyone will punch them. Women are going to start punching each other, probably more often than the guys. They get pumped up more, I know, I am one. I'd be brutal in combat. The woman doing the article didn't use that quote. She went with the angle of men not accepting change." Her eyes widened. "Oh, oh, hey, did you check out the new You-Go-Girl epoxy Roxie boards I designed? It's so very Roxie! They're along the wall up front. Women lean toward the epoxy boards because they're way lighter, narrower, and shorter. They like three fins. They want more color, floral patterns and glitter. They go crazy over glitter. And hibiscus! They love hibiscus drawings, hibiscus decals, stickers, jewelry."

I pulled out a longboard that had a hot pink floral pattern and purplish-silver glitter on the deck, emblazoned with a horrid air-brushed painted lettering that resembled frosted wedding-cake writing: 'Santa Cruz'n Surf Diva.'

"Pretty rancid, huh?" said Shiloh. "But the You-Go Girls are nuts over any board they know a man would never ride."

"No argument there," I said, sliding the board back.

Shiloh saw a customer and rapidly whispered, "Here comes Andrea ten years from now, Execudiva II: 'The Reckoning.' These women are assembled out of the same box! It's either the ponytail and baseball cap or blunt haircut, dyed-blonde hair. The thin gold diamond earrings, a pearl bracelet. Talking on their diva mics. Why do all these dot-comers have to be doing two things at the same time? They're never here and they're never there."

Execudiva II *did* resembled an older version of Andrea. But, in a highly unflattering way, which pleased Shiloh, but disturbed me, and probably pleased Shiloh more. Execudiva II was very attractive, but the eventual mudslide of time and whatever life she lived had—over the last forty years—had drifted the softness off her flesh, which left a bedrock of skin that needed to be silted over by make-up. She had a Rolex, a BMW, and the bummed-out business look that went along with it. We smelled her perfume from the rear of the shop. She strolled along the racked-out line of surfboards like she was reviewing troops.

"So we'll see you at Ridge, we set up a vertical tasting of their Montebello Cabernets—it's a special event with the winemaker. They're going to open the 85's for us," said the woman talking on her diva mic. "Ken Dixon from Oracle will be there, and so will Ed Cravalho from HP. I also made reservations at The Wild Hare in Palo Alto. We'll hook up after spin class. My personal trainer says I should add a pilates workout to my routine."

Shiloh whispered to Skin Dog and me, "I'm so over it, watch me take this trannie." She sauntered over to the woman, and cheerfully asked, "Hi, if you see anything you like let me know."

"I need a board for my daughter, and I want one too. All my friends are taking up surfing," said Execudiva II, briefly glancing at Shiloh as if she were an afterthought. Then she resumed her conversation on the diva mic. "It's the house I wanted. My stocks went up. I don't care about price, so when the renovation costs went up, it didn't matter to me. After all is said and done what's another $280,00? For the stairway posts, we're using Zircott—it's a Mexican ebony, $500 a foot. It'll be a six-foot wide staircase curved with an 18-foot Romeo balcony. I'm having it painted deep adobe red, decorated with Mexican glass and tile, four fireplaces, and a home theater. Our bedroom has vaulted ceilings and a walk-in closet, which is just the way our honeymoon suite was in Hawaii. And we have a little drain in the laundry room so our chocolate Lab, Anisette, can make her doody in there."

"The boards go for around eight hundred," said Shiloh.

"What?" angrily snapped the woman, who reassumed a pleasant tone and continued her diva-mic conversation, "I mean compared to Santa Monica the prices for beach homes here are cheap. And with all the work we put into the house, our place is easily going to be worth $3.5 million. It's solar friendly. We have dual-pane windows. We're asking for a reassessment because some palm trees planted by the county partially obscure our ocean view." She glanced at Shiloh and asked, "How much?"

"The boards go for nine-hundred dollars."

"Speak up?" she asked.

"I'm sorry was I interrupting our conversation?" said Shiloh.

"What?" the Execudiva II snapped again, then shifted back to her diva-mic conversation but spoke in a sweet voice again. "There's the Japanese rock garden with coy fish, a bathing deck with Jacuzzi, four-separate temperature-controlled rooms, a cigar room, a climate-controlled wine cellar, granite kitchen counter tops, and a pizza oven. I have yoga mats on order. Our espresso machine—hand carried from Madrid. A marble tub from Carrera where Michelangelo got his marble for the Pieta. Ba-bye."

"Excuse me?" asked Shiloh. "You want..."

Execudiva II walked over and ran her fingers along the rails of the boards and pulled out an eight-foot long "Santa Cruz'n Surf Diva" baby blue board.

"This board is the best board in your shop," she said, firmly. "This is the one for me."

"It's the right length," Shiloh said neutrally. "But for you to put it between your legs, you might need something wider."

The woman picked up the board, admired herself in the mirror, and said, "A wider board won't fit under my arm." She paused. "And I like the sparkles. God, Baby blue, do you have Island seat covers in that color to match? I need decals!"

"Well, yeah," said Shiloh. "I know you like the board, but a board's designed for floating you in the water, if it's narrow you won't be able to paddle it too well, and it won't float you so I—"

"Do you hear this?" the Execudiva II indignantly said to me. "She's disagreeing with me!" I shrugged. She snipped at Andrea. "More than eight feet won't fit in my car." She paused. "And you were telling me the price would be?"

"Nine hundred and fifty," said Shiloh.

"Fine."

"Before I scat, I'll take this for my five-year old son," said Execudiva II, walking over to the clothing rack and plucking up a sixty-dollar hooded sweatshirt. "And my sister wants to take up surfing too." She grabbed another. Then she reached for a cap.

"And I'll get this for my husband on Father's Day." She saw the earrings and said to herself. "These are quaint. I can use these as gag gifts for my costume party." She also went for a baby blue-paneled wetsuit and a baby blue leash cord to match her baby blue board, to match her baby blue BMW (which from what I could see, didn't have sparkles). "I'd like a tutor for my daughter in a private surf lesson so that when she goes out in the ocean I know she safe with an experienced person in the water." She threw down a wad of cash on the counter, as if she were shedding dead skin from her hands. She hit her phone's speed dial and spoke into her diva mic, "This is Cody's mother, when I picked him up at daycare yesterday, the Tupperware lid from his lunch bowl wasn't there." She took the change and walked away. "And he was missing a sock too." She paused and added, "Look, I don't have time for all of this minutiae, I have to go to the dry cleaners and pick up my husband's dobak."

Ralph entered the shop and patiently held the door open for Execudiva II. She didn't acknowledge him, or his gesture, and disappeared into the fog of whatever concept she had of herself.

Shiloh said, "God, these people are just so awful." She paused. "A girlfriend of mine works in daycare. She says execudivas never ask how their kid is. Instead, they complain about little shit because of guilt they don't want to face. They think they're good Moms because they can afford to send a kid to day care."

"If you think she's bad, you should see her husband," said Ralph who carried a bag filled with tacos and burritos. "He came in the bank with Evita there. They paid $2.5 million for the house. Put one million down in cash. They could have paid for the whole thing. They were crowing like roosters. And they went out of their way to impress me with that particular fact, and said their broker told them to put the rest in tech stocks. Talk about bucks. Tack on the $10,000 a month in taxes, the mortgage payment, and the utilities, the gardener. the nanny, the cleaning people, and we're talking $70,000 in upkeep a month. And these two are buying their dream house, right? A house purchase should be a glorious event. A dream house is something to celebrate. But they're all stressed out, and he's ripping into her the whole time for putting too much mileage on their BMW."

Shiloh asked, "Was her house baby blue?"

"You know," Ralph said, smiling. "I didn't ask."

"Oh, I got to meet up with another class," Shiloh said as she left. "I have to bring back some foamies to the shop tonight. We can celebrate me being on the cover. Go out for Mexican? Or, I can always bring a tri-tip sandwich by. I'll see you tonight."

Shiloh got into her white van. It was exactly the same as mine, but had the words 'Santa Cruz Wave Divas' alongside a logo of a woman with an hibiscus flower behind her left ear, surfing.

'Because' by The Dave Clark Five played.

"She's in love with you brutha," said Skin Dog.

"Yeah after she had a run at Bystrom with his boat in Hawaii. Shiloh had her chance," I said. "It's just not happenin'."

"Say what you want, that the love that's never goes away, that's a love you have to kill" said Skin Dog. "I know when I see it. It's what I thought I had but never ever got, that love lasts." We listened to the song for awhile. "Beautiful song, isn't it?"

A pained and confused voice came from the front door.

"Where's the old couch?" asked The General.

We hadn't seen each other much since our falling out on the water. But The Crew could never stay mad long. We respected the friendship more than each other. He stood by the register. He held a half-eaten burrito wrapped in tinfoil.

"I wanted to sit down and eat my lunch and watch a surf movie," continued The General, inspecting the shop like it was a crash site. "You're watching business news for the stock ticker? The shop boards are gone too. I thought you'd never sell—"

"They're on loan at Surf Dot Com, I didn't sell them."

"An office that wants to look like a surf shop and a surf shop that wants to look like an office, yeah it is," said The General, placing his burrito on the glass counter. He grimaced at the surfboards. "Epoxy boards! I can't believe you are selling epoxies. They're junk. Glorified pop-outs. You remember when surfing was big in the sixties? They came out with pop-outs, mass-produced surfboards from molds. They were just floaty pieces of shit. These epoxy boards are no different. They're too light. They're too stiff. The rails can't sink into the wave. They can't bend or flex, so when the whitewater hits them they slide out. I tried to noseride one of those epoxies and felt it right away. These people out in the water don't know the difference, none of them will surf long enough to know their epoxy board doesn't work. It's not a board, it's a thing. One time I was down at the beach, and a clueless guy stood on the sand, boasting about how indestructible his epoxy board was, and how it would last forever. Man, these dot-com people think everything they have is going to last forever. To prove his point, the guy laid his board on the beach and jumped on it. The damn thing exploded!"

"Hey, what can I tell you?" I said. "They sell."

"I've seen a lot of your custom boards in the water. I hear people bragging out how Vic Burr personally shaped the stick for them. And just by coincidence, all those longboards happen to be 9'10." And, I believe, that's the longest length those computer machines can shape a blank. And that means you're not shaping your own boards. You're not, are you?"

"Am I on trial, here?" I asked, flicking up my hands. "Should I have Driveway Dave present as my attorney? Hey, if I put a board I shaped next to a machine-made one, even you couldn't tell them apart. They're just as good."

"So, instead of putting your name on the boards, why don't you say, 'Machine made?'" The General paused. "Because you know machine-made is a negative. You know machine-made isn't right. The best stick I ever had was slightly warped. Every board made by a shaper always has a certain tweak of his in it. There's something about the human flaw in a board that gives it that special uniqueness when it's matched with the right warped person. It makes it real. You're not shaping, you're counterfeiting! I can't believe you of all people are standing there and telling me a machine-made board is better than a blank shaped by a guy covered with foam dust who has been grinding and surfing for over forty years. No way, man, I've seen you shape the rails of a board with a two-inch piece of sandpaper, walking back and forth on a nine-foot blank, and moving that raggedly piece of sandpaper up and down the rails, feeling along the sides by just using three fingers. That's a touch. That's a feel. That goes in the board. That's why your name is on the stringer. Who cares no one can't tell the difference? You know there's a difference and you're signing your name to a forgery. Your class is stamping out surfers the same way. You're cookie cutting snakes and burn artists. Tell me again there's no difference between those boards or them and us. If you say that to me, then, you're lying."

"Are you calling me a liar in my shop, *hombre*?"

"Yeah, I am. You're lying to the one who counts—you," said The General, holding his mark. "You don't know the difference anymore. Once you make deals with dot-com guys who have money belts, you don't call them on the cheating and the lying. You know why? Because you have established a relationship where there's checks and balances and everything evens out: their checks and your bank balance. He's getting you, and you're taking the money. Then you get away from dealing with the real issue, which is what you're both doing. You're ruining 38th Avenue. You're making it worse. All these classes, where you're blocking out people, and shoving students into waves. What are you teaching them? You're telling them to paddle out there on a surfboard to take more waves. You're telling them that everyone is supposed to get out of their way. And you give them a certificate and validate them being out there. That's not soul. You're not making surfers. You're making money. When you take money from people, and yank them up on boards, etiquette goes out the window. After they graduate from your class, they're like salmon. They come back to where they were born. But they don't die. They just keep laying eggs and bringing more people into the water who are just like them."

"It's going to happen anyway," I said with resignation. "Hey General, I'm just trying to save my shop."

"What shop?" said The General, looking directly in my eyes. "You blew the egg out of the yolk. There's nothing left of your old surf shop now. Who would want to hang out here? This used to be a surf shop. All you have now are pop-outs, foamies, clothes, and wetsuits. There's not one thing in here you couldn't get anywhere else. This place could be a store in a mall."

He walked out the door. The General left his half-eaten burrito on the counter. I guess there were two things he couldn't stomach. I flicked the food into the garbage. It left a pool of grease on the glass counter.

I WALKED DOWN the Pacific Garden Mall to meet Andrea. It was called the Garden Mall because the roughly seven-block downtown district had a variety of trees planted along it. The stretch was filled with bookstores, coffee houses, hair salons, beauty schools, used record stores, overpriced restaurants, cheap Mexican food joints, sushi bars, health-food grocery outlets, a deli, head shops, clubs, vintage clothing and designer jewelry boutiques, local breweries, an artisans gallery, gay bars, pizza places, business offices, chain stores, comic book shops, spas, a nine-screen movie theater and an "art" film house. When I got to the corner of Pacific Garden and Cathcart Street, I passed a six-foot high cyclone fence with shattered wooden slats interwoven within the wire mesh (The slats were broken because bums used the wood for fires.). Through the openings in the fence, was a vacant lot with a huge crater surrounded by eight-foot high weeds where a building once stood. It had been a vacant lot for almost ten years. In 1989, on October 17 at 5:04 pm, the 7.1 Loma Prieta earthquake killed three people downtown, and took out over sixty shops and stores, giving some merchants a convenient opportunity to claim irreparable damage on their buildings, take the money from FEMA, level the structures, upgrade them, and cash out—a real bro deal for some. (One condemned landmarks, was the 1894 Cooper House, and had been retro-fitted *before* the quake but was condemned anyway. The building seemed pretty rock solid; crews took three days to demolish it with a wrecking ball the size of Guam. The Cooper House was replaced with a 100,000 square-foot, five story office building.). It was no longer the downtown I knew. Gone were all the distinct funky turn-of-the-century, low-level, Gothic and Victorian masonry-and-brick buildings with the cupolas and domed roofs. Gone were the meandering streets, big trees, over-grown brick planters, and courtyards. In went straight streets, walled into a tight hallway by sky-blocking, Art Deco, beige-colored, ogre-like buildings with Spanish mission touches, such as, arched entrance ways, and ceramic tile trim. These modern structures were easily four stories higher than their predecessors. They had chain stores on ground level and numerous offices or apartments on the upper floors. There was nothing genuine or distinctive about the new look, except that the buildings resembled plastic computer monitor casings. The new downtown was like the rest of Santa Cruz; it was renovated beyond repair. But there was one element the downtown revitalization couldn't alter: the *altered*. Pacific Garden Avenue was packed with a horde of full-time weirdos on a casting call for a movie nobody wanted to star in except them. The strip was shoulder high with a steady tide of grunge-looking gutterpunks, transient troubadours, burnout hippies in army fatigues, bubble-blowers, glass bottle and musical saw and spoon players, hackysack-kicking drug dealers, balloon-twisting clowns, jugglers, bad ventriloquists with ugly dummies, street poets, and incense-burning drifters dressed like gypsies—who looked like they had no future—and sat cross-legged with dirty feet on frayed hemp quilts and offered tarot card readings to tell you yours. Squatting, weaving, and sometimes staggering through this self-conscious circus, was the usual trail mix of lone shamans who torrentially muttered diatribes about God or conspiracies, and held torn chunks of cardboard with slogans written with shoplifted magic markers. Their dog-breath dementia was accompanied by street musicians who desolately stood with open guitar cases at their feet and moaned protest songs or badly composed love ballads, while World-Beaters played an absolutely unaccomplished fusion of congas, rainsticks, steel drums, rattles, djembes, Turkish darkbukas, gourds, or asthmatically blew into digeridoos, which I guess is an very large aborigine kazoo.

On every other corner, earnestly possessed political activists sat behind folding tables adorned with banners. Their eyes cast a spell of shame to coerce pedestrians into signing petitions on issues, such as supporting "Food Not Bombs," fighting US suppression in a Third World country, overturning the sentence of a black guy falsely imprisoned because of his race, the right of the homeless to sleep downtown or camp in a park, the need to "Free Tibet," legalizing medicinal or any kind of marijuana, and fighting a law that prevented street performers, panhandlers, as well as political tablers from being near a business entrance.

After I passed Upper Crust Pizza, I hurdled through the first sloshy wave of deadbeats. A pregnant, teenage girl sat on a street bench by a closed kiosk. She wore a faded high school jacket. She had oily, long brown hair, and a puffed out face that looked like it had been stung by something. A young, hungover punk, rested his stained-turbaned head in her lap. They twitched together. A drunken Mexican duo in dingy clothing wailed "My Funny Valentine" (which were the only words of the only song they knew). They were in their thirties. The man attempted to play the guitar. I couldn't tell if he was trying to sing, or if he was in pain because he couldn't disentangle his fingers from within the strings. His partner, showed a toothless smile as she kept time to another world on a rusty garbage can lid. The couple was passed by an I-and-I dreadlocked Rasta guy in a rainbow trimmed knit cap, which looked like a vacuum-cleaner bag. He who wore sunglasses, headphones, and some type of flowing African garb. Mr. I-and-I Rasta glided down the sidewalk, powered by acid and stardust. His dreadlocks looked like snakes made of lint. Near his head, his right hand held a one-foot space shuttle model, as if he were holding onto it and hitching a ride on its flight through Santa Cruz. Behind Mr. I-and-I's vapor trail was a woman in a red archer's cap with feather boa and a Lone Ranger mask. The closing act was a man in his twenties, who dressed and looked like Jesus Christ, but probably wasn't on speaking terms with His Father. The traveling messiah-without-a-following piously dragged a six-foot wooden cross on his shoulder. Actually, the retro savior wasn't really carrying the cross, he was *pulling* the cross—it had casters on its bottom, and a sponge cushion where the cross weighed on his shoulder, a foot rest, and round pegs for hand grips (Four options that weren't available on the original model.). When the guy passed me, a hole in the back of his robe revealed his swaying testicles, which were covered with a genital-type soot. My next hurdle was comprised of freelancing local characters: the panhandlers in front of the Whole Leaf Market, an organic food store, where the inorganic loitered. There were about fifteen of them and they occupied a stretch of about thirty feet. Most were able-bodied kids in their teens to mid-twenties dressed in black, tattooed, and heavily pierced. The skin-headed kids cultivated a world-weary gaze of contempt within the frame of a Goth street punk pose. Most looked like they had been shaken out of a dumpster. Their zone was filled with discarded coffee cups, half loaves of bread, candy wrappers, junk food bags, and open guitar cases. Most of the punks were high, wanted more of the high, or just bored or sick because they were neither. Some slurped free soup given to them at another corner, and tried to hit on passing girls by urging them to smile, while others belligerently ask women for change, and if denied, softly snarled, "Bitch." I couldn't care less about these kids' self-inflicted plight, and tried very hard to show it. A pale twenty-nothing girl with a rooster-comb Mohawk strip down the middle of her shaved head glared back at me. She was dressed in a black leather jacket with silver studs plastered with numerous slogan buttons, and loudly hawked a wad of mucous from deep in her throat and onto the sidewalk in front of my sandaled feet. I stopped. Above me, came a loud squawk. A lemon grazed my ear, and landed with a muffled thump in on the sidewalk. The fruit rolled in the gutter next to six other lemons with identical bite marks on them. I looked up at a thirty-partially-something scrawny guy dressed in torn shorts and a white T-shirt in a twenty-foot tree. The soles of his bare feet were black. He had a long brown beard, and a large, circular mass of uncombed bushy hair. He looked like he was a castaway who had been stranded on a deserted island for ten years. He pulled down a branch, plucked another lemon, bit into it, then angrily squawked and flicked the rejected fruit onto the sidewalk.

"Yo, Vic."

It was Marty Wormhold, who was a meter maid. He wore a white helmet. He stood next to his L-shaped, three-wheeled, traffic enforcement van, and happily wrote a ticket. Wormhold was in his late forties, weighed easily two-hundred-and-eighty pounds (none of it muscle) and could barely fit in his uniform, a white shirt tucked into a pair of khaki shorts. Not a pretty sight.

"Howz'it," I said listlessly.

"Eh, getting off to a good start," he said, pointing at the UCSC sticker on the rear window of a new SUV. "Oh yeah, UCSC, now you're making points with me." He grunted. "They can use their L.A. Daddy's Gold card to pay for this ticket."

Wormhold was a local. He never married. He lived above his parent's garage and took care of his aging Mom, and a younger brother who had Down's syndrome. The guy who pushed his Mom in a wheelchair through shopping aisles and took his 32-year old brother trick-or-treating was a nice guy, but didn't match up to the Wormhold. I was dealing with now. This was The Wormhold who called-into several conservative talk radio shows all the time, and complained about illegal immigrants, lesbians and gays, unions, and regularly criticized the 'progressive" Santa Cruz County Board of Supervisors in the Letters to The Editor section of the Santa Cruz Sentinel. I tried to avoid him. For a guy who was into talk radio, he never listened to what you had to say, nor would he ask. Wormhold just went off on a topic. He never left an opening because he wanted you to hear everything he had to say, and by talking rabidly, you couldn't get away from him, and had to hear it. I was trapped.

"It's gotten so bad in Santa Cruz these UCSC people now see themselves as locals. If anything, the college destroyed this town before the dot-comers made a run at it," said Wormhold. "When the University of California of Santa Cruz came in around 1965, the Chamber of Commerce thought it would mean more money for the local merchants. You know, inter-collegiate football and basketball games and stuff. But then the sixties hit, and what happened? The 2,000-acre campus overlooking the town became known as the 'People's Republic of Santa Cruz' with a voting block of radical students and faculty who booted out our locals in government and elected a slate of 'Progressives.' And what did they do? They prevented the construction of additional roads to get in and out of town on Highway One or Highway Seventeen because those routes would 'increase people's dependence on the car instead of taking mass transit.' This is a tourist town, the main thing is to get the people in and flush them out! And in the same breath those same progressives vote down renovating abandoned tracks in the Santa Cruz Mountains for a commuter rail system to San Jose because a railroad would increase housing and commercial development. Their solution to traffic problems is to remove side-street parking, eliminate car lanes, and put in bike lanes on major street arteries, causing even more traffic congestion. So, what do these great minds do? They think the increased traffic congestion justifies the need for even more bike lanes to reduce the number of cars. And what are their big claims to fame? They vote to keep the US Navy from bringing a destroyer into Monterey Bay on July 4th. Declare Santa Cruz a 'Nuclear-free' and 'Hate-free" zone. Make symbolic proclamations on national issues instead taking care of potholes and flooding. They supported feminist protesters and drove out the annual Miss California Beauty contest because the event 'degraded women into sexual objects.' But it's okay to have female muscle-building contests at the Civic Center because those events 'challenged the accepted sexual stereotypes of women in society' even though it's pretty obvious lesbians are going to see women reduced to cuts of meat *they* approved of."

"How's your Mom doing with the—"

"The supervisors are also big on hiking trails and public-right-of-ways through private property to get to parks," continued Wormhold, preventing my escape attempt., "One of my favorites moves of theirs is when these progressives wanted to 'promote understanding and international ties' by declaring a "sister city" in a foreign country, such as Alushta, Ukraine; Jinotepe, Nicaragua; Puerto La Cruz, Venezuela; Sestri Levante, Italy; or Shingu, Japan. Come on, what's that about? So some supervisor or a committee member can visit these distant sister cities on taxpayer or political junket money to represent Santa Cruz on a 'humanitarian mission'? They support anything that brings in more tourist and ruins the town for the locals—"

"I heard your brother is on a new medication that—"

"You know, none of this legislation would have happened without UCSC in the mix, " said Wormhold, who kept the same pace of anger throughout his speech. "I mean the way I see it. The influence of UCSC is a worse long-term threat to Santa Cruz than Cisco Systems or the dot-comers of Silicon Valley. UCSC has a steady turnover of more than 15,000 students, 3,800 staff people, and but only 5,000 parking spaces. There's planning, huh? It's the largest employer in the county. And what do they produce? Other people who graduate and want to work there! Oh yeah, they're going to make a better world. Then why don't they allow the voters to decide on who serves at the college? You know how big UCSC is legally allowed to grow?"

"I'm supposed to meet—"

"I'll tell you: 35,000 students! And that's in a town that already has 55,000 people. You can't tell me the college administrators' long-term goal isn't to increase their power and salaries by boosting student enrollment. Without consulting town officials or the electorate, the college leased a 172-bed Holiday Inn for a ten-year period to house undergraduates, and caused the city to lose hotel-tax revenues. State money taking local money! And even though UCSCers say they're environmentalists, the college is chopping down redwoods and plowing up agricultural campus land for parking garages, and dormitories."

"Huh, really. Cool, that's you. Nice, yeah, but I need—"

"And they develop the shoreline with marine labs. It's right near my Terrace Point trailer park, the residents thought it would be a nice thing to have. I warned them. One hundred and sixty thousand square feet later, they build this research center to study *their* Monterey Bay 'sanctuary.' What? So some grad student can make friends with a seal? And you know students aren't going to live in those labs. It'll be perk housing for faculty and administrators because of the lack of affordable ocean-views for MBAs in Santa Cruz. Didn't bother the researchers to ruin my ocean view! To UCSCers the bro deal is academic. As far as I'm concerned being enrolled at UCSC is like getting an all-day ride pass in Santa Cruz for five to seven years. It's okay to want to change the world when you're young, I made mistakes when I was young, but I have to live with mine. Why should I have to pay for the mistakes of someone else's youth every year? We're stuck with the consequences of their actions. The UCSCers just run up the taxpayer's bill for social programs, then they graduate, skip out and stick the locals with the tab."

I waited to see if he was done. I knew he didn't want to hear my opinion, and if I tried to say anything, he'd launch into another tirade, and anyone who heard him, would think I was his friend. What was amusing is Wormhold's political beliefs didn't deter him from taking a job with the county for the medical benefits and the retirement plan. He hated all people moving into Santa Cruz and raising property values, but he was indebted to them for his job. After the rich Instant Locals occupied their McMansions, or set up business offices downtown, they circulated petitions to prevent anyone else from parking in their neighborhoods. The Supervisors ruled the roads were public, however, in the public's interest of preventing traffic congestion and the abuse of parking, the board agreed to put up permit-only parking signs, and sold those permits, which meant even if you lived in the town, you had to pay to buy a permit to park in another section of town (Wormhold told me the only ones who didn't have to pay for parking were the Supervisors, because they made the law.). And what did you get in return for your parking fees? You created a job for Wormhold, who would ticket you. Wormhold lived to ticket anyone—one time, he came into the shop on his lunch break and boasted how he ticketed parents who illegally parked their cars in front of a pre-school when they ran in to get their kids. He said the kids should wait outside. When I said the parents probably didn't want their six-year old kid standing outside on the street where a dirtball might abduct them, Wormhold just laughed and defended himself by grunting the parents deserved tickets anyway, claiming they were just SUV-driving Soccer Moms who cut him off in traffic while they talked on cell phones and balanced Grande Starbucks lattes on their knees. He was an asshole.

In Wormhold's eagerness to give the UCSCer a ticket, he was filling it out while there was still time left on the parking meter.

"You can't write a ticket until the meter expires, right?"

"Eh, it's a minor detail that will resolve itself in two minutes," said Wormhold, writing down the license plate number.

Just then, a white face-painted clown with orange hair, a round red nose, an American-Flag jumpsuit, and a jacket covered with balloons, stopped, and put a quarter in the meter.

"Whoopee!" the clown said in a high-pitched cartoon voice. He squeezed off an air-horn honk, and waddled off in huge, floppy, orange shoes. "Feed a meter. Power to the people."

"Hey, clown," said Wormhold, furious.

"How do you know he's not the guy who owns the car?" I asked. "He *looks* like a UCSC student to me."

"No, it's this clown who calls himself Mr. Twisted, he's been feeding meters on me all morning," Wormhold growled. "I had him arrested for doing that yesterday. It's against the law to feed people's parking meters without permission. He twists balloon animals for kids at the Farmer's Market on Wednesdays. I'm going to sic the cops on him there."

"Good place to handcuff a clown, in front of children."

"Yeah, he's—"

There was a squawk from above. A lemon whizzed down in a yellow blur and conked Wormhold in the helmet.

"Hey!" Wormhold shouted and looked up at the squawking, treed castaway, who hissed at him.

"Later," I said, getting ready to shoot the rapids of tourist-and-customer frightening street-wise weirdos.

A panhandler blocked my way. I stopped.

"Yo, rookie, can you lend me a few bucks?" said this huge pear-shaped bum. She was in her late fifties. Just another one of the homeless who somehow managed to be broke but remain perpetually fat in Santa Cruz. She had stringy hair on her small head. Her round face had blotches of long whiskers growing from it. She wore a torn ruffled skirt and a stained shirt you could see through. She didn't wear a bra. I don't know what kept her alive.

Some people disliked the panhandlers, but I enjoy turning down people for money who I don't like .

"Can't help you."

"Fuck you," she replied instinctively.

“Yo, Vic, having difficulties with the residentially challenged?” asked a familiar voice followed by a laugh.

I walked toward Officer Kim. She was dressed in khaki shorts and a white shirt. She was in her mid-thirties, thin. I shaped her an 8’6” egg to surf Scotts Creek. She stood alongside a mountain bike near a passed out drunk, who was lying in the alcove. Officer Kim checked to make sure no one was looking but me, then she withdrew an Ace of Spades out of her pocket and flicked it on the drunk. “Death card,” she said, laughing. She held up an entire deck of playing cards, and every one was an Ace of Spades. “When I worked graveyard we’d flick them on the drunks. Old habits die hard.”

The bum grumbled at me, “I don’t need you or anybody.”

“El Diña, that’s enough!” said Officer Kim.

“Nazi,” growled El Diña, who stomped away in her dirty sneakers towards the Metro bus station.

“Ah,” Officer Kim smiled and said to me. “That’s the third time I’ve been called a Nazi, and I’ve been called a fascist five times. God bless you, El Diña! You know that new outfit you have really brings out the dilation in your eyes.” She said to me. “What a joke, huh? She’s one of the many CEOs of bumdom in this town. She gets free bus passes. And when her clothes smell so bad they wouldn’t let her read magazines and sneaking her shot of Wacky Jack in the public library, church groups give her clothes. She gets food vouchers, free groceries, or a meal at one of three soup kitchens. But she doesn’t *need* anybody. Right.”

The drunk who was supposedly passed out at Officer Kim’s feet sullenly mumbled, “I don’t need anybody either.”

“Yeah,” said Kim to the drunk. “That’s why you dialed 911 didn’t you, DiTomasso? Said you were suicidal. I come down here. You act passed out so you can get taken to the hospital on a thousand-dollar ambulance ride to sleep it off in the emergency ward.” She looked at me and said, “DT here, gets his three hots and a cot, he’ll get released without charges because the system won't earn any money from processing him.” She laughed. “He’s been arrested over four hundred times, right DT?”

“Hey, today’s Tuesday, right?” asked the drunk. “That means tomorrow is pancakes.”

Kim laughed and said, "See, he knows the jail menu!"

"I saw some guy throwing lemons at people from a tree near the market."

"Oh yeah, Doylie, he's auditioning for the current bro deal."

"Auditioning?"

"Yeah, for SSI—Social Security Income. El Diña's an SSI CEO. They teach each other how to get it. The trolls act like they're crazy, so the county gives them four hundred dollars a month disability. Then the trolls fake like they have a back injury to qualify for pain medication. They turn around and sell their medication on the street. An $800 a month total. They use it to pay for booze or drug of choice. Yeah, get their Methadone at the county building on Emeline, then chip it with heroin by the railroad bridge at the boardwalk. Each bum you see is on file with the county. They're all accounted for. We know their names, meds, who they hang out with. Blows my mind. Amazing. The bums panhandle us and the county panhandles the taxpayers. Santa Cruz, the city built on bro dealers." She snorted. "Awhile ago, I read an article about a longhaired local surfer harassing women in Good Times." She paused. "The woman who wrote the article came down and filed a complaint on you. But I handled that particular case. She's sitting there saying how she was in the water and didn't do anything. She assumed I'd take her side. From talking to her, I figured out she burned you. I asked why she burned you and she said, 'What does that have to do with anything?' I said, 'Because you lied in your report. You said you didn't do anything, and you did do something.' She got all mad and wrote another complaint to my Captain. I explained it to him. He took my side. But there are other cops who are new and not from here and don't know anything about surfing. They would have gone after you. Fortunately, she met me first."

"I haven't seen you in the water that much."

"I got hurt," she said, slightly wincing. "I responded to a bar fight call at The Crepe Bistro and a drunk bull dyke took me down and screwed up my back. And what was funny is, I'm a dyke. I mean come on!" She laughed. "I'm white, part Native American, Mexican, and a lesbian, if there's ever a riot. I'll never get hurt because I can take either side." I couldn't help but laugh.

She was so chipper about bad things. She muttered to me, "Here comes yet another fine citizen from the deep."

A bum approached us. He wore a soiled tie-dyed shirt and jeans, and carried a scepter tipped with a tiny silver rodent head. He looked like he had been turned inside out while wearing his clothes. He had a frayed, black cap with mouse ears.

"Hey, Officer Kim," the bum said shyly.

"Hi, Wayner, what's up?"

"I just got reviewed by my case worker and they said I was a diabetic, and changed my medication."

"That's a good thing, right?"

"Well, I've been presenting myself as a schizophrenic," Wayner replied. He genuinely seemed disconcerted.

Nearby, six UCSC students were staring with a combination of disbelief and disapproval at the headlines of front pages within the newspaper vending machines. One UCSCer moved to the slot with a two quarters, but hesitated, as if depositing the coin and opening the door would contaminate their perfect Santa Cruz existence with current events from the outside world.

Wayner left us, quickly walked over to the students and said, "Why lie? I want a beer."

The students were charmed and gave money to Wayner.

An ambulance cruised down the street. Officer Kim waved it over. The EMTs got out and came over.

"Showtime DT," said Officer Kim. "Your limo's arrived."

A trio of UCSC girls dressed like peasants and wearing African masks leaped and danced past us. They clanged finger cymbals, shook bells, and banged mallets on tongue drums. I wouldn't really call it dancing, they looked like they were being dragged across the sidewalk by parachutes.

"I guess they're getting in touch with their white middle-class roots," said Officer Kim. "It's like everyone comes from all over to Santa Cruz just to be stupid." She walked away, smirking. "I'm not a cop anymore, I'm a game warden. There are trans *trans* gendered people here. Halloween is the only day they're properly dressed for. Yesterday, I busted a clown for putting quarters in expired parking meters. A clown! I think the Supervisors are afraid he'll develop political ambition. The day before, I had to bust UCSC women demonstrating against The Gap by going topless. Drew a big crowd of bums, who I don't think really got the social significance of the protesters' message. The day before, I collared a punk for throwing pieces of bread in the sidewalk at people. Today, I busted a woman who was protesting a fashion show at the Civic Center. She dressed in cold cuts—and the meat looked better than she did." She nodded at a thin, white guy in his mid-thirties, who had a crew cut, and dressed in a pressed gray conservative suit with a clean white shirt and red tie, and scuffed brown dress shoes. He had blue mascara on his eyes. Officer Kim cautiously whispered to me without moving her lips, "That guy is the only one who really freaks me out down here."

"Why does he freak you so much?"

"Because he's not *trying* to be weird."

I laughed.

"Yeah, I don't get that many bum at my shop because there isn't a recycling center nearby."

A dispatcher voice came out of the squawk box on Kim's belt said, "A lifeless person on a park bench in front of The Logos Bookstore."

"'Lifeless'. A drunk. Probably El Diña," she said, mounting her bike. "Today a troll OD'd on heroin in a Porta Potty, shoulda buried him in the damn thing."

"Watch out for lemons."

"Tell me about it," she said pedaling away. "And clowns."

I went into the StokaMocha and waited in line for Andrea's coffee. It was a UCSC bistro playpen. The students were just a blurred swarm of knapsacks, used books, bikes, and glares, who lived in a world of semesters, consortiums, co-ops, syllabuses, and roommates who didn't do their dishes. The students made a hard-core effort to be unattractive and even less sexually identifiable. And, I actually couldn't tell if it was an improvement or not. I mean in Vietnam we would have gotten written up for doing to a gook corpse what these people willingly inflicted upon themselves— piercings, tattoos, partially shaved heads, or test-pattern hair dye jobs. I stood by a table of typical too-hip-to-shit UCSC students. One was a blonde dreadlocked, nineteen-year old guy, who inexplicably wore an over-sized, droopy, red-and-white striped three-foot high worm of a hat, modeled on the one worn in the Dr. Seuss story "Cat-In-The-Hat." He also had on a UCSC T-shirt and its banana slug mascot on it. With his looks, I could see why he favored creatures that left slime trails. Cat-In-The-Hat's girlfriend wore a nose ring and had a blue barb-wire tattoo wrapped around her upper right arm. She had cropped hair, dyed red and blue. She wore a midi T-shirt, bellbottoms, and 70's-era high-platform clogs that were ridiculous now, and were ridiculous back then. She was a little too heavy to be wearing a midi. Her slight gut rolled over and formed a puffy ledge over her jean belt. Her navel piercing looked like an air valve. When she leaned forward in her chair, I could see a winged tattoo above her butt crack. She chewed on an avocado-and-sprouts fajita and stared off at nothing.

Cat-In-The-Hat held up an issue of City On The Hill, a UCSC weekly newspaper nobody but students read. It had a picture of Ralph Nader on the cover. Behind Nader was a circle and a slash imposed over the words 'Cisco Systems.'

"'We are dealing with corporate narcissists who are expanding their corporate activities and enriching themselves personally with stock options and other executive compensations on an ocean of corporate welfare,'" said Cat-In-The Hat, quoting Nader out loud. "Nader is right. If that guy runs for President in 2000 I'm voting for him. There's a guy who represents change." Cat-In-The-Hat looked around, obviously hoping a nearby dot-comer would overhear his remarks and engage him in a debate. But no one rose from behind the cover of a laptop screen to debate him. So, he just loudly continued. "Cisco claims they are designing the site around mass transportation. What a joke. So why are they building 22,000 parking spaces for an employee facility, and sticking their hands out for state and federal welfare to build an infrastructure that will include widening The 101 to six lanes? Those people with their dot-com millions will ruin the character of Santa Cruz. Dot-comers are financially and gravitationally ruining the UCSC campus. We have hyper-competitive Asians students. They're against student evaluations and want courses to have grades. Grades only prove people test well!"

"You're being judgmental," Clogs said.

"What's that mean?" replied Cat-In-The-Hat, who spotted me, but pretended not to recognize me.

Judgmental? I could give these UCSCers a good example of being judgmental right now. I recognized them. Two years ago, I used to live next door to Cat-In-The-Hat and Clogs. They were in UCSC house on the Westside, near Bay and Escalona, which was just down from the college. They were two of ten roommates in the house rented to them by professor Gerry Paton, who taught 'Advanced Logic,' and had underpaid teacher's aides do his class work, while he kept his job by writing an academic paper for a journal no one would read. Paton lived in subsidized faculty housing on campus. This bro deal, in addition to his salary, gave the professor enough disposable income to pursue a student-housing slumlord degree. Long before the dot-com boom, Patton, and other faculty members, purchased rundown, residential homes, and charged enormously high rents to students, who paid $750-a-month a piece, lived ten in a house, and had loud parties that started at two in the morning. Their buddies left parked vehicles on the block for weeks until I started smashing out car windows. At the end of the school year, I caught Cat-In-The-Hat and Clogs trying to leave their mattresses and art projects in my back yard. And like a lot of UCSCers, they abandoned their dogs and cats, which were taken to animal shelters, but because the pets weren't easily adoptable puppies or kittens, the older animals were euthanized. No wonder the UCSCers pretended they didn't see me.

I stood at the counter, but the help ignored me. The staff, three heavily pierced, tattooed, and pale young women, had slight pot bellies, but still wore midi tops and low-waisted jeans, which made their upper hips looked like yeast-expanding dough. The staff ignored the growing line of customers, sang along with Aimee Mann and talked to each other about what dance club they were going to tonight with their roommates. Their backs were turned to me. When they stood next to each other, their three individual eighteen-inch horizontal tattoos that ran along the base of their spines, stitched together into a pattern sample of the wallpaper in Satan's master bedroom. The register had a picture of the guy in 'Eraserhead' and below it were two neatly typed signs, "Bathrooms closed due to vandalism," and "No checks or credit accounts." Near the register, was a tip jar filled with a gallon of water, containing dollar bills and a mound of change; a sign on it said "Support Counter Intelligence."

Finally, one of the sad-eyed ladies of the lowlands approached the counter and blankly stared at me, as if she were waiting for me to serve her. She had a silver hoop in her septum aligned with a matching hoop through her purple, upper lip.

"Why is your tip jar filled with water?" I asked.

"So people can't easily grab and steal the jar."

"The trolls, you mean.'

"Trolls?"

"The bums."

She looked harshly at me and said, "They're people too."

"Oh, sure," I said, noticing her pearl tongue stud.

"I think it's good that the homeless are downtown, it brings attention to the issue," she said, glaring.

"Nice," I said. "A large French Roast without a glare, please."

"That's $1.75," she said, taking my five-dollar bill.

She gave me change. I kept it. I stood there. She indirectly looked at me, but threw in a splash in a of contempt. I stared at her silver hoops and wondered if she could double as a shower curtain. An immensely depressing Greg Brown song played.

"Where's my French Roast?" I asked.

"You're 'The Fool.'" she replied.

"I'm the fool, *hombre*?" I asked, flaring on my stinkeye

"You're coffee is under 'The Fool' card," she said, pointing to a co-worker, who was ghosted replica of herself. The pale girl poured boiling water into one of ten coffee-filled filters, which were positioned in a stainless steel shelf at the far corner of the counter. Each dripping filter had a paper cup below it. Above each cup was a different face card, that identified each order.

As I waited for the coffee cup to fill, the UCSCers conversations dripped onto my brain: "that question promotes stereotypes....I was playing pinball. And using the flippers the ball come through it forming a perfect Pascal triangle...That might be another way to write your thesis...I haven't decided on marine biology or being a ski instructor... Tomorrow is my mid-term for dance...I'm conflicted...How would you describe okra to someone who is living in France?" The coffee cup was just three-quarters full. I couldn't handle hearing these people. UCSCers were dot-comers without the software. I was afraid the grad student talking about okra was going to elaborate on another topic. I grabbed the cup and fled.

I stood on the sidewalk near a sushi kiosk between Stokamoka and Le Nick. I watched the crowd go by. Not everyone was a nose-ring freak, an obnoxious UCSC student, or a bum. I saw happy shoppers, families, couples, kids, people-watching tourists, and locals whose names I didn't know. And I thought, if I didn't surf I would think Santa Cruz with its Mediterranean climate was the greatest place in the world. I mean, these people were clearly happier than me, and I grew up here. They competed in wharf-to wharf outrigger or running races, sand castle contests or clam chowder cook-offs. They camped at Cowells or Big Basin, hiked through Pogonip, mountain biked at the Wilder Ranch, bird-watched and kayaked at the Elkhorn Slough, took pictures of elephant seals at Año Nuevo, and admired the Monarch butterflies coating the eucalyptus trees at Natural Bridges. These people ate at all the different restaurants, checked out bands at clubs, went to see plays and lectures and visiting artists at UCSC and fundraisers, and supported the Kuumbwa jazz society, and were friends of the library. They visited touristy things like The Mystery Spot, or the boardwalk, and got their faces painted at whatever county fair or art-&-wine festival was happening that month, ate at Fire Department pancake breakfasts, and shopped for organic foods at Farmer's Markets. They day-tripped to look for jade in Big Sur, skin dived in Monterey, knocked around San Francisco. They toured old Spanish missions, historical sites, museums, the Monterey Aquarium, the Mount Hamilton observatory, and Hearst Castle in San Simeon. They checked out the Garlic Festival in Gilroy, the Begonia Festival in Capitola, the Santa Cruz Blues Festival, the AT&T Pebble Beach golf tournament, the Salinas Air Show, Woodies On The Wharf, the Half Moon Bay Pumpkin Festival, the lighted boat parade at the yacht harbor around Christmas time, and First Night New Year's Eve celebrations. They attended professional games at 3Com, the San Jose arena, Candlestick, and the Oakland Coliseum. They sailed, fished, golfed, disc golfed, played tennis, and went skiing at Lake Tahoe. My feeling about those activities was simple: it kept those types of people out of the water.. All I wanted to do was surf my waves. That was the sole reason I lived here. I was a surfer.

"I don't need this job. I make over $165,000 a year," trumpeted a dot-com geek. He stood with his date at a kiosk and wolfed down a California roll. "See that Targa? Mine," boasted the geek. "I went to the Porsche dealership and said I wanted red. He informed me they didn't have that color in stock. I said, 'I came to buy a red Targa and I want it now.' The salesman said, 'It'll take two weeks.' I said, 'I'll give you twenty five thousand dollars more if you have it by the end of the day.' I got it."

"You must be very important," said a six-foot Asian woman who had lustrous long black hair down to her hips. She was thin but had large breasts. She wore a sleek, short, black dress.

"I'm a millionaire with my stock options. I have a killer stock portfolio," the geek nasally said. "And I'm bright! I do it for the challenge. By the time I'm thirty I will have enough money to build out and form my own company. No one will ever tell me what to do. I'll call the shots. I'll be the next billionaire. Those are the people in this world who make the difference."

I couldn't believe a woman that hot—or, any woman, could listen to this idiot go on about himself. Then I flashed on her shoes: unpolished white come-fuck-me pumps with scuffed heels. I've seen women who wore shoes like that when I went on R&R in Thailand. Those shoes also explained why the woman wore a little bit too much make-up, and why her dress was pilling and had dust balls on it. and why she had large breasts on her small frame. I realized why the great Zander wasn't referring to himself in the third person. The all powerful IT didn't want anyone to see he was downloading a hooker. He saw me and quickly walked away.

"Huh," I grunted.

A minute later I felt a hard shove on my shoulder. I turned. It was Andrea. At first, I didn't recognize her. Andrea had dyed her hair blonde and wrapped it back into a thick ponytail. She wore bluejeans, sandals, and a Vic's Surf Shop T-shirt. She was trying to look just like me.

"Wassup! Sorry, I'm late, but every three feet I had to step over an open guitar case," she said. "I felt like singing, 'Tiptoe Through The Burnouts.'" I laughed. "I'm on a date with a my surfer person." She paused. "So, see anything interesting?"

"Nah, same old same old," I said, handing her the coffee.

I didn't say anything about Zander, if that's what the poor guy had to do to get laid, it was his business. When I looked to see if Zander was still around, I noticed all the guys eyeing Andrea. She was dressed ratty. But she still stopped everyone. I kept thinking I've never been out with a woman this beautiful.

"Everywhere I go, when I say I surf, everyone is surprised. They say, 'Wow, and you're a *girl*?'" she said. "Let's queue."

We stood in line. I smelled sandalwood. I turned. The two UCSCers, Cat-In-The-Hat and Clogs, stood behind us. They were two of the many reasons I rarely ever went to this place. The moviegoers were usually UCSC maggots, professor types, trannies, and dot-comers. Le Nick had four screens. The theaters were small. The rows tight, The sodas watery. But the popcorn had real butter. Le Nick's staple was a steady bill of campy midnight flicks, documentaries, coming-of-age movies, animation or film festivals dealing with gays and lesbians, revivals of a director's work , women-discovering-themselves-as-women dramas (which always had a guy getting punched or hit in the balls and a woman's first 'real' orgasm), along with your basic out-of-focus, avant-garde foreign movies with too many subtitles, and bad plots but had artistically choreographed violence, sex, masturbation, and a racist rant—that was supposed to show how racism was wrong, but played to it, plus vomiting (as part of a drug withdrawal or overdose scene). I really hated being here.

The attendant in the ticket booth was a squat but firm woman in her twenties who was cultivating a real mustache and goatee.

Andrea gave off an oh-my-God expression of disbelief, covered her mouth with her hand, looked away from the ticket booth, and quipped, " I guess the circus downsized their bearded lady staff, because they had to give a raise to The Frog Man." She paused. "Nice to see her off leash."

I laughed.

"This is trippy," Andrea said excitedly, pointing to a poster of 'The Birds in the coming attractions window, which was one of the films being shown in a Hitchcock Film Festival. "Check this out, it's so ep! There's my car! It's exactly the same. My gull-wing Mercedes. It's the one Tippi Hedren drove." She pointed at a newspaper article near the poster. "This is so *kewl*, 'The Birds' movie is based on a real-life incident that happened here!"

Within the display window, above a newspaper clipping, was an introductory card that read: "'The Birds,' directed by Alfred Hitchcock, who became a local resident in 1940, when he paid $40,000 for a 200-acre ranch at the end of Canham Road in Scotts Valley. The 1963 film is based on a story of the same name by Daphne du Maurier. But two years earlier, the seed for making the movie came from a real life bird invasion in the Pleasure Point area of Santa Cruz." Below the introductory card, was an yellowed newspaper clipping from the Santa Cruz Sentinel, which was dated August 18, 1961.

Seabirds Attack Santa Cruz

by Dave Dunleavy

After feasting on anchovies, thousands of sooty shearwaters, flew kamikaze style into shore side buildings from Pleasure Point to Rio del Mar during the night.

Around 3 AM, Pleasure Point and Capitola residents were awakened by birds slamming against their homes. Residents rushed out with flashlights, but rushed back inside after hundreds of birds flew toward the light. At sunrise, thousands upon thousands of dead, and stunned seabirds littered the streets. Disgorged fish covered the roofs and lawns, leaving an overpowering stench.

Mike McMahon, UCSC zoologist explained what caused the bird invasion, "The shearwaters in their frenzy of feeding, picked up a bacteria from the anchovies. They feed in flocks, when the fog came in, they became confused and headed for whatever lights they could see, such as streetlights, and overhead house lights. Their frenzy killed them."

A flock of dot-comers swooped by the movie line carrying shopping bags and drinking smoothies. They resembled looters more than shoppers. They slowly walked in the middle of the sidewalk, obstructing anyone who tried to get around them. The digital packet twittered on cell phones or to someone in their group. There was an underlying edge of sophisticated one-upsmanship to the way they pelted each other with high-flying titles, places, name-dropping, price tags, or on what they owned, or what they bought, or would soon buy...

"In France we stayed at the Tour D'Argeant—"

"You haven't been to The Royal Palms, Eden Rock?"

"You must go to Saint Barts."

"Have you been to Pac Bell Park in The City? It's hard to get tickets. We *know* someone. They stopped serving beer after the seventh inning. 'Since when?,' I asked. They said, 'Ten years!'"

"I traded in my wedding ring for a platinum one."

"You think your car is hot? In November, Derrick is getting a Mercedes, it's so over-the-top."

In the center of the scouring flock, a black-military-shoe-khaki-pants-dot-com-logo-ed-polo-shirt guy geek, who had a trimmed smudge of a chin beard, angular glasses, spiked-and-jelled short hair, bent over and sneezed without covering his mouth. It was gross. I could see the spray. The group didn't mind it.

"Look at those dot-comers," contemptuously said Cat-In-The-Hat. "They're so hypocritical. They think they're above everyone else. They live in a bubble. They're libertarians. They don't want government regulating them. They think they're independent of everything. They act like they invented the web. The U.S. Defense Department developed the Internet."

"Yeah, but you don't like government either," said Clogs.

"I'm a secular humanist," The Cat-In-The-Hat said.

Andrea hungrily rose to the UCSCer's baited remarks and defensively added, "Excuse me but *I'm* one of those people,"

"So I have an opinion?" snapped back Cat-In-The-Hat, whose eyes began to gleam because he provoked someone into an argument. "Even with the Cisco campus they say it's for research and development—"

"And..." said Andrea, sarcastically.

"Cisco doesn't research and develop anything, they purchase technologies developed by other people," said Cat-In-The-Hat, who lived to increase the intensity of his hostility. "The guys who founded the company lifted it from research funded at Stanford, Gates purchased DOS, the Netscape guy was accused of stealing browser technology developed by other associates—"

"Your point?"

"All you are is a bunch of marketers who produce nothing and consume everything—"

"Whatever," Andrea said, looking away.

Cat-In-The-Hat was still incensed, and retorted to Andrea, "'Whatever,' what and oh-so original retort."

Clogs laughed.

Andrea responded with a caffeine-laced bitchy screed, "You two go to UCSC, don't you? That's funny, you don't *look* like someone who goes to UCSC. I like the dreadlocks—you must be one of those trust-fundafarians? Oh, by the way Dr. Seuss, getting the cobweb tattoo for your elbow. Hold me back! No one's ever thought of that one before! I mean why are you two here? Couldn't find eight more people to make a drum circle?" She shifted to Clogs. "And FYI, pudgy, I really like the barb-wire tattoo around the arm. I mean I've never seen that oh-so-original one before either! Did you come up with it all by yourself? Or did you bump into someone else in a mosh pit at a ska show and it smeared on you?" She paused. "And I'd rethink the nose ring, dear. I mean it's a nice look if you want your head to look like a hand grenade. And what's that tattoo say above your butt crack? 'Contents may have settled during shipping'?" She paused. "You know, I can see what you two have in common—a brain cell."

"Oh, like is that a shot?" Clogs asked, staring blankly.

"What are you going to do, girlfriend? Hit me?" Andrea jeered, leaning her beak an inch away from Clog's nose.

The UCSCers turned away. I was stunned. I'd never seen a woman rip somebody apart like that.

"Boy, you went off," I said as we got our tickets.

"Fucking UCSC maggots," she scowled and snorted. "Telling me where to get off, that's just not happenin'."

God, I thought, she's even starting to talk like me.

The art film, "Drury Redux," was about an alcoholic career woman building a huge mansion with a swimming pool. It was set in Westport, Connecticut, which must be a horrible place because everyone seemed to be drinking a lot, trying to cheat on each other, and thought indoor tennis was fun. I knew I wasn't going to like the film right away, because the opening soundtrack was cello music, and the cello is the most depressing sounding thing ever invented. You want to put me in a bad mood, play a cello. Fuck the cello. Anyway, it was about the Drury family, Kate Drury, a career woman who becomes a success, has a huge office at the World Trade Center, and commutes back to her home. But her professional achievement has been at the expense of her teenage daughter, who she has neglected. The daughter is "bi-polar," resentful, turns to drugs, and becomes a "lipstick" lesbian, which I guess is an off-duty heterosexual because the other lesbians didn't really accept her. The daughter was close to her dog, which was the only time I liked her and the movie. At the end, the mother finds the daughter standing on the high dive above the mansion's empty, newly built swimming pool. The two have a verbal confrontation I didn't pay attention to. Then the daughter—to either prove her point or win the argument—jumps into the empty pool and dies. In the last shot, the mother wails, clings to her lifeless daughter, and rocks back and forth at the bottom of the concrete pool. Heavy cello music.

"What did you think?" Andrea excitedly said as we walked to her car, which was parked in front of 'The 99'.

"The popcorn was good, sodas watery."

"No, what did you think of the movie?"

"What happened to her dog? She seemed so close to him."

"The dog? It just didn't fit into the flow of the story."

"So, life doesn't have flow. If something flows then it isn't the whole story. If it's too smooth, it's a lie. When I got out of the service and was bumming around for a year just surfing, I didn't fit in after I got back from Vietnam. I was just getting by, catching up on the waves that I missed, and living in an old slant-six Plymouth Valiant by the Lighthouse at The Lane. I lent my car to Zipperhead who had to take his girlfriend to the eye doctor and he rolled it. And there I was with no skills, and living out of garages because I didn't know too many people anymore." I paused. "Those Valiants run forever, I still see them on the road. In a way, I don't think I ever recovered from that moment."

"But the dog wasn't really the main point of the movie," Andrea said, slightly exasperated. "Well, how did you feel about the movie?" she added in a probing way, as if she were trying to extract an emotion from me.

"The movie was depressing," I said. "You were even crying"

"It's supposed to be depressing."

"You go to a movie and *expect* to cry?"

"It's about a woman who pays the price for self-involvement. She never connected to her daughter. Sometimes you can never connect—ever. That's the price."

"Yeah, I got that," I said, pausing. "Plus, I hate cellos, they're always depressing and put me in a foul mood."

"Yo Yo Ma isn't depressing. Have you heard his music?"

"No, but if he plays the cello I'm not going to listen to him."

Andrea laughed, shook her head, and we walked in silence for a few steps.

"The film has more going for it than just a war movie."

"Hey," I said and shrugged. "All I know is I paid seven dollars a ticket to see a movie to find out that life isn't worth living. Now that seems really dumb to me. I feel good after a shoot'em up."

"Well, why would a veteran go to see a war movie if Vietnam was so horrible?"

"I guess, for the same reason someone who had a shitty family would go see a movie about a shitty family where someone commits suicide. It's something you went through."

"The movie we saw is all about irony," said Andrea.

"Irony?"

"Yeah," she confidently said. "People become the enemy they fight against, and as a result, they end up losing everything anyway. That's the irony."

"So you think irony is something that's permanent?"

"Yeah."

"Huh, I guess you have to go to college to believe that."

She found this funny.

We came upon another group of UCSCers who were reading the headlines in the window of the newspaper vending machine. "I can't stand people who do this," Andrea said and strutted over to them. She put two coins in the machine and handed a Santa Cruz Sentinel to a student. "Here, live on the edge, it only costs fifty cents." She strutted away, rejoined me, and pulled out her cell phone, which was cherry red and smaller than the last one she had. "I have to check my voice mails." She stopped and listened. I stood to her side on the curb.

Cat-In-The-Hat and Clogs walked around us. He mimicked Andrea on a cell phone. He muttered an inaudible crack to Clogs, who laughed. Without looking, the oblivious UCSCers stepped into a crosswalk in front of a moving car, which slammed its brakes. When they went by the stopped car, and saw the driver glaring in disgust, the two walked even slower to irritate him.

"Walking here," Cat-In-The-Hat said, scolding the driver.

"You can be so sarcastic," said Clogs, laughing.

"Yes, but only on a verbal level," replied Cat-In-The-Hat.

"Let's go to The Catalyst," said Clogs as they left, "then hit the Palomar, and finish out at the Red Room for lemon drops."

Andrea clicked off her cell phone, put it back in her purse, nickered and said, "Ehhhh-xcellent. One of our angel investors came through and we're getting a second round of funding."

"Wait. You don't stay in business by selling anything? People just give you money?"

"It keeps the company going. You—"

"Darlin', I need an angel too," interrupted a breath of scotch with a voice. It was a bum, whose clothing resembled weather stripping. He held out his dirty hand.

"Oh yeah, like that's going to happen," Andrea said scornfully.

"I know what you are," said the bum. "A dot-com yuppie."

"I'm not a yuppie," Andrea huffily replied, stamping her foot.

The bum intently peered at her and calmly asked, "Do you have a pasta machine?"

She was quiet.

"Yuppie," he victoriously said, smiling. "See? You are! You are!" He wandered off, and said to the next pedestrian, a UCSC student. "I need an angel." The kid flipped him a buck. The dirty hand got a handout. The bum shot a thumbs-up to Andrea and said with a gray-toothed smile, "Darlin', thanks for the tip. As long as there's angels the devils will always be in business."

Andrea didn't notice. She had a habit of never looking back. Out of nowhere, she asked me, "Do you own your building?"

"I rent," I said, surprised at the question. "Why?"

"You can do more with it. You need a plan."

"A plan?"

"The first thing you have to take care of is paying yourself."

"How do you pay yourself? What does that mean?"

"Real estate is a good place to park your money."

"Park? The only thing I park now is my new van," I said and proudly pointed at it.

"Wow! That's huge! Your van is bigger than Weever's," she said, running over to peak through the passenger window. "Why do you keep you're windows down? People could—"

Ranger's head came halfway out of the window. She had both paws on the edge of the door and barked roughly. Andrea was startled. She jerked away from the door. I laughed.

"It's okay, Range," I said, petting her. "Whups, Daddy is going to get you an ice cream sundae with a lot of whip cream." I said to Andrea. "She loves whip cream. All dogs love whip cream. When I go to ice cream parlors I get two sundaes, and they ask, 'Why two?' And I say, 'One for me. One for my dog.'"

"That animal sure likes you a lot," Andrea said in a queasy way. She pressed her lips together. Her attractiveness hardened into a rough look that took the beauty out of her face. I think she sensed this. She pulled away from it, nervously laughed and flipped her ponytail.

"We always had a dog when I was growing up," I said, scratching Ranger's chest harder. Her left leg thumped. "I've always been a dog guy. Some people say they want a dog, but they have back-yard dogs. They go to work and keep them in the back yard. You have to be with your dog. My Mom got me the dog. After Mom passed, my Dad treated me worse than a dog. 'Go away, go outside.' That's all he said. I was just a kid—nine years old, and it's winter, and it'd be dark and he'd say, 'Stay outside.' It was nighttime. He'd tell me to go outside." I paused. "Just so he drink and could have his girlfriends over. He always sat in his Barco-lounger watching TV. When he wanted another beer he'd crunch his empty beer can and say, 'Slap, another brew.' He hated Slap. I always talked about Slap's shop."

"Slap?"

"He was the one who owned the surf shop in the sixties when I hung out there all the time. That's the building you're in."

"Your Dad felt threatened. Slap was your father figure."

"I don't think so, I had a father, and one was enough. And if he was like a father to me, I'd have known it. When my Dad got mad at me because I wouldn't do something his way, he'd thump me in the head with his gold ring." I held up my finger. "This ring. He made it when he was on a ship in the Merchant Marine. He took a twenty-dollar gold piece and banged around its edges with a spoon to make the band come up, and then he drilled a hole in the middle of it. When he died, I got the ring. We had him cremated. During his funeral service, for some reason I remembered how he would always get drunk and criticize other people. He always kept on telling us the Hartmans, our neighbors across the street, weren't happy. You should have seen these neighbors. Their kids had great clothes. They had a nice car. They kept up their house—you know, painted and all, nice lawn, bushes. And they went to Disneyland once a year. They had great bikes. One day, in school, I started a fight with one of those kids and beat him up good. Then I felt bad about it. And I came home and my Dad was sitting on the front steps, looking across the street and staring at the neighbors. He was drinking a Coors, and grunted, 'They're not really happy.' I told him, 'Hey, Dad, they are happy—*we're* the ones who are unhappy.' He chased me all around the house, to flick me in the head with that goddamn ring. I hated being hit by that goddamn ring. But he couldn't catch me. He could never catch me. That's what was flashing through me at his funeral. When I held his urn at the funeral service, I was wearing his ring on my finger. Before I handed Dad off to be buried, I thumped his ring against the urn. After that, I stopped drinking and taking drugs, I just did. I mean I was wild, dropping acid and going to the Haunted House at the Boardwalk, stealing police cars, but I stopped, just like that."

"I think I just got bit by a flea," she said, brushing her right hand across her upper left arm. "God, there's fur everywhere."

"Want to go to Marianne's for some ice cream? I can get Range a sundae."

"So he's coming with us?" Andrea said stiffly.

"Ranger is a she." I said, and gently guided my whuppers to the back seat. "She goes everywhere with me."

"Yeah, but on a date?"

I firmly repeated, "She goes *everywhere* with me."

"You know, I don't feel comfortable leaving my fly-by ride downtown. Why don't you walk me to my car? I'll meet you there. We can take the ice cream back to your shop and we'll watch a video someone took of me surfing."

"All right."

We walked back to her car, Andrea suddenly stopped, pointed at some geek, and whispered, "OoooohmyGod."

"What?"

"That's Rameesh Gupta," she said, as if she were humbly approaching an oracle.

Gupta was a skinny guy who was a combination Asian, Indian, and American—he even seemed to be developing another racial tone as we neared him. The guy's limbs looked like they were grafted on. Nothing about him blended into any defined shape. He stood on the curb, straddled an expensive racing bike, and methodically sucked water through a straw of a plastic squeeze bottle. His body looked like it was coated with neon Lycra. He wore a protective white helmet that had a tiny, blinking red light in the back of it.

"He is a genius. He speaks several languages."

"What? French, Spanish, Italian?"

"No," she snapped. "Unix, Java, Linux, C++. God, you realize what he is worth?" she continued in a tone of envy-coated admiration. "He did a start-up that managed online content and sold it. Gupta is one of the few who made it early on with stock options. He made something like 700 million."

"Seven-hundred million dollars," I said. "You know, I might be able to retire on that."

"He's got a place in Woodside, and another place in Maui."

"Gupta!" she called out, which made him flinch. Andrea stood a foot away from him. "It's me! Andrea Kanable. I did a Power Point presentation once for you." He said nothing. But he was listening. "You scored. You're out! Really out there."

"Yes," he said without any inflection, his arms dead at his side.

"That's great," she said. "I mean that is just so cool."

Gupta said nothing. He was completely inert.

"So what are you up to?" she eagerly asked.

"Not much," he said, lamely and with effort.

"Well you must be doing something?"

"Yes."

There was a long pause.

"What are you doing?"

"A friend of mine and I go biking."

"Cool."

"We ride a couple paths every other day."

"Cool."

There was another long pause. Gupta didn't think it was rude not to keep up his end of a conversation. He reeked of bike geek sweat. He saw me, but didn't introduce himself, which I deeply appreciated. I had my fill of "genius" for the day.

"So you're getting in shape," she said. "All that riding, cool."

"Yes," he tonelessly replied. He looked down at his thin right calf, like it was a spare part he could replace. "I strained a muscle, yesterday, I guess. I'm stretching out more."

"Stretching out is good for you. Flexibility. You know, yoga."

"Yes," replied the bike geek, a vacant look in his eye. "I might go to Italy and bike." He paused. "You know, set a goal."

"Italy. Wow."

They stared at each other. Gupta wasn't being rude, that was all he had to say.

"Well then," Gupta said. He pushed off on his bike and clumsily pedaled off in an empty limbed way.

"Amazing, huh?" she said, then added with undisguised contempt and disbelief, "And he's a fucking idiot."

"You just told me he was a genius who spoke— "

"Someone like that ends up with all that money just so he can remain a geek forever," said Andrea, who punctuated the observation by flapping her lips. "You know when I run into geeks who are architects, research scientists, cardiologists, or NASA engineers, I know I could never be like them. But most of these successful dot-com start-up CEOs are high-school dropouts or MBAs who have never even ran a business before. I mean I *know* I'm smarter than them. He's still a fucking idiot." She paused. "I mean what's the point?"

When we reached 'The 99'. The place was jumping. Inside the club, I heard music with a rap beat playing. Through the windows dot-comers slammed down Piranha beer as they played some type of contest, where a guy asked questions. One table of dot-comers was alternating between sips of Cabernet Sauvignon and martinis.

"It's trivia night!" Andrea said.

Inside the 99', a few drunk Wassups recognized me, yelled my name, and assumed some stupid surfing poses. Just outside the place, next to Andrea's car, stood a young Asian geek with a road kill-from-space hair cut: dyed purple-and-yellow spiked hair. He was dressed in a dot-com polo shirt, khakis, and military shoes. He sipped a Cosmopolitan in front of a red Lamborghini, and gazed at it. That's all he did. I couldn't believe it.

"That's David-with-an-e-after-the-d. Davide tips the bar staff to keep a space open out front so Davide can point it out to people at the bar," whispered Andrea, leaning her firm body against my right arm. She asked, "Wanna go in?" I didn't feel like being the oldest guy in a bar with a young girl, but I might have gone in if Reddo was working the bar; he wasn't. And I wasn't good at trivia. I didn't understand it, really.

"I'll pass."

Several dot-comers came out of the 99'. A song by Fastball called 'The Wave' played on the club's outside speakers: "The road they walk on is paved with gold." The dot-comers' pupils were the size of dinner plates. The guys and girls rubbed each other's arms. They were tweaked and amped on something besides booze. "...It's always summer they'll never get old..."

"Wassup," the dot-comers said to me.

One of the dot-comers, a gorgeous Asian woman in her twenties, came over and stroked the defined line of my firm, upper biceps and murmured, "Please don't take offense, but I hope years from now, after I'm married, my husband will be in as good a shape as you at your age."

"It's okay," I said, and smiled.

"Hey bubbles," she cawed, who withdrew her soft hand, pointed to a nearby corner, and moved on. "Bubbles."

Andrea leaned against me and said, "I work with them, and they only say hello to you." She smiled. "And M-A-I-J-A flirting with you like that, I guess that's the price of fame."

"If I am the price of fame, you can afford me."

She laughed, but then said in a low voice, "If she's going to be my competition, maybe I'll have to get a little more aggressive."

The dot-comers followed the bubbles and chattered...

"Yo, I have free passes for 'Faust.' for tomorrow."

"Hey, they're going to get a Macy's. Finally I won't have to drive Over The Hill to get some decent clothes."

"You can't get a good salted bagel in Santa Cruz."

"Santa Cruz needs someone who can make a good Philly cheese steak with onions."

"The pizza in Cali sucks—they're casseroles. I think it has something to do with the chemicals in the water for the bread."

"What's 'Faust'?"

"Hey, check out the cool bubbles!"

The wired dot-comers trotted to a nearby corner. They stood in front of a longhaired, burn-out. He wore jeans, and a tie-dyed shirt. The guy was a re-rerun hippies in his twenties—bare feet and everything. He dipped several different shaped hoops into a large metal pan filled with a thick soapy fluid. He swept his skinny white arms to fashion a galaxy of small bubbles within a larger bubble. It was pretty impressive. He made several bubble universes. The see-through non-solar systems wobbled, stretched, and floated above the dot-comers. The wind lifted the galaxies higher.

"Yeah, look at the bubbles, they keep going, and going."

"They're not breaking, it's so cool."

"And they're just going up and up and up."

"Let's each pick one and bet to see whose goes the highest."

"Did any of them burst yet?"

"I can't tell, I can't see, I'm losing mine in the darkness."

"Wow, this is classic, it's classic," said one of the dot-comers, swaying and pointing to the darkness. "It's so classic."

A couple stroked each other's face and gazed at one another.

"Some people are easily amused," said Andrea, smirking.

"I guess."

"They're on E," she said, laughing.

"E?"

"Ecstasy. It goes for about thirty bucks in the Beach Flats. It's a pill. I've done it on an experimental level. E releases all the serotonin in your body, the chemical that makes you happy," she explained it, as if her body was merely an operating system. "On coke you get the dopamine, and on heroin you get the endorphins. E gives you the rush but you still feel low and slow. A fine enough feeling for me, but the guys want to get hard, so they take Viagra."

"Guys who are in their twenties are taking Viagra?" I asked. "Now there's something I never needed in my twenties."

Andrea smirked and said, "Have you ever noticed people who do drugs and people who do computers are both called users?"

"No."

The dot-comers made wishes on their chosen balls of air. And, as nice a Santa Cruz was, not one of them wanted to make a life here...

"We're thinking of running a B&B in Seattle. Somewhere below the snow line but above the fog line."

"I'm going to sell our place and get a horse farm in Montana and live in Hawaii during the winter."

"I'll own a winery in San Luis Obispo. Color me gone."

"Santa Cruz is just a jumping off place until I hit my number: $2.5 million. When I arrive. I'm out of here."

The bobble-headed dot-comers stood in place, bounced up and down on the balls of their feet, and rocked from side to side, like anchored buoys on a rolling sea. Above them, their chosen suite of inflated galaxies ascended into the darkness. The techies swayed and obliviously stared upwards, as if each one of them was simply tolerating everything and everyone around them, until the day would come, when they would finally be beamed up into the exclusive bubble of their self-fulfilled world, where they be able to drift away from the gravity of ever having to actually be anywhere or anyone else forever.

I got back to the shop before Andrea. I moved the computer desks, and set up a futon and pillows on the floor in front of the big-screen TV. I left the door open. When Andrea entered the dimly lit shop, Ranger barked, then kinda grumbled, went over to her food dish, and immediately ate everything in it. 'I Had Too Much To Dream Last Night' by The Seeds played.

"Andrea," I said, lying down on the futon. "I left the Chocolate Chocolate Chip ice cream over behind the register, could you bring it over, please?"

Something on the register caught Andrea's eye. She picked up a small silver and enamel badge. The badge had a 1795 model Springfield Arsenal musket on a light blue bar with a silver border, which was on and over an elliptical oak wreath.

"What's this?" she asked.

"My CIB."

"CIB? I thought you didn't like abbreviations?" she said in an unsteady, goofy voice.

"CIB stands for Combat Infantry Badge. The blue bar and the musket represent infantry. And the oak symbolized steadfastness, strength, and loyalty. I earned a Bronze Star, a Purple Heart, and probably a couple others. They gave me the certificates for all of them. But my Combat Infantry Badge was the only one I wanted to wear. When I went stateside I wanted all the fat-assed, rear-echelon motherfuckers who sent me to Vietnam to see it."

"It's all dirty and chipped," she said, returning it to the register. "If it means something to you, you ought to clean it." I said nothing. She seemed confused. "You know they have a portable Vietnam wall that tours all over the country. It was in Santa Cruz awhile ago. Did you see it?"

"Yeah, near the cemetery on Graham Hill Road. I went. I bought a fruit cup, because that's one thing all the guys wanted over there: fresh fruit. I looked at the names on the black wall. I couldn't find anybody. How do you find a JJ, Tank, Buzz, Stoner, Benji, or a Moose? After my first firefight, I was the only one to walk out of the jungle. I decided to stop getting to know people real well. I mean they'd die. I vowed after that, never to go to anybody's funeral. I had to get through this. Guys said, 'Burr, you are one cold motherfucker.' All I just wanted to do was get back to California and surf. I did. At The Wall I saw all these upset people sticking flowers in the cracks, and leaving ribbons, newspaper clippings, and badges. It was nice. You have to respect that. But there were some guys who never mustered out. They were my age and dressed in full-on military fatigues. No way would I ever wear those again. These guys were with real young girlfriends who were also wearing military clothing. It was creepy. They were like professional mourners. They stood there crying. It looked like they were crying because they couldn't get *past* the wall. They flashed on my CIB. They stared me down, waiting for me to cry. That's the big thing, a lot of people expect you to admit all these horrible things you did, and start crying. Like it's some healing process. Maybe it's more of a healing process for them because they never went or saw what I saw and felt guilty for what I had to go through. But what does that have to do with me crying? That was just not happenin'." I paused. "I did my crying over there, I did my crying over there."

Andrea had no idea how to respond. It was her turn to reveal something of herself. She wasn't going there.

"Let me check out what's in the fridge," she said, skipping into the back room and opening the fridge. "All that's in here are Pepsis, cold cuts, beef jerky, and frozen Butterfingers. I mean no beer or wine? Is that all you eat? Meat, caffeine, and sugar?"

"With all the chemicals I was exposed to in Vietnam I think that's all that's holding me together," I replied, lying down on the futon with my back pressed against the pillows.

"It must have been hard to adjust."

"I remember thinking American women were large compared to the Vietnamese women."

"I meant mentally," she said, smiling, entering with two Pepsis. "Do you have to put everything on a physical level?"

"It's a start," I said.

"Younger Girl" by The Critters came on.

Andrea's phone beeped. She answered it, listened, extended the phone to me and said, "It's Weever. He wants to speak to you."

"Me? How'd he know I'd be with you?"

"Me. I did. But only after he told me about this totally killer idea for a surf class."

I reluctantly took the phone.

"Yeah," I said.

"Hey bro," said Weever.

Bro.

Already, with the bro. What did he want?

"I met these CEOs of other dot-com companies who saw you on the web page," said Weever. "They want you to take them surfing."

"So just have them sign up for the class."

"Hey, we're talking top-drawer guys here, major hierarchy, bro. They don't want to take a class in Santa Cruz. These guys are major net worth. Asking these guys to be in a class and surf in Santa Cruz would be like asking them to use somebody else's bath water. These Type A's don't attend classes. When you're as successful as these guys and making the kind of money they make, you don't pay to learn anything. Why waste our time in Santa Cruz, bro? You could pick the spot. Costa Rica, Peru, Australia. We can escort all these rich people on trips and surf on their dime. Half the time they'll be too out of shape to surf, and we'd have these world-class surf breaks all to ourselves."

"We?"

"Yeah, I'm setting up the deal, a quid pro bro, bro."

"Do what you want," I replied listlessly.

The stereo played 'It's All In The Game' by Tommy Edwards.

I handed off the phone to Andrea, who listened to Weever, then said, "Yeah, I'll talk to your new hires." She clicked off. "God, that e-hole makes such a big deal about me not working late every night. He comes in at noon. And he's in charge of all these new hires and thinks he's so important. The whole thing is such bullshit. All these new hires but no one really seems to be working. Drake has to build out. You got to spend a lot to play at a higher level of empire building. It's a high burn rate. The more staff, the bigger the company appears, the brighter its outlook. Surf Dot Com must obviously be making profits if we're hiring, right? It's part of the market-share game. I've seen it at so many dot-coms. I know the whole MO: get big fast and go home. I've learned, you act busy, never ask for more work, and let them build their empire. Just don't get in the way. Yeah, the virtual empire builders." She paused. "Weever's deal sounds good."

"Yeah, it does, if he wasn't attached to it," I said. "It never occurred to me to take surf camps around the world. I'd hire someone to do classes here and go off on three week trips."

"Outsourcing, already huh?" she asked. "My local surfer person is upgrading to empire builder. I'd love to go around the world and surf first-class waves. Imagine how good I'd become."

"Where would you get that kind of time?"

"You kidding? With all the people there now. I could probably be gone for a month and no one would know," she said and searched her satchel. "Oh! You have to check out my surfing session! I was even wearing a mic so you can hear me." She pulled out her videotape, put it into the VCR, and sat down next to me. Andrea's surf video opened with several shots of the crowd at Pleasure Point. All I could see was a competitive swarm of incompetents who tried to jump on everything that moved. Most of them could barely stand on their boards. They popped out of the foam like splinters the ocean squeezed out from an infection. The next shot was Andrea in a neon-orange paneled wetsuit, which she had pulled down to her hips. She wore a Roxie flower-pattern bikini top, and paddled for a wave. She burned another woman coming down the line. In the video, Andrea waved her arms and shouted, "This is so Ep. I'm surfing. Tucker, here I am! Whew-ho!" The woman she burned collided with a surfer. Andrea didn't even turn around. It was Shiloh.

"Who's Tucker?"

"Just a friend of the family, my Dad likes him because Tucker graduated from Stanford." She smiled. "Oooooh, is someone in the room getting jealous? I like jealous. Increases my value."

"You burned Shiloh," I said, irked about Tucker, so I criticized Andrea. "You can't go for everything. You look left first—"

"Did *she* look left?"

"Knowing Shiloh, yeah, she did —"

"I don't see a line out there to stand behind," replied Andrea. "I'm bright and I work hard and long at what I undertake. I have to prove myself."

"Prove? It's surfing. Prove what?"

"I hold myself up to a higher standard than others. I give everything my all. I try to exceed. It's a standard that sets me apart. That's what bright people like me do, we achieve. We work hard at everything and we attain it.. When I get out in the water it's my time. Everyone else is getting waves and cheering each other, but when *I* go for the waves the surfers yell at me. Those people say there are rules, but those rules were written by them and for them so they can get what they want. Why should I have to take their crap? My time is just as important as anybody else's time out there. I bought my wetsuit, my board, and when that wave comes through it's my low-fat double espresso caramel macchiato to go. So I'm a bitch, what's the big deal? When I want to get in touch with my feminine side I'll have PMS. My mother said there's plenty of time for the soft stuff later."

"Soft stuff? What's soft stuff?"

"My mother didn't go to college. But she wanted me to go."

"Yeah, but what's soft stuff? You said soft."

"Soft stuff? You know, kids and nurturing. That's soft, right?"

The Syndicate of Sound played 'Hey Little Girl.'

The Wave Diva van pulled in front. The only light in the shop was coming from the TV screen. I think Shiloh thought I was alone watching a video. She open the door and walked in.

"I figured you be hungry. I brought you a tri-tip sand—" Shiloh stopped talking. She stiffened at the sight of Andrea. They were both wearing the same clothing.

"We're just kicking," said Andrea, possessively arching her body on the futon and adding insincerely. "You're welcome to stay. It's not like you're interrupting anything or anything."

Ranger came over and stood between them.

"I didn't realize *Burn*ette was here," said Shiloh.

"Burnette?" Andrea snapped.

"Yeah, Burnette, that's what locals call you in the water because you burn everyone on waves," said Shiloh, pointing at the video of Andrea surfing. "Look at you. You can't even turn. You just angles across the wave, standing on the nose, posing like you're so hot-shit cool, but the whole time, looking like some Roxie-bimbo hood ornament." Shiloh turned and wheeled on me. "She's one of those clueless trannie You-Go Girls you said you always hated, Vic! You know, the Mercedes Instant Local, and the tough look, and driving her boyfriends van and being a jerk in the water cause she's doing some local. On a scale of ability from 1-to-10, Burnette is a 2—maybe. But with you backing her in the water she opens her mouth and she thinks she's a 10." Shiloh spat at Andrea, "You're the worst kind of cool there is, you think you're cool, but all you are out there is dangerous."

"And?" replied Andrea.

"It's not about anyone but you out in the water is it?"

"Your point?"

"My point? What do you think my point is?" said Shiloh gently working her fingertips into her natural blonde roots at the top of her head as she added, "Why don't you allow the brown to come up through your hair so you can give me an answer?"

"Whatever," said Andrea. "Don't look at me like that? I'm not going anywhere. Is home girl, hit me? Get a life."

"Just don't ever try to turn and burn me again," said Shiloh, who stomped out of the shop, and slammed the door. "Over it."

Ranger stood and stared at Andrea, looked at me, gently picked up the bone, and then went back to her corner.

"The girl has mega issues," snapped Andrea, narrowing her eyes as she threw a dagger glance that went hilt-deep into Shiloh's back. "And that blonde hair of hers. I bet the carpet doesn't match the drapes."

"Shiloh's a Westsider, I wouldn't mess with her."

"So she's a Westsider. Ooooooh, hold me back."

"Hey, don't go rail-to-rail on a Westsider who has history."

"I can take care of myself on the home-girl front."

"You just might have to."

"And what does she mean by calling me a trannie? Last time I checked we all lived in the same country. Maybe I should have never done anything with my life, just have a part-time job and be a full-time loser who feels superior to everyone else because they're locals. They're just rednecks with surfboards who's only claim to fame is sitting on their butts in one place their whole lives." She paused and looked awkward. "You're an exception of course." She scowled. "But her? Hello? Pardon me for having a future." She angrily swished her ponytail, and snorted, "Maybe I should give her five dollars, so she can buy herself some ambition." Andrea's cell phone bipped. She deftly flipped it open on the second bip. "Hey you!" she said in an upbeat voice. Her indignant tone was completely gone. She laughed. "No, you didn't wake me up." She paused, looked at me, and added to her unseen friend, "I was just trying to get pregnant." She giggled. I ate my ice cream, but didn't taste it. "Where you guys going to be? How about after tae kwon do? He what? No!" She laughed. "Which club? That guy is insane. He's the shit. So hit me, where you guys going later tonight?" She pulled her arm with the cell phone through one sleeve of her shirt, and then stuck the phone out the shirt's neck, and pulled the shirt over her head. She wore a white-laced bra. She kept talking. "No way. I PDF'd that file to you. You should have no problem opening it." She flipped off her sandals and wiggled out of her blue jeans. "I have it on a zip drive in my fly-by ride, I'll bring it over in say ten—no, fifteen minutes." She wore lace-white thong panties. There was a one-inch butterfly tattoo above the crack of her butt. She laughed. "Yeah, catch you on the back side."

Andrea tilted her head from side to side, flicking her ponytail from one shoulder to the other. She still held her cell phone. She saw me admiring her. Man, there wasn't an ounce of fat on her.

"You have a tattoo?"

"I have a small scar from a mole I used to have there, so I wanted to cover it," she said, smiling. "Have you ever seen Pirelli underwear?" She ran her finger along the waistband of her thong panties. "They're Italian. Three hundred dollars a pair."

"They look real good," I said, nodding appreciatively.

"Aren't you going to *do* anything?"

"Well, yeah," I replied, not moving.

"Usually, when I take off my clothes, guys are all over me."

"What can I tell you? I'm an older guy, I don't believe in wasted energy."

"Well, I do!" she shouted, flicking her cell phone on the futon, dropping to her knees, pulling down my pants, and putting her mouth on me. Ranger protectively growled and bounded from the her corner to defend me.

"No Range!" I pleaded.

"Oh God!" shrieked Andrea, who withdrew, curled up in a ball, and covered her head with her arms.

"No! No! No!" I shouted, struggling to pull up my pants past my erection. Ranger was about to pounce. I grabbed her collar. She lunged at Andrea. "Down!" I commanded. Ranger settled. She was confused. I released her. Her head drooped and she skulked back to her corner spot. Andrea uncovered her head. "She thought you were attacking me." I laughed. "Rangey."

Andrea uncurled and said, "That dog's just a hair above the over protective edge, don't you think?"

"Ranger's not used to people getting this close to me. It's important to be able to protect. Hell, even I was pulling up my pants! When Ranger gets worked up, even I don't know what she *might* go for."

"I bet you can't take me down," Andrea said, laughing and quickly springing to her feet. Her breasts didn't jiggle. They swayed side to side and settled. God, were they perfect. She assumed a crouch. "I'm working toward my black belt."

"Is that where you learned the Oh-God-cover-your-head-curl-up-in-a-ball take down move against Ranger?," I asked motioning her toward me. Andrea remained in a frozen crouch. I waited. She didn't advance. "Well, are you going to fight, or what?"

"No, you have to come at me first," she said, not moving. "I don't know how to attack yet."

I advanced. She tried to throw a kick. I caught her lower body with my hip, grabbed her right arm, extended it behind my shoulders, and effortlessly used her own weight to flip her. Andrea found herself on the futon, lying flat on her back. She looked up at me, impressed and aroused at the same time.

"Woof, woof," said Andrea, who sprung up on her knees, and undid my pants again. Within seconds, she slipped a condom over me with her tongue.

I looked down at her work and said, "If you learned *that* in karate, I'm taking the class with you."

She laughed, smiled, stretched out on the futon, and tilted her head from side to side. Those panties may have cost three hundred dollars, but they came off like any other brand. It was mad dog time.

"Wait," she said like a referee.

Andrea rolled out from under me and reached inside her satchel. She removed her laptop and pulled out a very large blue plastic bottle from the bottom of the bag.

"Astroglide," she said, like it was a snack she craved.

"Astro—what?"

Andrea squeezed the 32-ounce bottle, but nothing happened because it was three-quarters empty. She roughly shook the bottle, squirted the lotion on the condom and started stroking her hand up and down on it. "This stuff is really good."

It took awhile for me to get back into the moment. She helped. She was all there. When we disconnected, it was as if we were blown apart from a force neither one of us expected to go off. We lied beside each other, rapidly breathing, drenched in our sweat.

She rolled toward me and bit my ear. “You’re my dawg.”

“I have to pee,” I said, which for some reason amused her. I sprinted into the bathroom. I looked at myself in the mirror. I was glowing. My muscles were glistening. My face had that conked and stupid just-got-fucked look. I heard ‘For Your Love’ by The Yardbirds playing on the shop speakers. I was pumped up. I couldn’t believe how uninhibited Andrea was during sex. Man, when she came out from behind that professional wall! Whoooooa! I wanted to get behind that wall again and again and again. I enjoyed it there. If she could be like that all the time with me, what else could she do with my life? When I was in Basic, the brass wanted to put me through officer’s training school because I out distanced everyone in my squad—even when I was in survival class and we were put in the woods for seven days, I was the only one who *gained* weight. But, I wanted no part of the military. No thank you. I resolved to be the best soldier possible so I could get back in one piece to Santa Cruz. I did. I could achieve. I had it within me to apply my inner talents and excel beyond the abilities of others. I could advance to another level. I thought of Andrea and her nylons and the perfume and the smell of her approaching storm and the money from the shop and the classes and the roller coaster ride and the new life I was paddling into. Yes, I could have her, the money, and still keep surfing in my life. I mean so far that’s the way everything was working out. I could have the same things Weever and his dot-com buddies bragged about. I could own a beach house in Pleasure Point, and another place in Baja or Costa Rica. Money could do that. My shop could expand. Surf magazines would do articles on me. More people would take my classes. I could have all things denied me. I suddenly felt an overwhelming desire to return and mad dog Andrea and scream out all these things to her. I rushed back and found Andrea was already dressed, coolly sitting upright on the futon and typing on her laptop.

“What are you doing?” I asked, surprised and offended. “I mean, what am I? An inflatable doll or something?”

“I’m only answering my e-mails,” she said. Her phone bipped. She looked at the number on her pager. “I gotta bail. The server is down, and they lost my content.”

"You're going back to work at ten in the evening?"

"The beeper never sleeps," she cheeped. "It's like pulling an all-nighter. We wait until the end and push it all through."

I put on my pants and followed her outside. She slid into her convertible and started it up. I bent down and we had a long kiss. Our incoming tongues melted into a long, creamy slope that flowed between us. We parted. I think even she was surprised at the tidal bore we created. We were silent. Our lives had changed direction. I stood by the car. She remained in the driver's seat. It unsettled her. Andrea stiffened. Her phone bipped again. It gave her a reprieve she needed from the moment.

"Gotta fly, bye" she quickly said to me, blew me a kiss, drove away, and answered her phone, "Hey you!"

I went back into the shop. Ranger sulked in the corner. I went to the futon. Andrea left a Post-It Note in the middle of the TV screen. I peeled it off. It said: "Focus." I watched the video. There were five idiots on a two-foot wave. They stiffly crouched in the middle of their boards like they were dropping down the face of a 40-foot bomber. When the dribbling wave broke and its foam gathered around their boards, all of them lost their balance, their legs went out beneath them. They fell, as if somehow an invisible coyote had taken them down from behind.

Just as I was about the turn the TV off, the camera cut to another scene. It was Andrea and The Fish in the water. They were sitting on their boards and arguing.

"Hey, you have to at least make an effort to get out of my way when I'm coming down the line," said Then Fish. "Instead of moving, you just lied there."

"That's the first thing you've said to me," she replied in a real bitchy voice. "A dead boat in the water always has right-of-way over a moving boat in the water."

"What do boats have to do with what I'm saying? This is surfing. And then you just bail off your board and almost take my head off."

"Duh, hello? That's the second thing you've said to me," she said haughtily. "I have a leash cord attached to my ankle, and that is the proper way to dismount a board. And, by-the-fly, I don't think I need to take directions from you."

"Well, you keep surfing that way, you're going to need directions from somebody, directions to the nearest hospital."

"That's the third thing you've said to me today, dog breath," she said. "I'm a beginner, back off. Just remember, when you're fucking with me, you're fucking with Vic Burr."

"You're so wrong, girl," said The Fish, paddling away "If you fuck guys like you fuck people in the water, I bet you're probably pretty good in bed."

"I bet when you're sitting on a surfboard it's the only time you have something hard between your legs," said Andrea.

"You'd make a vibrator limp, girl," said The Fish, leaving.

Andrea floated and simmered. She clearly resented not getting the last word in. Man, she was fuming. She deserved it, though.

"All The Fish wanted was an apology," asked The General, who sat up on his board next to her.. "But you wouldn't give it to him would you? You'll only say you're sorry if it will benefit you in the long run, right? What can a guy like The Fish ever do for you? You're an angry person, I can see it. What makes people like you? What did your parents do to you? If this is how you act in the water I can't imagine how you are on land. Don't people like you ever get tired of going through life just blaming everybody else for why you're miserable? Is that why you'll never apologize? Because it's easier to blame other people for your unhappiness? What are you mad at, who are you mad at?"

"Another party heard from," replied Andrea, looking away. "Cry me a river. You're just a bitter, old man."

The tape ended. The TV kicked on. I was watching an episode of "Friends" I clicked that off real fast.

"Huh."

I felt bad about yelling at Ranger. Then I smelled it. There was a pile of dog poop near the futon.

"Range!" I yelled, going over to her corner.

She lied between her empty food dish and plastic water bowl. Her head rested on her stretched out front paws. I knew why she did it. I just couldn't punish her.

"Babeee," I said sympathetically, cleaning up Ranger's mess.

She came over to me quickly—too quickly, both her back legs gave out.

"Range!"

I gently lifted Ranger's back legs and she used her front legs. I wheel-barrowed her back to the futon, and set up a blanket for her, refilled the water bowl, and put what was left of the melted pint of ice cream in her dish. Whups tilted her head and looked back at me. But she didn't eat the ice cream. She rested her head on her front paws, stared at me with her brown eyes and made a soft groaning "oooooooorn" sound through her closed mouth. I sat down beside her and said, "I know Rangey, I know." I scratched wherever she couldn't reach. "You're an old lady, who doesn't know why she doesn't feel good. That's what you are, yeah. And old ladies sit there and everyone is nice to a an old lady whup whups." She tilted her head a different way to each inflection of my voice. Her tongue moved rapidly in and out as she panted with effort. I knelt over Ranger and pet her. "Whups," I said, scratching the center of her rib cage—that was her special spot. Ranger extended her front left leg out and thumped her back right leg, its nails scraped the rug. "Yeah whuppers, yeah."

I lied on the futon with Ranger as my pillow, and listened to 'Everyone's Gone To The Moon' by Jonathan King. Sometimes at night, when me, myself, and I, are all in the same room, we don't get along—we're wise to each other. I just couldn't drift off. I didn't want to read. I didn't want to shape a board. And I couldn't go to the ocean. I just couldn't close my eyes. I kept looking at the clock. One. Two. Watching it all go around. Three. Four. The sixties kept playing—'Turndown Day' by The Cyrcle, 'The Letter' by The Box Tops, 'Big Bad John' by Jimmy Dean, 'Come On Down to My Boat Baby' by Every Mother's Son, 'The Horse' by Cliff Nobles and Co., and 'Ferry Crossed The Mersey' by Gerry and the Pacemakers. Each tune was like clicking a bead of a rosary. I spun my father's gold ring around my finger. I stared at the ceiling. The oldies kept rolling and soaking into me—'Silence is Golden' by The Tremaloes, 'So In Love' by The Thymes, 'Groovy Kind of Love' by The Mindbenders, and 'Searching For My Love' by The Bobby Moore Group and the Rhythm Aces. No matter who you are. In the middle of the night, when all your screw-ups plow into you, there are deep moments of anxiety you can't escape. The oldies kept coming 'How Can I be Sure' by The Rascals, 'Wild Weekend' by The Rockin' Rebels, 'Big Bird' by Eddie Floyd, 'To Sir, With Love' by Lulu, 'Catch The Wind' by Donovan, 'I Think We're Alone Now" by Tommy James and the Shondells, 'Cherish' by The Association, and 'In The Year 2525' by Zager and Evans. I thought of Shiloh. She liked Ranger. Shiloh was an excellent surfer, a Santa Cruz local girl. When she looked at me I knew she loved everything about me. Shiloh was right about Andrea being everything I didn't like, but Bystrom was also everything Shiloh said she didn't like too. She wanted to start up with me, but only after she made a run at Bystrom in Hawaii. Then, when that failed, she came back, and settled for me. But did he dump her or did she dump him? The difference was, my choice was working for me. I kept mentally clicking along through the oldies: 'I'd Love To Change The World' by Ten Years After, 'Reach Out In The Darkness' by Friends of Distinction, 'If You Want To Be Happy" by Jimmy Soul, 'You've Lost That Loving Feeling' by The Righteous Brothers, 'My Pledge of Love' by The Joe Jeffrey Group 'My Boy Lollipop' by Millie Small, 'Time Won't Let me' by The Outsiders, and 'Hooked On A Feeling' by B.J. Thomas. Each song represented a pure emotion I felt encapsulated in a memory from my life, I drew on those songs. But now, I was fighting my past. I was weighing on me. That's why I couldn't sleep. I was halfway down a path I'd never taken. I had gone as far as I could with myself. A woman like Shiloh, who was content with just me, wasn't going to advance me any further. And the way Andrea talked to The General? Well, if I listened to him, would he save my shop? How? By giving me a halibut he caught? I don't think so. Finally, I started to drift off to 'Baby It's You' by A Band Called Smith. I dreamed I was on a surfboard at Pleasure Point all by myself. A huge triangular fin of a shark rose in the water. I felt fear, knowing the Great White was going to swallow me completely. But I didn't panic. I remained on my board. In slow motion, the shark took me whole into his mouth. My wetsuit, spread out, thickened, and cushioned me. The shark couldn't chew through it or swallow me so he had to cough me back out, and I worked my way back to the beach.

THE CREW WAS GOING FULL TILT in the surf shop. Driveway Dave entered our weekly revenue into an Excel spreadsheet. Ralph day traded on-line, threw us into stocks, set up our 401Ks, and a college fund for Squirrel. Chops wore a diva mic and ordered food for a two-week surf camp we were setting up for the next day. The Legend stamped envelopes that contained student photographs. Skin Dog opened cardboard boxes with a razor, pulled out shirts, sweatshirts, surf racks, board bags, Ugg boots, and sports watches. Sonny hung clothing. Just outside the front door, a couple Mexican teenagers—who were friends of Fernando—washed and rinsed off the wetsuits, and stored blue foam rental boards in a large shed behind the shop. I sat at my laptop by the front counter near the cash register. I pulled off a yellow Post-it Note Andrea left on the monitor. It said, "Don't do a job, make a job." She kept leaving me motivational messages in odd places. I found "Be the answer not the question" on my van's steering wheel, "Don't follow the sun, be the sun "on my surfboard, and "Dream with open eyes" on Ranger's food dish. Actually, Andrea and I had a relationship she described as "backwards compatibility." We left each other alone. It improved our relationship because there was nothing to argue about. She got her way, and I got mine. Andrea finally gave up on trying to drag me to different places. I just wanted to work at the shop, conduct classes, and surf. She went out with her friends. I mean, why would I want to watch people get drunk and high at 'The 99'? Or stand around at some rave where people danced on rugs in the redwoods way up in Bonny Doon at three in the morning? I was even getting into using the computer; in fact, I enjoyed it. It was a buzz, like I had too much caffeine. I was thinking faster, and words came to me more easily. I was being given prosthetic brain cells. I didn't have to talk or deal with vendors. I simply went on the Internet and placed the shop orders. It was surprisingly effortless. Nothing got between me and what I wanted. I'd lock onto the computer for hours. I downloaded movies and MP3s through peer-to-peer file sharing, did my banking on-line, and got surf reports to anticipate swells for the classes. I was organized, making money, and for the first time in my life, effectively running under my own power. Everything was going great. The only drag was dealing with Shiloh, who never ceased criticizing Andrea, and kept drawing me into stupid arguments over little details connected with shop orders. But today, I had a reprieve from Shiloh. When the surf was flat, Shiloh handled all the classes. She took them kayaking at the Elkhorn slough, tidal pool exploring at Pleasure Point, or on nature walks at Point Lobos to "develop an understanding of the ocean's cycles." And, the students went for it, amazing.

'Kicks' by Paul Revere and the Raiders played.

"They're going to do a story on the news on how Surf Dot Com's is having their second stock offering tomorrow," said Ralph, glancing at the TV screen and back to his monitor.

"Yeah," I said, typing with two-fingers to check on a purchase order. "Hey, Skin Dog, is that box the sports watch order? It should be fifty watches, and a bill for twenty, because we had thirty on backorder. That's purchase order 1296, right?"

"Yeah," said Skin Dog, amused more than impressed. "Hey, since when did you get so organized, brutha?"

"God, yesterday Vic was on that computer for six hours," said The Legend. "I couldn't even get him to go out for lunch. Vic is going geek on us."

"That's because he's used to playing with inanimate objects," said Chops.

"Instead of you, who inflates them," I quipped.

"Whoa!" said The Crew, as if on cue.

"Vic comes up with a line!" said The Legend.

Chops dropped to the ground as if he were hit by my remark, and flailed about the floor and said, "He got me." He acted like he was trying to pull shrapnel from between his shoulder blades. "Pull it out. It's napalm and it's burning into me. I'm having flashbacks, flashbacks. The sappers are coming over the wire. Who's eating rice? I hear voices. Is there white rice in the room?"

Sonny said evenly, "Andrea's wisecracks are rubbing off on you." He snorted. "A real nurturer, she."

"She wanted me to go to this Renaissance Fair at UCSC today," I said.

"Oh, that's you," said Chops.

"Vic? Go to UCSC?" said Skin Dog in complete disbelief. "That I could see."

"Yeah, with an assault rifle," said Chops, drawing a laugh. "There will be a lot of heads lining that particular parameter."

"Tonight Andrea and I are going Over The Hill for some dot-com Com launch. She and Weever set up and meet-and-greet where I present myself to rich guys who want to go surfing in Costa Rica. They'll pay for lodging and the food and the flight."

"Costa Rica?" said The Legend. "That would be bitchin'."

"I can understand you going to Costa Rica," Chops said, who seemed amused and surprised. "Wait, did you say you're going Over The Hill, driving up Highway 17? You?" The Crew laughed. "To San Jose?" The Crew laughed again.

"No way am I spending the night there," I said. "Even when I was nail banging Over The Hill, I never spent the night there. I had to wake up in Santa Cruz." I paused. "I used to have nightmares of waking up in San Jose."

"Now, when we wake up in Santa Cruz, we wake up in San Jose," said Sonny. "Over The Hill has rolled down to—"

"The a second offering story is on!" said Ralph, pointing to the image of the Surf Dot Com building on the wide-screen TV.

I hit a key on my computer, turned down Paul Revere and The Raiders, grabbed the TV-remote, and cranked up the volume on the CNBC financial news.

"Just a day away from Surf Dot Com's second offering, SDC's CEO, Drake Sather, announced a contract with Adapient, a satellite and microwave equipment firm," said a female reporter in a business suit. Stockbrokers traded on telephones behind her on the exchange floor. "Along with Adapient, SDC also announced contracts with Sapient, maker of analog wireless chips, along with Expient of fiber-optic switching fame. This acquisition and merger expands the start-up's virtual network and increased capacity, boosting SDC's stock price to an all-time high of $203 a share. Another high-tech winner was Adapient. The start-up's stock shot from $28 to $79. And, Expient's recent IPO went from $2 a share to $58. With the projected demand for data and voice transmission based on anticipated network capacity, all these developments make tomorrow's SDC second offering the most eagerly anticipated event in the high-tech world."

Ralph clicked the financial news off. I turned on the music. 'The Battle of New Orleans' by Johnny Horton played.

"What's all this shit coming from the printer?" grumbled Driveway Dave, who shuffled through a stack of papers in the printer's tray. "A JPEG of two black girls doing it, Squirrel!"

"It's mine," said Squirrel. "Check out the dildo they're using. It has two heads!"

I walked over to Squirrel and said, "I thought you were working on updating the web page."

"Busted!" guiltlessly said Squirrel, whose eyes were fixed on his new laptop's computer screen. He had a Tootsie Roll stuck halfway out into his mouth, a bag of Cheetos in his lap, and a Pepsi in his left hand. He double-clicked the mouse with his free hand. "Some of these company e-mails are real dirty. It's unreal. Man, these computer geeks have tons of porno!"

"You're tying up the printers with all this shit? And..." said Dave as he sifted through documents in the pile of printouts. "What's this? 'Bros of Drake'?"

Bro

"Hey Squirrel," continued Dave, "why, you're downloading inter-office stuff from Drake Sather's files."

"'Bros of Drake'?" asked Sonny. "What the hell is that?"

The phone bipped.

"Put it on the speakerphone," I said. "Don't say anything, It might be Weever, I don't want to deal with him today."

But it wasn't Weever. Instead, we heard a golf swing, and men talking business:

"That's all in the 'Bros of Drake' account."

It was Drake's voice.

I turned down the music and motioned everyone to be quiet. The Crew and I stood around the speakerphone and listened.

"Shit," grunted a guy after a bad golf swing.

"Reboot, bro..." said Drake.

Driveway Dave whispered, "They're hitting balls off Drake's deck—that's what they're doing."

"Our ass is covered at Credit First San Jose Suisse. After the second offering, I'll be able prune back the cash burn," said Drake. "But, not before the second offering. Our lock-out to sell SDC stock options ends just before the market opens that day."

Another Drake buddy said, "I did the research and rated the SDC's stock as a 'buy'—but being a bro, I have to tell you personally, the stock is junk."

There was laughter.

"After we sell our options we'll have to restate earnings," said one of the guys.

"Restating earnings is no problem," said Drake. "Our contract with you at Adapient will keep Surf Dot Com's and Adapient's stock high, along with the guys at Expient. It's no big deal, Adapient just announces it before the offering, then after we sell our stock, we announce Adapient couldn't comply with the specifications, i.e....the performance specifications are so high Adapient can't meet them, it's not our fault they couldn't put the deal together, yada yada yadda." He paused. "Reboot—"

"Damn," grunted another guy, who swung a club. "Fat."

The cell phone disconnected. The Crew and I stared at the speakerphone.

"What was that?" said Sonny. "Why would Drake want to put us on a conference call? Are we being set up?"

"No, that's not what happened," I said. "Andrea showed me that Drake sometimes accidentally hits his cell phone's speed dial. I guess it dialed us this time."

Dave put down the documents, removed his reading glasses, and said, "God, he's just cooking the books, that's all."

"No news there," said Sonny. "So are we."

I turned the oldies up, catching the tail end of The Animals playing 'Don't Let me Be Misunderstood.'

"Oh man," said Dave, who shuffled through the papers. "To keep Surf Dot Com's stock price high, Drake has had to find ways to artificially increase earnings. SDC's trades banner ads with other companies and puts those companies on Surf Dot Com's web site, and counts those ads as revenue figures. Drake even listed shipping and handling costs under marketing budgets to inflate his margin. He's taken loans and put them into accounts receivable, and records the loans as sales. And even when he legitimately sold a deal, he put in gross revenue figures instead of the actual cost of the transaction, to show a profit when he really lost money. And there's more. Surf Dot Com shifted money from their accounts to Adapient, which they own, and then Adapient purchased their networking services from Surf Dot Com with Surf Dot Com's own money, and Drake reports it as revenue." He paused. "It's a shell game."

"Boring," said Squirrel.

"Enough," I said, thumping his forehead with my ring finger.

"That's weak," Squirrel muttered. "That's so weak."

Ranger quickly came over. She waited. Squirrel froze. I turned the music up. 'Mister Custer' by Larry Verne played.

"Squirrel, how are you getting this stuff?" asked Dave.

"Warblood. It's the game," Squirrel said, rubbing his forehead where I bapped him with the ring. He looked at me and added, "I told you it was *more* than just a game. All you guys thought all I was doing was just killing people." He paused. "I'm doing more than that. I'm killing people and I'm spoofing."

"Spoofing?" asked Dave, puzzled but curious. "Meaning..."

"I'll show ya," said Squirrel. "Check out my screen now."

The Crew gathered around him.

"See those peon guys," said Squirrel, pointing at a line of gnome-looking creatures who were removing gold bricks from a mineshaft and carrying them into a stone castle. "Zander incorrectly assumes his peons are gathering gold for his heroes."

"Heroes?" asked Sonny.

"The heroes have more powers than the soldiers in the troops they command," said Squirrel, who seemed surprised we weren't familiar with every detail of the game. "Heroes cast spells, cause earthquakes, and throw fireballs. But to upgrade them to those powers you have to use your peons to gather gold from the mine." He paused. "But, those aren't peons. They're Trojans."

"They're called Trojans?" Dave said. "Didn't you just tell me those figures with mining the gold are peons?"

"Nooooooo, but that's what Zander thinks they are," said Squirrel. "That's why it's a spoof. My Trojan is a hella spoofing program. I designed a code to make it appear that way. Those aren't gold bricks, they're data packets I'm removing from Surf Dot Com's database. That's how I get all my porno. This guy Zander on Battlenet doesn't even know I'm doing it. Because I spoofed him."

"Battlenet? I thought you said you were playing Warblood?"

"Battlenet. Get real. Everyone knows Battlenet. It's a worldwide network of online servers. When I log on, I can find any opponent to play Warblood any time of day. There's an IT in every company who plays it. I've gotten into the Pentagon, the CIA, banks, stock brokers, and a lot of dot-com companies." He paused. "The only bummer is when the ITs go off-line, I can't get into their database until they go back online again."

"Can't you get caught at this?"

"Most of the time, no one knows until the transaction is over. But sometimes a big security company uses packet sniffers."

"Pot stickers?" asked The Legend, lost.

"No, packet sniffers," said Squirrel.

Dave furrowed his brow and asked, "A packet sniffer is what?"

"A packet sniffer gives out the bit stream and the name of the packets in it," said Squirrel. "The sniffer program can see through my spoof and identify that the gold bricks aren't gold bricks but are data packets from the company network database."

"So, this is how you get into their company systems?" asked Dave, still confused. "And this works by..."

"The Trojans," said Squirrel, showing his exasperation by issuing a lengthy and loud exhalation of air. "When I'm playing this Zander guy. I'm using his own peons to carry data packets through Surf Dot Com's firewall and into my hard drive." He hit a key and split the screens on his monitor. One window displayed the Warblood game; and the other window showed lines of text, which grew a line each time a gold brick was mined by a peon. "I've gotten through Zander's firewall, and he doesn't know it."

"What's a firewall?" asked Skin Dog.

"A firewall is supposed to protect a network from outside hackers like me. I'm an outside user, which means that I'm kept outside Surf Dot Com's network and can't gain access because of Zander's firewall. The only way I can officially get into their network and access the database is with the authorization of a person behind the firewall, who is usually a System Administrator or an IT." He paused. Squirrel noticed we were confused. "It's like Zander's behind the wall of a castle and he has to lower the drawbridge for us to get in."

"Oh," The Crew said, trying to concentrate on Squirrel's explanations. And because he rarely made sense, it took a lot of effort.

"This Zander guy is the IT who administers the network and initials all requests for files in the computer's system," continued Squirrel, who was thriving so much in the attention he was getting, he confused it with respect. "He's designed the firewall to prevent outsiders from getting through it. What the ass-clown IT doesn't know is, when he plays Warblood against me, Zander creates a hole in his company's firewall. Zander's the weakness in his own system. That's the opening for my Trojans."

"Are they ribbed for your pleasure?" asked Chops.

The Crew laughed.

A grim-faced Sonny said to Chops, "You don't disappoint. I knew you would say that." He paused. "Not funny."

"So these Trojans of yours can just go right into the system of all these company ITs who are playing this stupid game against you?" Dave said, smiling. "Impressive."

"Yeaaah," Squirrel replied, who stretched out 'yeah' so it sounded like a sarcastic "cha-yaaah" sound. "My Trojan is a hacker program. It accesses everything they do, including all the security passwords, and keyboard changes. If they access a bank account, use a credit card, I can get their IP address. I get it all."

"Are there any more of these 'Bros of Drake files?" said Dave, who referred to the page in his hands.

"Look at this," said Squirrel, who hit a few keys. "Hella cool, this Drake guy has more porno than me."

"Get the Bro-of-Drake files," I said. "Never mind the porno."

"But he's got a file of chicks with dicks," Squirrel pleaded.

We hesitated on that one.

"Show us," patiently said Dave. "The *files* not the dicks."

Squirrel deftly hit a series of keys. The split screen changed from the battlefield to a full window with lines of text-file lists.

Dave took control of Squirrel's mouse, scrolled through the lines of files, and asked, "Are you playing war games against guys who are working at Adapient, Expient, and Sapient?"

"Yeah," Squirrel said, picking his nose.

"Now, I see why these dot-com stocks are so overvalued," interrupted Ralph, examining the documents by the printer. "The 'Bros of Drake' set-up is a Surf Dot *Con*—not Surf Dot Com. Adapient, Sapient, Expient, and all the other whatever-*ients* that are connected with Surf Dot Com are just fronts. Remember when I was telling you about how everyone gets greedy and thinks stupid when they see a guy play roulette, who bets all his money on the number ten, wins, then let's it ride, and ten keeps coming up again and again and again? So then the other people get tired of seeing someone else get rich and they start betting their money and leaving it on the number ten. Well, what if the real reason the guy keeps hitting on the number ten is because his *bro* is running the roulette wheel and told the guy to keep leaving his money on the number ten, because they both know how many times the number ten is going to come up?"

"Holy shit balls," said Skin Dog. "A carny hustle."

"All these guys are artificially keeping the stock price high," said Ralph, who was clearly pleased to illuminate us with his evaluation, "so they can sell their shares at a profit before everything tanks."

"But what if the stocks don't go up but go down?" said Ralph.

"What would happen then?" asked Sonny.

"Well one of two things," said Ralph. "One, we lose everything and Drake and his bros get rich. Or two, Drake and his dot-com buddies lose everything and we become rich." He paused. "I like the second option better than the first option. I'm a little biased."

"Howz'it?"

"First to accomplish this your company needs a very good attorney," said Ralph, who pointed to Driveway Dave. "And a very brilliant Chief Financial Officer." He pointed to himself. "So for the sake of argument, and the lack of a better term, if a certain someone—let's call him Squirrel—hacks into Surf Dot Com's network, obtains all information we have here about the 'Bros of Drake' and Surf Dot Com's true state of books, and then our little hack monster here e-mails that info to investors, the employees, brokerage houses, and the media—"

"You'd burst Surf Dot-Com's bubble!" said Driveway Dave, laughing. "Beautiful."

"If they have to declare bankruptcy, than all the creditors come after me and the shop. I lose, right?" I asked. "So how does bursting their bubble help us?"

"Vic's right," said Sonny, who addressed Dave. "Remember, you told us about that clause in that agreement he signed with Drake, what was it called?"

"'Senior Liquidation," Dave said.

"We're going to kill seniors?" asked The Legend.

Sonny leveled a steady gaze at The Legend and said, "Do people knock on your head to come inside your skull to pick mushrooms because it's so damp and dark in there?"

"Fine with me, they can help themselves once they're in there," said The Legend. "I hate mushrooms. They're a fungus."

An instrumental oldie played.

"I know a way around it, an investment strategy," Ralph said, who became distracted by the oldie. "Hey, I know this song, I used to hear it all the time, years ago, never knew the name."

"Al Hirt. 'Java,'" Skin Dog said authoritatively. "He's dead."

"Enough of Al Hirt!" said Sonny. "Can we get back to figuring out how we're going to make money, please?"

Ralph said, "Okay, fine. First, we can get the skinny on Surf Dot Com's other companies, and my guess is that every company SDC is connected to is cooking their books the same way Surf Dot Com is—"

"Ralph, are you saying you'd sell SDC stock short?" asked Dave, who laughed. "I see where you're going? "

"Selling ourselves short is going to make us money?" loudly asked The Legend.

"We're not selling ourselves short, we're shorting the stock," said Ralph, correcting The Legend.

"Selling short. How does that work?" asked Sonny.

"No, we're shorting the stock," repeated Ralph.

Sonny stared at Ralph, nodded like he understood, paused, and said, "How does that work?"

"Okay," said Ralph, who leaned back in his chair. "First, we have to leverage out all of the shop's assets, which means everything, including our 401k. Then, we go to a broker, and based on all our assets, borrow stock from him."

"The broker lends the stock to you?" asked Sonny.

"Yes, we borrow the stock from the broker, then sell the stock and at whatever its current price is."

"So we sell what we borrowed? That's investing?"

"Yes," said Ralph, who hit a few keys and turned his monitor around. An image of a calculator was on it. "Let's say the stock is at one hundred dollars a share. And you borrowed a thousand shares from the broker. And you sell them for $100 a share." One hundred thousand appeared on the calculator. "Then Squirrel goes online and all the investors and brokers find out Surf Dot Com, and its other companies misstated their projected revenues by...," he paused and looked at a document, "I'd say, and this is a conservative guesstimate, about 47 percent."

"Wow, 47 percent. That's almost half," said The Legend.

"Really, Legend," said Sonny, "Your mind astounds me."

"Can you do what Ralph said, Squirrel?" I asked.

"Fuck yeah, they'd be ghost?" said Squirrel.

Ralph continued, "Once SDC's true losses are revealed, investors will dump it. The SDC shares we borrowed at $100 a share and sold for $100 a share will plummet in value."

"Then what?"

"Let's assume the Surf Dot Com's stock drops to $1 a share," said Ralph. "We purchase the stock back at $1 a share and return those shares we borrowed to the broker who takes the loss."

"What happens if we do nothing?" Sonny asked.

"The 'Bros of Drake' will rake in all the money for themselves by executing their stock options on the unsuspecting public before the stock dumps," said Driveway Dave.

"But it's still illegal, why should we be the ones to lose on that 'senior' thing?" asked Sonny. "They're the crooks, not us."

"That's what Drake and his buddies are counting on," said Dave. "Remember insider trading scandals in the eighties? Banks knowingly made bad loans to company guys who got rich, but taxpayers would up bailing out the banks because banks can't go bankrupt. It would upset 'consumer confidence.' Only this time it's not taxpayers paying, it's investors. After Drake and his bros declare bankruptcy, they'll probably just get a slap on the wrist. A gangbanger robbing a convenience store in Salinas would do more time than those guys. The Bros will defend themselves by claiming they did nothing legally wrong, which, depending on how good their attorney is, will be true. Then, there will be an investor class-action suit on fraud, where after legal fees, maybe some investors get pennies on the dollar, and the creditors will take steps to seize your shop, the van, and your dog."

"Nobody takes Ranger."

"I think he was kidding about the dog," said Sonny.

"Nobody kids me about Ranger."

"Fine," said Sonny, who turned and asked Ralph. "So if we short the stock?"

"After all is said and done, and not working in all the fees and shit, let's just say we come out with a tidy $99,000 in profit."

"A reverse bro deal!" said Skin Dog. "We do to them from the bottom what they want to do to us from the top."

"A turn and burn!" Chops said. "We snake them out of their Internet wave and stuff them in chump change."

"Jez, $99 out of $100 by selling short. That's almost a 100 percent profit," said The Legend.

"Your math ability continues to amaze," said Sonny.

"I can handle the rest of the deal," said Driveway Dave, smiling broadly with his yellowed teeth. "After we short the tech stocks. I take that money, establish a trust, and set up a system where you guys will never have to pay taxes ever again."

"And if the plan doesn't work?" I asked.

"You would lose the shop," said Dave.

"What shop?" I said, looking at the computers and the women's apparel, the epoxy, foam, soft-top, and machine-shaped boards lining the walls. "The shop I fought for isn't here. I might as well take the chance." I paused. "It's happenin'."

"But there is one thing I can't do," said Ralph, looking straight into my eyes. "I cannot personally profit from this. You have to just pay me a straight salary for my work."

"What do you mean you can't do it? It's your plan, brutha?" said Skin Dog in disbelief. "If you don't believe in putting your own money in, why should we put in ours?"

"I can't. I can't use my money," Ralph said. "I'll help you, but I can't use my money."

"Listen to this guy," said Sonny. "I say fuck the plan, let's declare bankruptcy first, and get out with what we have."

"And then what? The money won't be enough, and we'll still be back in the same situation," said Chops.

"So we had a nice run, accept it," said Sonny. "I mean you want Ralph handling our cash now?" He paused. "How can we trust him? He could be playing us for suckers."

"What's that suppose to mean?" angrily said Ralph. "I've placed all you guys in stable investments. I worked with Dave so we could incorporate all of you as a separate company. I have taken nothing extra, nothing. The only thing I received is pay for the work I've done. Ask Dave. I've built the shop's portfolio up to $1.2 million. Dave's seen the books. Ask him, go ahead."

"It's all true," said Dave.

"I don't know what finance guys do, but I do know dope deals," said Sonny to Ralph. "And when things don't go according to their original plan and go sketch, that's when you get busted. This is sketchy. Let's divide everything up." He jerked his head at Ralph. "Besides, he can't even surf that good."

The Legend said, "I don't think Ralph surfs so bad."

We were silent. Terry Stafford's 'Suspicion' played.

"Wow," said Chops, pointing at the speakers. "Art meets life."

"Sonny's right, Ralph," I said. "Why? Why can't you put in your own money? Why?"

Ralph looked down, took one deep breath, and said, "My wife and I have been separated and I haven't even seen my kids for six months. They want nothing to do with me and I can't blame them. I always tried to give an impression I was divorced because it avoided the real issue, or talking about it. I had a gambling problem. That's why we separated. That's why I played with your money, not mine—if I used mine, I'd be gambling. I had to see if I could resist." He uncomfortably looked up and around at all of us. "I'm ashamed to admit it. I was a mean person."

I tilted my head and said, "You being mean, Ralph? I can't picture it. Look at what you've done for us so far? It doesn't fit. I could see it, if you were a weasel, but you're such a nice guy."

"Yeah, I'm a nice guy" Ralph grunted. He narrowed his green eyes, placed his pudgy face a quarter-inch away from mine, and smiled. He had a sharp glint in his pupils. He spoke in a flat frosty way, "I'm a nice guy, so you wouldn't mind calling me on a bet? I'm such a nice guy you wouldn't mind losing twenty bucks to such a *nice* guy like me?"

"Whoa!" I said, shocked by his flat eyes and dry-iced tone.

"I had lied to my family so much, and caused my wife so much pain. One time I was gone for fifteen days in a poker game. They had no idea where I was," Ralph said, walking over to his board, which leaned against the back wall. He felt its sides and looked up to its nose. "I called her at seven in the evening and told her a friend was coming to give me a ride home, then I called her at nine and said the guy had a car problem. I couldn't leave, my bad luck was turning good. Then I called her at two in the morning. And I lied and told her the guy's car had a timing belt problem and we were in a garage. And she believed me because she loved me. I had done this thousands of times. But it was the ridiculousness of the story that made me hit bottom, five hundred miles from home, at a poker game. But she believed me because she loved me. And because she loved me and believed me, she was making herself vulnerable to anyone who she should tell the story to, and she would be considered a fool." He paused. "The nice guy threw his wife's heart into a pot of strangers. A nice guy lying to his wife. That's not something a nice guy does. I never went home that night. I was too ashamed.

I needed to change. I remembered Santa Cruz. Surfing was a place I could always come back to. It was something I had. I was lucky, at least I had a spark of something. I had great times here in the sixties and the seventies at Pleasure Point. So I came back, and walked in here with no friends armed with a bag of hot dogs. And without hardly even knowing me, you filled my canteen when it was empty. I met you and this shop and The Crew and I thought these guys are really cool. These guys are alive, living the life. They know what it's all about."

"Wanna bet?" asked Chops, drawing a laugh.

"Yeah, I know," said Ralph, pleased with the familiarity of Chop's dig. "The odds." He paused. "I left out the most important part." He smiled and growled out. "You guys put back the gurrrrrrrrrrrrrrrrrrrr in Rrrrrrrr-Ralph!"

"Okay, enough of you, there's still an issue we haven't addressed, Dave," said Sonny. "You want to burglarize a house of cards. But you're forgetting it's *their* house of cards. You've worked for these people. You know these are dark forces we're going after. They live for their money—it's all they have. If we cost these people money, the dark side will track us down. When their house of cards falls on them, they will look for our trail. We have to leave tracks they can trace. If we do a turn and burn like that we have to leave footprints. They'll find us."

"Wrong!" said Squirrel, smirking. "You are so wrong. No one can trace me. Impossible."

"How come they can't trace you?" asked Sonny, walking over to Squirrel. "But you have to leave footprints."

Squirrel flapped his lips in a juvenile pffffft sound, and said cockily, "I go through proxy servers. I have one in Russia, one in Thailand, and I can mask my protocol. The only thing they can find out is the hardware. But they can't locate where I am. I'm using thousands of variations."

"We're going using thousands of Asians?" asked The Legend.

"No, variations not Asians," said Squirrel.

"I guess it all comes down to what we want out of this for ourselves," said The Legend. "I guess I'd like to travel around, take pictures, maybe do a surf film or something."

I want my shop back," I said.

"'I'll tell you what I want," quickly chimed in Sonny. "A long time ago, when I was in the islands. There was this old Hawaiian. I thought he was old because I was in my twenties. And he was in his fifties, and at the time, that was old to me. He sat on the beach at Waikiki. He'd stare at the ocean all day, completely at peace. I was only twenty-three back then. I was burned out on Hawaii, having a good time. We did these things called Mandrakes. They never made it over here. They were 250 milligrams, fifty-percent Quaalude and fifty percent hypnotic. I kept thinking, here I am a guilt-ridden neurotic Italian, and I take a fifteen-cent pill and I'm thinking way better of myself than I could natch—naturally, by myself. I didn't want to be like that old moke. I wanted to see the world. I have. I traveled to Afghanistan, and Turkey, Algiers, Nicaragua, and Peru."

"Following the harvest no doubt," said Chops.

"I'm not the only one in this room who picked up the fruit that dropped from that tree," Sonny solemnly noted, scanning a few of us, who raised eyebrows. "I've been all over. Today, what that old Hawaiian was doing looks pretty good to me. I can sit on that beach all day, staring out at the ocean. Even with the crowds, I'll still get my share of waves." He paused. "But that's not really all of it." He suddenly showed the first display of vulnerability I had ever seen in him. "It's not what I want, it's what I don't want. I don't want to be ever be a burden to my two boys. I don't want to ever hold them back. I want them to rise."

"What the hell, what do you have to lose, anyway?" said Chops. "You don't have friends." He paused. "Personally, I'll donate my share to a homeless shelter in Santa Cruz."

The Crew laughed except Sonny, who said to Chops, "You know, I've never found you funny, and I don't think I ever will."

"Thank you," said Chops, who continued, "I'd just be doing the same thing and just getting better at it. Play music full time. I wouldn't have to take shitty gigs because I'd have money. Surf. See, if I have anything to offer." He paused. "Either that, or just go to school and learn to be a computer graphic artist."

The Crew laughed.

Dave said, "Maybe, I'd get back into doing some legal work again, some pro bono stuff. Make the bad people with money miserable, you know, give them problems. Fight for the little guy, you know, be a fool."

The Legend said, "Skin Dog, what would you do? Get a bigger trailer?"

"What the hell," said Skin Dog, who smiled. "You know what they say, brutha, it ain't home until you take the wheels off."

The Crew laughed.

"What about Shiloh?" I asked. "She's part of this too."

"Do you want to call her?" asked Ralph.

"I don't think that's such a good idea, she's pissed at me."

"You want me to talk to her?" asked Driveway Dave. "I'll give her a choice of either getting money or going in on it with us."

"Fine by me," I said, shrugging.

"So we're all in, now what, brutha?" asked Skin Dog.

"We're playing the same game on Drake and his bros that they were going to play on us," said Dave, who was stationed at another computer, and hit key after key to print out file after file. "Keep those peons digging Squirrel."

"And insider trading?" asked Sonny. "Can they get us on that?

"We're not insiders," said Dave. "In our existing positions with Surf Dot Com there is no way we would have access to this information. We're not company officials. We're surfers. And how can it be fraud if the information we're putting out is true? Plus, according to Squirrel, there's no paper trail linking us to these guys. They would have to prove intent on us, and we have no intent, we have a motive. But as your attorney in these matters, it is my responsibility to inform you that you need to find a silent partner to purchase this stock for us."

"I have someone," I said.

The Crew quieted down. Dave began cross-examining me.

"Someone who isn't running the surf class?"

"Yeah," I said.

"And someone who isn't connected to this shop?"

"Yeah."

"And has no business dealings with Surf Dot Com in any way, matter, shape, or form?"

"Yeah."

"The General?"

"No."

"Well, then who?"

"It's probably better for all around if you don't know."

The Crew stared at me.

"There is a possible glitch," cautioned Squirrel, who hit keys and launched a few fireballs at a screaming and retreating enemy. "I can get totally into all the nested files drilled down in Zander's system. I already have his codes and the passwords. But, he still has to be online playing this game. If not, I can't get anything."

"Andrea to me Zander's not around today," I said. "He's going to be at some Renaissance thing at UCSC. Wouldn't it be better if he wasn't there, so he couldn't tell what you were doing?"

"Yes and no, mostly no."

"Why?"

"I told you, when Zander plays the game like he's doing now, he gives me the opening in the firewall."

"Yeah, so..."

"After he logs off, someone has to go over to Surf Dot Com and log Zander back onto Battlenet so I can play him. Then I can get busy, and fill the game with peons and get into all the systems of every dot-com start-up that's connected with Surf Dot Com. I can clean out all their databases! But, like I've been telling you, if Zander comes back and figures out I've messed with his system. He can use his packet sniffers and he'll find out what information I had access to."

"That's just not happenin'," I said. "He won't return. I'll go with Andrea to the Renaissance Faire. I'll meet her at Surf Dot Com, when I'm there, I'll log Zander's computer online."

"I'll write up a list for you on how to do it.," said Squirrel. "It's real easy. I even have the guy's battle-net password. All you have to do is make sure Zander doesn't return to work."

"He won't."

"What are you going to do?" asked Chops, amused. "Mount his head on a pole? Frag him?"

"How the hell do I know what I'm going to do? But, like I said, him stopping us is just not happenin'."

Ralph went through the documents as they came out through the printer and snorted, "This stuff is amazing." He looked down and studied a particular page and handed it to me. "If you're going to see Andrea, you want her to see this. It's about her."

The document Ralph handed me was entitled 'Questionable Assets'. It was a list of Surf Dot Com employees. Andrea's name was at the top of the list.

"What's 'Questionable Assets' mean?" I asked.

"It means Drake's planning cutbacks and, she's one of them," said Ralph.

Edwin Starr's 'War' played on the shop speakers.

"I am locked and loaded," said Squirrel, who rapidly hit keys. "I am the bomb." He hit another key. The printer started kicking out documents.

"You're right, Squirrel," I said, proudly placing my hand on the kid's flabby shoulder. I observed the battle. "This is definitely more than just a game."

"Damn Skippy," he paused. "Fo' shizzle my nizzle."

"What's that mean?"

"You don't want to know," said Squirrel, laughing.

The Crew gathered around the screen and watched Squirrel's knights gallop through a pastoral field of sweeping fields of grain and grunting livestock. Squirrel's legion was suddenly surrounded by ogres, and winged dwarves.

"It's time to take out my can of whoop ass," said Squirrel, who briefly took his fingers from the keyboard. He yawned, and then made a big show of pressing down a single key with a one-finger flourish. "Dot Boom."

The battle screen was consumed with blinding bolts of rays, fireballs, and flashing swords. A dark cloud filled the screen. Slowly, the fog of war lifted. The landscape was decimated with fires and explosions. The scorched ground of the digital world was littered with hundreds of enemy skeletons lying on mounds of pixeled-out gray ashes.

THE DISCO BALL'S GLITTER sparkled a watery reflection on my shop boards, which hung from straps attached to the rafters above the cubicles in Surf Dot Com. The irritating thump of techno-arrhythmic music was replaced with a mellow ukulele tune. Israel Kamakawiwo'ole, an Hawaiian guy, sang 'Somewhere Over The Rainbow.' I passed the War Room. The door was open. I spotted Weever. He sat in a chair alone near the speakerphone. He looked like he was squinting. But it was more than that. There was something off. He didn't even notice me. He was wincing. Weever looked like he had found, claimed and ruled his own private layer of depression. I mean we all look that way once in awhile, but this guy was deep into it, and sinking deeper. He was misery without a map. He wasn't going anywhere. On the speakerphone a group of children sang: "From a distance, the world is blue and green." The chorus sang, "God is watching us, God is watching us." I figured it out. It was his kid's school performance. He felt guilty because he wasn't there for his children. I actually felt sorry for Weever. I didn't want to intrude. I said nothing. I softly back-pedaled away.

I approached Andrea's cubicle. She was talking on another new cell phone that was a different color and even smaller than her last one. Her back was to me. She was no longer dressing up. She was dressing down. More and more she resembled a Pleasure Point surf bum. Her blonde hair was pulled off her neck, and bunched upright on her head like a small dust broom.

She wore one of my frayed, hooded sweatshirts, a pair of sweatpants with holes in them, and sandals. I held the 'Questionable Assets' sheet in my right hand.

"You had an off-site launch, I'm down with that," she trilled. "I was at this launch last week and because of all those fucking Asian women I couldn't even get a guy to even look at me. No big loss either, all these geeks, you know, the roll-your-own hackers. But there were tons of tchotchkes. What was in the swag bag? I—oh, oh, oh, wait, you'll never believe who is coming over here to go to the Renaissance Faire with me at UCSC. Vic! Yeah, my surfer local person. It's so ep! And tonight we're going Over The Hill to San Jose. Locals hate Highway 17. I mean nobody in Santa Cruz wants to drive 17 to work. They'd rather get less money, and work two jobs just to live here so they don't have to go Over The Hill. When I took this gig, my headhunter warned me, she said, 'Whatever you do, don't get trapped on doing everything in Santa Cruz. You'll forget the forest for the trees.' And she was right! People here think Santa Cruz is the whole world. Santa Cruz is like that island in Pinocchio where all the boys stay too long and become donkeys. People in Santa Cruz stay here too long and become these creatures that don't fit anywhere else. Talk about narrowing your bandwidth.Their virtual isn't undoable. Vic's a perfect example. Outside of surfing and his shop he never wants to try anything new. His only friends are surfers, and they're just like him. Everyone else he knew dropped surfing and moved on with their lives, developed other interests But not him. I think that's why so many people knows Vic but why has so few close friends. Get Vic to go up to Tahoe to ski, forget it. Vic won't dance. Vic won't go to concerts. Get him to leave here, impossible. Unless if going to Corralitos to buy homemade jerky at a meat market qualifies as leaving town. And get this, when we go out he always takes his stupid dog."

Stupid dog? I retreated a few steps out of her sight line. I could still hear her.

"I mean like the guy is totally attached to his dog—it's obscene. I mean it's maudlin. If I hear him baby talk, 'Whups' or 'Whuppers' one more time, I'll totally hurl. I mean I know animals have unconditional love and all that, but a dog can only love you like a dog not like a person. It's a disposable relationship at best." She laughed. "Yeah, you're right, I'm one to talk. Right, disposable is the key word. I guess that's why he and I get along. You know me, Ms Backward Compatibility. I always go through a new guy every six months. I mean, hello! Earth to Santa Cruz. Earth to Santa Cruz. He's going to have to grow. He's coming along, though, but it always has to be through surfing. There is a whole world out there. Otherwise, that's just not happenin'."

And here's another thing that was just not happenin', I thought, folding up the 'Questionable Assets' document and putting it in my back pocket. I snuck quickly past Andrea. Her back was to me. I hunched down and entered Zander's cubicle. I went to his computer and moved the mouse. The screensaver of Pamela Anderson disappeared. I looked at his desktop, found the Battlenet.com icon, and clicked it. I looked at the paper with Squirrel's instructions and logged Zander online. The Warblood game appeared. I watched peons scurrying back and forth, carrying gold bricks. Slowly, the number of laboring peons kept increasing. I smiled. Squirrel was taking it to the streets.

"Zander is that you over there?" said Andrea.

I slid underneath the IT's desk. My face was near some stale French fries and a half-eaten Big Mac, which were atop piles of frozen-food boxes in the wastepaper basket.

"Zander?" Andrea said, then resumed her call, "Oh, it's nothing Tucker. So, our second option is tomorrow..."

I crept quickly past her cubicle. She turned in my direction. I ducked into the Chill Out Room. I faced The Webmasters. They were absorbed in a project: melting Gummy Bear candies in the microwave. Fernando was there too, cleaning the sink

"Dude, check it out!" said Jef-with-one-f, staring into the oven window. "It's so rad. The guy is all morphed."

"Fucking looks like Zander, dude," said Gregg-with-two-gs.

"Keep it in the pocket, G," replied Jef-with-one-f. "Dude, we use a red Gummy Bear next time. Yeah, that is Zander, dude."

The two shouted, "All right now!" They followed it with a rhythmic handclap, stopped, made a fist, briefly tapped each other's knuckles and said, "Go Cardinal!"

The Webmasters looked over at Fernando.

"There's a job," disparagingly scoffed Jef-with-one f, nodding at my laboring friend.

"How'd you like to be doing that at fifty?" added Greg-with-two-g's, who probably thought Fernando didn't know English.

The Webmasters saw me and said sarcastically, "Wassup?"

I ignored them and said, "Fernando, como esta?"

Fernando turned around and smiled," A-meeee-go."

We shook hands and he smiled at me with his missing front teeth. The sight appalled Jef-with-one-f and Gregg-with-two-gs, who probably never knew anyone who was missing teeth.

I jerked my head toward the Webmasters and replied, "Tiene cabezas in el culo."

They have their heads up their ass.

"Ooooooh, pinche Victor, you're bad, a-meeeee-go," Fernando warmly said, and chuckled. He loved it when I used dirty phrases he taught me.

The Webmasters didn't understand us, but left when they suspected we were ridiculing them. Andrea laughed outside. Fernando noticed my eyes suddenly react in anger.

"A-meee-go," he said sadly. He was disappointed in me. "You don't love her, a-meeee-go."

"I thought she was good for me."

"But you did not love her."

I said nothing.

Fernando scraped the gunky, gummy bears out of the microwave and said, "Ama a quien no te ama, responder a quien no te llama, y andaras carreras vanas."

Love whom does not love you, go to her who does not call you, and you will be running around in vain.

"Hasta." I said, leaving.

When I got to Andrea's cubicle, she shifted from her cell phone to diva mic. She stared at a close-up picture of her face on the computer monitor. She clicked keys and changed the pixels in the image to narrow her waist, add blonde streaks to her hair, give her skin a darker tan, and put deeper blue into her pupils.

"I'll e-mail you a JPEG of me surfing on a wave, later, Yeah, I surf!" she said. "Gotta fly, bye."

"Andrea."

"Hey you," she said spinning around in her chair to face me. "Primed to do a faire? I have to make sure the banner is placed right. Zander is on site representing us. He's challenging people in sword fights. He's even streaming it on the web site. We'll take my car. Leave Ranger in your van. Did you talk to Weever about Costa Rica? I've never been to Costa Rica." She paused. "I'm sorry. I'm talking too fast, my wings are flapping from two low-fat double espresso caramel macchiato. I've been setting up all the caterers for the second offering blast for tomorrow, I had to order togas for the entire team—and, a purple one for Drake, of course. Plus armor outfits for two guys."

"Second offering?" I said, acting confused.

"The second offering," she repeated.

"Oh yeah, that's right," I said. "It doesn't mean anything to me, I don't have any stock." I paused. "I only get paid in cash."

"God, if you get paid in cash how do you make any money? Anyway, we're holding the stock offering bash on the second floor of Drake's beach house. His place is still not done. The second floor is where I'm putting in tables. I had to throw down carpets. It still just has plywood floor on it. The first floor looks finished and that lighthouse turret thing is all done, but a lot of the house still has framing on the third floor. Go figure. I put in a projection screen, full bar, food and bubbly."

I gazed up at a shop board, but snuck a peak at Zander's monitor: gold-carrying peons swarmed across the screen.

"Are you mad at me?"

"No, not you."

"The Second Offering party kicks off when the market opens in the morning with Mimosas and Bloodies. Did you see our latest price? We went to $225 on the strength of expanding our network. I can't imagine how high it will go when Drake puts out more shares on the second offering. It's so ep! I exercised my options last week. But I'd be a fool to cash out. Do you have any idea how much I'm worth?"

"Yeah, a rough idea," I grunted, which is how I figured she thought a 'twisted' veteran with a 'stupid' dog would react.

"Is everything all right?"

"Fine," I lied. "I have a headache, I guess."

"Check this out," said Andrea, spinning back around in her chair to face the computer. "I've been working on this photo all morning." She clicked a key. "Before," she said. I saw the complete picture. It was a shot of Andrea surfing a wave on a longboard. .Behind Andrea on the wave, a woman screamed at her; and in surfing front of Andrea, was another woman, who flipped her off. "After," she said, hitting a key. The screen went blank for a second. The pixels reassembled into another image. The two women vanished. The only person left in the picture was Andrea, who resembled the perfect vision of a California surfer girl—deeply tanned with blue eyes and long blonde hair and riding a wave. Andrea nickered and purred to herself, "Ehhhh-xcellent." She laughed. "I look like the cover of a Roxie girl clothing catalog! I'm on the nose too." She turned around, smiled at me, and added, "Isn't it so *kewl*? I just eliminate all the people."

"I guess they were questionable assets," I said.

"What?"

"That's you. That's really you, *hombre*."

I started third-personing. I looked at the shop boards drifting in the dot-com sky. I felt suspended too. I kept my shop, but lost my shop. What I was doing with my life was no different than what Andrea did to the pixels on the screen. I ruined friendships by crowding out surf spots with my classes to make money. What I did was wrong. And what did I get in return? The admiration and flattery people I never respected—Whew-hoos, Wassups, and the You-Go Girls, who honked their horns as they drove by me, or acknowledged me on the street, and in the water to impress their friends: the dot-comers were cool because they surfed and knew a local surfer *person*. And, I couldn't help but notice they never said hello unless someone could see them say hello to me. If the dot-comers were by themselves, they found a way to avoid me. And what was my legacy? A new bumper sticker and a decal joined the list of markings that identified the wanna-be-cool Instant Local: one was my surf shop logo; the other one, was the Santa Cruz'n Surf Diva's logo. I looked at Andrea's edited and revised image. What had I cropped from the dot-com world to make Andrea look good to me? And what else had I cropped from my life to fit her into my virtual Santa Cruz world? Shiloh, that's who, Shiloh. But was my virtual world undoable?

I lifted up my hand, flicked my finger, and thumped my father's ring against my forehead.

"Hey, that looked like it hurt," said Andrea, surprised.

"Yeah, it did," I said.

Andrea and I walked separately down a straw pathway that ran through a 16th-century recreation of an Elizabethan country fair and marketplace. There were thatched huts and huge burlap tents with long banners flapping atop them, placed on a couple acres of an open field on the UCSC campus. Hundreds of milling people were dressed like they were in the Middle Ages: earth-colored clothes made of wool, woven cotton, raw silk, flax, leather and linen. The guys wore muffin caps, muslin, straw, or feathered and squashed hats, as well as breeches, loose long-sleeved shirts with drawstrings, jerkins, cod pieces, knee-high socks and boots or moccasins. Some were equipped with sheathed daggers and swords. Other turkey-leg wielding fairgoers carried goblets, tankards, and mugs. Women went for low-cut tops with some type of underwear lining, and ankle-length gauzy dresses, scarves, ribbons, and lace, with Birkenstocks or Kung Fu slippers. The women had a set group of characters: weavers, candle makers, beer-flagon carrying barmaids, or peasants baking bread and roasting meats in black metal kettles, which were suspended by chains from rods over wood fires. Very few of the people would have been good looking in any other time period. Then I remembered a form of music I hated as much as the cello: Celtic music, which was painful. But, after all, this wasn't my scene. I mean, everyone else loved it, and sang and drank. They seemed like nice enough people just having fun. And who was I to say anything? Andrea and I were identically dressed in 'Vic's Surf Shop T-shirts, jeans and sandals. We were the ones who were out of place.

"I swear if they ever did a pewter and leather recall this would be a good place to start," Andrea said, studying the crafts booths. She assumed a British accent. "My noble Lord of Pleasure Point, pray tell, you've never visit'st ye olden Renaissance fair?"

"No."

"Are ye having a good time?" she said in her normal voice.

"Oh sure."

"Then tell your face about it," she said. "If someone asks who you came as, I'll tell them you came as 'The Plague." She paused. "Is something wrong?"

"I'm fine. Fine."

We passed an arrangement of mud-shaped fairies at an intersection constructed with corners made of stacked hay bales. A signposts said we were at Archangel Crossing and Crown Meadow. A court jester guy dressed in short pants and stockings balanced on a short plank of wood placed atop two wooden barrels. We stopped near stages and artisan booths of handmade wood with sod and straw roofs. We watched fire-eating mimes and ropewalkers. We scanned a snack bar menu:

Eat, Drynke & Be Merrie

Faire Viands

Sweete corn
Ye stuffed spud
Pizza
Freyed ice cream
Canterbury Pork Pockets
Steake on a Stake
Toad-in-a-Hole
King's Nuts
Hearty English Ale
Mead and Honey Wyne
Wilde Turkey Leg
Shepherd's Pye
French Fries
Coke

"Does'th ye desire any golden leeks and onions?" Andrea said. "Oooooh, the menu has Toad-in-the-hole. Hold me back! Color me there. Nothing like a greasy sausage banger cooked with cabbage in Yorkshire pudding to get this maiden in a bawdy mood."

"Oh God, do I smell anchovies?" I said, sniffing and narrowing my eyes. "I hate anchovies."

"Close stuffed sardines," she replied. "I'm saving my appetite foe perch in yellow cooked pears too. Yum. I—"

Andrea was interrupted by a particular knight doing battle.

"You are vanquished, knave!" declared a familiar voice, which tried to be omnipotent, but couldn't shake its whiney edge.

It was Zander. He was engaged in a sword fight against a pale and overweight guy who looked just like him. They wore football helmets with metal face grills. I knew which one was Zander, because the IT's helmet had horns on it. The combatants' arms, legs, chest and shoulders were covered with plastic plates that looked more like baseball-catcher shin guards than armor. Beneath the plastic were chain-mail shirts, and under the mail was some kind of sweatshirt, which couldn't conceal the knights' sagging and flapping fish-white bellies. The two grunted, puffed, and awkwardly whacked each other with wooden swords. They had scuffed-up shields made of a spongy material that muffled the blows. All they seemed to do was hit swords instead of each other. Dot-com geeks in SDC polo shirts and khaki pants, held tiny cameras and filmed the battle for the web page's Internet broadcast.

"Gandoff, you smashed my beeper!" Zander said angrily to his foe. "This isn't Quake or Doom, this is as real as it gets."

Suddenly, approaching trumpets played a fanfare.

An archer, who had a false goatee, pointed at an approaching procession, and said, "Hark, 'tis the royal court."

A whirling dance troupe came towards us, followed by strolling minstrels banging felt mallets on goatskin drums, blowing wooden flutes, and strumming guitars that looked lie triangular shoeboxes. The festive Celtic horror sounded like the musicians were falling down a flight of stairs while trying to play their instruments. In the middle of the troupe, protected by a retinue of red-jacketed guys, was a pale and heavily powdered lady with a black wig, and a crown, who wore a purple velvet gown. She said high upon in a throne-like sedan carried by servants. She held up her hand. The procession halted.

"Check out the Royal Guard," Andrea said, nodding at the red jackets around the queen. "They look more like extras in a bad high school play."

We were soon surrounded by bar maids, jesters, knights, friars, gypsies, blacksmiths, merchants, glassblowers, squires, farmers, mimes, musketeers, town criers, and ladies-in-waiting who had teenage pages holding up the long train behind their dresses. There were even a few pirates, which surprised me.

"Looks like the same crowd that hangs out at the downtown mall in Santa Cruz," said Andrea.

"That's funny," I said, not laughing.

Zander stopped his fight, walked over, and addressed the queen. The engraved coat of arms in the middle of his breast plate said "Surf Dot Com." The gallery made Zander come alive. He made broad gestures and spoke in one of those deep and stupid Shakespearean voices.

"Good morrow your Grace, Sir Surf of Dot Com is honored thou has'th made a pilgrimage to our enchanted shire," Zander said, bowing grandly to the Queen.

"He's in his element—methane," said Andrea. Her phone bipped. A minstrel gave her a dirty look. She flicked the phone open and said "Hey you!" She paused. "I'll tell him."

"What's up?" I asked as she snapped her cell phone shut.

"That was a security firm Zander hired to do some type of packet sniffing," said Andrea. "They said a 'benign entity' is accessing SDC's database. I have no idea what it means. It's all techie stuff. They need Zander back on the campus ASAP."

"But he's having such a good time," I said. "You can't—"

"I don't know what it means, but evidently it's real critical." She paused. "Sir Dot of Com must pay fealty to yon cubicle."

"It can't wait?"

"He has to fly post haste."

Now, that just wasn't happenin', I thought, Zander can't return to work. He'd discover what Squirrel was doing. The Bros of Drake would win. Then, I got an idea. A good one.

"That fat dork doesn't know shit on how to use a sword," I derisively shouted, pointing at Zander.

The peasant children around me laughed.

"This is a serious martial art," said Zander, who was so offended by my crack, he briefly broke character.

"Come on, you suck," I said.

The peasant children laughed again. Minstrels played lutes and did rim shots on their drums.

Zander got back into his medieval character and said to the royal court, "Oh Highness, this knave's temerity before thee, verily displays he be a barbarous prattler indeed." The Queen benignly smiled and nodded her approval of the knight's witticism. Zander checked to make sure the web cameras were focused on him. He addressed at me, "Doth this dried meat wag emerge to do battle from a woman's chambers!" Then he spoke to the crowd. "And doth this low-born upstart dare to assail the occasion of our pageantry?"

"Yeah."

"Since honor means little to a rogue such as thee," imperiously said Zander, turning his head from me to Andrea. "Perchance thou would'st do battle with me for the favor of this young sportive damsel in the name of chivalry?"

"Yeah sure," I said, shrugging.

"I challenge thee to do battle," said Zander, removing a gauntlet from his right hand and flinging it in the dry dirt at my feet. I stared at it. The protective glove had a 24K gold engraving of Surf Dot Com's logo. "Don some armor to suit thy words to the name of action."

"Armor?"

"Doth ye have'th second thoughts?"

"I don't need armor. Just give me a sword, horn head," I said. "And stop talking like that." I paused. "It soundeth stupid."

Zander muttered, "For a man of your means, the price of poison is never too high."

The snare drummer in the crowd did another rim shot. There was more laughter. More lutes.

I said to the musicians, "After him, you guys are next."

They found this funny and laughed.

Andrea rushed to my side and said, "Oh, wear this in battle for your fair damsel, it will bring you great fortune for I fear for thee." She tied a scarf on my wrist. She smiled and whispered, "I saw someone do it in a movie." She chuckled and walked away saying, "And don't worry, if you fail in your quest for the grail, and Zander tries to besmirch me, my chastity belt is set on stun."

I marched to face The Mighty Zander in the field of battle. The crowd circled us. We stood opposite each other. Zander was thirty paces away from me. He swaggered like a colossus atop a slight slope. He held his gloved hand aloft to quell the crowd. There was a ridiculously respectful silence.

"The rules governing this contest are simple," ceremoniously declared Zander in a deep voice within his plastic helmet. He played to the web cameras. "Art thou ready to be bold, scurvy knave? All will soon witness Sir Dot of Com's wrath reigning down upon thee like a pox. There are no rules. To the death."

I borrowed a Homer Simpson page from Squirrel's limited book of repartees. "Boring"

The peasants and the Royal Court laughed. There were more drums. Some tambourines. And unfortunately, more lutes.

"For honor," Zander bellicosely bellowed. "Lay on!" He charged and spun his duct-taped wooden sword over his head. His plastic armor clicked and his chain mail clanked. He wailed his battle cry, "Yaaaaaaaaaaaaaaaaaaaaaaaah."

I didn't budge. I stood still, kept my sword low, and calmly balanced the balls of my feet to the weapon's sway and weight. He was six feet away. He cocked back his sword. I briefly wondered if I should do to him, what I was planning to do.

"Yaaaaaaaaaaaaaaaaaaaaaaaaah," screamed Zander, swinging his sword at my head.

I ducked. He just missed my head. I dropped to one knee. When Zander passed, I sharply whipped my sword around, whacked his calves, and cleanly cut him down from behind. Zander fell to his knees. I was pumped. It was welcome-back-to-Vietnam time. I raised my sword and swung it with all my might. There was a hollow thunk. A crack.. My wooden sword broke in two pieces. His helmet flew off. It landed ten feet away, minus one horn. I victoriously stood over the vanquished IT.

Zander gazed at me in an uncomprehending, downloaded daze. His head bobbled atop his neck. His eyes rolled up. His jaw went slack. He listed on his knees. With his arms at his sides, he fell forward, face down in the straw. His plastic armor clattered. The chain mail on his chest rang out with a final ca-ching.

"Awesome," shouted the peasant children.

A mob gathered around us.

"Somebody get a doctor!," shouted a sorcerer dressed in a black cone-shaped hat, and a gold-star embroidered purple robe.

"You're a fuckin' idiot," yelled a friar in a New York slur. "You could have killed him."

"What are ya, retarded?" shouted a pirate in a Boston accent.

I removed my helmet and said, "He tried to take my head off! Don't blame me. He's the one that said no rules."

Andrea rushed over and said in a shocked tone but snickered through it, "My Lord and master, what have you done?"

"When he took at swing at my head, I just lost it," I said, looking at Zander, who was receiving mouth-to-mouth resuscitation from a pirate, which the pirate seemed to be enjoying.

"Let's fly before they kill us," whispered Andrea.

We ran from the fair and into the woods. She sprinted ahead and directed me into a redwood grove. I was still pumped from the duel. We stood in the center of a ten-foot circular forest floor, completely enclosed by several two-hundred-foot tall redwoods. The dry heat baked the air and cooked up a raspy, wooden, resinous smell. Nobody pursued us.

"That was ep!" said Andrea, laughing. "God, you lit that guy up. I'm actually looking forward to going into work just so when I go into the office Zander won't be there for once." She leaned back against one of the trees. "I love redwoods," she sighed. She turned, pressed her chin on the bark, and looked up. "Redwoods are locals. They thrive here. I think it's because of the fog and the moisture. Nothing kills these guys. They survive fires. They can be blackened, hollowed out, and they're still alive. They're amazing. You know, redwoods don't grow like pines from pine cones. Redwoods network. They have a root system that's connected, and when something attacks the root, another tree grows. That's why they grow in a protective circle around the biggest tree. Just like the way The Crew hangs around you." She studied the barren circle of dirt. "They logged the big one out."

"The big one? What do you mean?"

"The first generation redwood was where we're standing. A logger yanked it out a hundred years ago to make some money. He left these guys. The first generation was milled."

"Huh."

"Look at the light coming through the spars," Andrea said, spinning around in the center of the trees. The sunbeams flickered around her moving figure, as if her image was a on a strip of film sliding over the white bulb of a movie projector. She gazed at the canopy above us. "It's like a cathedral. You can't see the forest for the trees." She turned, leaned her back against a redwood, angled her hips toward me, and gave off a hard look that didn't have to be explained. "I got you in here, didn't I?"

She undid her belt buckle, then mine. She was all there. But I was angry and deeply mad-dogging everything else but her.

Andrea dropped me off at the Surf Dot Com parking lot. It was nearly four in the afternoon. We saw small waves coming through Cowells. Shiloh's van was parked near the Dream Inn hotel. She had a class out. Andrea wanted to surf with me. I lied and said I had to pick up some boards. I wanted to get back to the shop to find out if Squirrel was successful. Andrea said she'd pick me up for tonight's party. It was a quiet drive to the other side of town. Ranger was sulking because I left her in the van. When I pulled up to the shop, the placed looked closed. The lights inside were dim. The front door was shut.

I gently lowered Ranger onto the sidewalk, and said softly, "Come on whups. There you go."

A teenager dressed in baggy pants, a heavy hooded sweatshirt, and a wool-knit cap, loped out the shop's door. He slightly lurched side to side as he listened to his headphones. He carried a plastic shopping bag. The arm of a new wetsuit stuck out of it. Knit-cap saw me, averted his eyes, and picked up his pace. I slowly opened the shop door. Rap music played. I crept into the shop. In the back by the computers, I heard the chain-sloshing sound of quarters being scooped out of the Pepsi machine's change box. Its front door was open. The shop keys were in the vending machine's popped-out, t-shaped lock. Squirrel knelt on the floor and shoved handfuls of quarters in his pocket.

I turned off the rap music. An oldie came on. 'Tie Me Kangaroo, Down Sport' by Rolf Harris.

Squirrel looked over his shoulder and said, "Busted."

I studied him, spun my Dad's ring around my finger, and said, "What's going on *hombre*?"

"Nothing."

"That's nothing?"

"Just getting some money for a pizza."

"You mean *stealing* money for pizza, don't you?"

"My bad," indifferently grumbled Squirrel. "I figured it was okay. I got everything you needed for Dave and Ralph."

"If you figured it was okay, then why didn't you call and ask me first?"

"I was going to tell you and all."

"What was that punk doing leaving with that new wetsuit?"

"A wetsuit?"

"You floated a wetsuit out of here to that piece of shit."

"If I was doing that why would I be taking quarters from the Pepsi machine for pizza?"

"I'll tell you why, because once you start stealing, you can't bear to ever pay for anything. It's pretty cool when you get away with something isn't it? But when you get caught you're not so cool are you? Cause all you are is just a fucking thief."

"So?" Squirrel grunted. "You're the guy talking about ripping off those dot-comers in your classes."

"That was work."

"Well, you sounded like you were stealing something."

"I bought you a laptop. You make good money here. I give you everything you want. All you have to do is ask. I've put away money to send you to college. And after all I've given you this is the thanks I get?"

"What's the big deal?" grunted Squirrel, who looked right into my eyes and said, "You can afford it."

"What?" I said, advancing toward him.

He tried to get up, but he tripped on one of his loose sneaker laces. I kicked him in the ass and knocked him down. Quarters flew into the air. Ranger chased and barked at Squirrel. A rolled up wad of twenties and a clear plastic baggie filled with weed dropped from his pocket. Squirrel tried to grab the cash and dope. Ranger snapped at his hand. He pulled it back. I yanked Squirrel up by his shirt and heaved him across the floor. The baseball cap flew off his head. He banged against the boards and fell. He started crying, but I wasn't sure from what.

I picked up the dope and cash, shoved it in his face, and said, "What is this shit?"

"Oh, like you never did it before," he snapped.

"Do you see this shit in my shop?" I asked, booting his ass and knocking him on his belly. "Do you see me drinking? Do you see me getting high? Do you? Not in this shop. Not anywhere."

"You're not my Dad—"

"If I'm not your Dad, than stop acting like my son," I said, ready to flick him in the forehead with my Father's ring.

Squirrel covered his head and pleaded, "Not the ring, not the ring! I hate the ring, I hate the ring."

I looked at my cocked finger. What was I doing? What was I becoming? I pulled the gold ring off, and whipped it into the corner of the shop, where it rang off an epoxy board.

"I'm sorry!" Squirrel sincerely blurted. "I'm sorry."

"Sorry for what? Sorry for—"

"Stealing," he said, still on his knees. "Sorry for being a fucking thief. All right! All right?"

I grabbed a T-shirt off the rack, heaved it at his head, and said, "Clean off your face."

Squirrel caught it. He cried and wiped his nose.

'Mountain of Love' by Johnny Rivers played.

I looked at the clear plastic bag of dope and the twenties in my hand. Is this what Squirrel was learning from me? But why was I asking myself questions I knew the answers to? I didn't feel good about hitting him. Whatever went into him went out of me. I felt drained.

"I'm sorry too," I said. "I'm sorry I hit you."

"I deserved it," said Squirrel.

"Yeah, you did."

Driveway Dave and Ralph burst through the front door, eating hot dogs and carrying thick folders.

"I give you the 'Bros of Drake,'" Ralph gleefully said, and spread his hands over a pile of folders, which he arranged like ascending steps on the front counter. He pointed at the lowest step. "This is Surf Dot Com. One company." He tapped the next raised step, a much thicker folder. "These are all the companies Surf Dot Com has contracts with." Then he pointed to the last step, a larger folder with over five hundred pages in it. "And, here in this third pile, are the companies the firms in the second pile are connected with." He looked at me. "And what do all these companies have in common?" Ralph held up a single piece of paper. "Every one of these deals is handled by the same bank and brokerage firm: Credit First San Jose Suisse." He took a bite of a hot dog and passed his hand above the paperwork stairway. "And in these piles, every CEO on each start-up firm's advisory board is a card-carrying members in 'The Bros of Drake.'"

Dave wiped the mustard off his mustache and said, "We pretty much knew Drake and his business cronies were giving themselves deals. But this is much bigger! Here's how the scam works. Every high-tech company in this pile has an advisory board. These advisory board members can give stock to each other or to relatives, and these advisory boards are not required by law to report any of this to the stockholders. The Bros-of-Drake are giving each other shares under the legal category called 'Friends of the Family.' And get this, if you're a stockholder who wants to find out who's on the advisory board, the company isn't legally obligated to provide the names of its members."

Ralph shoved some French fries into his mouth and added, "The 'Bros of Drake' get first crack at Surf Dot Com's stock. And why are Drake and his buddies getting first crack at another company's IPO or second offering? The answer: Credit First San Jose Suisse. Suisse is the bank that backs Surf Dot Com's stock. In order to get the money from the bank for their IPO or second offering, The Bros agree to give the Credit First San Jose Suisse's brokers and bankers, kickbacks and higher commissions on the sales of SDC's stock. That's how it begins. It also helps that the investment firm, which reviews and rates the legitimate value of SDC's stock, also just happens to be a branch *within* Credit First San Jose Suisse, which stands to make a huge profit from the sale of SDC stock because they also lent Drake and his buddies the money for their company. Okay, the next move is when the brokers at Suisse's investment firm generate a buzz about SDC's stock value by recommending it as a 'buy' to investors, which the brokers know is based on cooked up books, phony profits, and doctored projected earnings. So, when the IPO, or Surf Dot Com's second stock offering goes public, investors fight over each other to buy it, and escalate the value of the highly touted stock. The Bros of Drake—who were given the stock earlier at bargain basement prices—sell their stock and make millions. But, it doesn't end there. Here's where the bubble blows itself up from inside out. The CEO insiders, alias 'The Bros of Drake,' who made big bucks because Suisse's brokers gave them the first crack at Surf Dot Com stock, are the same CEO Bros of Drake who also sit on the advisory boards of *other* dot-com start-ups, and these Bros Of Drake have Credit First San Jose Suisse underwrite the funds for their new dot-com start-up's stock offerings. In exchange for the underwriting agreement, the brokers of Suisse's investment firm give out first-crack shares to the CEO 'Bros of Drake' in the form of special brokerage accounts. Then Suisse's investment firm rates the new start-up's stock as a 'buy' and the whole process expands again. It's more than a bro deal, it's a bro deal cubed." He laughed. "But, once Squirrel does his damage by releasing all this information, the greed that once had investors scrambling for the hottest tech stock, will be turned inside out, and every investor will be fighting to get *out* of all high-tech stocks. That's where we come in. Not only will we score by shorting Surf Dot Com's stock and all of its other start-ups, but we'll really score big time when I also put shorts out on the so-called bullet-proof high-tech companies, such as Cisco, Yahoo, Sun Microsystems, and several others, because those stocks will take a dive in reaction to the downward spiraling of the market." Ralph gestured to the workstations. "Now, we're the ones who have the technology!"

Dave noticed Squirrel picking up quarters from the floor. He sensed the something-went-down vibe and said, "Hey, are we interrupting? Did something happen?"

"Squirrel was floating a wetsuit to some punk out of the shop and stealing quarters from the Pepsi machine for pizza. It's an issue. But right now, you guys have the floor."

Horns honked. Car doors slammed. We looked outside. Sonny, The Legend, and Chops, rushed past us to the back of the shop, went behind a shoji screen, and grabbed their boards.

The Legend's eyes were darting as he said, "There's a South with a little West pushing in. It's classic 38th."

Skin Dog added, "It's going to be a good score until dark."

"Perfect little three footers just rolling through there," said Chops. "It's a small ass with a double D out there."

"Nobody's on it.," said Sonny, Not a single sinner out there."

Ranger watched them and became agitated. She sensed we were going to the beach. She mewled and barked.

"I'm on it," I said. "I have to get my wetsuit, it's in the back," then I added to Squirrel. "After you're done there, take the board down from outside, bring in the wetsuits, vacuum the shop, and clean out the toilets in the bathroom." I paused. "After that, order a couple pizzas for everyone with those quarters."

"Pepperoni?" Squirrel said, perking up.

"I don't care what you get as long as it's meat. But no anchovies. I don't want baitfish swimming in my cheese."

"Andrea's here," said The Legend, leaving with The Crew.

"You guys charge it, Ranger and I will catch up."

Chris Montez sang out of tune on 'The More I See You.'

Andrea's gull-wing convertible parked in front of the shop. A ten-foot longboard was wedged at an angle beneath the dashboard against the passenger seat, which had tropical red-and-white hibiscus Roxie seatcovers. The Crew acknowledged her, and sped away. Andrea legged it into the shop. She wore a low-cut, black evening gown, and red spiked heels. With two hands she held the longboard at arm's length off to her right side, as if she feared it would contaminate her. Ranger quickly went to her dog dish and devoured all her food.

"My board had a little accident," she said, nodding her head at a three-inch fin gash from the rail to the wooden stringer at the nose of the board. "It was all Shiloh's fault too." Andrea placed her damaged board on the floor. Her phone bipped. She flipped her cell phone open and said, "Hey you." She handed the yellow phone to me. "Weever. I told him to call me when I got here."

"Yeah, Bobby," I said neutrally.

"This morning I was talking to some CEOs and CFOs who are key players in Pan-American stuff," said Weever to me. "They saw SDC's web page, and read about you being a combat veteran. These CEOs want you to take them to Vietnam."

"Vietnam," I said excitedly. "I never surfed Vietnam. I've always wanted to surf Vietnam."

"When you meet them tonight you'll give the project arms and legs," said Weever. "Vic, once you're there as a baseline, they'll get their arms around the concept, and the rubber hits the road."

"Vietnam," I said, completely psyched, forgetting whatever reservations I had about Weever or Andrea. "Man, I'd love to surf China Beach. Vietnam."

"Vic, I'll let you go now," said Weever. "Oh yeah, by the way, I was wondering...I still want a classic board."

"We'll work a deal," I said, and quickly added. "Later, bro."

Bro.

I pulled the yellow phone off my face like it was a banana slug.

"This is so Ep!" said Andrea, who smiled. "I wanted it to be a surprise. I thought it would be a good closure thing for you. And not only that, some big-time movers and shakers are going to be at this bash. A lot of net worth. This could be a big opportunity to advance your life to the next level. You don't ever have to be stuck in Santa Cruz. Think out of the box. Don't let this place be your coffin."

"Bro" I numbly said, as if I had cold-cocked myself.

"What's wrong?" asked Andrea.

"Bro," I soberly repeated it. "I just said bro." I paused. "There, I said it again."

"Bro? Duh, hello? Bro's a word. It doesn't mean anything," she said.

"Then why is it a word? Why is anything a word?"

Andrea shifted her attention to the way I was dressed and said, "You're not going like that are you? This soiree is at a totally ep four-star place. We don't want to look too Santa Cruz." She bounced her head from side to side, and whined, "Do we *have* to take Ranger tonight? I don't want dog fur on my dress."

Ranger barked and scratched at the glass on the front door. She wanted the beach.

I felt like I regained consciousness and said, "IJAH."

"IJAH? What's that, some reggae term? First with 'bro' and now with the 'IJAH'. Could you enlighten me, puh-leeze. IJAH Hello? Translation? Listening."

I opened the door, let Ranger out, and said, "I'll give you the 411 by spelling it out for you ASAP: I-J-A-H. Translation: It Just Ain't Happenin'."

"What precipitated this?" Andrea said, giving me her where'd-my-low-fat-double-espresso-caramel-macchiato-go? take.

I put Ranger in the passenger seat, threw my wetsuit in the back, and returned into the shop.

"Excuse me," she said, snapping her hair back in a miffed flip. "The question requires an answer."

"I don't really matter, do I?" I said accusingly, folding my arms across my chest and standing three feet away from her. "None of this is about me is it? It's all about how much money I make. Isn't it? You're all about the money."

"It's not about money," she insisted.

"Yeah, it is," I insisted back.

Squirrel muttered from the back of the shop, "Damn Skippy."

"It's not about money," snapped Andrea. "It's not, not, not."

"Then tell me how is the Vic standing here who just wants to surf and take his dog to the beach any different than the Vic who you want to dress up and go Over The Hill with you? I'm the same guy. But I *do* know why. It's because just being a guy who runs a surf shop and shapes boards in Santa Cruz isn't good enough for you is it? The person I really am still doesn't make enough money for you. Do I? It's about money. Say it, say it."

"It's not about money, it's not! I just happen to run my life like I run my business," said Andrea, who was agitated but struggling to conceal it. "I need someone who is equal to the income I have. It's important to be financially independent so we can bank on each other. It's positive backward compatibility that moves forward. It's a good fit. It works. My personal standards also apply to myself. Expectations. Goals. It's more than money. I don't ask for much." She paused. "I'm easy to get along with."

"Shouldn't *I* be the one to say that?"

"It's not just about money," she said, stamping her heels. "It's simply a quality-of-life issue. It's not about money."

"We don't want the same things," I said, We were rail-to-rail, but standing opposite each other. "What you want, is not what I want. What you want is not important to me."

On the stereo 'I Feel Free' came on by Cream.

Andrea couldn't come up with a response. I had her. She stood there, scrunching her eyes shut, doing a browser search to find the work-around last word to dismiss me. She couldn't. But when she listened the sixties music, she found her work-around last word. And then the hackles and the claws came out big time.

"You're just a *hippie*!" she disdainfully lashed out in a raspy growl of revulsion. "That's it. A hippie surf-bum!" She paused, clearly repelled by me. "It's tragic. You're wasting your life. With your skills you could be so much more! So, so, so much more!"

There was a silence between us; it spread like a stain.

"I don't love you and I'm going surfing," I said, walking out the door to my van.

"Word!" cheered Squirrel from the shop. "Mad props."

"Shut your pie hole," Andrea said to Squirrel, then followed me and spattered out, "I bet this has been the story of your whole life, isn't it?" I said nothing. She sneered and continued, "Anytime the world gets real, and you're forced to make something of yourself, and life gets too complex with adult choices, you shutdown, hide behind your stinkeye and your beloved whuppers and go surfing. Now there's a fucking skill set for the ages. Sure, just go surfing!" She muttered, "I should have known better, it's like my Mom said, 'You can't reheat cabbage.'"

"It's okay, I hate cabbage," I said, closing the van's side door.

Andrea kept scornfully drilling into me, "Before you met me, what had surfing given you? With all the waves you've gotten, what did you have to show for it? No real career. No children. But it's my bad because I make something of myself and get money. And it's your good because you don't make anything of yourself and get waves. Nothing ever gets between you and your dog and your precious waves. You can commit to waves and a dog but throughout your whole life you've never committed to a person have you? There are two things I know: surfing doesn't teach you about life, and a dog doesn't teach you about love."

I said firmly, "You don't get it."

"What?" she shouted, infuriated. "I don't get it! I don't get it. Now, that's a joke. Me? I don't get it." She added in a nasty, snippy way, "So what don't I get? Tell me, Tell me what am I suppose to get! Tell me, tell me! What am I supposed to get?"

As if on cue, Shiloh's car pulled up behind my van. The door slammed. She rushed over to us. She still wore a wetsuit. Her hair was damp. Shiloh was full of pepper piss and had a red ass for Andrea.

"You burned me on my last wave," said Shiloh, aggressively leaning into Andrea. "You just dropped in front of me."

"And?"

"I ate it on the wave, lost my board, and hit some guy. I had to take him to the emergency room to get stitches."

"Your point?"

"You hurt people and keep going."

"Whatev—"

"You go girl!" Shiloh growled and threw a punch that solidly connected to Andrea's jaw, shooting her neck up an extra inch. Her cell phone went flying. Andrea staggered backwards. She helplessly jabbed with the rear-edge of her red spiked heels on the concrete sidewalk, toppled, and tumbled into the bushes. Shiloh stood over her, bent down, shook a fist, nickered, and sarcastically purred, "Ehhhh-xcellent!"

"I'll have you arrested for assault," said Andrea, wiping the blood off her nose.

"Go ahead, call a cop and file assault charges," Shiloh hissed. "You'll probably win in court. But, I bet you'll never say, 'whatever' to someone's face after you pissed them off again will ya? See if I care. You dot-com Instant local You-Go-Girl trannie Roxie-out bitch!"

"Whoa," I said. "Hey, I—"

"And you. I'm over it!" Shiloh said to me, crying. "I'm over it all. You're just as bad. Over you. All over you."

She bolted to her van, pinned it, and drove off, leaving a little scratch with her tires.

"Yeah, right, you go girl," muttered Andrea, slowly limping on a broken heel to her car. "As if."

"Warned ya, don't go rail-to-rail on a Westsider with history."

Squirrel stood at the shop's front door and said to Andrea, "It's for real girlfriend."

"Fuck you, rodent," said Andrea, picking up her cell phone.

"Huh," I said as she got into her car.

"And Vic, why are you still here?" said Andrea in a kinda of obnoxious sophisticated voice. "Aren't you going to pursue your true love? You know, chase true love down? And give true love a soul kiss like in some bad movie and true love will go surfing with you. I bet Shiloh would do it too. Women like that need to have a man in their life for self-esteem. You can marry and raise a communal family of surf-bum-hippie underachievers."

I stood with my hands in my pockets.

Her eyes narrowed, she said in a slightly quivering voice, "I thought you were a nice guy."

"Yeah, sometimes I even manage to fool myself."

Andrea hit the gas, and without looking, quickly pulled her fly ride out in the road. She made an illegal U-ey, cutting two SUVs off, one going in each direction. The SUVs honked. She flipped them both off, raced fifty feet to an intersection to a four-way stop, and then jumped her turn. A cop was right there. He hit his flashers and immediately pulled her over.

I wondered if she would cry to beat the ticket.

"Hot wheels from hell here comes another set," declared Skin Dog, paddling over the first of six waves.

It was definitely a good swell. The lines were clean, evenly spaced creases. The way the waves came from the West off the sand bar just didn't get any better: nice shoulder-to-head-highs, peeled out into perfect left and right handers that tapered all the way to the beach. When I punched through the wave and came to the surface, it was like I had traveled back in time. 38th was the way it used to be. Smiles everywhere. It was just us, again. It was so unreal. Everybody was moving. It was voom, voom, voom. Wave after wave after wave. We paddled back out and hooted and whistled and howled as we watched each other's rides. You could park it on the nose, or you could carve and drop if you just wanted to make the sections. It was so good. Nobody even bothered with the lefts.

As I trimmed across a wave with my toes parked on the nose, I spotted a solitary You-Go Girl on the inside, paddling for the same wave. Oh no, I thought, she's going to burn me. But when the You-Go Girl saw me, she politely stopped paddling. She smiled at my cutback. I let the wave reform, threw the board around to the right, and walked to the nose. She watched all my moves with a growing gleam of admiration in her eyes that made me feel good. I kicked out and paddled back towards her.

"Wow! You got on the nose and walked back," she said, then suddenly burst out in one breath, "It's just like those old sixties movies like 'Endless Summer' cause I'm just learning I see people out here surfing and I don't want to get in their way so I just stay inside that's where my girlfriend and I used to come out together but then she stopped going and I was afraid to go out by myself but I like the ocean so much and being here and I just ride the inside until I get tired which happens real fast cause I only get out once a week but every time I come out here I have such a great time and the water is so clear today I saw a dolphin or is it a porpoise I still mix up what the right name for is and I know it and even saw a seal surf and I'm just beginning and all."

I don't know why she stopped talking, my only guess was it took her just as long to inhale air as it did to exhale words.

I'd say she was nineteen. She was an attractive, full-figured. Her wetsuit was pulled down to her hips. She wore a baby blue-and-white hibiscus-patterned Roxie bikini top.

I slid off my board and stood chest deep in the water.

"Let's switch boards," I said. "There is no way you're going to catch a wave on that pilc. That's not a beginner's board."

"The girl who sold it to me said it would work. Don't the flames look cool?"

"The flames aren't going to help you. Your board is too short, too narrow, and not thick enough to float you right."

"I know it's small, but I thought it would make me paddle more and I'd get stronger and better quicker."

"No, paddling and *catching* waves makes you stronger. You need glide, a longer board. Maybe later as you get better you can ride a shorter board. Look at it this way, in skiing you don't start out with advanced skis, right? Kinda the same thing."

"I didn't think of that because I don't ski and—"

"Just try it," I quickly said to cut her off from going into another one-breath-verbal-brain dash again.

"This board is big," she said, straddling my board, smiling. "When I go for a wave on mine the wave just rolls under me."

I saw a small two footer rolling in

"Paddle."

"Now?"

"Yeah, paddle," I said. "Paddle."

"Now?"

"Go, paddle! Stand up when you feel the wave push you. The board is designed to work when you're standing not lying on it."

Without looking, she started paddling to shore.

"Paddle. Paddle. Paddle! Go, go, go. You're there," I said, watching my board pick up the wave. "Stand now!"

She quickly bounced up, stood and cheered jubilantly, "Hey!"

As I watched her, an upwelling of pleasure rolled out from inside me, as if I was surfing a wave for the first time. I never felt it teaching classes. All I saw was the money. She rode straight into shore on the foam. Then she fell. She surfaced, clearly surprised how a longer and wider board made a difference. Her unrestrained joy was refreshing. She was stoked.

"Was that a lot easier?" I asked her when she returned.

"Bitchen'!" she said, giving me back the board. "You're right, I rode all in and saw the rocks and the tide splashing—"

"Come by my shop over off 38th and Portola," I said, cutting her off before she went off on another verbal tear. "I'll sell your board and I'll cut you a deal on a longer board."

"Okay," she said.

Suddenly, numerous jelly fish-like creatures floated between us. They were less-than-a-half-inch cobalt-blue sacks of air, which had cellophane flaps on them. The wind hit the flaps and made them flop and flap across the water.

"What are these things?' I asked.

"Velella—"

"Velveeta?"

"No," she said, laughing. "They're Velella vella, a hydroid." She picked one up. "Velella is a polyp colony turned upside down and the hydranths are underneath the float. We're studying them. They are differentiated into three main forms, with functioning tentacle-like food, capturing individuals at the rim, as a central polyp that digests the food, and as gonozooids that produce tiny medusae. The colony releases numerous medusae, but mature ones have only rarely been found in the plankton."

"So you don't know what they do either."

"Actually, no."

"They look like tiny bubbles," I said. "Bubbles with wings."

"They're dying," she said, picked one up by its air sack. "I'm majoring in marine biology at UCSC, I do some work at the Long Marine Lab. Velella vella, are called 'by-the-wind sailors' because they just float on the surface. Usually they just drift back and forth on the open ocean in tropical and subtropical waters between the continents. Check these things. See the little clear flaps? It's a transparent sail on the back of their air chamber. That's the blue part is the air chamber that enables them to float like that. They just drift. I have a hard time remembering what their function is. Jellies. No brains. No hearts. Spineless. Feeding and living off the surface wherever the wind takes them. Now the wind's beaching them, and that's why they're dying. They're not dangerous, but don't handle them by your face or eyes, irritation can result."

"When I got back from the war, I tried to go to college," I said. "But I just couldn't keep still in class. I just couldn't." I paused. "It was weird. I had all the words and the vocabulary inside me. I've always read a lot. But I couldn't access it. I just couldn't translate it out. It was weird. I knew I had it in me, but I couldn't do or say it. I was sealed, like a human wound."

"You ought to come by the marine lab sometime. Thanks for being so cool."

I smiled, watched her go in, and paddled back out and said, "Huh."

For the next two solid hours, no one else was on 38th. We must have gotten over forty waves apiece. The Crew went back to the shop. I was the last one in the water. My arms were all spaghetti-ed out. The setting sun cracked open on the horizon and spilled out a slick of twilight oil on the ocean's glassy surface. The hills along the coast were streaked with orange. And all the windows of every house reflected the sunset and framed it. I kept surfing. I couldn't let go of this moment. It would have to let go of me first. A purple darkness steadily brushed the sky. The full moon threw enough light to see the waves. But the incoming tide was slowly filling in the bay. The waves were becoming bouncy and moundy. They began backing off. They rolled and closed out on the beach. I was good to go. I got all of it. I wanted to leave on a good vibe.

I paddled through the moon cast silver-tinted darkness,

toward the beach. Then, I heard splashing. A head bobbed along the surface. At first I thought it was an otter.

It was Ranger!

She struggled to keep her head up out of the water and doggie-paddled to me. I couldn't believe it.

"Whuppers!" I excitedly cheered and laughed. "You're in the water! What you doing out here, whup?" We paddled alongside each other. She never went in the water—never. "You came out to see me. Whup whups, you came out to see your Daddy!" I was so caught up with Ranger being in the water, I neglected to notice a three-foot closeout behind us, which wiped us out in the shallow water. I lost my board and rolled on my back through the sizzling foam and onto the sand. Ranger playfully jumped on me, barking, and wagging her tail. The waves combed over us. I deeply laughed. I sat up in the sand. "Whuppers!"

We rolled around like that for a little while, then I got my board. The waves washed up the Velella-whatever-the-hella-they-were organisms. The ocean's surface was being capped by a thousands upon thousands of these dying blobs. They formed a blue slick topped with flickering shiny flaps covering the surface. It looked like an unappealing cold soup. Splashes smacked and punched small holes through the slick. At first, I thought fish were feeding on the vellella fellahs. But I was wrong. I heard a mean-edged, drunken laughter coming from the second floor deck of Drake's dot-com McMansion. With an unsteady foundation beneath the Über Geek and his dot-com buddies, the Bros of Drake confidently hit new golf balls into the dead.

"Reboot!" shouted Drake, followed by the swish of a steel shaft, and a click of contact.

Ranger and I walked ankle-deep in the lapping waves, popping the bubble-like creatures under our bare feet.

THE GOLDEN AGE of Surf Dot Com's second offering commenced with the grand entrance of the Über Greek, Drakus Maximus. He was ceremoniously attired in a purple toga. The diva mic on his head was adorned with laurels. The digital emperor stood on a raised dais before his following of white toga-clad geeks. A row of shop boards framed the cornflower blue Surf Dot Com banner above his head. In front of the high-tech ruler, on either side of him, were two crew-cutted muscular guys dressed like Roman gladiators, who folded their arms and glared straight ahead. They had a mean and protective edge in their eyes. I could tell these guys weren't just playing a part, they were real bodyguards. Behind Drake, was a wide-screen TV tuned to the CNBC business channel. To the right of its screen, was a three-by-three foot digital scoreboard that tracked Surf Dot Com's stock price at $378. The stock price's glowing number cast a red smear of light on the two long white-cloth covered tables, which were packed with raucous dot-comers who had plates of Thai food, and unopened bottles of Clos La Tech Champagne. In the back, The Crew and I casually leaned against the bar, which was near a vacant DJ booth by the stairway exit, Squirrel thumbed through the booth's collection of records. In a half hour, the stock market would close. We drank our sodas, nibbled meat off finger-food ribs, and waited. The dot-comers' feet pounded the floor, but failed to produce a unified beat. They sounded like a stampede. The flooring vibrated. The incomplete McMansion slightly listed. The third-floor framing swayed. The Crew and I uncomfortably felt the building's brief and unsteady roll, but the dot-comers didn't. They were dizzy, spinning in another world.

"Surf Dot Com, Surf Dot Com, Surf Dot Com!" feverishly chanted the dot-comers, as if they were trying to summon the future to move faster.

The Über Greek extended a golden chalice above his head. The group quieted. Drake drank from his cup of over flowing bubbles and howled out, "Who sees the wave?"

"We do!" responded his toga geeks.

"What are we going to do?" he asked in a louder voice.

"Go for it!"

"Surf's Up!" triumphantly shouted Drake, assuming a surfing stance.

The dot-comers erupted again in their driving chant, "Surf Dot Com, Surf Dot Com, Surf Dot Com!"

"And one more thing..."

The group laughed again.

Drake rose from his surfer stance and solemnly said, "I want to thank this team for all your efforts, you worked long hours, and put this dream together. Our interface and reality will bundle at the market's close on this sunny California day. Critics said we shouldn't have our partied before the market closed, but we are history in the making. We are present at the creation of a unique paradigm shift. Surf Dot Com opened at $235." He pointed to the large scoreboard with the company's current stock price. "And at this auspicious moment, we're at $378."

"We rock, we rock, we rock!" rabidly howled the dot-comers, who shook their champagne bottles, prematurely popped their corks, and spurted bubble spume over each other.

"Let's go to the Surf Dot Com stock price scoreboard," said Drake, acting like a telethon MC. "A drum roll please."

The dot comers rapidly pounded their tables.

Ralph checked his watch, nudged me, and whispered, "Here it comes." He paused. "Dot-crunch time."

"One more thing..."

The dot-comers drummed harder, faster, and louder.

Drake pointed to the scoreboard and triumphantly said, "The current stock price for Surf Dot Com has gone from $378 up to..." The red digital number on the scoreboard blinked, went blank, and posted a new number. "$270!" gasped Drake, who spit out champagne. The drum roll dwindled across the room, followed by a back beat of groans, gasps, and coughs from dot-comers who gagged from the Clos La Tech bubbles that backed up their noses. "The price has to be a glitch," said Drake. He cleared his throat and sputtered, "Reboot!" The number dropped from $225 to $80. "Reboot!" screamed Drake at the scoreboard, as if ordering the price to behave. The number dropped from $80 to $35. "Reboo—hey, what the fuck is going on!" said Drake into his diva mic, ignoring everyone and stomping up the third flight of stairs that led to his turret. He slammed its door. The guards stood on either side of it.

The Crew tapped soda glasses. Reddo filled Ranger's water dish with Pellegrino. Squirrel did his oh-cool face and put a record on the turntable. Driveway Dave lit up a cigar. The dot-comers stopped drinking champagne and went into action. They whipped out cell phones and called brokers, scanned Palm Pilots to check e-mails, and typed on laptops to get on the web. The Crew and I retrieved my shop boards and carried them out to the van. When we returned to the second floor, the dot-comers were riveted to the TV news on their company's demise.

"Dot coms are dot bombs," said an attractive female journalist from the stock exchange floor. "Tech investors were stunned today by the revelations of insider trading and market manipulation at Surf Dot Com. The rapid price decline of SDC's high-tech empire, including Adapient, Expient, Sapient, was caused by the release of inter-office documents, which disclosed SDC and other high-tech companies overstated their earnings, burned through all their VC funding for the quarter, and will never hit their numbers. Surf Dot Com's stock price closed at $3 a share."

"Score!" we shouted around the bar, shot our arms up in the air, and jumped up and down. "Turn and burn!"

The dot-comers stared at us. We didn't care.

Ralph crossed his arms over his chest, and smugly imitated Drake for The Crew, "Wait, one more thing..."

The business reporter continued, "The SDC revelations began a chain-reaction that has sent all high-tech stocks tumbling on the market. Cisco Systems stock from a high of 178 to 15."

"Overvalued," shouted Ralph. "I'm two for two."

"...Yahoo has gone from 205.63 to 24.44—that's a huge 88.1 percent drop..."

"Score!" we shouted.

"Overvalued," Ralph said. "Three for three from the floor."

"...Amazon 75.25 to 10.44, an over 86 percent drop... Inktomi 241.50 to 11.44—a 95 percent drop."

"Score!" we cheered, high-fived, and whooped.

"Overvalued," Ralph said, gloating. "I'm five for five, I'm batting a thousand."

"...CMGI 154 to 4.22 that's a 97 percent...Exodus Communications 89.81 to seventy-five cents...Ariba trading at $3 from 173.50, that's down 97 percent."

"Score!" we howled.

"And the hits just keep on coming," said Ralph, snobbishly adding, "Oh, by the way, did someone page Mister Eight-for-Eight?" He paused. "God, I'm good. All this and looks too!"

"Hey, we don't ever have to work for somebody else again!" proclaimed The Legend.

"Who sees the wave?" shouted Sonny.

"We do!"

"Vic's Surf Shop, Vic's Surf Shop, Vic's Surf Shop," The Crew chanted.

"Grandmaster Squirrel is in the house," said Squirrel, who hit the stereo system on the DJ's booth. It played 'Tubthumping' by Chumbawamba. "It's on, it's on."

The speakers rang out with a chorus, "We'll be singing when we're winning."

"Victory dance," said Chops, pulling his pants down to show his underwear, and did a rap move. "Let's get jiggy with it."

We sang along with the song, "We get knocked down, but I get up again. You're never ever going to keep us down."

The Crew followed Chop's lead. Skin Dog lifted up his shirt

and rolled his gut. Sonny shook his hips. Driveway Dave grabbed his crotch. The Legend spun around on the floor. Ralph did disco finger-pointing moves. The adrenaline that came into our bodies flowed faster than we could burn it off. We were laughing from sheer exhilaration. We kept on with the dance of all dances: our style. For what is a groove but a rut with a view?

"Hey even Vic's dancing," said Chops. "Vic's dancing!"

Squirrel huffed a rap beat, and sang with the chorus, "He takes a Pepsi drink, he takes another Pepsi drink. Vic sings the songs that remind him of the good times, Vic sings the songs that remind him of the bad times."

I jerked my arms, flapped my elbows, and hopped. I had no idea what I was doing. I looked stupid. And, I hated looking stupid. But, when you go from zero to hero, you gotta move.

"I haven't felt this good since I got out of the army," I said, laughing. "You know, this really is a pretty fucking great song."

"Reboot!" commanded Drake, as if we had desecrated his temple. "Silence!"

We stomped harder, danced even more wildly, and shouted at him, "You knocked us down, but we got up again, you're not ever going to keep us down!"

"You fools made money? You!" said Drake, astonished. He descended from the dais, flanked by guards. "You losers made money on the stock market?" He paused. "You sold short?"

Ralph stopped dancing, placed his hand on his chin, and said sympathetically to Drake, "Oh, I guess you guys went long." He paused and added cavalierly, "Ain't that a bitch?" Then he broke back into his free-form dance.

We sang out, "We get knocked down, but we get up—"

The bodyguards took the microphone away from Squirrel, and turned off the sound system.

Suddenly, an avenging figure burst up the stairs and pointed a finger at Drake. It was Zander. He wore stretch pants, a 'Ren and Stimpy' cartoon t-shirt, and sandals with rainbow straps. His scalp was heavily bandaged.

"God, what happened to that guy?" said Ralph.

"I took Zander out with a sword," I replied.

"A sword?" asked Driveway Dave.

"Long story," I said.

Zander stood in front of the dazed dot-comers and accusingly railed, "Don't listen to this dry heave! This weasel slime fuck is reaming us. Drake is filing for bankruptcy. We're 'questionable assets.' Who knows how much money this super steaming pile of shit and his CEO suits are walking away and leaving us pushing turnips out of our asses. We're being boned. It's a massive fuck."

"That's not true," said Drake.

The lie detector attached to his phone eeee-ed from within its belt holster.

Zander kept going, "We're window dressing! This asswipe and his asswipe buddies have been giving each other millions in loans for 'short-term cash needs' and bonused out each other's salaries to buy their cars, second homes, trips, private jets—"

"Percentage wise I haven't gotten that much," Drake said.

The device on his hip eeee-ed louder.

"Damn," Drake muttered to himself. "Reboot—"

"The emperor has no stock options, the emperor has no stock options," declared Zander, pointing at Drake, who stood there as if he was naked. The IT charged Drake. "The emperor has—"

A guard quickly dispatched high-tech Zander with a low-tech jab to the IT's head, dropping him. The distressed dot-comers jerked, as if they were struck. They remained seated.

"This is a departure," said Drake. "So we hemorrhaged. But think of the publicity. It puts us in play to be purchased." The device on his hip eeeeee-ed louder—it got stuck, he tried to shout over it. "Surf Dot Com has brand equity. There are mergers and acquisitions. It's very likely our competitors will purchase us just to get our database of over three and a half million customers." The device on his hip registered the intensity of the lie with a louder and more prolonged eeeeeeeee-ing that climbed up an octave. "We are a lever that can move the world—"

The betrayed dot-comers shouted their leader down: "You said we were family...I took all my meals there...You promised we'd have jobs for life...I brought my sleeping bag in...I agreed to stay on at half pay in exchange for more options."

"We went for the dream people," Drake said, then sputtered. "We—we, we went for the dream, we..." He suddenly broke character and viciously brayed, "Wah, fucking wah, fucking wah!" The dot-comers became quiet. "Give me a break, you spoiled babies. Who the fuck are you geeks kidding? Not one of you pampered brats ever planned to go the distance with this company. I've seen all of your e-mails. None of you believed in what you were doing, not one of you. You only believed in your success. I'm not an MBA, but do you think I'm stupid? You worked hard. How do you defined working hard? Because you stayed late? Woooooh, I'm impressed. That's what you want to be known for, isn't it? Staying late. Blow me! Most of you came into work at eleven in the morning, played foosball or some stupid video game for an hour, then went to lunch, came back, did your e-mails, and called your friends. Then you went out for another bite, came back, and crawled under your desk to sleep off a couple drinks. Then you woke up, had a snack or a cappuccino in the break room, returned to your cube, and surfed the web. Then maybe you worked a little, or talked to each other about work from seven until eleven at night, and then you went out to a club to party. Some of you even came back to the office drunk and high. You work? It takes you people twelve hours to put three hours of work together. Don't give me your bullshit and act like you're shocked that all I wanted to do was make money. What were you trying to get this whole time? I don't feel any love here? Do you? Each one of you was doing something else half the time on my dime, anyway. Yeah, some of you were working 24-7, because you were graphic artists doing freelance work for someone else, or software engineers writing code to design your own software programs to make yourselves rich. You were all tunneling out the whole time and waiting for your fuck-you money. Well, here's your half of it: fuck you!"

Driveway Dave walked straight to Drake and handed him a document. We backed Dave up so the guards wouldn't make a move on him. The guards saw Ranger and exchanged looks.

"What is this shit?" Drake asked, glancing at the papers.

"My discharge," I said.

"Actually, it's a release agreement," said Dave.

"Release?" jeered Drake.

I flamed on my stinkeye and said, "I want me back."

Ranger sat at my feet and aggressively growled.

Drake shook his head in amusement, and said, "There's no release for anyone." He laughed. "I don't take prisoners. It's part of our contract. Why if you're such a good lawyer, how come you never heard of 'senior—"

"'Senior liquidation preference,' quickly interjected Driveway Dave, who added judiciously. "Yes, it's a clause in our agreement, In fact, I believe each employee here also signed an agreement with that particular provision in it too." The dot-comers leaned forward in their seats. Their beepers went off, but went unanswered. "For those of you here unfamiliar with it, 'senior liquidation preference' simply means if a company is sold or its assets are liquidated in a bankruptcy, the investors get their money back first, which means the rank and file, i.e., you guys, get nothing." He paused and smiled. Then I noticed an emotion in Dave I'd never seen: pride. Surfing and being with us over the years helped him rearrange his priorities. Driveway Dave had rediscovered himself as an attorney and acquired a fresh professional poise. "Our concerns on the 'senior liquidation preference' clause are addressed in my client's release. A check for $125,000 is attached to it. We're even."

"I don't need your money," Drake snapped dismissively. "I'll get it anyway. There's no death by a thousand cuts here."

"So you're declining to sign," asked Dave. "I'm going to have to pursue another avenue."

The Crew and I advanced.

Drake spat, "I don't respond to idle threats."

"This isn't idle, this one is moving," said Dave.

Drake pointed at us and said, "Guards, escort these surf bums and this twisted vet out of here."

"Did you say twisted, *hombre*?" I said, standing with Ranger in front of The Crew.

The bodyguards froze.

"If either of you make a move," I admonished the guards. "I will kick you both in the chest, knock you to the ground, and then my dog will go for your balls." I paused. "Then Ranger will go for your throat, and once she does, she goes crazy." I paused. "After that, I'm not responsible for her actions."

The guards didn't budge. They exchanged glances, then looked at Ranger and back to me. They remembered—especially, the guard with the 1983 canine-tooth scar on his chin.

"Throw them out," yelled Drake. "Did you hear me? What am I paying you pinheads for?"

"Not enough to protect you from *this* guy," answered one of the bodyguards, retreating down the stairway.

The second guard, followed the first one, and added to Drake, "Easy for you to say, you never surfed Rivermouth with him."

"Reboot!" yelled Drake, suddenly grasping he was alone. He looked nervously over our shoulders. The dot-comers were thawing out from their stunned shock. They came toward him, a few held empty champagne bottles. The only barrier separating the emperor from a dot-comer uprising was us.

"I assume you want to revisit our original proposal," said Dave, extending a pen to Drake. "I have a notary present." Dave gestured to Ralph, who was chewing on a piece of jumbo shrimp slathered with cocktail sauce.

"This is extortion," Drake hissed.

"I fail to see any of that language in this release," said Dave, stroking his mustache, which had some guacamole on it.

"Get out of my way," Drake ordered.

Ranger growled. She was ready to spring.

"If you take one more step, this *twisted* veteran will kick you in the chest, you will fall to the ground, and then Ranger will jump on you and go for your balls." I paused. "Then she'll go for your throat, and once—"

"Getting physical isn't going to solve anything," Drake huffed.

"I'm not looking for a solution," I replied.

Chops added, "Drake, I think you'd have a hard time being understood by a jury when you're testifying in a slightly higher voice against us without your balls."

Sonny laughed and said to Chops, "Now that was funny! Why? Because I want it to be true."

Drake studied the document, then stopped halfway through it. He looked at us and whispered in a tone of restrained admiration, "You hand me this release all drawn up." He paused. "You knew this was going down. You were somehow involved in all of this."

"As you well know, *intent* is very difficult to prove," said Dave.

"There are witnesses," said Drake.

"Oh yeah, they'll be real sympathetic to you in court," Driveway Dave replied, raising his eyebrows. "So will a jury."

"There's one key point you've forgotten counselor, every agreement has to be to the benefit of both parties," quickly countered Drake, who lowered his voice into a conspiratorial undertone, "I'll sign that release on the condition you get me out of here."

"Sign first," I said.

"I'll sign that release, Off site," said Drake. "But not now."

"That might take away your incentive," said Dave.

Drake looked at me, smiled and said in a disassembling way, "Vic, babe, I'm trying to cut a fair co-venture here. A deal that will benefit both parties. A deal."

"What kind of deal?" I asked, distrustfully.

"A bro deal," Drake cheerfully said, stepping towards me with outstretched arms, as if he were either trying to embrace me, or to show us he was unarmed.

Bro deal.

"Okay?" said Drake, smiling, getting closer. "Okay, bro—"

I quickly kicked the Über Geek in the chest and dropped him to the carpeted floor.

Ranger pounced on him.

"Get your dog off me, get your dog off me," squealed Drake, who desperately curled into a ball. Ranger tore apart the CEO's toga. "Reboot! Reboot! Reboot!"

"I told you, I told you what would happen," I said, shaking my head in disapproval and chastising him. "I told you..."

Ranger growled and ripped into Drake's money belt. Bundles of dollar bills covered his body, as if the dot-com CEO was just a skeleton covered by a bankroll of other people's money. The dot-comers gaped at all the cash. They started getting worked up, like caged animals near feeding time. Drake sensed it.

"I'll sign, I'll sign," he said in a terrified voice, grabbing the pen, and scrawling his signature on my discharge.

Dave took the document and looked at the signature. Ranger moved up toward Drake's throat.

"Reboot," he warbled us. "I signed. Call her off! Call her off!"

"I'm sorry, but you still have to initial this second page," said Dave, handing the document and pen back to Drake, who quickly scrawled his initials on the paper. Dave examined the document, looked at me, and nodded his approval.

I called Ranger off.

"Good dog, whups," I said, bending over and hugging her.

The deposed and humiliated Über Geek squirmed on the floor. His glasses and headset were twisted on his face. His purple toga was torn to shreds. His voice activator was still stuck. Without his stock option promises, the hustling wad of nothing was stripped down to a giant eeeeeeeeeee-ing lie.

We backed away and let the dot-comers close in.

"Hey, we had a deal! said Drake. "I signed."

"Huh, nothing in this agreement says that," said Dave, looking at the signed document. "I merely suggested you wouldn't be predisposed to signing the release at the premises." He shook the papers. "You wanted a bro deal, you got a bro deal."

The predatory dot-comers slowly encircled Drake. They rapaciously hawkeyed the bundles of hundred-dollar bills lodged within the webbed threads of several money belts coiled around the Über Geek. The dot-comers' hunger was aroused, as if the cash was an undigested meal in a disemboweled animal. They craved that money. They were entitled to their money. Yes, *their* money. The money that now mocked them. The money that reminded the dot-comers that they had been snaked out of their stock-option dream wave by Drake and his Bros, a wave of money formed by the dot-comers' lives. Suddenly, they were behind the curve, not ahead of it. The dot-comers had no way to catch this wave. The clutch on their paradigm shift had burnt out. They were champagne-soaked, stock-optionless, and drifting in bubble-bursting foam toward their thirties or late forties without a life preserver. The brilliantly overpaid who arrogantly accused others of not getting it, realized *they* were the ones not getting it. Their only remaining option was to enviously watch snakes and burn artists "Whew-ho" and "Yo-Go Girl" themselves as they rode—what should have been the dot-comers' wave—towards a mansion with an ocean view in an exclusive, gated community, which the dot-comers could never enter. The dot-comers were forced to deal with the consequences of their own actions as adults. They faced this brutal reality the only way they knew how: they erupted into a raging tantrum.

"Our money!" screamed the dot-comers. "Give us our money!"

Drake jumped up, clutched his money belts with both hands to hold onto his cash. His eyes darted toward the street exit. The dot-comers blocked it. Drake looked to his right, saw an opening, knocked down Aedhmer, and scrambled up the third-floor steps to the McMansion's tower.

"No so fast, bro!" shouted Weever, who threw an object.

An empty champagne bottle hit Drake in the forehead. He stopped, then staggered up the stairs. He began bleeding. The dot-comers swarmed and pounced upon their fallen emperor. They brutally stripped off his money belts. Rolls of cash thumped to the floor and bills drifted into the air. When the dot-comers clawed at the bills or dropped to their knees to grab the rolling wads of cash, Drake broke free, reached the tower, and slammed its door behind him.

"For honor!" shouted Zander, who withdrew an iron from the golf bag near the bar. He brandished it like a sword, and sprinted up the stairs. "There has to be more money in the tower. That can't be all of it. There has to be more. There just has to be!"

"Surf Dot Com, Surf Dot Com, Surf Dot Com," clamored the revolting dot-comers as they rammed their shoulders against Drake's tower door.

There were too many people on the third floor. The Crew and I felt the floor roll and buckle. The framing creaked. Windows shattered.

"It's all going to go boom," said Dave. "Traveling music."

We hustled down the swaying stairs to the sidewalk and ran across the street. We looked up. The three-story frame bent more and more from the left and the right. It was going to go.

I looked around at The Crew and said in a panic, "Where's Squirrel?"

Squirrel and Reddo came down the building's steps. Squirrel struggled with a huge glass bowl. Reddo carried a case of wine.

"Hey, I snagged some shrimp," shouted Squirrel, smiling. "I threw some extra cocktail sauce on top."

Reddo stood next to us, put the wooden box down at his feet, and said to us, "I wasn't about to leave a case of Heitz Martha's Vineyard Cabernet Sauvignon 1985." He laughed. "Fuck him."

A gull-wing Mercedes screeched in front of Drake's building. It was Andrea. She was dressed like some Vestal Virgin and showing a lot of cleavage and leg through a specially designed toga. She talking on her diva mic She looked through us, got out, and slammed the car door.

"I'm on site now, I can't access my e-mails, there's some virus," she said to someone on the diva mic as she rushed on her red heels towards the building. "Tell me about it. I'm getting calls from everybody. And that asswipe, he..." She heard the pounding and the chants and looked up at the building, which was swaying like it was being tossed on a rough ocean. Then she saw the money coming down and people in the street gathering up the bills. "This is not *kewl*. This is not *kewl*. This is..."

The House That Dot Com Built simultaneously creaked, cracked, and split open. Its third floor pancaked onto the second floor, followed by the combined layers of third and second floor, which pancaked to the ground. Its galloping rumble became one giant echoing and rolling explosion.

Drake's tower toppled toward her.

"Not *kewl!*," screamed Andrea, running.

The tower crushed her gull-wing, fly-by ride.

A huge, rising, Medusa-Jellyfish-shaped cloud with dusty tentacles formed from the debris of the dot-com wreckage. Its ghostly gray mushroom-like hood rapidly flapped downwards, as if the specter was an exposed dark soul, fleeing from the light of day for the protection of another scheme to conceal itself. The evaporating, cloud-clustered blob rose higher and higher, propulsively powered by the self-consuming shrieks, spinning dollar bills, and wailing whines from the harsh, stinging air that filled the vacuum of the fallen sky.

THE $3.99 'LOCALS ONLY" breakfast special was back at Bings. So were the dot-comers. But the only dots left in their lives were round quarter-inch stickers of green, blue, and red, which were strategically placed in the middle of their foreheads. It was a 'Pink Slip Party.' A green dot meant you were looking for work. A red dot meant you were hiring. A blue dot meant you just wanted to party and have fun. The dots resembled bullet holes, and, they could very well have been bullet holes. The dot-comers held their cell phones pressed against their ears like they were applying ice packs to head wounds. Their dye-tinged hair seemed singed by a recent blast. They aimlessly lingered among themselves. The displaced dot-comers were bleary eyed. Not only had their dreams backed up on them, but, after seven spree-filled years, they were also suffering from a hangover of spending too much money. They desperately checked their laptops, voice-mails, beepers, and Palm Pilots, hoping for a resumé response. They found nothing. There was no reprieve. The windmill on the railing tried to blow a bubble, but each one stretched out and popped. The refugees without a home page were downloading a different world...

"There goes my fucking horse farm."

"They outsourced my job to some a raghead in Bangalore who's only getting $8 an hour."

"My husband won't be able to travel as a chaperon with my son's marching band to Hawaii."

"I didn't get severance. My unemployment ran out. They even took away my frequent flyer miles. I'm living on my IRA."

"I had to sell my Beanie Babies on eBay."

"My recruiting firm went out of business."

"I'll never be able to bungee jump all around the world."

"I don't want to have to commute."

"You're my accountant. I'm begging you! Just find a *way* I can still keep my Lamborghini!"

Reddo smirked as he refilled my Pepsi at the bar and said to me, "Look at them, the masters of the New Economy, reduced to sucking dick for beer money."

"You know, I heard some people made out," I said with a half smile.

"Yeah, I hear some people did," said Reddo, glancing at me. He chuckled. "No one's going to throw a pity party for these clowns. Outside of their cars and their houses, what did these people leave us with? I don't see any scholarships, stadiums, charity balls, or hospital wings, sure they did it to promote their dot-coms at black-and-white balls, but it all ended there. Would you say Santa Cruz is better now than before they came? Not me. Feeling sympathy for these digital dweebs is like feeling sorry for a shark who has heartburn from eating your arm. This town will never be the same." He paused. "I think that's why we'll outlive all these people, it takes a long time to forgive them." Reddo threw his hands up in the air. "Hey, you know the guy who bought the place I rented and we got kicked out? He tore the cottage down, put up a McMansion, and wound up paying over $2.8 million for the whole deal. Well, Mr. Dot and Mrs. Com lost their jobs, divorced. They only got $800,000 for their place. Last I heard, they're fighting over their house-money shares in court. He's doing Photoshop seminars and using a check-cashing service in Fremont so she can't get to his money. Yeah, she won't get it, but the checks go through and he'll have to pay. They all think they can get away without paying, man. The house was scooped up by a big money guy in Chicago, who only uses it two weeks out of the year to play Pebble Beach, Spyglass, and Pasatiempo. My wife and I are back in the place as caretakers and walking the guy's Chocolate Lab. Yeah, some revolution. The only thing that's changed are the landlords."

"Huh."

"Shiloh is back from Hawaii. She's got a gallery in Capitola."

"I heard," I said, sipped my Pepsi and stared off. "She hasn't talked to me. She went through Driveway Dave or Ralph for her checks and stuff, which is fine by me, I guess."

We were silent for a few seconds. Reddo started to say something, but hesitated. The gulls squawked, seals barked, and the waves sizzled around the wharf's pilings. A lifeguard class of teenagers jogged past the restaurant. The boys wore red Lycra swim trunks and the girls wore red polo suits. They were young, untested, and full of summer hopes. The girls were gorgeous. The guys were flat-stomached and invincible. A few carried those orange rescue cans with tow lines to throw at drowning people. They laughed. It was a beautiful day.

"I'm sorry about Ranger," gently said Reddo.

"Thanks," I croaked, pushing my bacon-less plate away.

A beeper went off. Six dot-com geeks spastically scrambled near us. They spilled their drinks as they frantically patted their khakis to check their beepers.

"Oh, that's me," I loudly said, checking the number on my belt beeper. "My travel agent. I'm going to surf Peru next week."

A geek said in a familiar detached style, "Wassup, dude?"

It was Jef-with-one-f. The dot on his forehead was peeling off its rounded edges—or, more likely, the Webmaster was peeling off the edges of his dot. He wore a pressed shirt and slacks, shined shoes. He was clean-shaven. He had gained weight.

"Howz'it?"

"I sold my board," said the Webmaster. He was drunk. Sold my Yamaha pocket rocket bike. Canceled my gym membership."

"Where's your two-gs buddy?"

"Gregg? He went on a surf trip. Haven't seen him since."

"Huh," I said, surprised.

"I'll find something in Boston," cockily said the Jef-with-one-f. "I'll earn half the money, live with my folks, and make out better. But, I wouldn't trade my California experience for anything."

"California *experience*?"

"I charged it, dude" said Jef-with-one-f, like he wanted me to believe he was a success, and everything that happened to him was by choice. "The true upside, dude. I surfed. I partied. I had my own place, a TV, a DVD. I mean, I learned about the business world and living on my own. I was part of all that excitement. I wouldn't trade that experience for anything." He snorted. "Santa Cruz has peaked. I can't imagine staying in this dump and resorting to driving Over The Hill just so I can have a so-called real job that only pays the bills. Shine that noise. I'm ejecting. No way am I going to live paycheck to paycheck."

"What are you going to miss the most about Santa Cruz?"

"'The 99'," he said instantly. "That place was tits."

Amazing, this guy wasn't going to miss the weather, the surfing, or the people. The only thing he was going to miss was a bar where he got wasted on imported beer, took ecstasy, snorted cocaine, played trivia contests against other geeks, and fucked dot-com girls.

"I'm twenty-eight, I can afford to take a high risk. I can still go anywhere. What did I ever have to lose?" Jef-with-one-f- asked. "How can you be a failure for the rest of your life at age 28?"

"Who knows? You could be the first," said Reddo, ringing up a drink order.

"Now, I'm going to follow my passion," Jef-with-one-f- said.

"Passion? Really," Reddo said. "No one ever gave me a job to follow my passion."

"No, I want to write."

"You write?" skeptically asked Reddo, clearly irked. Reddo had traveled through France, sculpted, and was a complete Hemingway freak. "You need experience to write. All you did was give up having a life. You need to have a life to write."

"Not if it's science fiction," confidently said Jef-with-one-f, drifting away in a sea of green dots looking for a red dot.

Reddo and I said "All right now!" We followed it with a quick rhythmic handclap, stopped, made one fist, lightly tapped each other's knuckles and said, "Go Cardinal!"

I slid a ten under the plate and bounced out of Bings.

"You'll won't be able to wear that hat at the club's father-son tournament," I heard a man say near me.

"So, I won't go to the club, Dad," whined Cat-In-The-Hat.

"Leave Cyril alone honey," said the woman who was obviously the Mom. "Let's not talk about that now, dear. He only gets irritated. This is a day of achievement. Why are you so down? This is a great day. A new world is opening up for you."

Clogs and Cat-In-The-Hat were in a deep funk. They looked like they were in the custody of a death squad. Their parents were dressed in Hawaiian shirts and shorts. They were laughing and taking pictures. The UCSCers parents seemed like more fun than their own kids, who were clearly miserable.

"I can see why you like it here, it's so beautiful," said Clog's Mother, holding a small digital camera. "It's raining back East. And the humidity is terrible at the shore. Your Dad and I are at a nice bed-and-breakfast in Capitola. Does anybody work in this town? We saw a lot of bums! And everywhere your Father and I went, in restaurants and coffee shops, or when we drove by the beach or tennis courts, there were people out in the middle of the day. What do they do for a living? We couldn't believe it." She walked to the edge of the wharf railing. "Oh look, seals! Let's get a shot of the graduates with the seals in the background."

"Mother," sniped Clogs, who dragged her feet alongside Cat-In-The-Hat, who pouted.

"Oh Kimberly, stop being such a pill," her mom said.

The lifeguard class ran by the UCSCers. I thought the forlorn graduates wanted to grab the tow-line from the rescue can, but the UCSCers were beyond its reach. They were being swept away by a parental riptide as they longingly watched their Santa Cruz recede. They reluctantly but submissively drifted back to wherever people like them came from.

I walked down the wharf, and passed the dot-comers' cars. Three out of four parked SUVs had "For sale by owner" signs on their windows. A Volkswagen Passat with Nevada plates had a U-Haul trailer attached to its rear bumper.

A guy brushed by me. It was Bobby Weever. His blonde hair was freshly dyed and he looked like he had a face-lift to remove his crow's feet. Outside of the distressed look on his face, Weever physically looked buffed-out, which surprised me. He wore pressed khakis and huge black square-toed shoes. But instead of a polo shirt, he wore a white dress shirt—and, a tie. He got into a car and tried to start it. The engine knocked, then quieted.

"Howz'it?" I asked, walking over to him.

"This Chevy is a goddamn piece of shit," grumbled Weever, peeling the green dot off his forehead. "I don't know why I even bother coming to these pink slip parties. It's just a total waste. I had to move to Watsonville. It was the only place I could afford to live. The day after we moved in, somebody broke into our garage and stole my golf clubs. And we can't even get DSL. I have a 56K modem. Me! It's embarrassing." But Weever wasn't done yet. He was still verbally trying to pull out the spear in his career wound. He became more and more agitated. "I was a risk taker. The others clung to their desks at their same old jobs. And what do I end up with? After 25 years in high-tech, I'm in survival mode. My last job was three months, I trained these L-1 Visa Bangladesh geeks, who replaced the staff at half of our pay. Now, I'm working a part-time data processing for not even half the money—I can't work at home, I'm in a cubicle. And my second job is at the desk in a health spa handing out towels!"

"You look good. I guess they let you use the equipment—"

"I'm working two jobs and paying for my own benefits, and I'm supposed to be grateful for it." Weever sneered, but he was still running strong on bitterness with a full tank of empty. He looked away and spat out, "Fucking Alan Greenspan."

"Alan Greenspan?"

"The head of the Federal Reserve Board," Weever said sourly. "He's the one who said Internet stocks were overvalued—he called it: 'irrational exuberance.'" He paused. "And you know who bought my place? Your buddy Dave, the guy who used to live in his motherfucking driveway. And the guy had the nerve to ask me for a bro deal. Me! I know what a fucking bro deal is."

I didn't gloat over Weever's plight. I felt sorry for the guy. After all, I almost agreed to do those classes with him. I had been seduced by The World of Bros too. We were both tainted. That's why I didn't even make fun of his name. The thought of him depressed by the speakerphone stuck with me. I was going to offer a few supportive comments. But then, he launched at me.

Weever glared and snarled with full-on resentment, "How did someone like you make out, and me, wind up with nothing?" He nipped out, "At least you can afford to buy a new dog."

"Nice tie, Weeeeeeeeee-*ver*."

The traffic reporter on the car radio said, "In the Santa Cruz mountains on Highway 17, an SUV flipped over a guard rail at the Summit on Northbound 17, traffic is backed up to the Mount Hermon Road exit in Scotts Valley."

"Boy is my life one big glorious bowl of fuck-me," grumbled Weever, driving off to his bubbleless world.

I spotted Andrea before she saw me. She stood by a dumpster across the street. We hadn't seen each other for six months. Andrea didn't look healthy; in fact, she strongly resembled every woman she criticized. She lost her tan. Her hair was no longer blonde or long. It was an auburn blunt cut. She wore angular, tortoise shell glasses, and dressed in a midi top with Capri pants and black flats. She put on some poundage. Her tight stomach had turned into a dough-like spread, which slightly spilled over the edge of her pants. The blue dot was on her forehead bent halfway down; showing its white backing; it resembled one of those dead, blue-bubbled, jelly Velella-vella fellahs.

"I was hoping when *we* got back from Europe all of this would blow off," she said into a cell phone, which was another color and even smaller than her last one. "When I came back I hit the ground running and sent out a thousand resumés and didn't get one bite. I started cold calling around. And what I have to endure during these interviews! They said because I jumped from one job to the next, I'm not capable of loyalty. I'm capable of loyalty!" Her lower right lip twitched, as if she flinched to avoid thoughts about herself. "I intended to stay at those jobs. But when someone gives you a better opportunity you have to seize it." She paused. "I got turned down at my last job interview because I couldn't explain what I said on my resumé." She paused. Her lip twitched again. "I'm not really worried. My current job situation isn't affecting me in the immediate sense. Actually, it's kinda fun not to have to get up in the morning, get dressed, and put on make-up. Oh, oh, oh, did you hear about Aedhmer? She's joining the Peace Corps., if you can believe that." She snorted. "The Peace Corps? Oh yeah, I guess Nigeria needs a web page." She laughed. "Nothing like showing a guy with a bone in his nose and a machete how he can do a power point presentation on pestilence. Hold me back. Oh yeah, that's going to make a difference." She paused. Her twitch came up again. "Hey, I got a call coming in from my headhunter person. Gotta fly, bye." She listened. "What do you mean I'm difficult to 'place?" Andrea said in disbelief. "Your job is to place me. My skills can easily translate into other markets. What about non–profits? Breast Cancer, Alzheimer's, the Red Cross? I can build brand equity and create a presence where it really matters in the community." She paused. "I can't believe this. I started at the top. I don't go back to the mailroom. I was never in the mailroom! That's not backward compatibility." She shifted into an accusing tone. "You're not doing your job. Last year at this time, BrassRing Dot Com, your job placement service, got me any position I wanted. I had two interviews a day. It was doable. I'd virtually find a job in a week and get stock options and signing bonuses. Fine. Fuck you very much. Gotta fly, bye." Andrea started to dial another number, but she saw me, and said apprehensively, "Hey you."

I thought that she might be worried that I'd bring up the three hundred dollars in parking tickets she ran up using my van, and stuck me with. But, I figured I deserved it. I didn't approach her. I kept my hands in my pockets to avoid a false hug.

"Andrea, you cut your hair."

"I needed transitioning from the outside in," she said. Her lip twitched again. She *had* acquired a facial tick. I don't think she realized she had one. "I'm detoxing, but in a nice way. I'm not depressed but I feel a lot more restricted and I'm getting totally pessimistic. Me! When I got laid off from Surf Dot Com, I just figured, fuck it, I'm bright, I have the resources. No big deal. I decided to give myself a little sabbatical to step back from what happened. I had some life questions I wanted to work out. I'm transitioning, I felt I had to listen to my creative side, the one that yearns for new challenges, and add to my experience reservoir. What I miss the most about work is the events. Getting the face-to-face interaction. Being able to have an intelligent conversation all the time, the so-called real world isn't like that."

"Huh," I grunted.

The lifeguard class ran between us. They were going for their second wharf lap. Their stride was strong. No one was out of breath. They were smiling. Their feet left the ground easily.

Andrea glared at the young girls. Her lip twitched again. She said, "But when I think back, and I think about how every day all I thought about was, 'What's the stock doing today? What's the new technology?' It just makes me want to hurl. The whole deal was a merry-go-round. It was going real fast, but no matter how fast it goes, it's still a merry-go-round, and it has to stop, and then they box up your stuff, take away your office key-card, and lock you out." She paused. "There's no low-fat double espresso caramel macchiato at the end of the rainbow." She paused. "Hey, if I didn't have the stock options, and if I didn't get bad advice on my money, I wouldn't have lived a lifestyle beyond my means." I waited for her facial tick. It came. "I'm saving money. I used to go out to restaurants five times a week, it's amazing how much money you can save if you cut back on that. I don't buy bagged lettuce. I toss my own salads. I dropped cable. And, I can do without my StokaMocha wings. I make my own coffee. Now, I want to connect with a world larger than me. I need a job that challenges me but still gives me the free time to explore different aspects of my life and grow. I mean, ever since college. I wanted to make 300k and retire at thirty. But, I've changed."

"That's nice."

"People are more important than things. "

"And?"

"I was successful but there was emptiness in my life," she said, then added with deep sorrow and regret. "I made a mistake."

"Your point?"

She paused and said with great resolve, "I should have gone into wireless."

"Whatever."

Andrea finally caught onto my sarcasm. Her eyes narrowed, her lip twitched, and she said snidely, "I get the irony."

"Yeah," I replied, pleased. "I kinda thought you would."

Her phone bipped out the opening chords of 'My Heart Will Go On." She reached for the phone the way an asthmatic would reach for an inhaler. Her lip twitched.

"Hey you, bonjour, Monsieur Tucker," she said in a French accent, then resumed her normal voice. "Yeah, tell me something I don't know, my portfolio lost 90 percent of its value." Andrea waved her free hand to either say goodbye or motion me to stay. "Right now, all my tech stocks tanked and are underwater. I feel like the cruise director on the Titanic after it hit the iceberg. I'm still happy with my stocks. I have all the right tech stocks. I have to believe my stocks are worth more than thirty cents. Tucker, you should see me now, I have a dot on my head and look like I lost in a game of paintball." She paused. "I'm so tired of bright people. I'd just like to be in a place where I can laugh again."

I flicked my hand in a dismissive goodbye, turned, and didn't look back. Actually, I was relieved. For a second, I was afraid she wanted to get back together.

Down at the wharf entrance, I saw the blue and red flashers of emergency vehicles. I hurried over to check the scene out. Clog's Dad was videotaping the activity. The sulking graduates looked off in the opposite direction. The other set of parents took pictures of each other on the beach, and laughed.

EMTs in blue jump suits were working on a guy in a gurney. It was Jef-with-one-f! He didn't look good. He was pale white, hyperventilating, and sweating. He seemed lost and frightened.

"Chestpain Dot Com. Yeah, we got another one," I heard EMT Ed say into his hand mike as he stood at the open driver's door of the ambulance. "AMR. Rig 35. We have a white male, age 28, calling in a Code 3, blood pressure is 160 over 110, diafretic. No loss of consciousness." EMT Ed saw me. He was in his early thirties. He surfed Three Mile a lot. A year ago, I shaped him a 9'2" thruster. He clicked off the mike. "Yo Vic, we're going to be getting a Southwest soon. The angle is right." He looked over at the flat ocean. "Hasn't hit yet, but when it does it'll be a good swell." He reassumed his official voice and spoke into the microphone. "Subject is radiating pain, chest tightening, weakness on right side... angina pector...is having an MI."

I waited until EMT Ed clicked off his microphone then I asked, "What's going on with this guy?"

"We're getting a lot of these when I pull double shifts up in the Valley," said EMT Ed, who smirked. "Chestpain Dot Com is what we code them now. A lot of these people are stuck with paying a bill they thought would never come due, and they can't handle it. Or they made money and they're sitting by their terraced swimming pool with a drink and realize their life is shit cause they have no friends and their wife is banging a business partner and their kids hate their guts. Eventually, even their own bodies reject them. Chestpain Dot Com. Probably hyperactive stress because of stuff: losing their house, the country club membership, not being able eat at the same restaurants. Stuff, just stuff! I'm even getting called out to Porsche suicides. When these dot-comers go bust and can no longer even make payments on their Porsches, they run the cars off cliffs or into canyons. That's their concept of providing for their family, leaving money and not being around for them."

"God, why don't they just blow their brains out?"

"Insurance companies don't cover suicides, but they do cover accidents," said EMT Ed, smiling. "It's just such *e*-waste. I mean look at this kid. For God's sake, I mean what can we do for a guy who is in his late twenties and has chest pains?"

"Do they die?"

"Not right away, usually, it's panic attacks most of the time, and if it's not, they damage their hearts," said EMT Ed, who slid behind the wheel of the ambulance. "Cardiac muscles don't rebuild. The doctors say a heart rebuilds, but you can't prove it by me, I've seen the autopsies, and the hearts have scar tissue. People who act like they don't need a heart find out the heart doesn't like to be ignored. The heart doesn't forgive that." EMT Ed shrugged. "Instead of believing a job would bring him happiness, he should have come to California believing a little more in himself, and a little more in people."

"Yeah, I guess."

The other EMTs ran an IV on Jef-with-one-f. They slid the gurney into the vehicle's rear hatch.

"Wait!" blurted the Webmaster in horror. "You're not taking me to a *community* hospital! I want to go to Stanford."

"Trust me, right now you don't want to go to Stanford," said one of the EMTs.

"Patient's name is Jeff Miller," said EMT Ed. "Jeff—you know, I'll spell it for you: J-e-f-f."

"That's Jef-with-one-f with one F!" whaaaa-ed a voice from within the ultimate waaaaaaaaah-ambulance.

It was time to run the monkey up the flagpole. I pulled down on the ropes and hoisted the triangular metal cage, containing Bro The Monkey, who screeched and angrily shook the bars. I almost regretted getting him. He was mean and that sucker was strong. And between either eating or jerking off, Bro threw monkey shit at anything that moved. But some things you have to do to get them just right. I fired a short salute, and quickly moved because I didn't want to be his next target. I stood at the entrance of the former Surf Dot Com building. I absently traced my finger on the glass panel where I removed the magnetic card access device and replaced it with a mail slot. Then, I re-read the old notice taped to the inside of the front door's top glass panel:

Surf Dot Com Clearance

Flat screen monitors. Color printers, Badminton sets. Water squirt guns. Foosball game. Ping Pong table. Laptops (Compac and Apple). Dell and Mac Towers. Baseball caps. USB hubs. Espresso machine. Treadmills. MP3 players. Big screen TV. Walnut conference table. Adobe programs. Clothing, pens, travel cups. Workstations. Power strips. Photocopiers. Fax machines. Headsets. Palm Pilots. Wacom pads. Canon digital and video cameras. Sony Play stations.

The auction happened months ago, but I didn't want to take the flyer down. I wanted to savor it.

"Vic's Surf Center," said Skin Dog as he came down the ladder to admire his work. "Whaddaya think, brutha?"

I looked at the restored, slightly altered sign that was back in its original location on the roof above the front window. The only change was "Vic's" had replaced "Slap's."

"Looks like your name always belonged up in lights," said Skin Dog, slapping me on the back. "You've come full circle."

"I'd like to think so," I said and paused. "I'd like to think so."

"He's going for the three point play!" shouted Chops, running to the side of the building. He lobbed a silver disco ball into the dumpster. The ball split in two and settled on the useless printers, chunks of smashed cubicles, plastic shards, and broken chairs, which filled the bin. "Vic, the dump won't take computers because the screens have lead, the batteries mercury, and those metals seep in the soil and will contaminate the water supply"

"Just put them all in the trash," I said looking at the high-tech waste. "People will do their dumpster diving tonight and take out half the shit, and we'll fill it up again tomorrow."

I stood there. My mind drifted back to Andrea on the wharf. I flashed on the "Monsieur Tucker" phrase in her cell phone conversation. Then I remembered the picture in her cubicle. The one of her with the beret-wearing geek in France. His name was Tucker. I guessed Tucker was Andrea's revised exit strategy. The beret geek from Stanford was going to provide her with a trampoline of emotional and financial support that Andrea needed him to continue her arc to Tennis Momdom. Backward compatibility takes another leap forward. Maybe that was why Andrea was so angry, because no matter what personal or career change she made every six-months, or what she achieved, she secretly resented where she was going to end up. She never had an arc; it was a fall-back position. Andrea had ambition but never enough courage to chuck her destined seating card placed at the members-only table of her parents' securely-zoned world. My life was the ocean. Hers was a chlorinated pool with lifeguards.

"Hey, what's up Vic?" inquired Chops, who noticed my mood. "You look like something's bugging you."

"I ran into Andrea on the wharf."

"Ah, that's it. No wonder," said Chops, chuckling. "She was always angry about something. I kept a respectful distance from her. I could tell she never liked me."

"Shit," I said. "She was my girlfriend and I don't even think she even liked *me*!"

We laughed.

Driveway Dave tapped his horn and parked his BMW next to The Legend's SUV that was next to my new van, which was still dirty from my last trip to Baja. It was parked beside Skin Dog's Harley. They were all repossessed vehicles we picked up for one third of their list price. Dave had just come back from court. He was freshly shaven with a trimmed mustache. He wore a sharp suit. He looked good.

Dave came over, stood beside me, and said, "It's a beautiful thing." He studied the sign. "To the Victor go the spoils."

"Victor, now there's something I haven't been called in awhile," I said. "Victor, yeah." I savored it. "So have you been busy in court? Dave?"

"I'm suing the county to redesign the yacht harbor's entrance to restore sand flows to stop the cliff erosion on the Eastside of town. I'm filing papers against them for putting in permit parking and restricting beach access. I'm pissing off all these jerks because I can afford not to get along with them," He said, unwrapping an expensive cigar, "Oh, BTW, I'm no longer Driveway Dave, my name is Split-Level-Beach House-With-An-Ocean-View-Jacuzzi Dave." We laughed. He did a rap move and shouted into the shop, "Yo Squirrel, I got bling bling!" He paused. "Check this out." He held up a postcard. "It's from Sonny. He's in Hawaii. He's says he's enjoying himself."

"Man, warm water," I said. "When I came back from Hawaii to here, I just fought putting a wetsuit on." I paused. "When you get two weeks of something different it's hard to switch back."

"Are you talking about the time you spent in a men's prison?" asked Chops, who smiled and marked up a point on an imaginary scoreboard. "I wish Sonny was hear to tell me that wasn't funny."

"Did Sonny say if Shiloh talked about me there?" I asked.

"No," uncomfortably answered Dave. "Where's The Crew?"

"The other guys are getting stuff for the shop."

A horn honked.

Fernando pulled up in a brand-new black pick-up truck. He wore a new white cowboy hat with a black band around it, along with a pressed blue shirt, a bolo tie with a silver clasp, and a huge Aztec-styled gold ring on his right index finger.

"A-meeeee-go!" he sang out. He sat in his truck and smiled. His missing teeth were replaced with a bridge. "Como esta? You need help a-meeee-go? I help you."

"No, we're all right," I replied. "Beside you already helped."

"I guess we all made mucho dinero, pinche a-meeee-go. It is a good beginning, half is done."

"Ya lo creo," I said. "Half is done? What's the other half?"

"You come to my Purisma place I take you to Punta Pequeño in Baja, mucho olas," he smiled, then his glance penetrated mine. "You have everything, a-meee-go." He sensed something. "No serás amado, si de ti solo tienes cuidado."

You will not be loved if only of yourself you take care.

"Lo entiendo, amigo," I replied. "I understand."

"Si te ví, no me aceurdo," said Fernando, his eyes gleaming.

If I saw you, I don't remember.

"That's the smart way to be."

"If anyone asks if I know you, a-meee-go, I tell them, 'I don't have that problem anymore,'" said Fernando as he pulled away in his truck. "A fly cannot go into a closed mouth."

"Hasta," I said, laughing.

"Now there goes *one* successful day trader," said Ralph.

"Yeah, he is," said a familiar voice.

"I found a shop board you might be interested in," said The General, who had the tail of a ten-foot surfboard on his sneaker; the board's nose pointed up. The stick was white and in the middle of its deck was an air-brushed, two-foot figure of Superman. "I'd like to put this on display here. I picked it up at the flea market in the drive-in last Sunday. Fifty bucks. The guy said he found it in the rafters of his garage when he moved into a house." He paused. "A solid score."

"That's the original board from Slap's."

"Yeah, it is," said The General.

"It's never been ridden," I said, running my hands along the rails. "And no wonder! This board is a piece of shit." We laughed. "But it's definitely a shop board, I'll hang it from the rafters above the front door, where it hung years ago."

"I'll do it, I can handle replacing the past," said The General, who picked up a ladder from the floor. "It's what I live for."

"I appreciate it. Thanks."

"Sorry to hear about Ranger," said The General.

"Thanks," I said mechanically.

"I remember when Skin Dog, The Legend, and I got her," he said. "Ranger was a great dog. She really was."

I sucked in my lips and said nothing.

When I entered the shop, 'Higher and Higher' by Jackie Wilson came out of the speakers. The former Surf Dot Com office was littered with report papers, scattered file folders, keyboards, and business cards from other defunct dot coms. The shelves were bare from floor to ceiling. In each former cubicle location, disconnected bundles of wire stuck out of small, round plastic openings in the floor; the wires resembled half-buried tendrils of dead aliens. We tore down most of the hallways and the walls, but I kept the shower and the kitchen. The shop boards were still on the floor. Zoof even came by and placed black candles and incense in each corner of the building to purge Surf Dot Com's energy from the place. In one corner, by the window, a candle burned near a blanket, by an empty plastic water bowl, silver food dish, and a dry, frayed yellow tennis ball.

"Yo Vic," said Squirrel, who sat in an Aeron chair at a workstation, which was placed behind the glass counter to the left of the shop entrance. "The DSL line is working."

"I'm still trying to get the big screen up," said Ralph, who was on his back on the floor in the middle of the shop. His hands tangled up in wire cables.

"Vic, when is lunch up?" asked Squirrel, who had a chunk of beef jerky sticking out of his mouth. "I'm starving."

"Yeah, you look like you're starving," I said, walking around the shop, and trying to figure out where the boards and displays would go. "The sandwiches will be here, I ordered them an hour ago."

My sandal stepped on a curled object. I reached down. I picked up the coral reef fragment Andrea used as a key chain; it was covered with crumpled Post-It Notes of her motivational phrases. I peeled the Post-its off. I turned the hard, dry, dead chunk over in my hand. Just like the reef this piece of coral came from, Santa Cruz would never be the same. The dot-comers chipped at it, took what they could, sold what they built, and left. They ruined Santa Cruz, but they didn't ruin *me*. I put the coral in my pocket. Maybe I could still make something out of it.

The Legend and Chops came through the front door with the old shop's beat-up green sofa. Chops asked, "Where do you want us to put this piece of high-quality merchandise?"

"In front of the TV where it always was."

"Hey, Vic, you got the Pepsi machine in. Are they cold?" asked Driveway Dave.

"Should be," I said. "Yo General, we have lunch coming, you can hang out if you want."

"I'll take you up on that," said The General, who stood on the ladder, attaching a strap to the rafter. "I—"

"Delivery!" shouted the sandwich guy to Squirrel.

"Sorry, I don't take deliveries," replied Squirrel, who stared at his laptop monitor, picked his nose with one finger, and typed with his unengaged hand. "Sandwich guy is here."

"Okay, Squirrel," I said, taking out my wallet. "What's the damage on—"

I stopped. It was Zander. The former IT was dressed in a white 'Togo's T-shirt. His head hung down. His gut slung over his black, draw-string sweatpants. I was surprised at how much more he resembled a delivery guy than an engineer.

"Munch time," Squirrel said, snatching the three large white bags filled with lunch. Squirrel placed the bags on the low maple table, which was covered with surf magazines.

"Hey Squirrel, do Skin Dog," urged Chops, smiling.

"Sure," eagerly said Squirrel, who never passed up any chance to get attention.

"Do me?" asked Skin Dog, confused. "What are you talking about?"

"Squirrel does an all-time impression of Skin Dog getting up from the couch," said Chops, smiling.

Squirrel sat on the couch, rocked back and forth, and did a play-by-play commentary of his every move, "Skin Dog goes like this to get going." The Crew laughed. "Then when he gets enough momentum, he bounces up." When Squirrel stood, several M&Ms fell from within the folds of his shirt to the floor. "Then whatever food he's eating falls on the rug."

The Crew laughed. Skin Dog shook his head and smiled.

"Yo Vic," said Squirrel, going through the bags, "The passwords are set up with the server. The LAN is networked to two computers and the register. We have a static IP address. We can also work off a server in the back." He paused. "I rock!"

"That's your IT?" asked Zander, who seemed offended a fourteen-year old kid who could do a great impression of a fat guy getting up from the couch also possessed same high-tech skills as Zander.

"I got the cable box connected!" said Ralph. He turned down Jackie Wilson, hit the remote control, and cranked up the TV "Hey, they're talking about Santa Cruz. I just saw Drake!"

A female TV reporter sat at a desk. She wore a white blouse but showed some cleavage. Behind her, flashed different pictures: warehouses filled with used chairs; the Pets.Com sock puppet dog; shuttered restaurants; empty hotels; McMansions with 'For Sale' signs with a hooked shingle below that said "Reduced;" and, vacant buildings along 880 in Sunnyvale with 'Space For Lease' billboards; an auction on a fleet of vans with Webvan logos; and, peasants in Guiyu, China, scavenging landfills of motherboards, and burning wiring to extract copper.

"Since April 14, 2000, the dot-com stock wealth of the 100 biggest tech companies in NASDAQ has cratered by a stunning $2 trillion, dropping the market by two thousand points," she said. "It's dot-come and dot-gone. Over 79,000 jobs have been vanished in Silicon Valley, with a 3-year projection of 200,000 jobs lost. The unemployment rate for Silicon Valley is 7.6 percent, which is the highest since 1983, and higher than the rest of the country. The dot-com prospectors hoping to strike it rich on web-site mineshafts are cashing out and fleeing The Valley in droves. Over 56,000 people have moved. Indian restaurants are closing up because the glut of HB-1 programmers can no longer keep their visas. Venture capitalists funding in this second quarter is at its lowest period in four years. Many remaining tech companies are outsourcing workers from foreign countries and relocating to areas where the cost of living is lower. Even Cisco Systems said they were 'postponing' the construction of their Cisco Campus in Coyote Valley and announced their first layoff ever: 8,500 people. At the height of the binge bubble, 204 Silicon Valley companies went IPO and sold an estimated $18.5 billion in stock. Today, seven out of ten, of those 204 start-ups, have joined the dearly e-parted, delisted, and dying. In fact, at least 40 Silicon Valley companies lost 99.5 percent of their value. Even, the prestigious dot-com job placement service, BrassRing Dot Com, is laying off 70 percent of its own employees, and suspended its job fairs and resumé databases due to the lack of interest of companies hiring high-tech workers. The only ones not feeling the pinch of the digital downturn on the exchange are the CEOs, directors and major inside investors of software, hardware, and telecommunications start-ups, who took home $3.4 billion, along with venture capitalists and bankers who received one dollar out of every four raised. Recent statistics show bankers made $2 billion in fees, while inside traders pulled down $8.7 billion for selling their shares."

"They're all just getting into the backlash," Zander peevishly snorted. He walked toward the TV, as if he were going to ram it. "Oh yeah, that dumb bimbo looks like a real journalist. Dyed blonde hair and lipstick. She's paid her dues in beauty school! How did she get her job? Sucking up bed sheets in her mouth with her ass in the air? Fucking media assholes. They're jealous, jealous, jealous!" He scowled and looked down at the rug. He was quiet for several seconds. "Zander has to deliver food and all because Zander doesn't have that little slip of paper that says Zander has a degree. Zander who trained the testers. Zander who can work with 98 percent of the operating systems on all computers." He shivered and looked down at his hands as if he was in chains. "Zander got yelled at today because Zander didn't wait for Zander's 'break' to go to the bathroom."

A photograph of Drake Sather flashed on the screen.

"In a related story in Santa Cruz, was it Surf Dot Com or Surf Dot *Con* Job?" continued the newscaster.

"That dick-wipe," hissed Zander. "Talk about morons, look at Zander. The day of the second offering Zander found a hacker got through the firewall because Zander was the flaw in Zander's system. Then Zander discovered Drake's plans. Zander had no business sense. Zander is in a world without a joystick."

The newscaster continued, "The Kahuna of Surf Dot Com, Drake Sather, alias Errol Dean Clark, who, in part of an on-going grand jury probe, is being charged for previous telemarketing fraud convictions in Yuba City, along with additional violations of stock fraud by The U.S. Attorney's Office in New York. The National Association of Securities Dealers are seeking disciplinary action in connection in Sather's relationship with Credit First San Jose Suisse. Suisse is charged with alleged conflicts of interest between the bank and its investment-research departments. Court documents alleged Suisse's investment units gave 'buy' ratings to Surf Dot Com in exchange for getting lucrative investment banking fees. Four Suisse brokers, among them, Santa Cruz resident Arlen Norby, a six-figure earner at the height of dot-com excesses, is accused of charging higher commissions as well as receiving kickbacks from investors for allowing them to purchase SDC's stock at its initial offering, which enabled the brokers to make millions."

The screen showed a photo of Arlen Norby with a surfboard.

"That's Bro Dork!" I said, wondering if he'd explain 'the rules' to the boys in the prison showers.

The newscaster continued, "The SEC is seeking a $15 million fine against Suisse's investment firm, which is $5 million less than what any of the four brokers earned last year, and less than half of the severance package most of them received. There are millions in stockholder class-action suits against Surf Dot Com, but sources said Sather's existing assets won't cover all the claims. The investigation was triggered by inter-office memos released by an unknown source on the Internet.." The woman paused. "In the go-go nineties, Surf Dot Com was once a hot tech stock selling for prices at over $300 a share." She paused again and smirked. "It's holding at four cents."

The Crew laughed. The General turned off the news, put in a surf video, and 'Telstar' by the Tornados played.

"You guys still don't get it," accusingly whined Zander, who continued in his distinctive lordly tone of snitty superiority. "You guys never got it. Surfing the web was a magical spot. Surfing it was pure. And a select group had that world al to ourselves. It was never about the money and getting a house. It was about fulfillment. It was about IQ. There was an honest exchange of information. All the bright people knew each other. It was such a free and easy lifestyle. It was about making good products, good jobs, and respect for one another. A value chain. R&D. All that freedom and energy and innovation! Testing boundaries. It was an exciting chance to get out of the six-by-six cubicle world and create something out of nothing. The web's technology was going to be the great equalizer embedded into the fabric of society and enable the middle class for the first time to—"

"Hey brutha, where are the mustard packets?" interrupted Skin Dog, searching through the sandwich bags.

"They're inside the napkins at the bottom of the bag," said Zander, who sourly continued. "It could have been a beautiful period. Those early days of 93'...but then came the point-and-click MBAs with their blue-chipped, gold-plated, platinum-tipped resumés, who left their consulting and investment firms and took up surfing the web and went into start-ups. Those MBAs overran our spot. Then everyone started riding the wave of high-tech for what they could get out of it. These transplants weren't real surfers. They were crowding us out on our waves. What did these MBAs and their concomitant lightweights know about surfing the web? They didn't understand or write code, or appreciate our culture. They destroyed it. The money is gone. And that's wrong. There are still great ideas out there that deserve VC funding. Experimentation results in innovation. That's why high-tech will come back. It's cyclical. Something will happen. It will turn around. It's bottomed out. The valley always goes through a shake out. Things will take off again. It's got to come back. It has to! Zander has the experience. Zander has the knowledge. Zander has the wisdom. Another wave will come. All Zander has to do is hang tough and be in the right spot at the right time for the *Next* Big Thing."

A monkey turd smacked Zander in the head. The Next Big Thing exploded in a brown splat, blowing out the IT's heavily combed-over bald spot.

"Incoming!" shouted Chops.

The Crew laughed.

Bro victoriously screeched from his cage.

"This is so fucked!" Zander groaned in disgust, finally getting it. The disabled IT delicately picked out the monkey shit and peanut shells from his hair. He hacked from the smell. "Gross!"

"You're lucky most of it was hard," Chops said.

Zander's shoulders sagged. Something inside him had cracked. His eyes looked like a creature who was caught in a trap and suddenly realized it chewed off the wrong leg to get out. The Crew had been there once or twice. We stopped laughing.

'Sunny' by Bobby Hebb played.

"You know what I think of now?" asked Zander in a dejected voice that surprised us all. "How during all that time at Surf Dot Com I was on meds, and the way that ratfuck yelled at me, and how I didn't make the time to go back to Iowa to see my Nana who was sick. Nana is German for grandmother. I thought it would work itself out, you know, and...she, she passed away. And I had the money to go too. My parents told me that just before she died in the hospital, Nana smiled and told them she had a nice visit with me..." His voice broke and his eyes welled up with tears. He spoke with genuine sorrow. "I wasn't there for her, she was always there for me. I didn't go back for her funeral either. I was too busy. She was around ninety-four, but she was never around long enough for me. I knew what she would say to me, 'There's no need to rush out here now. I'm not going anywhere.' She was always so practical. She was always so proud of me. Nana thought I was a genius cause I was always taking things apart and putting them back together. She admired how neat I kept everything and had respect for my tools. Father was mad and disappointed I wasn't a jock. Mother thought I was just a big baby. But Nana would always come into my room when I was working on a computer program and bring me sandwiches and some of her sun tea in a special Flintstones jelly glass." His voice started breaking again. But he didn't wipe these tears away. He was proud of them. "Nana told me, 'I love to watch you eat, because what I made for you was making you stronger." His voice warbled. "Today's my birthday. I always used to get a card from my Nana. It always had a little money in it and a note to treat myself to a nice meal." Zander closed his eyes, took his right hand, and pressed a finger on each inside corner of his lids at the bridge of his nose. He shook his head, took a deep breath, wiped his face, sniffed, and added without any trace of self-pity, "I'm a failure." He paused. "I failed at what she loved in me."

I didn't know what to say. I felt real bad for this Zander guy. I mean, I had beat on the guy with a stick. I was all set to dislike him forever. And here he was, in my life, and I liked him.

"Yeah, I was making stupid money," said Zander, who smirked. "I mean I was working 80 hours a week. I was getting paid so much money it was really stupid. I saw all these dot-comers making the money and getting caught up in it. I swore it wouldn't happen to me, and then I got stupid too." He hung his head and then looked at us. "You know, I was rude to a lot of people. I was super stressed out. Tired all the time. I was snapping at everybody. I didn't like the person I became." He nodded and looked back at me. "I mean, didn't you ever try to become something you thought you should be but really weren't, and regret it? I regret it. You have to let people make up for it, everyone deserves a second act, just to see, just to see if they can really do the right thing with their lives." He paused. "I bet, I was probably rude to you too. I'm sorry."

No one said anything.

"You know I might have an opportunity for you at the shop," I said, leaning against the counter. "That is, if you're interested. Squirrel has to attend school. I need time to shape boards and surf, so I'll need someone to work the shop. When it's slow, you can design and write code here, play your games, whatever you want to do. I mean we have computers here, and a DSL line. When I'm off on surf trips, you can housesit my place at Pleasure Point, that's a perk that comes along with the job."

"A job?" said Zander. "You're offering me a job?"

"Have you ever worked a cash register?"

"No."

"Done retail?"

"No."

"Handled inventory?"

"No."
"Sales?"
"No."
"So you really have no functional job skills at all?"
"No."
"Or people skills?"
"No."
"Well then, you're hired, because those are the perfect job qualifications to work in a surf shop."
"Yeah, cool, great" said Zander, smiling.
"Yo Vic," Squirrel shouted, "Check out the surf cams."
Above the counter, along the upper wall were three screens with gold name plates above them marked "Cowells," "The Lane," and "Pleasure Point."
"Check out Cowells," said Skin Dog. "The surf is coming up. There's a nice bar out and it's working."
We saw three-to-four footers, clean lines. They were perfect peelers. Then, the screens went blank.
"Fuck me," seethed Squirrel. "Computers! I get the right software, download the upgrades, and it crashes for no reason."
The Crew grabbed their boards from the floor.
"Goin'," said Skin Dog.
"I'll catch up to you guys later, I have to hang here and wait for some foam blanks to come in."
Squirrel said, "I'll wait."
"No, you have to go to school."
Zander tapped me on the shoulder and blurted eagerly, "I'll watch the shop for you."
I looked at the monkey shit in his hair and said, "I think you ought to shower first, there are towels back there."
"I can take a shower later."
"No, take one now. I'll wait a few minutes."
"Oh, okay," he said. "I guess I am a little ripe."
An oldie 'Little Bit Of Soul' by The Music Explosion played.
"Squirrel," I said, "When you put the system back up maybe you can get some help from Zander—"
"Jimmy," interrupted Zander. He said his name calmly, as if speaking his real name relaxed him. "My name is Jimmy."

When I got to Cowells, I expected to see The Crew out in the water. But instead, they stood along a low concrete wall by the cinder-block bathroom in the parking lot between the Dream Inn hotel and the entrance to the wharf. They leaned against their boards, heads bowed. I walked through the parking lot and saw huge vans with surf murals on them, each had a different logo, Klub Ed, UCSC, Surfing Las Amigas, Go With A Pro, Stokerettes, Endless Summers, Surfer Girl Power. I figured they were sponsors for some surf contest or something.

"Howz'it?"

The Legend pointed to the ocean and said, "Six surf classes with twenty students a piece. They just paddled out there." He paused. "We stopped doing classes, but it looks like someone ripped a page out of our playbook. The instructors are even wearing colored hats like we did."

"They're almost all women," said Chops. "I guess Shiloh was ahead of her time."

The water was filled with over a hundred people. The instructors were female dot-comers who took Shiloh's classes. The instructors could barely surf, some even staggered on their boards, but their pupils didn't notice. I guess the dot-comers who wanted to keep their Instant Local buzz discovered how to throw women and children into the ocean and soak money out of them. There were women everywhere. The beach was riprapped with blue foam boards. The students, and instructors were either stretching out, lying on their boards in land-simulation drills, or setting up separate folding tables with food, and firing up barbecues. The classes looked like opposing armies.

When the waves rolled in, surf-class instructors in yellow floppy hats and their students ruthlessly paddled on blue foam boards and dropped in front of red-floppy-hatted instructors and their students, who also dropped in front of neon-orange-floppy hatted instructors and their students. On the beach, several photographers in different colored floppy hats, tenaciously edged out each other to get the best camera shot of their students.

"Surf classes snaking and burning other surf classes," I said.

"Think it's karma?" asked Chops.

"No, but, *that* is," said The General, pointing.

We turned and watched a surf safari of eight rusted Volkswagen buses pull into the parking lot. The VWs roofs were stacked with longboards. The surfers emerging from the buses were in their late-twenties. They all looked like *me*! Even the women. They had sun-bleached, shoulder-length hair, tanned faces, and defined muscles that strained against their wetsuits. Beside each surfer, was a German shepherd with a frayed, dirty, green tennis ball clamped in its mouth. They all had a Ranger!

"Wassup!" they all shouted to me, and took their boards down. A few dogs dropped their balls and barked.

I just stood there stunned. I really never saw this coming.

"You planted a seed," said The General, chuckling. "Little did you know it was *being* you."

A Wassup came over and stood opposite me. He acted like I was supposed to recognize him.

"Howz'it?" he said.

I froze. This Wassup-turned-Howz'it looked like a younger replica of me. It was like staring back into time. The guy was my height. His blue eyes were level with my blue eyes. He had a walnut-brown tan. He wore a short-sleeved Spring wetsuit. Under his arm, he carried a white longboard that had yellowed from the sun, had numerous cracks, and water-soaked dings that looked like cigarette burns. In his left hand, he held a gym bag with a water jug and bowl in it, along with a tennis racquet that had a chewed-up handle. A young German shepherd was at his side. With a uncomfortable jolt, I recognized who the Wassup-turned-Howz'it really was.

"Gregg-with-two-g's?" I asked tentatively.

"Yeah, it's me," he chirped, smiling. "We've all been down in Baja. Been all over it for months. Went down to Cabo. Zippers was going off. But with the Internet, within eighteen hours, everyone from San Diego flew down and was on it. The biggest assholes came down in SUVs with satellite phone systems. Those same stupid surf classes were down there too. Some of them were Germans. A lot of middle-aged women too. But they're genderless, which means they yell at everybody." He shrugged. "Big deal, we still got our waves." He paused. "Do you remember our repurposing session?"

"Yeah, I wanted to punch the shit out of you."

He laughed and said, "You intimidated me. I was jealous of you. So, I acted like you weren't important. Here I was, repurposing you and I didn't have a purpose. You had a life. I didn't. You fought in the war, and were broke, and you had no skills and learned about carpentry, and shaping boards."

I looked down and said, "It didn't go exactly like that. I did a few *other* things too that I wouldn't want to talk too much about."

"But you built a life out of yourself. How many people have the courage to do that? I was just a piece of software. I wasn't a person. Deep inside I knew it. I was haunted. You had friends you've known for years and years. Who did I have? Just people I worked with. And they were my friends only because I might bring them along to my next job, or throw them freelance work. I looked at them the same way. Hey, I had no idea. I was born in a crowd. I grew up playing in traffic. I just tried to play off the crowd. You showed me how to get a taste of another world." He looked down at the ground. "It takes a lot of effort to be that kind of guy. There's no work-around or short cut, you have to put in the time. When I got laid off, I was given the time, and I thought maybe surfing will show me what to do. Anyway, I was surfing at The Wall in Baja, out there in the ocean with the waves and it just came to me. I found it. I thought, 'You know, I want to become a dentist. That's what I want to do with my life.'"

"No shit.," I said. "Huh."

"In my heart I'll never get lost in the crowd again," Gregg-with-two-gs said. He shouted over his shoulder to his troop of Wassups, "They're not driving us out of the water."

Gregg-with-two-gs charged the surf with a dog at his side. The Wassups followed him. They carried longboards, gym bags, and ran towards the ocean with their German shepherds. They chanted their war cry, "It's just not happenin'! It's just not happenin'! It's just not happenin'!"

"Who knew?" I said, completely confused. "Who knew?"

The Crew lined up before me. They smirked.

"What?" I asked. "Now what?"

A small, cold nose touched my bare feet. I looked down. A wet, black German shepherd puppy stood between my legs, and wedged its head under my crotch. The puppy proudly displayed a dirty tennis ball in its mouth. I laughed. The damn ball was almost as big as its head. I lifted my left leg over the dog, placed my board on the asphalt, bent down, and scratched the puppy's head. It licked my face. I smiled.

A soft shadow wavered over us. I looked up and saw Shiloh. She wore a black spring suit. Her hair was wet. She shifted weight from left foot to right foot.

"The puppy got wet, she was out there swimming," Shiloh said nervously. "She doesn't have a name, yet. I rescued her from an Animal Shelter place. When I heard about Range, I started looking for a certain dog. That was the hardest part, leaving there without an animal, leaving those animals behind. But, I kept going every other day. Then yesterday, when I thought there wasn't anything, just as I was leaving, a paw reached out of a cage and touched my leg. I bent down and saw her. She was wagging her tail. She had a yellow tag on her collar. They were going to put her down that day. And I think she knew it. I looked at her through the bars and said, 'Not today! Not you. Not today!'"

"A-meee-go?"

I turned around and was surprised to see Fernando. He stood with three other Mexicans. They were all dressed like him—a new white cowboy hat with a black band around it, a pressed blue shirt, a bolo tie with a silver clasp, pressed bluejeans, gold belt buckles, and brown cowboy boots. They all held guitars.

"Why did you come back here, Fernando?"

"You need a song, a-meeeee-go."

"A song?"

"I told you half was done. This half is called 'Think of me.'"

Fernando and his band members strummed their guitars and plaintively sang a soft ranchero-like, love ballad:

"Piensa en mi."

Think of me.

"Si tienes un hondo penar, piensaermi."

If you're longing for someone think of me.

"Si tienes ganas de llorar, piensa en mi."

If you feel a deep cry of suffering, think of me.

"Yaves que beñero tuimagen divina."

I see you as someone divine.

"Tupas bula boca que siendo do tan niña."

I see a mouth that promises youthfulness.

"Me enseño a besar."

Teach me how to kiss.

After a chorus, they strummed guitars and hummed.

"That's your song, it is from you to someone else," Fernando said. "You need a song to sing, a-meeee-go. That's what I have to leave you for what you have given me."

I sucked in my lips, pet the puppy, looked into the friendly eyes of Fernando, and said without an edge, "Gracias, hombre." I paused. "Me pasa esto."

This is happening to me.

Shiloh warily said, "I was throwing the ball for her. She's an ocean dog. And she loves whip cream." She paused. "Do you want her?" Her voice warbled. "That's the real question. Do you want her?"

"Damn Skippy," I shouted, springing up and sweeping Shiloh into my arms. I drilled her with a deep and long kiss and we clung together. Our hands dug into each other's shoulder blades, as if we were climbing up one another. We went higher and higher. I inhaled her. I let it all in. She and I were all there. And we enjoyed the view. Our lips parted, but nothing else did.

"Burr, that was hot," she said, laughing.

I held her. I laughed too.

"Actually, before you came Vic tried to do the exact same move on all of us," said Chops.

The Crew laughed.

The puppy dropped the ball and barked.

Shiloh said, "What do you want to call her?"

"You name our dog," I said and put Shiloh down.

"How about Sam?" said a voice behind us. It was Broadway. He looking for deposit bottles in a plastic green recycling barrel. "Sam! That was the name of the monkey in Slap's place. I don't know why, it just locked in. Sam! It's always the simple things you can't name."

Skin Dog pointed outside and proclaimed, "Hot wheels from hell here comes a set."

Twelve waves came through. The shape was perfect. The swarm of surf classes went for every wave in the set, dropping in, burning, and snaking one another, swearing, and colliding.

"Everybody's surfing, everybody's cool," said Chops.

Ralph said, "They're too busy hating each other to notice us."

"They're cursed," said The General. "Those people will always come out of the water the same way they went into the water. Actually, they come out worse, that's their curse."

"Who cares about them?" said Ralph.

"Let them consume each other.," added The Legend.

We watched the mounds of the swell pass through The Lane, transform into creases at Indicators, and break on the sand bar along the far cliff edge, just below the shutdown bathroom. The waves held their shape, peeled for a few hundred yards to shore, and smoothly taper down to nothing in front of us. That's all we saw: the waves. The waves that brought us to where we were right now. Where would those waves take us today, and tomorrow? Even if we stayed in Santa Cruz forever, those waves would always take us somewhere else.

"Over it," said Shiloh.

"I'm all over it," I said, smiling. "Let's hit it."

"Hey, we have the technology, we always did, brutha," Skin Dog said, gently rapping his knuckles on the deck of a longboard. "All we needed was a surfer, a dog, and a van."

"Yeah, we did," said The General.

The Crew and Shiloh and I followed the puppy down to the beach and into the ocean. We paddled out to get our stoke and let the others swallow the magic.

Whups

THERE'S A MISSING PIECE in everyone's story, part of something left unsaid or deliberately concealed, which gives ill-fitting humans the flaw they need to dismiss a book, an achievement, a belief, a conversation, a news story, a movie, a career, a surfboard, a love, and sometimes even an entire life. They see the missing part as a flaw. It prevents all the pieces from neatly fitting into an easy category. This missing piece didn't fit in with the flow of my story. But I knew people would see it was missing. That's the way life is. People never see all the mistakes in life you catch, but they'll always call you on the ones you miss. But they forget, sometimes the missing piece provides a curve that gives you a defined shape. I mean, growing up, I didn't fit anywhere but at Slap's and Cowells. After the war, I didn't even fit on the waves, really. Until I had Ranger, I didn't fit together with the ocean; or even people, and they didn't fit together with me. I could have left this part out. But no way was I leaving Ranger out. Not Ranger. That's just not happenin'.

Inside Mobil Mark's van, I sat stiffly on a blanket. His van was parked in side lot by a Rotten Robbie discount gas station, which was across from the Moe's Alley blues club near the Soquel Avenue exit ramp of Highway One in Santa Cruz. Mark had taken care of Ranger since she was a puppy, and now, he was seeing her out. I held Ranger in my arms. She was nervous but she trusted me. She shouldn't have.

"This dog's alert," gasped Mark, studying Ranger's eyes, then looking over at me. "When an old dog comes here at this stage, they're out of it. She's all there."

"I know," I groaned. "I know."

I stared off at the morning bumper-to-bumper traffic on Northbound Highway One. In the slight, low-lying fog, the car's brake lights looked like red cinders drifting up a chute, as if the commuter's journey was incinerating them. Ranger shifted slightly against my chest. She tilted her head to the left and looked up. She was wondering what she did to upset me.

"Are you sure you still want me to do this?" said Mark.

"Don't ask me that," I dryly pleaded, the words parching my mouth and constricting my throat. "Don't ask me that." I paused. "She has no legs. When her back legs went, I'd wheelbarrow her, but then her front legs went. And there she was just laying in her own, in her own—it just wasn't right to have her be like that. She doesn't deserve that." I sniffed and whimpered. "Before we came, I made her to one last sundae with loads of whip cream before we came here. She ate it all."

"I'm going to inject her with a pain killer, it's called sodium phentabarnatol," he said slowly. "It will go to her heart. It will be very fast, maybe less than a minute." Mark held the syringe and delicately stressed every word. "And just so you know, there's a chance of some movement afterwards. Sometimes it happens. It's just nerves, it's not her."

I stroked Ranger's neck, looked at Mark, and nodded the go-ahead. I started sobbing. He slid the needle into her back leg and injected the fatal fluid.

"She won't feel anything.," he said, withdrawing the needle. He slid out of the van, stood near me and respectfully turned away. "I'm here, though."

"Whups." I said.

Ranger looked up at me. Her eyes were focused. Suddenly, she went limp. She slipped from my arms and landed on her side in my lap. I wasn't ready for that.

"Range!"

My whuppers looked up at me, confused. She didn't know why she lost control. She was so helpless.

"Whups," I blubbered.

My tongue turned into sandpaper. I closed my eyes. They felt like a thin flame slit across them, which set off a fire of hot tears. My nose ran. My chest heaved. My throat was sealing up, nearly choking me.

"Babeeeeeeee," I said, pressing my lips into the soft skin within her pointed right ear. "Whups."

Her eyes were still clear. Damn it, they were clear. Clear!

"Good girl, good girl," I sighed, my eyes winced. "Oh Range, I didn't want to do this. I didn't want to do this."

Ranger, my pillow.

"Whuppers."

Ranger, who tilted her head at different angles in recognition of every word I spoke.

"Whups."

Ranger, who loved going to the beach.

"I didn't want to do this. I didn't want to do this. I didn't want to do this..."

Ranger, who always rose to protect me.

"I'm so sorry, Range. I'm so sorry..."

Her breathing got shorter.

"Whup, whups."

I buried my head in her fur. I pet her. She felt different. Her muscular tension let loose. She felt like a bony pelt. I couldn't feel her heart but I knew it was still beating. I stroked and stroked her side. She didn't respond.

"Ranger, Range, Rangey, whups, whuppers... "

She was still. I pressed my head against hers. I drew her up into my arms. Her front legs folded up against her chest. Her lower legs limply dangled. Ranger had gone to a place where she could never bring a ball back to me.

"Range."

My tears flowed like lava sap. I convulsively sobbed. I pressed and twisted the flat of my tongue against the roof of my mouth. My shoulders heaved and heaved. I slid from underneath Range, and put her down on her green wool blanket. I stroked her head. My body slumped. I stood outside the open doors and looked at her still figure. Her eyes were wide open. Her pupils were large but not moving. Then I flashed back to the day she swam out to me. She had never done that before, ever. Then, I realized Ranger was saying goodbye to me, giving me the one thing I always wanted her to do, but wasn't really a part of her. Yes, she was saying goodbye. My whups was saying goodbye. And I didn't know, until I was out of Range.

Mark turned around. He reached over and pressed his fingers on the inside corners of Ranger's eyes. Then he listened to her heart with a stethoscope. He looked at me, and nodded, then he looked down. He said softly, "She's not here." He started to cover Ranger with a blanket. I couldn't let him cover her face. Mark backed off.

I leaned across Ranger, hugged her limp body, and pressed my lips just below her right ear.

"All you had was love for me, Rangey," I whispered. "All you had was love for me. Goodbye Range, I love you. I know you loved me, whups, I know. Good dog, good dog."

I placed the blanket over Ranger's head. I turned away and sat on the edge of the van. My legs loosely hung over the bumper and mechanically swung back and forth. The tips of my sandals brushed and grazed the asphalt. It was two days after my birthday. Without turning around, I rested my right hand on the blanket above her chest. I knew she felt my touch somewhere. She had to feel me. Ranger had to have a soul. These tears of mine didn't have a practical function. There was no foreign object in my eyes. Why would I cry this much if she didn't have a soul? How could I cry like this if I didn't have a soul?

"There was nothing you could do," said Mark. "You did the only thing you could. There was nothing you could do."

"Ranger was alive when I brought her here. Now she's dead. I feel terrible." I said flatly. "No wonder God has off days."

There was a silence.

"If you want, you can just sit here awhile," consolingly said Mark, patting me on the shoulder. "I'll get you a soda. Would you like one? Would you like a soda?'

"I have one in my cooler." I said, scrunching my face together and sobbing.

"Okay, I'll get it for you."

I wetly sniffed, wiped my face and said to him, "I thought. I did all my crying in Vietnam, but I never did cry over there. I never did. They wanted to see me cry. They wanted to break me. But I didn't cry. Not for what I did. Not once. Never."

Mark stood there and replied, "Maybe you just needed to cry for someone else."

I looked down.

Mark walked away. He wobbled, slightly. He was almost as shaken as I was.

"Whups," I sighed, yearningly looking up into the fog for a spiritual sign that never came.

When I leave this world, I wonder if it will be like paddling in from the ocean after a great surf session. And, there would be Ranger, sitting expectantly on the beach, where she had been patiently waiting for me all this time. Her loyal tail wagging. A green tennis ball in her mouth. And when Ranger saw me on my board, she would start happily barking in short, rapid bursts. And on healthy, strong, powerful legs, bound from the shore into the water, and swim out to join me. And with Ranger alongside of me, we'd paddle back towards a strange coast. And the wave behind us would close out, spilling us onto shore together again. And we'd be in the wet sand with the surf breaking over us and I would be laughing and rolling with Ranger and I was just a boy on the beach again in the waves of Santa Cruz before the war took me away, took me away, took me away, away.

In Memory of

Ranger

The Ultimate Surf Shop Dog

About the author

Fred Reiss has written two books, *Insult and Live!* and the highly maligned *Gidget Must Die*. He graduated from Antioch College. He's worked a variety of challenging dead-end jobs, such as a journalist, stand-up comic, winery tasting room supervisor, surf shop employee, and morning radio talk-show host. He has performed on national TV. He currently works in radio, and intends to keep surfing in Northern California.

About the illustrator and artist

John Severson, founder of Surfer Magazine, who defines his life as "Born knowing little, I discover the surf and make a magazine. It's successful. I sell it and go surfing. The end."

Sevo